The Antikythera Code

Andrew Clawson

Get Your FREE Copy of the Harry Fox story *THE NAPOLEON CIPHER*.

Sign up for my VIP reader mailing list, and I'll send you the novel for free.

Details can be found at the end of this book.

Chapter 1

Germany

One punch knocked the guard down. A second kept him there. Harry Fox shook his stinging hand and looked around. Nobody came running.

Punching people was no fun. Not even for the one doing the punching. Moonlight glinted off the unconscious guard's holstered sidearm as Harry manhandled him into the back of a delivery truck and dumped the man beside an oversized metal container. One with airholes in the sides. He wasn't here to kill anyone. Harry only wanted the book. Nobody had to get hurt. Well, not badly, at least. The guard didn't move as Harry stripped off the man's uniform, opened the container lid and rolled him in, wearing nothing but his underwear. The container lid closed with a *click*. Harry tossed a sheet over it and buttoned his newly acquired shirt. Someone would find the guard. Eventually. After Harry was long gone.

He took a breath and looked at the other containers in his truck. Two rows of short tubes pointing up. Twenty in all, each a few feet long and a foot in diameter. A breeze rustled the canvas roof covering the box truck bed as he stepped down onto the dry ground. He checked the canvas roof again. The truck was an old army cargo truck, one with no solid roof. Exactly the sort of truck Harry needed.

A cloud crossed the moon, its shadow running across the ground to make the spotlights shining from the tall building next to him that much brighter. Harry looked up at the monstrosity. It was a long way up. A German castle, five hundred years old. Dark stone brooded over what during the day was a picturesque estate of wide green fields and thick woodlands. Towers rose at each corner of the rectangular structure. One in a rear corner stood taller than the others, the chapel tower with a massive bell inside. His gaze lingered on that tallest tower for a moment. *This can work.*

Static crackled and startled him. Harry grabbed at the stolen radio clipped to his belt. He listened to another guard speak in German, then turned the volume down. Harry's German was atrocious. As long as he didn't have to speak directly to anyone, he could get by with a few phrases over the radio. Anything beyond that was pushing it. Get in, get the book, get out.

The guard's blue uniform should buy him cover. He confirmed the guard's keycard was clipped to his belt loop, raised the collar and headed for the side door, patting his pocket to confirm the small electronic device was inside. His plan depended on it. His truck was parked at a corner of the massive castle, the corner diagonal from the tall belltower. That would matter in a few minutes if all went according to plan. Get in, get the book, get out.

The pack strapped to Harry's back was the same dark blue as the guard uniform. Hard to believe such a slim backpack held the key to his escape. He pushed the thought from his head and walked to the front door, a massive wooden affair Harry would need a tank to blast through. Fortunately, he had a keycard. He waved the stolen card in front of a reader, which flashed from red to green. Harry pushed on a handle bolted to one of the ten-foot planks, and the door opened without a sound. Harry slipped through, closing the door behind him and moving quickly to a shadowy alcove nearby.

A staircase wide enough to drive said tank up faced the front entrance. Hallways on either side of the stairs led deeper into the castle, while open doors and entrances dotted the walls on both sides. Harry pulled up a map of the castle's interior in his mind's eye. He was here for one reason. A reason sitting inside a locked display case in a viewing hall on the second level. Harry lowered his chin, hunched his shoulders, and marched forward like a guard on patrol.

His footsteps echoed off the stone walls as he moved at a steady pace past the wide staircase and down the left hallway. What centuries ago would have been a dreary and smoke-filled passage now had recessed lighting along the ceiling to guide him. Harry kept his head low in case another guard happened past, never looking up at the surveillance cameras along the wall. The castle owner took security seriously. A private company had the contract for guarding this castle, with nearly the same personnel on staff every day. One positive was the guards weren't supposed to chitchat. There was no water-cooler talk on duty. Not when Leon Havertz was paying the bills.

Harry passed three entranceways as he walked. The fourth he took, turning and continuing his fake patrol until he found a staircase leading up to the second level. Electric sconces lined the walls. Harry moved up the stairs toward the landing, above which the moon gleamed through a window of thick glass. His feet had barely touched the landing when a sound grabbed his ear.

Footsteps. Coming from above. He forced himself to keep his eyes down and his feet moving as another guard came around the corner above him and began walking down the stairs. Harry hugged the wall.

"Alles klar?" Everything alright? The other guard's rough greeting sounded as they passed.

Harry didn't think. He reacted. *"Alles klar."* It's alright.

The guard kept walking. Harry's chest tightened as he kept climbing, his fingers moving to touch the lucky amulet hanging around his neck. A gift from his father, one with a mystery he'd only recently unraveled. The other guard's descending footsteps stopped. Harry didn't turn; he slipped a hand into his pocket, his fingers sliding into the ceramic knuckledusters he kept there. He could turn and jump down at the guard, take him out before anyone else showed up. But then what?

Harry risked a glance over his shoulder. The guard stood on the landing, looking out the window, his back to Harry. Harry let out the breath he'd been holding. He quickened his pace to the second-level hallway and turned a corner, pausing a moment until his heart slowed. His brief, guttural response had fooled the man. One chance meeting was enough, though.

Harry straightened his back and began walking again, moving straight ahead, into the heart of the castle. Suits of armor stood guard on one side of the hallway, polished to shine under the electric chandeliers above. The suits were smaller than most people would imagine, only the largest of them big enough for a man Harry's size to wear, and he wasn't tall. The other side of this passage was open, bordered by a thick stone railing, beyond which Harry could see down into a large hall. The castle blueprints he'd studied told him to expect this. They did not tell him to expect it would be occupied. Raised voices filled the air and Harry went still. Voices coming from the hall downstairs.

Keep going. The best way to stick out in this guard's uniform was to act as though he didn't belong. Harry forced himself to keep moving, slowing his pace as he edged closer to the railing to get a view of the lower level. A group of four men sat in high-backed chairs around a blazing fire. A fifth man stood, his booming voice reaching to the darkened rafters as he shouted in German. No, not shouted. Sang. The man was singing, and Harry didn't need to speak the language well to know this guy was butchering some traditional German tune. Not that Harry wanted to understand. He was more interested in the man singing.

Leon Havertz came from old German money. Over two hundred years ago the Havertz family had a title conferred upon them by Emperor Bismarck. That title had vanished under the Reich, though Havertz didn't seem to have received the message. Leon Havertz was a man in need of ceremony to stand on, and not only because he needed to use a stepping-stool if he wanted to reach a top shelf. Harry watched the balding, diminutive man from whom this roaring voice emanated. Nobody that size should be able to blow the windows out with his tortured singing.

He turned away from the view and continued walking.

Harry didn't see the chair until it was too late. One moment, he was looking at Havertz over the railing; the next, he tumbled ass-over-elbows to the floor. He froze. The singing continued unabated. Harry looked front and back, found no guards coming, and jumped back to his feet. He kept going as though the tumble hadn't happened, and Havertz sang on with vigor.

Another stairway beckoned ahead, and as Harry turned to begin climbing it, he passed the final suit of armor standing watch in the hall. He angled his head. *There's a mannequin in there.* So that's how they kept the suits standing.

No guard approached as Harry ascended the stairs. A large tapestry hung on one wall. One bearing a name other than Havertz. Leon's ancestors had purchased both the castle and all that came with it when they received their empty title. If Leon had been as open as his ancestors were to buying and selling artifacts, Harry wouldn't need to skulk around this castle risking his neck and avoiding armed guards. But Leon Havertz wouldn't sell Harry the book, so Harry Fox needed to steal it.

It had all started when Harry found a note scrawled inside a bible. Not just any bible. The bible of Charlemagne's personal abbot. A handwritten note inside it spoke of a storied treasure tied to the Father of Europe, one hidden long ago and never found. That note had ultimately brought Harry here to this German castle on this moonlit night. He needed a book Leon Havertz owned to continue following Charlemagne's trail. An illuminated manuscript Leon Havertz kept in this castle.

The third floor was much darker than the lower two; the only lights were dim bulbs along the ceiling. The glass chandeliers up here were unlit. Harry glanced around the corner and found the hallway empty. No promise it would remain that way for long, due to the guards' randomized patrol patterns. Ten guards were always on patrol to keep Havertz's castle secure. Harry had thought it was overkill until he'd learned what Havertz kept in his home. A collection of relics and cultural artifacts to rival a museum. All for his private enjoyment.

Harry pushed any thoughts of pilfering other relics from his head as he walked down the hallway, alert for the sound of guards. This was the highest level, where Havertz's private quarters took up most of the space along with his personal relic collection. Harry moved at a steady pace, passing an elevator door in a dimly lit alcove, as he headed toward the north side of the castle, his footsteps clicking on the stone floor. The air was noticeably colder now; keycard readers glowed red outside of each door.

Harry needed the third door. It was the display room where Havertz kept his favored treasures. Harry waved his stolen keycard in front of the reader. It beeped and he twisted the doorknob. The light stayed red. The door stayed shut. He frowned and tried it again. Same result. What the heck? A look over his shoulder found the hallway still empty. He went back to the last door he'd passed and waved the keycard in front of its reader. The red light turned green and he pushed the door open with no issue. Why couldn't he open the relic room door? The guards were supposed to have access to all castle areas.

He stepped back, and the door began to close on silent hinges. A flash of light caught his eye, and Harry stuck a hand out to stop the door from closing. A flicker of light showed through the room's window. Harry walked into the darkness, closing the door quietly behind him before heading to the window. He leaned over and peered out to the ground three levels below. Not three stories like modern buildings. Three levels of a castle, with twenty-foot ceilings on every floor. Sixty feet down from this window to the gravel drive. His canvas-topped box truck was still parked there. For now, it was not attracting attention. That wouldn't last forever.

The relic room holding the book he needed was beside this one. Harry looked around and found this was a sitting room, with chairs in front of an unlit fireplace, book-filled shelving on one wall and a table in the corner. Ivory and ebony chess pieces sat on a thick board. He took all this in with a glance before turning back to the window. A simple latch secured it. Harry opened the window. He leaned out. He looked straight down. *Perfect.*

A ledge ran along the castle wall directly below the window. More of a decorative sill, really; calling it a ledge was generous. Half his foot could fit on the outcropping if he were lucky. A single row of stone led to the adjacent window, and beyond it was one of the small corner turrets. Nobody would step out there for any reason. Nobody except Harry Fox.

Harry had to hope the windows of every room at this level were equally unsecured. All he needed was to get on the ledge, make the short trip over to the next window, slide his pocketknife between the windowpanes to lift the latch and he was inside.

As long as he didn't fall off the ledge. Harry grinned. *No need to think that way.* He stepped out onto the ledge. One foot, which he had to turn sideways to fit onto the stone, then the next. Both hands stayed glued to the window frame. The window of the relic room was twenty feet away. Not far when he'd looked at it from inside the castle. A veritable odyssey out here. Harry took a breath, pressed his backside against the wall and started shifting. One foot, then the other until he could no longer hold onto the window frame. He kept sliding over at a steady clip, his fingers digging into the mortar lines for the illusion of support.

Bang. A gust of wind threw the open window behind him inward so it smashed off something inside. Harry winced. No breaking glass, but another gust came and the window swung inside once more. He picked up his pace. A guard might hear that and come to investigate the noise. Unless Havertz's dreadful singing covered his tracks. Harry almost laughed.

One foot slipped loose when he stepped on an abandoned bird's nest. Harry froze, mortar cutting into his fingertips as he gripped the wall. The thundering of his heart would draw the guards if the banging window didn't. The nest dropped down into the darkness as Harry slowly pulled his foot back and paused, cold air harsh in his throat with each gasp. *Easy, Harry. You're almost there.*

He pushed on, never looking down until finally, one fingertip touched the windowsill. Out came his pocketknife. The blade flipped up and Harry slid it between the panes, wiggling it up and down until the latch released and the window swung inward. A familiar scent hit his nose as he clambered up and over the sill with exaggerated care. The scent of smoke. Perhaps from Havertz's fireplace downstairs.

Harry closed the window behind him, leaving the penlight in his pocket. Better to work by moonlight than risk having someone spot his light under the door. Harry kept still as his eyes adjusted to the dark room. What he saw when they did kept his feet rooted to the floor. None of his research had prepared him for this.

His heart pounding, Harry walked to what looked at first like the dark outline of a man, nothing more than shadow. He risked using the penlight. Its beam turned the man to gold and sent waves of flashing light over the walls and ceiling. A suit of gold-plated armor. Gilded panels interspersed with polished metal gleamed in the light. A gaudy plume of red feathers decorated the helmet, while gemstones dotted the breastplate. Harry noted the golden beard carved into the face protector. How anyone could move in that stuff was beyond him. It had probably belonged to a king who drank wine and sat on his horse while the battle raged far away.

He turned and looked around him. Display cases lined the walls, dark spotlights above them to showcase the collection. A pair of gold-and-silver pistols sat on an adjacent display stand. Pistols that appeared to be the earliest version of a six-shooter Harry had ever seen. He didn't bother to read the informational placard on the stand as he began to walk slowly around the room. Same with the description of a pair of swords on the next stand, one a curved samurai blade and the other a Viking sword with a ruby in the pommel that could have ransomed a king.

Harry paused to look up at the marble statue that came next. Bearded, muscled and holding a jagged thunderbolt, Zeus stood seven feet tall and had been carved in ancient Greece. Harry's light moved to the final artifact in this row, held in a place of honor in a corner of the room under a protective glass case. It was an illuminated manuscript commissioned by Charlemagne and previously owned by Charlemagne's personal abbot, Agilulph. Agilulph was the man whose scrawled note had set Harry on this journey.

Harry stood over the case. Colors of a richness those living in the ancient world could scarcely imagine leapt off the page. Harry drew in a short breath. "Elephants," he whispered to himself. "Sara was right."

Even the gray ink seemed to glow, lustrous and vibrant. Harry shook his head. There would be time to admire it all later. He put the penlight between his teeth and reached for the glass cover. The upside of Havertz keeping his prizes in a castle with a squadron of guards on duty was that it seemed like enough. That's why the only thing holding this glass cover in place was a simple latch. Harry lifted it, the same as he'd done with the window. It flipped open. No passcodes, no keys. He raised the hinged glass top, grabbed hold of the open book and lifted it out.

Harry tucked the book under his arm like a football, closed the glass cover and headed for the exit. He cast a long look at the Viking sword, its decorative ruby as big as a golf ball in its pommel. *Maybe next time.*

He unlocked the room's door and slipped into the hallway, re-securing the lock as he closed the door behind him. Now to get across the castle and up to the corner tower. Then he'd give Havertz a real show before he left. The German could have avoided all this if he'd been reasonable. Too bad for him. Harry tested the door handle to be sure it had locked. The scent of smoke hung in the hall as he turned. Havertz was in for a surp—

Two guards stood in the hallway. The faint scent of smoke hung on their clothes. Both had a look of shock on their faces, the look of men sneaking a cigarette in a far corner room of the castle when they were supposed to be on their rounds. Two guards who never expected to encounter a man coming out of the relic display room. Two guards with pistols holstered on their belts. Both men stood as still as Harry.

One of them blinked. He leaned closer, peering at Harry through the shadows. *"Jurgen?"*

Harry ducked his chin even lower. He grunted a monosyllabic response and turned his back on the two. Harry shielded the book with his torso and started walking. One step, two steps, forcing himself not to move too fast. The two guards said nothing, and Harry let out the breath he'd been holding. *It worked.*

"Jurgen." Harry ignored the name and kept walking. The guard repeated the name, louder this time. Harry waved a hand without turning around and grunted again.

A flashlight beam came to life behind him. Harry's shadow stretched out in front of him. The guard's now raised voice followed. *"Halt."*

The stairwell was too far ahead. Even if he ran for it, these guys could have every guard in the castle on his tail in seconds. He had only one play. He stopped.

He turned and marched back toward the pair before they could respond. The light was in his face, so Harry lifted his own penlight and aimed it right in their eyes. A protest formed in one guard's throat as Harry came at them, feet pounding. He reached into his pocket, slipped his fingers into the knuckledusters and started yelling at the two guards.

"Guten Morgen! Wo befindet sich die Bilbiothek? Kaffee wit Milch!"

They were the first three German phrases that popped into his head. Wishing them good morning, asking where to find the library and ordering coffee with milk confused them just enough so Harry could get within arm's reach. The guard who had been speaking still had his mouth open when Harry clocked him flush in the jaw with his knuckledusters. The guy dropped. The other guard stared with wide eyes as his friend collapsed, looking up in time for Harry to send him down for the count as well.

The second guy had barely hit the ground before Harry was running hard for the stairwell. Everything depended on him getting to the far tower before those guards recovered and raised the alarm. He rushed down the first flight of stairs, stopped on the landing and looked out the window. Nothing seemed amiss. His truck was still parked there—*Uh oh.* A flashlight beam snapped on and lit up his truck's side. Harry saw a guard approach the vehicle. Harry turned the volume on his radio up and ran down to the second level, slowing as he rounded the corner, and marched along the walkway overlooking Havertz's still-raucous gathering below. The fire crackled, mugs crashed together, and the abominable German folk singing continued to fill the air.

Another guard walked out of the stairwell moments before Harry walked past. Harry nodded and grunted first. The other guy did the same and kept moving. Harry turned the corner, ignoring the stairwell in favor of a hallway that kept him on this level and put him closer to the tower he needed. He was halfway there when his radio burst to life.

"Eindringling! Eindringling!"

A guard appeared from a doorway ahead. Make that two guards. Harry kept jogging toward them as they watched him approach. He raised a hand and pointed past them, shouting as he picked up speed. *"Augen! Augen!"*

The guards hesitated. Why was their comrade yelling *eyes* as he ran at them? They couldn't know it was because Harry didn't know how to say *look* in German and this was the best he could do. What they did understand was something was wrong. One drew his sidearm as Harry raced toward them. The second tried to as well.

They were standing too close to each other. Their elbows smashed together and each howled in pain. Harry kicked one gun loose and punched at the other. Both firearms went flying. He jabbed the closest guard in the gut, doubling him over so the knee Harry brought up caught him square on the chin and sent him down. Harry turned to take care of the second guard.

Who was faster than he looked. The standing guard's fist landed smack on Harry's nose, knocking him back. Harry stumbled, shaking his head to clear his vision as the guard closed in. Harry saw another fist coming and threw his arm up, catching enough of it to send the blow glancing off his chin. He didn't catch the next shot, which caught him on the cheek and knocked him back another step. Harry twisted, a punch whizzed past, and he threw an elbow at the guard, who ducked. Harry shot forward to headbutt the guard in the nose when he looked up and the guy fell back, howling wetly, as Harry threw a hook that caught the guard square in the side of the face and dropped him.

All three of their radios erupted with frenzied German. Harry raced for the stairwell that led upstairs. He made it halfway before the sound of pounding feet and shouting guards came from above him, the noise sending him running back the way he'd come. His breath was coming fast now with the weight of the pack on his back. He burst out of the stairwell, turned the corner and passed a suit of armor as he rushed down the hallway overlooking the floor below. He saw that Havertz and his companions had huddled together in front of the fire and were watching Harry race around upstairs as Havertz shouted into a radio. None of them realized Harry wasn't a guard.

The armor. Harry stopped and went back to the armor, set his book down in a dark shadow and went to work. Off came the arms, the helmet and chest plate as Harry worked feverishly but almost noiselessly. The legs were next, and before any of the guards he'd heard in the stairwell appeared, Harry had freed the mannequin from its metallic case and was holding it in his arms. He used his stolen keycard to open the closest door, ran in and went straight to the window. Holding the mannequin like an awkward, lanky football, he drew his arm back and hurled it through the thick window. There was a satisfying din of shattering glass, followed by the thump of the mannequin hitting the ground below. Harry doubled back to grab the book, and as the noise of approaching guards sounded in the hallway Harry stepped behind a thick tapestry on the wall and stood still.

The guards ran past. Harry poked his head out and watched them dash into the room he'd just been in. One of them cried, "*Mein Gott!*" and Harry ducked back as the guards came running out again and headed downstairs. They were in for a surprise when they discovered the body on the ground was mostly plastic. Harry slipped from behind the tapestry, hugging the wall as he moved down the hallway and turned toward the stairwell heading upstairs.

"Halt!"

The shouted order came from below. He looked down to find a guard pointing at Harry. *"Buch! Das Buch!"*

The book. He'd spotted the book under Harry's arm. Out came a pistol and Harry ducked as the guard fired and a bullet pinged off the stone railing. A second shot did the same. So much for sneaking around. Harry lowered his head and took off at full speed. Two more guards joined the one firing below. Shards of rock erupted off the wall, the dust stinging his eyes as the ping of missed shots punctuated each step. Harry lifted the book to cover his head as he dove the last few feet toward the stairwell door, rolling as he hit the ground and crashing off the wall before skidding to a halt inside the stairwell. *Safe at home.* He clasped the book to his chest, then got up, tucked it under his arm, and made to take off once more. There was a metallic *ping* as something dropped to the floor. He looked down to see a spent bullet had fallen out of the book.

His footsteps echoed off the stone walls as Harry took the stairs two at a time up to the third level, following the route he'd memorized, until he arrived at the narrow stairway leading to the bell tower. His keycard opened the heavy wooden door, cold air greeting him as he raced up the winding stairs to an open landing on top.

The giant metal bell was suspended below a conical tower roof. He was high above the ground now, and the wind blew briskly here. Harry ran over to the stone wall and looked down to where a group of guards now stood around the dummy he'd thrown from the window. They were only a few feet from his cargo truck with its canvas roof. Harry grinned. *Get ready.*

He took off his pack and set it down, unzipped the top and removed a folded piece of fabric with straps attached to it. Harry secured the illuminated book in his backpack, then cinched it tightly around his torso and shrugged into the straps attached to the fabric. He tucked the fabric into a strap to secure it, stepped up onto the stone wall and reached up. A gutter running around the roof was within reach. Harry carefully pulled himself up to the roof as the first banging sounded on the closed tower door below.

Time for the grand finale. Harry pulled a small electronic device from his pocket, one no bigger than a deck of cards with a single button on it. Harry powered it on, and a solid red light illuminated. He crab-walked up to the peak of the pointed roof, leaning low, and when he reached the very top, he stood and turned. The shouting from below was loud now; the guards were nearly on him. Harry grabbed the folded fabric from his strap and looked at the dark horizon, then down to the cargo truck far below. He pushed the button on his device. The light turned from red to green and Harry ran as fast as he dared.

The edge of the roof rushed up fast. Harry ran at the darkness, took one last step on the roof and leapt into the void as the cargo truck exploded, rockets tearing through the canvas roof and screaming towards the sky.

Harry didn't watch them detonate as he careened into the night. He pulled a handle on his pack and flinched as the engine on his back came to life and the fan concealed in his backpack went to work. Harry threw the folded fabric skyward. The air caught it and the paraglider chute filled to stop Harry from plummeting seventy feet to the ground. The parajet engine on his back shoved him forward as the night sky around him filled with brilliant reds, blues and yellows. He dared a glance down at his truck, from which a steady stream of fireworks erupted in a wondrous display.

No bullets tore through the dark fabric of Harry's chute. None punched holes in him. He kept his eyes ahead, the fan on his back churning to push him up and on into the night, gliding in near-silence to the north. A compass strapped to his wrist glowed green and told Harry he was on the proper heading. Two minutes from now he'd touch down in a field beside a river, leave his pack and get into the boat he'd docked there. A boat taking Harry—and his book—one step further along Charlemagne's path.

Chapter 2

Manhattan

"Is this a bullet hole?"

Sara Hamed looked up from the book in front of her.

Harry swallowed. "Yes."

She nodded, her eyes lingering on Harry for several beats. "I see." That's all she said before looking back down.

Harry inhaled a lungful of sterile museum air. Dry paper crackled as Sara used a gloved hand to turn the page of the illuminated manuscript. She did not turn to look at him again for some time, her gaze on the book now on a table in her office.

Harry sat quietly while she turned the pages, focusing on the imagery at the beginning of each chapter. He lasted less than three minutes.

"What do you think?" he asked.

Sara flipped another page. The faint, familiar scent of lavender hit his nose when she pulled a strand of hair behind her ear. "About this book?"

Harry bit off a retort. "Yes, Sara. The book."

"By *the book*, you mean this manuscript that was created over a thousand years ago and features some of the most awe-inspiring images I have ever seen. A manuscript any museum would want for their collection." Now she looked up from the page. "A manuscript you drop on my desk with no explanation as to how you came to have it."

Harry opened his mouth.

"A manuscript we have discussed at length over the past month," Sara continued before he could speak. "And which you told me was in a

German castle owned by an odd and likely dangerous collector who has enough money to turn down an outrageous offer from a disgraced oligarch."

Harry did not open his mouth this time.

"Is that *the book* to which you refer?" she fired at him. He nodded. "Then yes, I have thoughts. None of which you will hear until you tell me everything." She punctuated that last word by stabbing a finger on her desk. "How did you acquire this piece?"

Harry Fox had bent the truth many times in his life. This would not be one of them. "I stole it."

That made her sit up straight. "Shut the door." He stood and closed her office door. "You stole it from Leon Havertz?" Sara asked. "You're joking."

"I'm serious," Harry said. "I have the bruises to prove it." He pointed at his jawline. "See?"

"Perhaps I could see them if you used a razor more than once a week. Tell me what you did."

Harry wasn't offended. She cared about his injuries. Probably. "Fine. And for the record, Evgeny isn't a disgraced oligarch. He had to leave Russia to survive. Leaving because the president wants you dead doesn't make someone a disgrace. He's a decent guy. In his own way." Sara's face made it clear he was pushing it too far. "Okay, okay," Harry said. "I stole a guard's uniform after posing as a delivery driver, snuck into Havertz's castle, relieved him of the manuscript and jumped off the roof." That got a gasp out of her. "Don't worry," he said. "I had a paraglider. Set off some fireworks to distract the guards and cruised to a boat I had stashed on the river. Nothing to it."

A few years earlier Sara Hamed had been an Egyptologist at the University of Trier in Germany. That's when she'd saved Harry Fox from getting his teeth knocked out by a couple of drunken skinheads. She'd had no idea what would come from that chance meeting. Her new role at the American Museum of Natural History, for starters. And an apartment in Manhattan. One she rarely used these days.

"You are the biggest fool I have ever met."

Harry flashed a half-grin. "A fool who manages to keep you around."

"I can't be with a dead man."

Ouch. "It wasn't dangerous," he lied.

"Were there more guards?" He said yes. "Did they have firearms?" Another yes. "How many times did they shoot at you?" He demurred. "Too many to count is what I'm hearing," Sara said. She looked at the ceiling as though for inspiration. "One day," she said in a soft tone, "your luck will run out. And then I'll be alone. I'm serious, Harry. Be more careful." She looked back down at him and her gaze softened. "For me."

"I will. I promise."

"Thank you." She tapped the desk. "You asked for my thoughts on this manuscript. I need time to review it."

"Is it the book we needed?"

"I'm certain it's what we need to continue following Charlemagne's trail." Sara flipped pages with care until the inside of the front cover was visible. "Look at this inscription." She indicated a line of concise handwritten Latin script made by an economical hand.

Harry read the passage aloud. "*This book honors the Great Charles, whose piety resounds in Heaven.*" He took a breath. "The *Great Charles* is Charlemagne, also known as Charles the Great."

"Correct. Abbot Agilulph possessed this book at one time," Sara said. "Agilulph, who laid out the reference points on Charlemagne's trail. A trail you discovered from the message he wrote in his personal bible."

It had all begun a little more than a month ago when Harry obtained Agilulph's bible and discovered a handwritten message inside suggesting relics from Charlemagne's reign had been secreted away. Harry didn't fully buy it, but he couldn't pass up the chance to investigate. Harry wanted the relics for a personal reason. Revenge.

"You agree this book contains the information we need to unravel Agilulph's last message," Harry said. He quoted it from memory.

"*The prizes of my Father travel with Columbanus to the Trebbia. Follow the knowledge of that learned servant of God. The true path is marked by the mythical beasts of thunder and fury who dwelled far beyond our lands.*"

"I do," Sara said. "Agilulph often referred to Charlemagne as 'Father,' and Columbanus was an Irish saint known for founding monasteries in Ireland and Italy. Including one on the banks of the Trebbia River in Italy. Columbanus stayed at the Bobbio Abbey after its founding to produce this illuminated manuscript." Sara indicated the book on her desk. "Agilulph is telling us to follow Columbanus's knowledge on a path marked by mythical beasts."

This part had tripped Harry up. Not Sara. "Beasts that aren't mythical. Elephants," he reminded her.

"They were mythical to Agilulph," Sara said. "Elephants hadn't been seen in Europe for nearly eight hundred years until Caliph Harun al-Rashid gave one to Charlemagne to signify the alliance between the Frankish and Abbasid empires."

"Thunder and fury describe an elephant quite well. And Africa and Asia are both far beyond Charlemagne's land."

"Which leaves us to find the true path." Sara frowned. "I suspect that answer is also in this book."

Harry sensed an opening. "Did you receive copies of the diaries from Evgeny?"

Evgeny Smolov, the exiled Russian oligarch. A man Harry had worked with on more than one occasion, never by choice. A man who simultaneously made Harry's gut turn cold and could also be almost decent, at least by oligarch standards. "He was supposed to send them to you."

"He did," Sara said. "Want to know what they say?"

"The short version." He pointed at the book. "We're on a roll here."

"The short version is the diaries belonged to Spartacus and his father. They detail how Spartacus became a gladiator."

Harry couldn't help himself. "How did he?"

"Spartacus intended to start an uprising, with the goal of engaging Rome and allowing Thrace to rebel for its freedom against a distracted enemy. He infiltrated the Roman army and allowed himself to be caught.

Because of his training and heritage, he was able to negotiate being sold into slavery as a gladiator instead of being executed."

"Spartacus believed Thrace couldn't defeat Rome unless the Romans were occupied with other wars. Force Rome to fight on multiple fronts and maybe Thrace had a chance." Harry shook his head. "This story rewrites the history books."

"Not unless we have proof. Without the actual diaries as evidence, it's only an interesting theory."

"Evgeny won't give you the diaries. He wants them for his personal collection."

Sara frowned. "Perhaps you could appeal to his lust for gold."

"He's already worth billions."

"I meant gold relics. As in the aquila. You have it?"

The same adventure on which Harry had uncovered the diaries had also led him to a pair of Roman aquila statues, the golden eagles carried by a legion to symbolize Roman might. None was known to have survived antiquity, until Harry discovered two of them. One of which was now in his shop. "I do have one," he said. "The other one is with Interpol."

"I saw the press release last week."

Harry had returned the first aquila to Taxiarchis Limnios, a man who worked for the Greek government, in the descriptively named Department Against Smuggling of Antiquities. The announcement a week earlier of its recovery from the tomb of a Thracian king had electrified the academic community. "You want me to offer Evgeny the aquila in a trade for the diaries?" Harry asked.

"The world now has one recovered aquila. Why not use the second one to reveal the truth behind Spartacus?"

Why not? *A couple million dollars out of my pocket.* That's what he wanted to say. He opted for a second choice. "We'll see."

Her look made it clear she didn't believe him. "You don't work for Joey Morello now," she said. "That's what you told me."

"I'm in business for myself now."

"As a relic hunter, or as an antiquities dealer?"

"Both. Either way, I'm my own boss."

A half-truth, and she knew it. Sara also knew when to let a subject go. "It can't be easy for you," she said. "Changing your way of life. I hope you realize why I worry."

Harry's gaze narrowed. "Why's that?"

"I want you to be safe." She reached over and touched the back of his hand. "I may have come to America for this job." Sara waved a hand to indicate the museum office and everything beyond. "But it wasn't the only reason."

"I know. The food's better here than in Germany."

"Very funny."

His phone buzzed and Harry looked down. "Uh-oh."

"Uh-oh what?" Sara asked.

"It's Evgeny." Harry showed her the phone.

"Offer him the trade."

He waved her suggestion away and connected the call on speaker. "Hello, Evgeny."

"Harry Fox, my friend." The booming voice nearly blew Harry's eardrum out. Apparently Evgeny was well into his champagne tonight. "We must talk."

An invisible fist squeezed Harry's stomach. "We must?"

"Yes. I have news."

"I'm working on a personal project now," Harry said. "The one I told you about."

"You will crush that bastard Olivier Lloris. Do not fail."

"I won't," Harry said.

"We will talk now." Evgeny barreled on as though Harry hadn't said a word. "I have made a discovery."

Harry ignored Sara, who was mouthing *Offer him the aquila*. "What did you discover?"

"I am richer than I knew." Evgeny chuckled. "Did you know I have artifacts from Pompeii in my collection?"

"I did not."

"They were burned." A dry laugh. "I joke," Evgeny said. "But it is true. When the volcano exploded, these artifacts were buried in the ash. Which is good, because they did not burn. They survived."

"What survived?" Harry asked.

"Scrolls from a private library on Pompeii."

I wish I'd found them first. Harry pushed the dollar signs out of his head. "A nice acquisition. What does it have to do with me?"

"They are in in my house." Evgeny didn't seem to notice when others spoke. "In Windsor." His voice dropped. "You have been there."

"I thought we were past that." By *that*, Harry meant him breaking into Evgeny's palatial estate to steal a crown that had belonged to Mark Antony.

"I am a man who remembers things," Evgeny said. "You should not forget that." Harry's pause had the desired effect. Evgeny returned to the subject at hand. "The scrolls are fragile, so they cannot be unrolled, which is sad. I would like to read them."

"Any idea what they say?" Harry asked. "There could have been other clues in the building where they were found that gives some idea of what's inside them."

"I would ask," Evgeny said. "But the man who owned the house is dead." The Russian laughed long and hard at his own wit. "I am joking. I am also serious. The scrolls could not be read. Now they can."

A vise clamped on his arm. Harry jumped, looking up from the phone to find Sara had moved to his side and looked ready to burst. He jabbed the *Mute* button. "What's wrong?" he asked. "You scared the crap out of me."

Her response was breathless. "Computed topography."

Harry did not blink. "Okay."

"He means computed topography." Sara stood back and jabbed her finger at the air. "Along with a custom artificial intelligence program."

Evgeny's voice filled the air. "Did you hear me?"

Harry unmuted the line. "You're telling me you can now read scrolls that burned in a volcano eruption?"

"I paid someone to do it. An American scientist. He used lasers and an artificial intelligence program to read them."

Sara mouthed *I told you.* Harry ignored her. "Money solves everything," he said.

"If not money, lawyers and guns."

Harry chuckled. "What do the scrolls say, and why do I care?"

"Because of one scroll. It talks about something important to you."

Harry leaned closer. Sara was at his side. "I'm listening," Harry said.

"You must read it yourself."

"The scroll?"

"I already sent it to you. Check your email. Read it and call me back."

"How do you know my personal email?"

The gravelly voice replied. "I know everything, Harry Fox."

The line went dead. Harry went to reach for his phone, but Sara grabbed his arm and ripped him out of his seat, hauling him to her desk and throwing him into the chair. "Open your email right now," she ordered.

Harry knew better than to argue. "What is computed topography?" he asked as he logged into his email account.

"A way to read ancient scrolls using infrared lasers to produce an image using artificial intelligence. The method was only developed last year. The laser picks up any ink on the scrolls, and the A.I. creates a digital version of what the scroll looked like when it was unrolled."

Harry stopped typing. "You're serious."

"Of course I'm serious." She glared at him. "Log in so we can read it."

Harry managed to get his password correct on the second try. "Here it is." He opened the file from Evgeny. Two images appeared on the screen, side by side. "It's one sheet," Harry said. "A full scroll would be much longer."

"The original scroll writing is on the left," Sara said. "In Latin. The image on the right is the English translation."

Harry's gaze flew over the first line of each. "It seems to be an accurate translation," he said. "Agreed?"

Both of them read Latin, though Harry was more adept than Sara. "Agreed," she said. "Now be quiet."

They read in silence. Harry was a tad slower, because Sara gasped a full second before he did the same. Harry reached out and touched the screen. "You see it?" he asked. Sara nodded. "Not Latin. That's a Greek word."

"The only one in the document," Sara said. "Or at least what we have of the document. We need the res—oh my."

Harry had caught up by now. "The name," he said. Sara didn't respond. Maybe she couldn't. "I recognize it," Harry continued. "He died in the eruption."

"Call Evgeny," Sara said. "We need the rest of this scroll."

Evgeny answered on the first ring. "Do you like my scroll?"

"Where's the rest of it?" Harry asked.

"With me."

"Send it over."

"Why are you interested?"

Harry closed his eyes. *Damn.* Should have seen this coming. "This is a job."

"It is a scroll."

"A scroll from Pompeii that mentions Pliny the Elder." Sara scribbled on a sheet of paper and shoved it in front of Harry's face. *Pliny wrote it.* "Chances are he wrote this."

"Full marks," Evgeny said. "I will tell you a secret. He did write it. What else did you see?"

"The name of a device no one has fully understood in two thousand years." Harry looked at Sara. "A relic even you can't buy."

"The Antikythera."

"No one understands its true purpose," Harry said. "It may have predicted celestial events. It may also have been used to measure time."

"Neither is correct," Evgeny said.

"How do you know?"

"I read the entire scroll. That is how."

"What does the Antikythera have to do with Pliny the Elder?" Harry asked. "He was a military man, a philosopher and a naturalist. He wrote…" Here Harry snapped his fingers. Sara scribbled another note, the title of a book that had slipped his mind. "He wrote *Natural History*. The first encyclopedia."

"I know this," Evgeny said. "Does it matter? I am not sure. That is for you to discover."

"I know we've become friends," Harry said. "But I don't work for you."

There was no humor in Evgeny's reply. "Friends can become enemies. You do not want to be my enemy."

Harry's blood chilled. "Come on, Evgeny. No need for threats."

"I do not make threats."

Harry looked at Sara. "Give me a second."

"I will wait."

Harry muted the phone. "What do you think?"

Sara knew about Evgeny Smolov. She knew what Harry used to do when she'd first met him, and she knew what he did now. Sara also understood the historical implications of having access to this scroll. She knew exactly what sort of risk entertaining Evgeny's offer entailed.

"I think I'm not the one who would be risking his neck."

"You've risked your neck a few times. Mount Olympus, for one."

Sara sighed. "Don't remind me. I suppose we owe it to Evgeny to at least hear him out." She wagged a finger in his face. "Don't promise anything, Harry. Make him send the entire scroll before you decide."

Evgeny Smolov had shot a man who was about to shoot Sara on Mount Olympus. Harry could never repay him for that. That didn't mean he couldn't play hardball. "Right."

He took the call off mute. "You send me the rest of the scroll and I'll consider it."

"No."

"I know you, Evgeny. If you're asking me to investigate this scroll, it must be big. Because Evgeny Smolov doesn't do little."

"I see what you are doing," Evgeny said. A pause. "No, I do not waste my time on little matters."

"Then whatever it is you're not saying will probably be enough to make me buy in."

"You will not refuse, I am certain." A new message arrived in Harry's inbox. "Read it and call me," Evgeny said.

As the line went dead, Harry wondered exactly what Evgeny meant by *will not refuse*. Would the scroll be that good, or did Harry not have a choice?

"It's only one more page." Sara pushed him aside and sat in the chair. "Where's the rest of it?"

"That must be all of it," Harry said. He scanned the first few lines. His mouth slowly opened. "Evgeny wasn't kidding." He read it. Sara didn't say a word, so Harry read through it again, still finding it hard to believe. "The Antikythera is for more than predicting the next eclipse. It conceals another secret."

Sara turned to face him. "Harry, do you realize what this means?"

"That we're the first people in two millennia to know the true purpose of the mechanism."

"It means Evgeny was right. This is big." A beat passed. "Which means it is also dangerous."

"You're not interested?"

"How could I not be? But that doesn't mean accepting this offer is wise."

Harry offered half a grin. "Since when do I make only smart decisions?"

"I'm serious, Harry. You run an antiquities business now."

"I do." Harry said. "Most of the time. A guy should have a hobby."

She looked at the screen. She looked back to Harry. "It's your decision."

"Wrong." He touched her hand. "It's ours. I can't do it without you."

"Why not?"

"Because you're smarter than me." He lifted a hand, palm up. "Usually."

She laughed. "You are impossible."

"Then it's yes." He composed a text and sent it to Evgeny. *I'm in.*

"We should review this elsewhere," Sara said. "My museum duties do not include spending time on freelance relic recoveries."

Harry's phone buzzed. He looked at the screen. "Evgeny offered to pay for everything I need. Imagine that." He stood. "Let's go to my store." Harry moved toward the door. Sara did not. "You coming?" he asked.

She touched the book on her desk. "What about Charlemagne? There's another mystery in here, and we're one step closer to solving it."

"Did you just say you support my plan?"

She glared at him. "I'm worried you'll get yourself killed settling an old score. But I also want to know if it's true."

Sara wanted to know if Charlemagne's water clock still existed. A water clock given to him by Caliph Harun al-Rashid. A water clock supposedly containing the keys to the holy city of Jerusalem.

"I won't let Olivier Lloris get away with what he did."

Sara gently closed the book, and Harry's phone buzzed again as a text came through. "It's Evgeny again," Harry said.

"What now?"

Harry looked up. "He said there's a present waiting for me at my store. A present tied to Pliny's scroll."

Chapter 3

Brooklyn

A sign across the building's front façade read *Fox & Son*. A ghostly hand appeared in the glass on the front door, and the sign flipped from *Open* to *Closed*.

Harry grabbed the package that had been delivered minutes before and walked past the stands displaying artifacts for sale. A gold octodrachm coin from the Ptolemaic kingdom. A fourth-century B.C. Greek necklace of gold and silver strands with silver coins embedded in them. A jade Chinese funerary urn from the Manchu dynasty, handcrafted at least five centuries earlier. And these were only the items he had on public display. Harry's store had quickly become a place where New York's rich and often questionable citizens acquired pieces for their private collections.

New York's best fence had played no small part in Harry's rise. Many of Harry's clients knew of Rose Leroux, she who controlled New York's black market for antiquities. A few well-placed words in the right ears from Rose and Harry's sales had gone through the roof. So much so that he planned on hiring his first employee. He couldn't run a busy store and chase relics at the same time.

Harry walked through a door at the back of the showroom and into a room where transactions were finalized. It was a small space with one display table and a computer. Another door led to his private office at the back of the building. Inside that were a larger table and desk, as well as a floor-to-ceiling safe built to withstand anything short of a nuclear blast. Sara was in his office leaning against the table, arms crossed on her chest.

"This is heavy." Harry set the package down on the table. "Hopefully a gold bar fell out of Evgeny's pocket as he wrapped this thing."

"The world of comedy suffered a loss when you didn't pursue stand-up." Sara put her hand out. "Knife."

Harry handed her his pocketknife and the wrapping quickly came off. Sara opened the box and found mounds of padding inside. "It's buried in here," she said, rooting around. "There. Found it." She lifted out a circular object secured in a velvet bag. Sara set it on the table and opened the flap, sliding out what Evgeny had sent them.

Harry leaned closer. "Is that—"

"The Antikythera." Sara pulled the bag completely off. "An exact replica of the mechanism. I'm certain, because we have one at the museum."

A circular metal device constructed of brass and dark metal lay on the table. Intricate gears were visible through the open face, while a series of Latin letters were inscribed around the perimeter, with one row of numbers and one of Greek mythological symbols below the numerals. It was an elaborate assembly of moving parts that could be manipulated to align the internal gears and cogs with the characters imprinted on the metal.

"He would only send this to us for one reason," Harry said in a low voice. "He wants us to use it on the scroll."

"The scroll refers to the Antikythera," Sara said. "Could it be a set of instructions?"

She turned and took a sheet of paper from Harry's printer. "This is the translation," she said. "In English." She began to read aloud.

To my friends on this island who provided security in my time of need, thank you. I entrust you with my life once more. Use great discretion in your handling of this scroll, for I will be executed if it is found.

The Great possessions sought by Caligula to validate his divinity are secure.

Caligula is not Jupiter reincarnated. He is a mere Emperor, and he is mad. To consider one's self a walking God is to assume untold and destructive power. Caligula can never retrieve the Great possessions. Should he succeed, unenlightened others will believe his falsehoods and bow to his demands.

A craftsman on Antikythera helped create this device. Use it to decipher the messages in my History to find the Great possessions if they must be moved to remain hidden from Caligula. Commence where the orator begins his training above the flowers.

"Forget about deciphering all of it for a moment," Harry said when she finished. "What are the letters and numbers at the bottom?" He pointed to a series of letters written in a single line. A row of numbers ran beneath it, lined up so one number sat below each letter. "It could be a code."

"Pliny basically says so," Sara replied. "Right here." She pointed to the final line in his scroll. "*Commence where the orator begins his training above the flowers.* I think he's telling us how to read the letters and numbers."

Harry had learned long ago to trust his gut. More recently, he'd learned to trust Sara. "Fine. I'll buy it for now." He waited. "Any idea what it means?"

She got that look on her face. The one that said *I know something you don't.* He really didn't like that look. "How much do you know about Pliny's writings on rhetoric?"

"Not as much as you."

She ignored his withering look. "Pliny studied the law before he served in the armed forces. After leaving service, he practiced as a lawyer while writing biographies, treatises on grammar and one other subject."

"Rhetoric."

"Correct. His writings on that topic eventually became a manual called *The Student.* Unfortunately, it is a lost work."

"Please tell me we don't need a lost work to decipher the scroll."

"We do need it."

Harry sighed. "Why don't you seem worried?"

"The manual has been lost, but other works contain references to it. Including material written by his nephew, Pliny the Younger. He wrote a summary of the work. The top lesson? That *the orator is trained from his very cradle.*"

"Cradle." Harry rubbed the stubble on his chin. "So *cradle* is where we start to decipher the code on this scroll. If it is a code."

"You don't think it is?"

"I'm just trying to think it through. This *flowers* part makes no sense."

"How is *cradle* the key?"

Harry didn't respond. He was too busy studying the text from Pliny's scroll. A series of Latin letters in a row, with seemingly random numerals beneath each letter. Below that, a circular line of ancient Greek mythological symbols. *Cradle* wasn't spelled out in the letters. None of the letters formed a single word that he could see, as though they were intentionally listed in nonsensical fashion. No, not nonsense. This meant something. Why else would Pliny have written them?

Harry closed his eyes. What could *commence* mean? To begin, obviously, but begin what?

Begin. His eyes shot open. "Begin counting," he said.

"What?" Sara asked.

"I think it means to begin counting." He pointed at the row of letters. "There are repeating letters in this list. *G*, *L*, quite a few *Ns*. But only one *C*. And the numbers beneath them don't repeat. They're not in sequence, but the lowest number is *one* and the highest is *twenty-six*." One side of his mouth turned up. "Know anything with twenty-six components?"

"The Latin alphabet."

"Which we use today." Harry tapped the paper. "I think this is a substitution cipher. And we need that"—he aimed his finger at the replica Antikythera—"to decipher it." He picked up the device. "This outer portion is made of several circular gears that move. One has numbers, another has Latin letters. Let's see what this gives us." He rotated the portion with numerals inscribed on it until the numeral *1* sat beneath the letter *C*. "Commence where the orator begins his training."

"*C* is the first letter," Sara said. "What about the third row of characters—the Greek mythological symbols?"

Harry pointed to one resembling a person holding their arms out. "Hydra, the water monster." His finger moved to the next. "This cup stands for Hebe, goddess of youth." He rattled off a few more. "Chronos, king of the Titans. Hades, god of the dead." Now he skipped to a specific one. "And here is Chloris."

"Symbol for the goddess of flowers."

"It even looks like a flowering bulb." Harry twisted the innermost dial to put the symbol for Chloris below the numeral *1* and the letter *C*. As he did it, something odd happened. "The other two rows are realigning themselves," Harry said. "I didn't touch them."

The letter and number wheels had moved independently as Harry twisted the innermost symbol row. "The inside gears made it move," Harry said. "Maybe we can use these letter, number and symbol correlations to understand the numbers in Pliny's scroll. Grab a pen."

Harry read each number from Pliny's scroll aloud, then told Sara which letter on the mechanism corresponded with it. Her pen scribbled furiously as he dictated to the end. Harry stood at her shoulder as she finished writing. He read her writing once, then again. "Maybe I was wrong."

Sara began speaking, one finger running beneath the decoded message as she went.

19 OBSERVE NATURE

"A number and two words," Sara said. She looked up. "You were right."

Harry checked them again. "I was? It still doesn't make sense."

"It does if you know how to use it," she said. "Pliny told us to *decipher the messages in my History*." Sara grabbed his arm. "He's telling us to look in his book. The number could be a page number, and the words part of the text on that page."

"I thought they were lost."

"All but one. *Natural History*."

Harry dug deep. He came up nearly empty. "I think I've heard of it."

"It's a compilation of nearly forty books covering topics from astronomy to art, mathematics and minerology, to name a few."

"We need a copy." Harry grabbed his phone. "I know a guy who specializes in rare—"

Sara cut him off. "That won't help."

Harry's hand stayed on his phone. "Why not?"

"*Natural History* was partially revised by his nephew after he died. Pliny the Elder published only the first ten books. The remaining thirty were actually published by Pliny the Younger. They may be different from the original text."

"Or they may not be."

"We can't know that with certainty."

"Then we need a copy of Pliny's original version."

Sara's hand fell from his arm. "Which doesn't exist."

"Where would Pliny have kept his original versions?" Harry asked. "I'll tell you. In his personal library."

Sara's voice was vacant, her gaze unfocused. "Which was destroyed when Mount Vesuvius erupted."

"Wrong. It was incinerated, the scrolls burned to a crisp." Harry lifted a finger. "Crispy scrolls our friend Evgeny Smolov owns, and now knows how to read."

Her head shot up. "You're right. It's possible they're in his collection and he simply doesn't know yet."

He picked up his phone and composed a text to Evgeny. He paused in his typing and looked at Sara. "You said Pliny was working on the unpublished books when he died." Sara confirmed she had. "Evgeny bought all those charred scrolls. If those books are anywhere, they're in Pliny's library."

"Don't get your hopes up," she said. "It's a long shot."

Harry tapped the last few words of what he needed and fired the message off to Evgeny. A soft chime sounded as he set his phone on the desk. "What's that?" Sara asked.

"The front door." Harry grabbed his phone and pulled up a live feed from the security camera out front. "It's Joey."

"Are you expecting him?"

Harry shook his head. "I'll see what he wants. Joey doesn't come by unless it's important."

Joey Morello was a busy man. Running the five families of the New York mafia limited a man's time for social calls. Harry pressed a button and the lock outside clicked open. "I'm in the back," Harry said through his phone, and Joey flashed a thumbs up. The familiar bulk of Joey's personal bodyguard filled the screen.

"Mack's here," Harry said.

Sara's face lit up. "He is such a nice man."

Only Sara would describe Mack in that fashion. "It's getting late," Harry said. "Are you going home for dinner?"

She nodded. "I would prefer to stay close in case Evgeny responds. But I need to check the currently available copy of *Natural History* against what we decoded. If it matches, we may not need the original version."

Harry lifted one shoulder with what he hoped was nonchalance. "You could stay at my place. Then stop by your apartment in the morning to get ready for the museum."

"Thank you for the offer, but I can't. I don't have anything with me."

"You can buy whatever you need." He lowered his voice. "I'll tell you a secret. You know those ridiculously expensive towels and the equally overpriced bathrobe you have at your place? I bought some for my place. In case you ever wanted to stay a few days."

"You're joking," she said, eyes widening. "You mocked me incessantly for buying those."

"I stand by my assessment. But if I want you to stick around, there are bigger battles to worry about." Harry raised a hand as though on the witness stand. "I swear it's true. Check the closet outside my bedroom."

She tilted her head. "You are serious."

Footsteps echoed from the showroom, growing louder. "I'll meet you there after I chat with Joey," Harry said. "Thai food sound good?"

That did it. Sara never turned down Thai. "I'll see you there," she said, shaking her head. "I'm not sure what you've done with Harry Fox, but please return him this evening."

A man loomed in the door to Harry's office, cutting off further conversation. The bodyguard had to duck his head a fraction to walk in, his shoulders brushing either side of the doorframe. Joey Morello's personal protector lived up to the truck that was his namesake. Mack.

"Aladdin!" Mack spread his arms wide as the wonderfully offensive nickname filled the room. "It's good to see you."

Harry couldn't help but grin. "Hey, Mack."

"Miss Hamed." Mack dipped his head respectfully.

Sara grinned. "Hello, Mack."

Mack winked, his gaze covering the room in a flash before he stepped aside to allow his boss to enter. "All clear, Mr. Morello."

The head of the New York mob walked in. Joey Morello might not have asked to replace his father on the throne, but even he couldn't deny that he now looked every inch the part. The suit, no tie; the dark, styled hair; the easy confidence and effortless cool.

"Harry." Joey wrapped Harry in one of the back-thumping embraces they favored. "Good to see you."

"You too, Joey." Harry braced himself as Mack joined in. "You too, Mack." That's all he got out before the air was crushed from his lungs and his feet left the floor.

"I'll never know what a good-looking—I mean, a very kind lady like Miss Hamed sees in you, Aladdin." Mack set Harry back on ground level and wagged a finger at Sara. "You ever get sick of this guy, you give me a call."

"You're first on my list," Sara said.

Joey touched Sara's shoulder. "Lovely, Sara. As always."

Sara looked at Harry. "You could learn from him. Good to see you, Joey. I must go."

"I'll walk you out," Mack said. "You need anything, boss, just shout."

Joey waited until Mack and Sara had left before he spoke. "What did

Evgeny send you?" Joey asked.

Harry had told Joey only that Evgeny had sent Harry a package related to the charred scrolls. "See for yourself." Harry indicated the reproduction on his desk. "It's called the Antikythera mechanism. Evgeny had a working replica created."

"I've heard of it." Joey stood over the brass and metal device. He didn't touch it. "Why did he send it?"

"We believe we know its true purpose," Harry said. "At least for Pliny the Elder."

Harry related how he and Sara had figured out that the mechanism could decipher Pliny's code in the scroll, and Harry's hopes for locating the unpublished versions of the *Natural History* books. Joey listened in silence.

"What if the published version of *Natural History* is the same as the unpublished version?" Joey asked when Harry had finished. "His nephew might not have changed anything."

"Sara thinks we need the original to be certain."

"Can't you check the books that are out there now, so you know?" Harry said that's what Sara was doing. "Good," Joey said. He rubbed the back of his neck, shifted his weight from one foot to the other, then leaned his backside against the edge of Harry's desk and crossed his arms.

Harry didn't need to be a detective to sense Joey's unease. "Something's on your mind."

"The Sicilian problem."

Only one Sicilian was causing Joey Morello problems. A man named Carmelo Piazza, head of a Sicilian criminal clan in his homeland. A supposedly respected man who had committed the grievous sin of being disrespectful to Joey Morello. In the world of bosses and clan heads, that ranked up there with being an informant. Even though Carmelo lived and operated across an ocean, theirs was a small world, and the word would get out. Men would ask why Joey had let it happen, which was all it would take to tarnish Joey's reputation. And in this line of work, reputation meant everything.

"Is Carmelo looking into me again?" Harry asked. The issue stemmed from Carmelo accepting money to ask questions about Harry Fox, who had until recently worked for Joey Morello. Carmelo should have gone about this the proper way, by going through Joey. Instead, he'd hidden in the shadows, asking questions in the hopes Joey wouldn't find out. Joey had, and now there was a problem. "I don't want to cause trouble for you."

Joey's mouth became a hard line. "Carmelo chose to insert himself into my business. Carmelo is the one at fault, not you. But no, he isn't snooping again. The problem is the same as before."

"You can't let him get away with this," Harry said.

"If the other family heads in New York learn I knew what Carmelo did and let it slide, they might ask if I'm the right person to lead them. I can't let it go. I must respond."

Carmelo's undoing had been asking the wrong man about Harry Fox and Joey Morello, a fellow clan head named Franco Licata. Franco's father had been close with Joey's father. Franco had called Joey and told him everything.

"What will you do?" Harry asked.

"I'm not sure yet." Joey waved a hand toward the desk. "You always have something interesting going on. Tell me more about the mechanism and this scroll. I'm intrigued."

Harry picked up the replica and demonstrated the decoding process for Joey, spelling out their finding. "We find page nineteen in Pliny's book and then read whatever message begins with *observe* and ends with *nature*."

"A message no one would ever suspect exists unless they had the device." Joey nodded slowly. "Pretty smart."

"The best way to hide something," Harry said. "In plain sight." He fell silent as Joey's gaze lingered on the device.

"Carmelo's inquiries into your activity included asking about Rose," Joey eventually said. "That fool involved Rose Leroux. She hasn't survived this long by letting people cross her and get away with it."

"How can I help?"

"You already have."

"I have?"

"By introducing me to Evgeny Smolov. We're working together on his laundering needs right now. I haven't used my cleaning facilities as much lately. Evgeny's business is filling the extra capacity."

Joey didn't mean a garment cleaning business. He meant money laundering, using any number of the small, legitimate businesses Joey owned. Dirty money coming in the back door and clean money going out the front. Evgeny would send Joey a pile of ill-gotten cash, Joey would run it through his business, and voila, return clean cash to Evgeny. For a fee, of course.

"How are those new ventures of yours going?" Harry asked. "Last time we talked, you were in the black."

"Still am," Joey said. "The future of my family isn't in illicit products or gentlemen's clubs. It's in online sportsbooks, wind energy and boutique banking." His face brightened. "And one of these banks is about to finally open its doors. You wouldn't believe the red tape I had to wade through to make it happen."

Harry gave a nod of appreciation. Joey Morello was modernizing the mafia. Did the Morello family still provide certain illegal services? Of course they did, and would continue to if there were customers for it. But he was also expanding to legitimate means of earning money, the most lucrative of which had been on windswept fields near Buffalo. "The wind farm doing well?" Harry asked.

"Better than I ever dreamed."

"You think Evgeny can help settle this problem with Carmelo Piazza?"

"I'm certain he could," Joey said. "Which is immaterial. I can't ask him. It's too early in our relationship. This has to play out at the right pace. Once it does, my position overseas will be strong. Nobody would think of doing anything like what Carmelo did to me."

Apparently, there were more unwritten rules in the mob than in baseball. "I see," Harry said.

"You working with him on this Pliny the Elder effort is appreciated," Joey said. "I know you have another project on the table. The one with Charlemagne."

A sobering reminder. "It's still on there," Harry said. "Front and center. I'm focused on Charlemagne right now."

"I thought Sara was working on the Pliny research right now."

"She is." Harry ran a hand through his hair. "Okay, maybe I'm working on two projects. I can't keep pushing the Charlemagne search aside. Not after what Olivier Lloris did to me."

"You need the Charlemagne artifacts to draw him in," Joey said. "I remember. I hope you remember he's a dangerous man, Harry. I know the type."

Olivier Lloris was a bad guy, no question. What he'd done was unforgiveable. Which was why Harry couldn't stop what he'd started. "I know," Harry said. "Same as I know you benefit from me keeping Evgeny happy."

"You don't work for me anymore," Joey said. "You do what you think is right."

"What's right is having my friend's back. Like you have mine." Joey said he agreed. "It could be Sara doesn't find anything in the *Natural History* book and we have to wait for Evgeny to decode the charred scrolls. Either way, I'm still working on Agilulph's bible. There's a message inside, I'm sure of it." He frowned. "I just haven't found it yet."

"And when you do?"

Harry grinned. "Then I'm back on the hunt."

"You worried about that German guy finding out who broke into his castle and stole the book?" Joey asked.

"Leon Havertz. No, I'm not worried. He has no idea who I am, and I used my Daniel Connery passport to enter the Schengen Zone." Daniel Connery was the name on a false passport Harry used when he needed to travel anonymously. His real picture with a fictional identity.

"Good man." Joey stuck his hand out. "I have to run," he said as they clasped hands and then embraced. "You need anything, just ask."

Harry said he would. Joey had barely stepped through the door when Harry's phone buzzed. He checked the message. His heart rate picked up. Evgeny Smolov wanted to talk.

Chapter 4

Germany

Shadows danced across stone walls as the man-sized logs flickered and burned in the fireplace, sap crackling as embers flew. Light reflected off circular glasses resting on the man's nose as he watched the fire burn from a high-backed chair. His narrow mouth tightened. The man who had done this would pay. A small hand reached out for an equally small glass on a nearby table, the amber liquid inside coming alive in the firelight as the man took a sip.

Leon Havertz was the master of his domain in all ways. His castle, home of his ancestors for several generations, was his respite from the world. Inviolate. At least until two days ago, when someone impersonating a deliveryman had ambushed one of his security guards, taken the man's uniform and infiltrated his castle. He had stolen the illuminated manuscript tied to Charlemagne. To sell it? Perhaps, but the risk was high. For some other purpose? That was what Leon suspected now.

He would know soon enough. His home might be ancient, but his security cameras were decidedly modern. The man had been careful. Very careful. But even the smartest criminals made mistakes, and Leon's head of security had assured his boss that if the intruder had made one, they would find it. And through that, find the intruder. Then Leon would have his manuscript back and that intruder would never commit another crime.

A high-pitched squeal filled the room. A sound to make the skin crawl.

Only hinges of a certain age made that noise. Hinges Leon refused to replace. Boots clapped on the stone floor behind him as Leon remained seated. His chief of security came to stand beside the chair, standing at attention until Leon turned to face him, moving only his head. "What have you learned?"

"I have an update, sir. The intruder's face can be clearly seen in one camera as he's escaping," the security chief replied. "Before he accessed the bell tower."

"From where he apparently vanished into thin air."

"We believe he used either a parachute or a gliding chute along with a propulsion system."

"None of which can be seen on camera."

"Correct, sir. The brightness of the explosion prevented our surveillance system from focusing on the object clearly enough."

"An object you cannot identify. It appears from my roof and may or may not travel toward the forest before it disappears from sight."

"That is accurate, sir."

"How is this useful?" At least his security chief had the sense not to reply. "A past failure on your part that cannot be remedied," Leon said. "Who is this intruder?"

"We received preliminary identification moments ago." The chief handed Leon a black-and-white snapshot showing the intruder in profile. Leon's gaze narrowed. "He is a foreigner."

"It appears so, sir."

Not even a respectable thief. A foreigner. Who had the audacity to sneak into his home like a rat and run through the halls. This man must be found. "Who is he?"

"Our contact in the European Travel Administration searched passport records. Discreetly. We believe we have a match."

"The name."

"Daniel Connery."

An odd name for a man who looked as this one did. "I would have expected a more ethnic name. What do we know about him?"

His security chief did not reply. Leon repeated himself. "Our contact identified a single Daniel Connery with the same biographical information living in the United States." A pause. "The man using this passport entered Germany one day before the burglary. Which appears to be impossible."

Leon sat up in his chair. "Why?"

"The Daniel Connery whose information matches the passport biography has been in an assisted living facility for the past six years. A car accident left him a quadriplegic. Daniel Connery cannot move his arms or legs."

"Meaning the thief stole Connery's identity. I assume you have continued searching for his true identity?"

"Yes. What we found is concerning. Given he is a criminal, we contacted Interpol and found nothing. We then circulated the image to contacts of a less reputable nature."

"Other criminals."

"Yes, sir. A positive identification came back from America. In New York City."

"The man is a criminal of means," Leon said. "Who is he?"

"His name is Harry Fox. He has ties to the head of the New York mafia. A man named Joey Morello."

The table beside Leon's high-backed chair held two items. One was his glass. The other was a wooden case made of burnished walnut, accented with silver clasps and gold filigree. Leon lifted the clasp and opened it. The two pistols within gleamed in the firelight. Dueling pistols. Leon picked one up and cast an appraising eye over a stag carved into the stock. "Why would the mafia send a man to steal from me?" Leon asked. "What else do we know about this man?"

"He is known to acquire rare cultural relics on behalf of the Morello family."

"Ah." Leon tapped the pistol on his leg. "That makes sense."

"What makes sense, sir?"

Leon waved his pistol at the man. "You are dismissed."

The security chief turned on a heel and walked away. Leon waited until the reassuring sound of his bootsteps faded. The recent overtures made regarding his collection now made sense. An anonymous buyer had contacted Leon through an intermediary seeking to purchase several pieces from his private collection. Including the illuminated manuscript. Had this Harry Fox person tried to acquire the manuscript without his employer's involvement? It appeared so, as the Morello family would understand the repercussions of stealing from Leon Havertz. Leon moved in circles not unlike those the Morellos did. He understood the rules of the game. As would Harry Fox.

Leon pulled a phone from his pocket, keyed in a passcode and scrolled through his contacts. He was a collector of cultural relics, but he did not dig in the dirt or break down doors to acquire his treasures. Leon had cultivated a range of contacts and suppliers to support his interest, and he obtained items as a gentleman should. He purchased them. How the seller came to own those artifacts was not his concern.

A specific supplier had come to mind as one well suited for this situation. A group of men well-versed in all methods of persuasion. Men whose services were always for sale to the highest bidder. Leon called a contact marked *IRM* and put the phone to his ear.

Ringing sounded for a moment before ending abruptly as the line connected. Soft breathing could be heard, but no words came through.

"Good evening," Leon said.

The reply was harsh and heavily accented. "What do you need?"

"I need to hire you."

"Where is it?"

Leon had only ever worked with these men to obtain artifacts. Some they already possessed; others they obtained at his behest. "Not an *it*. A man."

Several beats passed. "No."

"I will pay you well."

One beat passed. "How much?"

"Half a million dollars."

"No."

"This will not be a difficult assignment."

What sounded like a man spitting on the ground. "We are not mercenaries."

No, you are terrorists. Leon had no issues with terrorists, provided they stayed out of Germany. "I need to locate a man. He stole from me. I want you to find him and retrieve my property."

"No."

Leon tapped his foot on the floor. "He is American."

The only better enticement would be if Harry Fox were Israeli. "Why us?" the man asked.

"You are uniquely suited for this." Leon took a breath. "Marwan, we have worked together many times."

Leon only knew the man's first name. Marwan, a man he'd never seen and whom he knew only through phone calls. A man who Leon knew was utterly devoted to his personal cause. The creation of an independent Palestinian state. "Your efforts require funding," Leon said. "Can you afford to turn this down?"

"Who is this man?"

Of course you cannot turn it down. "I will send you the details once we have an agreement."

"What did he take from you?"

Leon briefly described how Harry Fox had infiltrated his castle and stolen the manuscript. "I want my property returned," Leon said. "Will you do it?"

"Does he still have the book?"

"Almost certainly."

Marwan muttered in his heathen language for a moment. "One million dollars," Marwan eventually said.

"Agreed."

"In diamonds."

Diamonds were easier to transport. They were also easier to trade for military-grade weaponry, which Leon knew was always in short supply for Marwan's group. The Islamic Resistance Movement needed all the funding they could get.

"Agreed," Leon said. "Half of the diamonds paid now, the rest upon completion."

"Agreed."

"One final requirement," Leon said. "I must speak with Harry Fox after you find him."

Marwan agreed and the line went dead. Leon composed an email on his phone and sent it to his private banker in Zurich. The banker wouldn't ask why Leon wanted to have the diamonds delivered to a Lebanese jeweler. One sympathetic to Marwan's cause, who worked to support their organization by funneling money to them through his jewelry business.

Leon sent the message and set his phone down on the table. He picked up his drink, leaning back into the tall chair. Marwan had his reasons for doing what he did, as did Leon. Before purchasing the first of many relics from Marwan, Leon had thoroughly vetted the man, not to be certain Marwan was reputable, but for quite the opposite reason. He wanted to be certain Marwan was as committed a criminal as he'd been told. He needed a man unafraid of doing whatever it took to acquire the artifacts Leon wanted. A man so committed to his own cause that he would do anything for the money. Leon didn't care that Marwan's fervor stemmed from relatives dying at Israeli hands.

Marwan's motivations were not Leon's concern. Marwan had agreed to find Harry Fox, recover Leon's property, then give Leon a chance to find out why Harry had gone to all this trouble.

Leon pulled a handkerchief from his pocket, patting a drop of perspiration from his forehead. He moved the chair back from the fire a few paces. Much better. He reached for his glass as his phone buzzed on the table. A message from Marwan. Leon almost smiled.

Fox is in New York. We will have him soon.

Chapter 5

Brooklyn

The clock on the wall read twelve noon when Harry set his phone down. He stood, stretched his back to a series of worrisome noises, then walked out of the spare bedroom he used as an office. He found Sara seated at the table downstairs, in the same place she'd been since early this morning. The same seat she'd been in last night when he came home from his shop, studying the same book in front of her. The illuminated manuscript taken from Leon Havertz. Their initial interpretation of how the Antikythera mechanism might point to hidden messages in Pliny the Elder's *Natural History* had yet to pan out.

"Work bothering you at all?" Harry asked.

Sara had called in sick at her job with the museum. Her condition? Fever brought on by the possibility of deciphering Agilulph's message and continuing on Charlemagne's trail. If there was such a message, it continued to elude them both.

"No," Sara said. "We hire good people. They don't fall to pieces when I'm not around." She looked up. "Has Evgeny called you back yet? You were in a rush to speak with him last night."

"The message from him seemed urgent," Harry said. "I have no idea why he's not getting back to me." Harry had texted Evgeny several times without response. It was now over twelve hours since they last spoke, and the exiled Russian had not responded. Normally Harry would be worried, except this was Evgeny Smolov. Harry was worried for whoever had detained Evgeny.

"I'm sure we'll hear from him. Speaking of hiring"—Harry leaned one hip against the desk, arms crossed on his chest—"I just had a final interview with my top candidate. I'm going to bring him on board."

Sara finally looked up from the manuscript. "It's time. You cannot run a business when you're in another country every other week. Who is this person?"

"A guy named Scott Marlow. He's not a total stranger. More a friend of a friend of a friend sort of thing." Sara's face made it clear what she thought of that. "I need someone I can trust," Harry said. "People I know vouched for Scott."

"Which is important, yes. But what skills does he have?"

"Despite what you may think, I'm not entirely foolish. Scott is more than a guy who knows to keep his mouth shut."

"Please tell me he's not part of Joey's world."

"You mean like me?" She had nothing to say to that. "I'm joking," Harry said. "And no, Scott has nothing to do with the Morello family or any organized family at all. His kid went to the same school as Joey and me, but we weren't tight. Scott's son wasn't into sports, so I didn't know him or his dad very well."

"I seem to recall your sporting experiences consisted of striking out in baseball and being beaten up in the boxing ring."

"I'll thank you to keep your opinions to yourself. As I was saying…" He powered on through her grin. "Scott's son was into building computers. The guy was an electronics whiz like his dad. Not surprising when your dad was the head of I.T. for the largest bank in the city."

"One moment." All levity vanished from Sara's voice. "Why would a man like that want to work for you at Fox & Son?"

"Something wrong with working for me?"

"I am serious, Harry. If Scott Marlow held the position you say he did, first of all, he should be incredibly wealthy. Second, that work has nothing to do with antiquities. So why work for you?"

Harry worried the inside of his lip. He suddenly found the floor very interesting. "It's complicated."

Sara sat back in her chair. She crossed her arms. "Humor me."

"Okay, it's not that complicated. What I've heard is Scott Marlow didn't like something the C.E.O. did, something about where they were investing company resources, so he did something about it." Harry looked up at her. "He published the bank's balance sheet online."

"And why is he not still in jail?"

"He never went to jail," Harry said. "He redacted a specific section of the ledgers covering private lobbying funds. He removed the names of any politicians who'd received payments from it. He let everyone know the bank was basically bribing politicians with shareholder money. Not who, or how much, just that it happened. Supposedly, Scott said that if he went to jail the names would be released to the press. The bank declined to press charges."

"*Supposedly*?"

"Okay, he did it. Scott told me."

"How did he connect with you?"

"He still lives around here," Harry said. "Word got around I was looking for help, and he applied. The guy's a major history buff, so he likes the idea of working with artifacts."

"While you like the idea of having a world-class I.T. wizard on staff."

"Yes." Harry wagged a finger. "But that's secondary. I know I can trust this guy."

"Which matters to you most of all," Sara said. "I agree."

Harry's finger stopped mid-wag. "What?"

"Well done. Quite the coup for your first hire. A trustworthy, unconvicted criminal genius."

He had not a word to say in response.

"I can only imagine who you'll hire next," Sara said. "Bernie Madoff's cousin, perhaps?"

"Very funny. You were the one pressing me to hire someone, remember? Something about making this a successful business, you kept saying."

"That would be a stable source of income and employment for you for decades. Yes, I recall."

"And you say I never listen."

"I'm sure Scott will work out well. Right now, there are more pressing matters."

"Like this manuscript you can't decode."

"I don't see you offering any solutions." She frowned. "It's in here. I know it."

Harry reached down and turned a scrap of paper so he could read it. "Let's start at the beginning. You found this passage in Agilulph's bible, and that's how we knew we needed the illuminated manuscript." Harry read the passage aloud.

The prizes of my Father travel with Columbanus to the Trebbia. Follow the knowledge of that learned servant of God. The true path is marked by the mythical beasts of thunder and fury who dwelled far beyond our lands.

"Columbanus is the Irish saint who founded monasteries in Ireland and Italy," Harry said. "Including one in Italy called Bobbio Abbey. The abbey used to have a book written by Columbanus and dedicated to Charlemagne."

"An illuminated manuscript that was sold to Leon Havertz to raise funds. A manuscript containing images of an animal that hadn't been seen in Europe for over three hundred years—a mythical beast of thunder and fury."

"Elephants. One of which Caliph Harun al-Rashid had given to Charlemagne as part of an alliance."

"Agilulph's telling us to use this manuscript," Sara said. "Which would have been at the abbey during his lifetime, accessible for study. Not owned by a man like Leon Havertz."

"And now we have it," Harry said. "Except we have no idea what we're looking for."

Sara pressed the heel of a hand against one eye, and then the other. "I need a few minutes."

"Take a walk," Harry said. "You've been at this for hours. Let me have a look."

She stood without argument. "I'll be back in fifteen minutes," Sara said as she removed her white cotton gloves and put them on the table. "I expect a solution when I return."

"In that case, come back in five minutes. I'm feeling lucky."

She told him exactly what she thought of that before heading outside. Harry put on the gloves Sara had left behind and carefully flipped to the first page of the manuscript. He didn't know what he was looking for, so he figured he might as well start at the beginning. Was it a hidden message inside the front or back cover? He'd seen that trick done before and didn't discount it, but his gut told him that wasn't it. The most likely scenario here involved Agilulph using the manuscript to hide a message in plain sight. Charlemagne had been a patron of Columbanus, the man whose money had facilitated building all those churches. Charlemagne had paid the bills, and Agilulph was Charlemagne's representative, so if Agilulph told Columbanus to write a certain passage or draw a certain image, the saint would have readily agreed.

Harry scanned the first page. He didn't find what he needed, so he flipped the next page, and then the next. The third page had it. *Elephanti.* Agilulph had pointed Harry and Sara to this manuscript by referencing elephants. That's what Harry suspected was the key to finding the hidden message. Either the word or an image of the mythical beast. A marker.

He kept going, scanning each page for the word and reviewing each with a critical eye when he found it; he did the same with any images of elephants. As the pages turned, his thoughts wandered, try as he might to remain focused. They wandered to the earlier conversation with Sara. To his casual mention of the towels and bathrobe she favored, which he'd bought to have at his place even though he suspected it would have been cheaper to have spun them from gold cloth. Despite that, he had them here for her. She'd agreed to come straight over last night, and that was it. A passing mention of how soft they were, sure, but that was not why he'd bought them. Had she missed his true message?

Harry had wrestled with the idea for some time now: how, or even whether, to let Sara know maybe she didn't need her apartment in Manhattan. That maybe he was thinking about the future, despite her clear impression he was incapable of doing so. That maybe he wanted her to stick around. Why else would he blow a small fortune on stuff she liked? It was practically the same thing as telling her.

The edge of a page slipped from between his fingers and fluttered shut against its neighbor as he looked without seeing. Harry blinked. *Did I miss one?* He flipped back and found an intricate elephant drawn on the page he'd just read. Or looked at, because his thoughts were far from this book. He'd looked right at the elephant and never even noticed. Same with the odd image of Charlemagne smashing himself on the head with his own sword. Or whacking the crown he wore, maybe. Either way, why would he do that? And what were those fragments flying off like shrapnel? They resembled chunks of stone. There was also a red oval beside Charlemagne's head with an angled cross over it. Harry rolled his neck. Focus, Harry. Or you'll miss something big.

Big like this elephant at the top. Or the map in the middle of the page. A map drawn by Columbanus on his travels through the Frankish empire, which stretched from the western edge of what was now France nearly into modern-day Romania. This specific page and illustration detailed what Columbanus called Burgundia. Today the lands were mostly part of Switzerland, though the geography had changed little. Harry picked out the settlements that would become cities, places such as Lyon in eastern France, Geneva in western Switzerland and Milan in Northern Italy. The mountains were clearly detailed; he could see the Alps in the southeast quadrant and the smaller ranges to the north, running through the city of—*hold on.*

Harry angled his head. A settlement was marked where a city would later blossom. That was correct. The mountain range running through it was also accurate. But the settlement was not marked with a name in the way every other location had been. Instead, an image had been drawn to show its location. A tiny image he'd missed before. An elephant. The town it indicated? Zurich.

"Why mark Zurich with an elephant?" Harry asked himself.

"What did you say?"

He shot out of his chair, turning to find Sara coming through the front door. "I didn't hear you come in," he said.

"I can tell." She kicked her shoes off and walked over. "What did you say when I walked in?"

"I asked why Columbanus would mark Zurich with an elephant."

She moved quickly to his side, following his finger as he first indicated the tiny elephant on what would become Zurich, then scanned the rest of the map to confirm no other location bore an image instead of a name. "I missed that," Sara said. "The elephant is so little."

"Look at how he drew the elephant," Harry said. "It's rearing up on two legs. I haven't seen any other ones like it. The rest of the elephants are all on four legs, and they sort of look like big cats with long snouts."

"Anteaters is what I thought of," Sara said. "Though Columbanus may never have seen the elephant given to Charlemagne, so he likely had to draw it based on description alone."

"This is intentional," Harry said. "We need to find an elephant like this one."

"Where?"

"In here." He flipped pages as quickly as caution allowed. "I think the elephant is a marker, a reference telling us to look for another one like it."

"What then?"

"I'll tell you when I see it." Another page flipped. "I bet—would you look at that?"

A rearing elephant stared up at them from the book. It had been drawn in the margin of a page, beautifully colored, intricately detailed, and the same as the rearing elephant marking Zurich. "His trunk is lifted, same as before. It's nearly touching this line of text." Harry translated the Latin into English.

And then I worshipped on the holy ground where the first King of Charlemagne's people defeated the pagans. On this ground the Lord's message was heard and the pagans vanquished. I worship the ground where the Great King of the Franks and his mount knelt before God's chosen.

Harry scanned the preceding few lines. "Columbanus never says exactly where he is," Harry said. "This is part of a long, rambling section. He doesn't give a specific place name further down, either."

"Charlemagne waged war against too many pagans to count," Sara said. "He even fought other Christians and may have called them pagans, or at least not true believers."

"Because they didn't submit to him. An old story."

"A useful one if you are in the business of waging war."

Harry didn't respond. He was too busy trying to think. "I remember something," he said. "About the Dark Ages in Europe and all the different tribes and small kingdoms that existed."

"Before Charlemagne."

"Yes, well before him, in some cases. There was a tribe that ruled the part of Switzerland that became Zurich. They lived there for centuries before Charlemagne." The name that had been on the tip of his tongue arrived. "The Alemanni tribe."

"I'm not as familiar with them as I should be."

"Excellent. It's my turn to be the teacher." He ignored her glare. "They were Germanic and existed alongside Romans as the empire declined. They should have been able to take over, but someone else showed up. King Clovis."

Sara drew in a sharp breath. "Clovis. The first king of the Franks."

"He united the Frankish tribes. By force. Clovis conquered the Alemanni several centuries before Charlemagne was born. Important, but not the best part. Guess which Frankish king was the first to convert to Christianity."

"Clovis."

It was all coming back to him now. "Clovis was the pagan king who converted to Christianity. The first king of the Franks." Harry lifted a finger. "But *not* the Great King of the Franks. That's Charlemagne."

"Charles the Great," Sara said.

Harry gestured to a chair beside him. "Have a seat. I'm going to tell you a story." He flinched when she feigned a punch. "It starts with Charlemagne waging war, as he was wont to do, and this time he was slaughtering and subjugating pagans near a church built by followers of his own grandfather, Charles Martel. It wasn't a great church, but Charlemagne had ties to it, which is why he stopped in the small town of Zurich on his way to commit other atrocities in the name of the Lord."

"Get to the point."

"According to legend, Charlemagne wasn't the most attentive guy."

"I've never heard that."

"The story goes that Charlemagne was riding his horse through Zurich to see this small church connected to his grandfather. As he approached the church, Charlemagne ran his horse smack into three tombs."

"You are making this up."

"Not at all. It's an entirely true legend, although it's probably pure fiction," he conceded. "Want to know why it's still important to us? Because the tombs Charlemagne ran over were the tombs of Zurich's three patron saints. His horse stumbled and fell to its knees, probably tossing Charlemagne to the ground where he hit his head. Hit it hard enough that he had a vision—likely the effects of a minor concussion—in which the Lord told him to build a greater church on the site."

Sara sat rapt with attention. "A church?"

"An expansion of his grandfather's church. A testament to God's greatness." Harry leaned closer, his voice low. "A church that still stands." He waited for a breath. "Grossmünster."

"It still stands?"

"I saw it with my own eyes. Didn't go inside, but I remember noticing two aspects of the church that may be relevant. First, there are seals on a pair of massive bronze doors. Seals with the image of Charlemagne.

Second, there's a big statue of him at the top of one tower, looking over the city."

"Suggesting even more ties to him inside." She pulled out her phone. "I can cancel my meetings for the rest of the week. I'll tell them something urgent came up." She looked up. "What are you waiting for?"

"Uh, nothing?"

"Then start looking."

"Looking for what?"

"Flights to Zurich. What do you think this is, time to relax? This book points to Grossmünster Church. We need to go there at once."

Harry did not get his phone out. He didn't search for flights. He waited, sitting still until Sara noticed the lack of activity. "Can't you find any?" she asked.

"It's not that." His tone made her look up. "Are you sure you want to do this?"

"Why would you ask that?"

"Because I have learned trying to read minds is a fool's errand."

Now she actually seemed to look at him. "Read my mind? What don't you understand? I want to go to Zurich. That's where Agilulph's message points us."

"I'm not talking about that." He shook his head, then the words came quickly. "What I'm asking is do you really want to go, because this could be dangerous." A volcanic expression came to her face. Harry raised his hands in self-defense. "Not that you can't handle danger," he said quickly. "You can. It's just that you don't always think what I do is the right thing."

Her expression barely changed. "I thought you weren't trying to read my mind?"

"I'm not."

"Then why are you telling me what I think?"

He opened his mouth to argue. He closed it. He crossed his arms on his chest. "You know I'm not trying to tell you what to think."

"Then what are you telling me?" She lifted a hand to prevent any response. "I asked you to find us flights to Zurich. I said I want to go. How am I not being supportive?"

"That's not what I mean. It's different."

Sara's face softened. "I know it's different. You aren't very difficult to read. This isn't about my feelings on you following Charlemagne's trail. Do I think your quest for vengeance against Olivier Lloris is foolhardy? Yes." She waved away his argument. "I also realize you are as hard-headed as they come, so I won't try to change your mind. If you believe you must find a relic to entice Olivier into the open so you can handle this, then I won't stop you. I support you."

"I thought you didn't want me to go. You have a lot going on." He waved a hand in the general direction of Manhattan and her museum. "You're in a new country. You're busy. Do you really want to come with me?"

"I do. That's not the question."

"It isn't?"

She shook her head. "No. You asked me if I wanted to come with you to Zurich. But that isn't what you truly want to know."

"How would you know?" He narrowed his eyes at her.

"I'm better at reading minds. And yours has pictures."

"I could do without the jokes."

"Duly noted. What you are really asking me relates not to Charlemagne or Zurich or any relic." She pointed at the staircase leading toward his second floor. "It's about towels. And an overpriced, luxurious robe."

Harry couldn't muster a response.

She crossed one leg over the other. "Your true intent wasn't lost on me. You bought those towels and the robe for me. Why would you buy towels you don't need and a robe you don't want? In the hopes I would feel more comfortable staying here. Which I appreciate. Why would you want me to feel more comfortable here? I imagine it is so I'd decide to stay here more often. Is that close to the truth?"

His face moved. His mouth stayed shut.

"I'll take that as a yes," Sara said. "Now I have a question for you."

He found his voice. "You do?"

"Yes. Are you asking me to move in with you?"

Harry Fox had faced down bullets, swords, spears, bombs, collapsing mountains and even a trident. Each time, he'd stood his ground, or if the situation called for it, run like hell. Either way, he'd handled himself. But now, he sat like a rabbit in the headlights. He didn't do anything.

"You'll need to speak up," Sara said. She waited a moment. "In answer to your unasked question, I'll consider it. There's no hurry. I have my apartment in Manhattan. Your house will be here. Does that sound reasonable?" Harry nodded dumbly. "Excellent," Sara said. "Now, those tickets?"

The train called Sara's intuition that had just run him over continued down the tracks, allowing Harry to pick himself up. "I can't."

"Yes, you can. Perhaps you meant to say you *won't*." Her voice became eerily calm. "Which would be a mistake."

"I won't do it, because this is my fight." He gained steam. "We talked about this before. Olivier Lloris hurt my family. He could do it again. The last thing I need you to do is be with me when I'm going after him."

"You're locating a relic to entice him. You are not chasing him down."

"Same thing. I do this alone."

She could say anything she wanted. Harry crossed his arms. She could read his thoughts? Great. She wouldn't have any trouble reading them now.

"You're afraid I'll be injured?"

"Or worse," he said. "It's not up for debate." He let her stew for a moment, then played the ace up his sleeve. "Besides, I need you here. I don't trust anyone else to help me with the Antikythera."

"What makes you think I will help you?"

"You can't stay away from it any more than you can stay away from me."

"A more incorrect statement has never been uttered."

Harry grinned. "You know what I mean. Evgeny Smolov may have it out for Olivier Lloris, but not like I do. Evgeny is focused on the mechanism and what it can tell us about Pliny's scrolls. The first pass didn't pan out. Evgeny is working on having the other charred scrolls read. If one of them is the original version of a chapter in *Natural History*, then we're in luck."

"And if he doesn't have it?"

"Then I have the smartest woman in the world helping me," Harry said. "We'll figure out a way."

"Flattery won't get you everywhere, but it is a good start." She tapped her foot on the floor. "Alright. I will work on Pliny's mystery. For now." She let out a long breath of air. "It will also be good for me to stay near Nora."

"Nora? Why do you want to be near my sister?"

"Why wouldn't I?"

"She can be a bit intense."

"And you're never like that," she said. Harry made it clear what he thought of the joke. "Nora and I are friends," Sara said. "We talk."

"Talk?"

"Is something wrong?"

"I'm not certain. Nora told me that her father has been distracted lately."

"Gary Doyle is a city prosecutor. He has no shortage of work. I expect he's still dealing with work from the Cana family case."

Not long ago, Gary Doyle's office had taken down one of the biggest mob bosses in the city, an Albanian named Altin Cana. Nora Doyle had played no small role in the matter, the end result of which was the Cana family ceasing to exist.

"It's not only that," Sara said. "Gary's open with Nora about work. But he wouldn't talk about what was on his mind. Whatever it is."

Harry had no idea what to say. Gary Doyle was married to Harry's mother, a fact he'd been unaware of until only a few months ago. Same as he'd been unaware his mother was even alive. Gary was a nice guy. Harry simply didn't know him very well.

A buzzing phone saved Harry. Or so he thought. He stared at the phone's screen. "You're not gonna believe this," he said. "It's Gary."

"Talk to him. I get the impression Gary doesn't have many people to talk to in his life."

"He's a lawyer. He talks all the time."

"He talks as a lawyer. He needs to talk as a person."

At times like this Harry wondered how he would ever keep a woman like Sara interested in him for the long term. "I'll do my best," he said, and connected the call. "Hello?"

"Harry, it's Gary Doyle. You have a second?"

Harry said yes. A minute later he was glad he had.

Chapter 6

Manhattan

"I got you a beer."

Harry took a seat across the table from Gary Doyle. Less than an hour had passed since Gary had called and asked Harry if he was free for a drink. Harry said he was, and then Gary insinuated this was more than just a social call. How much more? Harry would have to wait to find out, so he'd booked it into the city and found the Irish bar where Gary said he'd be waiting. True to his word, his mother's husband even had a pint waiting for him on the table.

"Thanks," Harry said. He lifted his glass. "Cheers."

They touched glasses and drank. Harry kept his eyes on Gary as Gary let his gaze play over the half-empty bar, taking his time. A jukebox on the wall played an old Blues Brothers hit, and the occasional crack of pool balls smashing together punctuated the silence. Harry didn't push.

"Thanks for coming," Gary finally said. He moved to run a hand through the mass of fiery red hair on his chin, the beard of a true Irishman. He stopped halfway, his hand going back to the pint glass. "I wanted to have a chat."

"Is this a good chat or a bad one?"

"I'll let you be the judge." Gary sipped his beer. "You may be surprised to hear this, but I don't have many people I talk with on a regular basis. Informally, that is."

Score another one for Sara. "I imagine you're pretty sick of talking by the end of most days."

"You have no idea how right you are." Another sip. "That's a different issue."

"Fair enough," Harry said. "What do you want to talk about?"

"How much attention do you pay to local politics?"

"As little as possible."

"I knew you were smart." Gary looked around again. "You know I work directly for the district attorney, who works closely with the mayor. The current mayor is a man of ambition." Gary paused. "I'll tell you a joke. What does the mayor say to himself in the mirror each morning? He says 'Good morning, Mr. Governor.' And his reflection replies, 'Good morning, Mr. President'."

Harry smirked. "Good one. So he's ambitious. Not surprising."

"What may come as a surprise is that the mayor is actively making his plan happen."

"How so?"

"From what I've been told, the current mayor will be resigning his role shortly. The lieutenant governor of New York is in poor health and is widely expected to step down next month."

"Which means the governor needs to appoint a replacement," Harry said. "Our soon-to-be-former mayor."

"Which leaves a subsequent vacancy in City Hall."

"Probably won't be a shortage of candidates."

"Starting with my current supervisor."

"Makes sense."

"The next several months will be interesting," Gary said.

Harry waited. Jake and Elwood fell silent. The pool balls cracked. Gary didn't continue.

Sara was right. Gary didn't talk much outside of work.

"Interesting for more than just those two guys," Harry said. "The dominoes will keep falling."

Gary made a noncommittal sound.

"Any idea who might be the next D.A.?"

"Whoever the governor appoints, and later on there will be a special election."

"Not many people vote in those," Harry said. "I'd want to be the guy who gets appointed. More name recognition, more time for the public to see you in action. It gives you a huge advantage on the campaign."

"All true."

Harry finished his beer. "The logical choice would be someone who knows the role, what's required to succeed. Someone with a proven track record." Gary didn't respond. Harry tired of waiting. "A current assistant district attorney, perhaps?"

"Perhaps." Gary finished his beer and signaled for another round. "But it will not be me."

"Why not? You just took down the Cana crime family. Your picture was on the front page. Great name recognition."

"Anonymity is often most appreciated after it is lost. And your mother wouldn't approve. She believes I work too much as it is."

"I don't think she wants the spotlight." He didn't add *for quite a few reasons*.

"Agreed," Gary said. "Which is a large reason why I have no interest in the role."

Harry wasn't buying it for a second. He also knew to keep his thoughts to himself. For now. "Speaking of Mom, how are you two doing?"

"Very well. She tolerates me as much as anyone could hope for."

Their next round arrived. Harry waited until Gary had a drink before speaking. "You know, we talk all the time. About pretty much everything."

Gary's face seemed to brighten. "She loves spending time with you."

"Can't say I blame her." That got a smile out of Gary. "We talk, and if she thinks I need advice, she gives it freely."

"We are both fortunate men."

"Including about my work."

Gary Doyle knew full well his wife's son ran afoul of the law quite often. Gary also knew not to ask questions he didn't want to have answered. He took another drink.

"There's one topic she's never asked me about," Harry said.

"What topic would that be?"

"Thessaloniki."

Gary looked at Harry. He knew full well the significance of that Greek city. More specifically, of Harry's escape from a police station there not long ago. An escape Gary Doyle's daughter had helped facilitate.

Gary twisted his pint glass slowly. "I suppose you wouldn't believe me if I said I don't understand," Gary said.

"Nope."

"Ah. Well, in that case, no."

"No?"

"No, I've never spoken with your mother on the topic." The glass spun again. "Sometimes it's better to keep your mouth shut."

Harry lifted his glass a fraction. "Cheers to that."

"You're a capable, resourceful man, Harry. Like the rest of us, you make a mistake now and again. If I'm able to help you out of a jam and no one gets hurt, I see no harm in keeping that between us."

"I don't care what my mom says about you. You're okay in my book." That made Gary chuckle. "Can this personal courtesy extend to when you're the district attorney?"

Gary didn't take the bait. "Nice try. Someone else can have the headaches that come with being the boss."

Harry took the hint. "If you say so."

Gary's attention was now on the wall to one side. He studied it as though answers to an unspoken question hid beneath the paint. "There is another reason I didn't tell your mother about Thessaloniki."

Harry raised an eyebrow. "What's that?"

"We both know what it's like to lie to people we care about. And to be lied to by those same people."

The sounds of the bar faded. Harry didn't like to think about this. Even though nearly a year had passed, the memory of it made his throat tighten and his stomach clench. "You mean my mom. She lied to both of us."

She had lied to Gary about her name, her past, about everything before the day they met. Including Harry. Who, until less than a year ago, had believed his mother had died decades earlier.

"Yes." Gary took a drink. "I know how it felt when I learned the truth. More importantly, I can see what the lying did to her. Once she told me the truth, she changed. Into a woman without the weight of another life pressing down on her."

"Lying about springing me from a Greek jail isn't exactly the same thing."

"True, but my concern is her well-being. She lost you for twenty years. Dani doesn't need to worry about losing you again any more than she already does."

Harry took a drink from his glass. "Thanks. I mean it."

"I hope you can forgive her."

Harry's gaze narrowed. "Does she tell you what we talk about?"

"No."

"Didn't think so." Harry lifted a hand, palm up. "I already forgave her. I don't agree with what she did, but I understand. Besides, it's in the past. We've all lost too much time. I'm looking ahead and doing what I can with the time we have."

"I second that."

"I want to get to know everyone better. Even you." Harry winked. "I've made progress with my mom. Nora, well, it's hard to tell if she enjoys my company or wants to throttle me."

"I know she enjoys your company."

"She said that?"

"Not in so many words. She respects you and knows you have our family's best interests in mind. Her respect for you was earned."

"I know she gets along with Sara."

"That she has said, more than once. Those two make quite a team."

"Sara's not bad. She's your biggest supporter."

Gary seemed truly caught off guard. "That's interesting."

"You, my mom and Nora. She's a big fan of us all for working to make up for lost time. I suspect it's because she's so far from her own family."

"Egypt is far away," Gary said. "As is Germany."

"She reminds me how quickly you can lose touch in a relationship, and how long it can take to get it back."

A strangely companionable silence settled at the table. Muted conversation went on around them, the jukebox kept playing, and in the corner a small group traded barbs around a dartboard. The silence did not last.

"There's another reason I asked to meet you," Gary eventually said.

"I guessed as much."

"Why do you say that?"

"Gary, you're many things. Unintentional is not one of them."

"Fair enough. It relates to Thessaloniki."

"Am I in trouble?" Harry asked. "Nora told me she called in a favor from that Interpol agent, Guro Mjelde."

"Who is based in Oslo. Guro asked a colleague in Athens to help you escape."

"Chara Markou," Harry said. "She frightened me."

"The sort of lady you want on your side when you're slipping away from corrupt police officers."

"Did the Athens police call you about a missing American who looks like me?"

"They did not. However, inquiries have been made, and I spoke with Guro about them. I don't believe they will amount to anything. Don't worry."

"That's good. If I'm not in trouble, what's this about?"

"I need you to know our office cannot provide any direct assistance for the foreseeable future."

Harry tapped a finger on the table. "Is this how you treat all your agents?"

"I see your point," Gary said. "Yes, you are a contractor on Nora's team. Which was necessary—"

"Because I worked for the biggest mobster in New York. I know."

"Which is not an issue with which I concern myself." Gary looked around again. "As I understand it, you are now fully in business for yourself."

Harry kept very still. "You're married to my mom."

"Yes. Why is that relevant?"

"Just reminding you because of what I'm about to say. Am I in business for myself? Yes. Have I cut off all contact, personal and professional, with Joey Morello? Not exactly."

"You are hardly the only businessman in the city with questionable associates. I assume you are aware of how to keep such relationships at arm's length?"

"If by 'arm's length' you mean 'plausible deniability,' then yes."

"Keep it that way. How this matters for you now is you should lie low for the time being."

"I deal in antiquities. It's a bit of a gray world."

"Then stay as far from the darker gray as you can until this issue dies down. Which it will within a few months."

Harry didn't have a few months. He didn't have a few days. Revenge being served cold was great and all, but he was too close to stop now. Not to mention the exiled Russian billionaire who expected results about Pliny the Elder's manuscripts. "I'll do my best," Harry said.

"Thank you. I won't forget what you did for Nora's team. In a few months we should be able to help again if it is needed."

"With anything I might stumble into?" he asked. Gary nodded. Harry tried to bite off what came next. He failed. "Might be an assistant D.A. with his eyes on the boss's soon-to-be-empty chair comes across a case he needs my help with. Is that the kind of assistance you're offering now?"

"Harry. That's not what I mean."

"If you mean I'm a little salty about being tossed into the fire so you can get on the front page, then yes."

"The Cana family was a menace to this city," Gary said. "Including to your associates. Your helping Nora's team to bring them down was far from altruistic."

"Point taken."

"I'm not interested in using you to become the next district attorney," Gary said. "Right now, I have no interest in the role. My only goal is to show you that you can trust me."

"Did my mom tell you to say that?"

"Hardly. I meant it when I said our professional relationship is mostly off-limits to her." Gary snapped his fingers. "Remember your adventure with Spartacus's armor?"

A relic hunt that had nearly got Harry and Sara killed on Mount Olympus in Greece. That was when Harry had met Evgeny Smolov for the first time. And it was also when Nora and Gary Doyle had helped Harry with his efforts.

"You never told her about that?" Harry asked. Gary shook his head. Harry worried the inside of his lip for a moment. "Thanks."

"You can trust me. Nora as well."

"I know she has my back."

"Then I appreciate you understanding this request extends to her as well. My ask of you is to realize our team cannot provide assistance to as great an extent as before."

"But you can still help me a little?"

"Please, I deal with lawyers parsing every word I utter all day. I can't handle it after work."

Harry raised his hands. "Okay, okay. I won't."

"Thank you. So you're aware, Nora is also under similar restrictions. She isn't going to make waves any time soon."

"Everything must be by the book."

"Correct."

Did Gary not want Nora to make waves because he was protecting her, or because he might soon find himself under increased public scrutiny? The kind of scrutiny that came with, say, being appointed district attorney? These thoughts remained unsaid.

"I understand," is all Harry said. "I won't push her on anything."

"Thank you." Gary glanced at his watch. "I kept you longer than intended. I'm sure you have better things to do than listen to me."

Harry stood along with Gary, and Gary paid their tab before heading for the exit. "It's good to chat. We're family, after all."

Gary stopped. He didn't look at Harry as he stood still for a moment, one hand on the front door. "Yes," he said without turning. "We are."

Gary pushed through the door, Harry behind him, and the men shook hands before heading their separate ways. Harry walked on autopilot, his thoughts still in the bar, running through what Gary had told him. And wondering what Gary hadn't told him.

Cars rumbled past as Harry stood at an intersection waiting for the light to turn. His pocket vibrated. He pulled his phone out. An international number showed on the screen. His jaw tightened as he connected the call. "Who is this?"

Chapter 7

Manhattan

"Where are my artifacts?"

The sound of Olivier Lloris's voice made Harry's body tense. He took a breath and stepped back from the curb, heading for the corner of a nearby building for a modicum of quiet.

"Being acquired," Harry said, once he was standing inside the alcove of a doorway. "This business doesn't happen on a specific timeline."

"What progress have you made?" Olivier asked. "I have a bible from Charlemagne's abbot. Nothing from the king himself."

"That's an invaluable piece."

"I have been promised more."

"A symbol of a peace Charlemagne brokered to secure his empire's future."

Olivier's words grew hot. "All I have is a book with scribbles in it. Nonsense about Saint Columbanus and mythical beasts. Gibberish."

"It's the key to everything else."

"Then where are my relics?"

Harry shifted his weight from one foot to the other. Normally he'd tell a guy like this to jump off a cliff, but this was different. To dispose of Olivier, he needed to keep him close by making him believe Harry was exactly what he said: a relic hunter looking to make money. "I'm getting close," Harry said.

"Prove it."

Fine. "I'll call you tomorrow. I have a new book. The one Agilulph's gibberish pointed me to."

The fire was gone. "You do?" Harry assured him it was true. He did not reveal how he'd found it. If Harry told Olivier he'd stolen it, there was a chance the Frenchman could figure out the collector was Leon Havertz. That could get messy. "It's an illuminated manuscript from Italy," Harry said. "Written by Columbanus."

"How does it connect to Charlemagne?"

"Charlemagne funded Columbanus's efforts to build churches and spread the word of God. Agilulph used this book to conceal the next step in his path to Charlemagne's relics."

"He worked to preserve the relics so that his heirs would be able to prove their claim to his throne," Olivier said.

This guy was sharp. "Maybe," Harry said. "I don't care why he did it. I only care that they're still out there for me to find."

"I must see the manuscript."

"Tomorrow," Harry said.

"Where?"

"I'll call you in the morning."

"In person."

"Sorry, Olivier. No way we're meeting in person. It's not that I don't trust you. I don't trust anyone."

"Why would I steal from you when I don't have what I want yet? You are the man who can provide what I want. I have no plans to prevent you from delivering."

A fair point. But getting this close to Olivier wasn't the smart play.

Same as it wasn't smart to lure in this deadly collector to exact revenge. Too bad. "You want to see the manuscript? Meet me in Zurich."

"I cannot go to Switzerland now. I am a busy man."

"Make the time. Or not. The manuscript will be in Zurich soon. If you want to see it, you'll be there too."

Olivier cursed. "Tell me the time and location."

Harry promised to send the information and clicked off. He slipped his phone back into a pocket and crossed the street, his thoughts churning. Was this the right play, and did he ever have a truly safe move with Olivier? No, so he'd risk it. What mattered was making sure Olivier didn't have another chance to hurt Harry's family.

Harry laughed at himself. Meeting the guy in person was about as good a chance as Harry could give him to do just that. Well, he'd make it work.

Harry rounded the corner of his street and looked up at his house. The porch light was on. A figure sat on the steps, their shadow running down to the sidewalk. He looked closer. *What the heck?*

"Mom?" Harry's voice rose above the noise of his footsteps as he jogged toward his house.

"Harry." His mother looked up from the book in her hands, then stood from the stoop. "I'm glad you're here."

"What are you doing out here at this hour?" He looked left and right out of habit. Nothing concerning. "Are you okay?"

"I'm fine." She squeezed his arm. "I was in the area and decided to drop by."

"It's late."

Dani Doyle shrugged, her black hair swinging around her shoulders. It was obvious where Harry got his tanned complexion. "I'm never too tired to see you."

"You didn't call."

"Am I required to make an appointment?"

He put his key in the front door and unlocked it. "I find it interesting that Gary just asked me to meet him for a drink, then I come home to find you waiting for me. It's almost as if this was coordinated."

"Is this an ambush? No. I simply enjoy your company."

Harry opened the door and gestured inside. "Consider me on full alert for any funny business. Want a drink?" Harry asked as he hung her coat on the rack, then followed her to the dining room table.

"Coffee would be nice," Dani said as she sat down.

Harry fired up the coffee maker and joined his mom. "Thanks for stopping by," he said. "I think. What's on your mind?"

"What do you mean?"

"I've seen that look before. Protest innocence all you like—you have an agenda."

"Perhaps Nora isn't the only detective in the family," Dani said. "I do have a matter to discuss."

"Let's hear it."

Dani sat back in her chair, arms crossed, as though she had all the time in the world. "Gary and I were chatting the other day."

Harry groaned. "I *knew* this was an ambush."

"I asked him about Nora's work."

"Nora's?"

"Yes. He gave me the same line he always does, that their work is confidential."

"What's that have to do with me?"

"Gary may say no, but Nora can be more open to sharing." The coffee machine beeped. Dani waited while Harry poured two mugs and brought them back to the table. "Thank you," she said. "I asked Nora about her work. She refused to share much but did mention one interesting fact."

Harry blew on his coffee. "What's that?"

"Nora told me she helped you with a problem you had in Thessaloniki."

Harry stopped blowing.

"And do you know what else Nora said?" Dani leaned closer to the table. "The answer is nothing, at first. I did not accept that, so Nora eventually revealed the 'problem' was you being in a Greek jail. A jail from which she helped you escape."

"It was more of a guided exit."

"How could you put yourself in danger like that?"

He could have said that being in jail was better than getting killed by corrupt cops. He did not. "I'm fine, Mom. Nothing to worry about."

"No, Harry. There is so much to worry about. I cannot believe you let that happen."

Harry's face grew hot. "You know why I was there in the first place?

Because Nora and Gary both asked me to help them." Not entirely true, but close. And Gary wanted to keep Harry at arm's length now? Fine. See how he liked getting tossed under the bus. "If it weren't for them, I never would have been there."

Dani put a hand to her mouth. "No."

"Ask him about it." Lines creased Dani's forehead. A thought struck Harry. *Maybe I shouldn't have said that.* "Actually, don't. Gary didn't know it would turn out like it did. Don't be mad at him. He was only doing his job."

Dani's voice barely reached across the table. "You think I'm angry with Gary?"

Harry shrugged. "Sort of looks that way."

"I'm not. I'm upset, and he will hear about this, but I'm more upset with myself."

"What?"

"It's my fault this happened. If I had never gone along with your father's plan, he might still be alive, and you wouldn't be forced to work with a mobster who puts you in danger for ancient trinkets and knickknacks."

Harry did not take the chance to correct her regarding their value. He smiled. "I *like* what I do. And you did what you thought was best for all of us."

"And look where we are now."

"We're together." He pointed a finger at her. "You." He turned it to himself. "Me. We're together, and whatever comes next, we'll figure it out."

"That's sweet of you. Inaccurate, but sweet."

Opportunity had presented itself. "Did Gary say anything to you about Mount Olympus?"

She frowned. "Not that I recall. Why?"

"No reason," he said quickly. Harry made a mental note to text Gary and tell him to stay strong, no matter how tough the questions. "Don't worry about me."

"It's my job to worry."

"Then try to keep it to a minimum. And be nice to Gary about all this. He's a good guy." Harry considered. "And we're family."

Dani angled her head. "That's the nicest thing you could say about him. What did you two discuss this evening?"

Harry put a hand on his chest. "I'm sworn to secrecy."

"I will let it slide." Now she laid her forearms on the table and took a breath. "I've done things I wish I could take back. It was wrong to leave you."

"We don't need to go through this again."

"Please, listen. I worry about you, but I support you. We've come to this place in our lives through my choices, not yours. You faced challenges you never should have faced, difficulties we shouldn't have forced on you. You are incredible."

Harry rubbed one hand with the other. "I know. But I do appreciate that."

"Your humility is equally impressive." Dani laughed. "I have two children who put themselves at risk in their jobs. You both do it for what you feel are worthy causes, so the best approach I can take is to support Nora, and to support you."

"I'll try to teach her a thing or two along the way," Harry said, then quickly continued. "Don't tell her I said that."

"I won't." Dani took a drink from her coffee mug. "Enough about the past. How are things with Sara?"

"Fine."

Dani raised an eyebrow. "Do better than that."

"We're good. She's busy at the museum. The store is, well, it's booming. You wouldn't believe how many rich people want cultural artifacts."

"I have an idea."

"It's busy enough that I'm going to hire someone to run the store when I'm…" His voice trailed off for an instant. "Busy."

"Do you have a person in mind?"

Harry said he did. "A man with an I.T. background. He's bright. And trustworthy. Impeccable references."

Dani's face made it clear she had questions. However, she kept them to herself. "That's wonderful," she said. "If there's anything I can do, ask. I have a lot of free time."

"I'll keep that in mind."

"I hope you and Sara have a little downtime together outside of work."

"We do, Mom. Pretty much every weekend."

"She's a nice lady, Harry. Remember that."

Harry almost stopped his eyes from rolling. "I will, Mom."

Dani lightly smacked his arm. "I'd hate for her to feel as though she isn't a priority. Did I mention she's very nice?"

"Duly noted, Mom. I'll do my best."

"Good." Dani looked at the clock on the wall. "I should go."

"Where's your car?"

"Just across the street." Dani stood and walked to the door, Harry right behind her. "You didn't see it?" She winked. "You're normally quite observant."

"I was looking at the suspicious character loitering outside my house."

"I'm happy to keep you on your toes."

Harry hugged his mom, following her outside and making her promise to text him when she made it home. Only after she drove out of sight did he close the door and turn the deadbolt.

Thoughts of bed and uninterrupted sleep were the only ones in his mind as he headed for the stairs. He'd made it halfway when his phone buzzed. He pulled it out and checked the screen. What he saw made sleep a low priority. Evgeny Smolov was calling.

Chapter 8

Brooklyn

The sounds of blaring horns and rumbling vehicle engines faded as the door closed behind him. The man peered out from beneath the brim of his newly purchased baseball cap. Half the tables in the neighborhood coffee shop were full, even at this late hour. The last rays of the falling sun cast long shadows through the shop windows as the man stood inside the door. He kept looking until he spotted one man sitting alone reading a book. A book with a blood-red dust jacket.

Marwan Qassam lingered by the door for several moments despite the all-clear sign from his contact. A bright red dust jacket on the book meant no concerns. A canary yellow dust jacket meant turn around and run. Marwan's associate in New York worked hard to keep a low profile, to fit in as a member of the community. When you quietly provided aid to a group classified as a terrorist organization, you had to be cautious.

"As-salaam 'alaykum." Marwan took a seat at the man's table.

"Wa 'alaykum as-salaam." His contact looked at Marwan over the top of the open book. His gaze stayed on Marwan's face a moment longer than necessary. Or rather, it stayed on a part that was missing. "I trust you had a pleasant journey."

"A lonely journey." Marwan's way of telling the man he hadn't been followed, either on his flight from Beirut or once he'd landed in New York. "I traveled with my cousin." Which meant he'd entered the country using a clean passport, that of a cousin sympathetic to Marwan's efforts as a member of Hamas. Most importantly, his cousin had no known connections to the organization, so his passport allowed Marwan to cross international borders where otherwise he could not.

"I am Bassel."

"Your hospitality is appreciated." Marwan kept his voice low. "Have you located the man I asked about?"

Marwan had sent Harry's photo and what he knew about the American to Bassel. What he knew was precious little.

Bassel set the book down. "This man has many friends in this neighborhood." Bassel lifted his eyes to indicate the borough of Brooklyn all around them. "His connections are strong. I did not find anyone who would speak openly to me about him."

"They fear the Morello family."

"This is a Morello neighborhood. In a Morello borough. In a city the Morello family leads. Harry Fox is protected."

"Do you know where he lives?"

"Yes." Bassel tapped the book. "His address is listed in here. With what else I could find." Bassel did not pass the book over. "First, tell me. How is the battle at home?"

Bassel likely had never set foot in Palestine, or even the Middle East. He was a man of America. A man Marwan would normally disdain. But Bassel was his host and Marwan had to treat him as such. If that meant humoring his pointless questions, so be it. "Active," Marwan said.

"I see the news," Bassel replied. "I see territory being lost. Men dying after the direct attack on Israel. How are things now?"

Marwan sat quietly for a minute. Bassel had the sense not to speak. "Difficult," Marwan finally said. "We have raised the world to our cause. But the road to victory will be long."

"Were you part of the invasion of Israel?"

"I was not given that honor. My role is special operations."

"Raising funds." Bassel dipped his chin. "I commend you, brother."

Bassel clearly understood that fundraising for Hamas didn't entail going around with your hand out, selling sad stories about the plight of

Palestine and the horrors of Israeli occupation. He knew that men with the skills to raise money for the cause were in short supply. Men who specialized in arms trafficking, stolen relics and smuggling anything of value. These were men of action, and quite often, of violence.

"It is my sacred duty," Marwan said. "Every day I support the cause is a day I honor my father."

"He is a martyr?"

"Murdered in a cowardly attack by the Zionist invaders." Marwan fought to keep his voice level. "They murdered my father and my uncle. They destroyed our family home and took everything from us."

"Including that?" Bassel looked at the left side of Marwan's head. At the knotted mess of scar tissue.

Marwan reached up and touched what remained of his left ear. "Including this. From a bullet in Syria."

"Allah favors you," Bassel said. "He protected you that day."

Marwan didn't respond. He lowered his hand from the gnarled remnants of his ear. "Where is Harry Fox?"

"What is your plan?"

"That is not your concern," Marwan said gruffly.

Bassel hardly blinked. "It is my concern. You are in my city. In my neighborhood. I am your host. Would you treat me with such disrespect?"

In Marwan's world he could do as he pleased. But here, he was a guest and the outsider. Marwan swallowed his pride. "Forgive me. I am too anxious to complete my job. I forget myself."

"Tell me the task at hand."

"I must find Harry Fox. He has an item that I will take from him."

"You may find that harder to do than you suspect."

"Why?"

"What little I have learned tells me he is resourceful." A pause. "Like you, in some ways."

Marwan's body tensed. "What do you mean?"

"Harry Fox helps finance the Morello operation."

"He is one man. Not even Italian. How could he support this crime family?"

"In the same way you support your movement," Bassel said. "One transaction at a time. He acquires artifacts. Locates, buys, sells them. This provides money to the Morello family. I am not certain, but it is possible he no longer works for them."

Not certain? "You know nothing," Marwan said. "How is that possible?"

"As I said, this is a Morello neighborhood. I cannot ask simply anyone about this man."

Marwan tapped a finger on the table. "The Morellos are a crime family. Crime families have enemies. Find someone who opposes them. They will talk."

"When I could not find anyone to talk about Harry Fox and his connection with the Morellos, I began to ask different questions. About another crime family. One that no longer exists." Bassel made a circular motion with one hand. "This territory was not always entirely under Morello control. Until a year ago an Albanian family controlled a section of Brooklyn."

"What happened?"

"The police arrested nearly all of them, including the leader. A man named Altin Cana. Today, the Cana family no longer exists. However, I located two Cana associates who were not arrested." A pause. "Two women. They did small jobs. They are the only leads I found who may speak with you."

"Where are they?"

Bassel tapped the book again. "Their last address is in here. With photos of each." He slid the book across the table. "It is the best I can do."

Marwan flipped the cover open and found two pictures inside an envelope, along with the other details Bassel had procured. "Cici. Iris." The names seemed to come with a sour taste in his mouth. "They will talk to me."

"Do you need anything more?"

"No." Marwan took the book in hand. "Thank you for what you have done."

Bassel did not stand from the table as Marwan rose and left, the onrush of noise and humanity greeting him as he walked out onto the street. He punched the address Bassel had given him into the prepaid cell phone in his pocket and started walking. It took him half an hour to walk to his destination. A half-moon was high over rowhomes lining one side of the street. A park occupied the other side.

Marwan found an open bench in the park that had a clear view of a certain house. The house where Cici and Iris lived. He sat and waited. Swing sets and slides were empty at this late hour. Marwan's eyes never left the front door of the house; he would wait all night if he must.

His wait lasted one hour. The front door of the house opened and a woman walked out. Marwan did not need to check the photos. It was Cici. A woman with pathetically over-styled hair and tight athletic pants. Marwan frowned, stood from the bench and walked quickly toward the woman, crossing the street as she locked her front door and began heading down the sidewalk. Marwan accelerated until he could have reached out to touch her shoulder.

"Cici?"

The girl jerked to a halt. She spun around. "Who's asking?"

"A friend of Altin Cana's."

Cici looked him up and down, her jaw working overtime on a piece of chewing gum. "Never heard of him." She twisted and kept walking, crossing the intersection to the next block.

Marwan stayed on her tail. "I assure you I am a friend of his."

"Get away from me, you creep." Cici kept walking as she spoke. "Or you'll be sorry."

"I only want to talk."

"Spill your guts to someone else."

"I will pay for your time."

Her pace slowed. Only for a moment. "Not interested." She sped up again.

"I pay very well."

She looked back, still walking. "You're giving me the creeps."

Marwan stopped. He pulled a hand out of his coat pocket. It contained a wad of cash. "A thousand dollars," he said. "If you answer one question."

Cici stopped in her tracks and turned to him once more. She didn't move any closer, though. "Who are you?"

"A man who needs information." Marwan lowered his hand. No need to wave the cash around. "I ask you one question, right here. You answer it, and I pay you. That is all."

Cici snapped a bubble. "You know who runs this neighborhood?"

"The Morellos."

"That's right. If you know who I am, you maybe know I need to keep my head down. So keep quiet."

Marwan lowered his voice. "Will you answer my question?"

"Depends." Another bubble snapped. "Give me the cash."

Marwan handed over a hundred-dollar bill. "The rest when you answer."

Cici studied the bill for an instant before stuffing it in her pocket. "Fine."

"Where can I find Harry Fox?"

The woman took a step back and lifted her hands as though warding him off. "No way, pal. Find another sucker."

She tried to turn. Marwan latched onto her arm and pulled her close. She started to shout, but he squeezed so tightly she could only get out a short yelp. He pulled her so close he could smell the fruity scent on her breath. "Listen to me. I do not want to hurt you, but I will. All I need is information. You tell me, I pay you, then I leave. That is your only choice."

"I'm not talking."

Marwan dragged her to the closest building, around its corner and into a dim alley. Moonlight glinted on broken glass. A trashcan fell over when he bumped into it. "Talk or this alley is your grave."

Cici's eyes tried to escape from her head as she struggled uselessly to rip herself free from Marwan's grasp. "Let me go," she shouted.

"Answer the question."

Her eyes locked on his. Marwan ducked an instant before she head-butted him, her forehead smacking the top of his skull. It hurt like hell, but he held on. This time he grabbed her with both hands and smashed her against the brick wall. "Talk."

An angry red mark was already appearing on her forehead. "They'll kill me."

"They will never find out you talked."

"That's what you think." She barked a laugh devoid of humor. "Even if you find him, the Morellos will hunt you down, and you'll tell them I talked to save your skin."

"You think I want to kill Harry Fox?"

Her mouth opened. "You don't?"

"No," he lied. "I want to recover my property from him."

She angled her head a fraction. "That's it?"

How stupid. "Yes."

"How do I know you won't kill me after I tell you how to find him?"

"You do not." She shrank away. "But I do not want a dead body in this alley and blood on my clothes. I want to give you the money. Then I want to leave."

She wanted to believe him. He could tell, could see it on her face. "Here." Marwan let go of her and stepped back. Not so far that she could escape; only far enough to make her think she was safe. "See?"

Cici stepped back and bumped into the wall. She wrapped her arms around herself. "Give me the money first."

It was not as though she could get away. Marwan pulled the money out and handed it to her. "Now, talk."

The money went into her pocket. She looked around as though

someone lurking in the alley might overhear. Then she leaned close to him. Close enough that he could have snapped her neck, had he been so inclined. "Don't try to get him at home."

"Why not?"

"He lives in the middle of Morello territory."

"Then where?"

"At his store."

"Store?"

"Harry Fox has a store where he sells stuff. Old stuff."

"Antiquities?"

"Yeah. Coins and statues and things. I never went in there."

"Where is it?"

She told him. Marwan fell silent, though he didn't move, keeping Cici pinned against the wall. Her eyes went in every direction for several seconds. Then she spoke again, suspicion tinging her words. "Everybody around here knows about the store." She narrowed her eyes at him as realization dawned. "You must not be from around here."

"If you say one more word, you are dead." Cici closed her mouth. Marwan stayed in place as he ran through everything she'd said. "What else should I know about Harry Fox?" he asked. "Tell me about his family."

"That wasn't the deal."

Marwan reached into a different pocket. Cici shrank back. He opened his fist to reveal another wad of cash. "I will give you five hundred dollars more if you tell me."

"He has a mother who he thought was dead for a long time, only she wasn't. I don't know where she lives. His dad is dead. Killed a while ago."

Marwan filed the bit about Harry's mother away. "Anyone else?"

"Yeah. A sister. She's a cop. Works for the city. Does stuff with those antiquities."

"Where does she work?"

"She worked with him when they busted the Canas."

"What is her name?"

"Nora. Different last name. I don't remember it."

He should be able to find this Nora. Marwan stepped back. "I know where to find you if you tell anyone of this meeting."

Cici was a lot of things. Unable to recognize a real threat was not one of them. She stepped around him, breaking into a run as soon as she was out of reach and disappearing around the corner. Marwan let her go. He knew fear when he saw it, and though Cici had more courage than he'd expected, she wouldn't talk.

Marwan walked out of the alley and back to the street where Cici lived. He considered the possibilities of how to corner Harry Fox. Of how he would retrieve the manuscript. He knew that the best way to convince a man to go against his will was to make it impossible to do otherwise. But how to do that?

Involve the woman named Nora. And it would not end well for her or Harry.

Chapter 9

Brooklyn

"You are in danger, my friend."

Harry kneaded his forehead with one hand as he stood halfway up the stairs. "Seems to happen whenever you're involved, Evgeny."

"You think I am making a joke? No. Leon Havertz knows who you are."

Lightning arced up Harry's back. His hand automatically touched the amulet around his neck, a soothing presence in trying times. "What?"

"Your identity has been uncovered."

"That's impossible. I wore a disguise. I never looked at a camera." Harry wracked his brain. "At least I don't think I did."

"I do not know how he knows. He knows your name and he sent a man to find you."

Harry ran down to the front door and checked the lock. He opened the coat closet. His shotgun was still in there. Unloaded, but the ammunition was on the floor. "How do you know?"

"You do not believe me?"

"I believe you." Harry moved the nearest window curtain aside and peered down the dark street. He turned and looked at the bullet holes that remained in the brickwork across the room. A reminder of a guy who had come for him once before. "How did you find out?" He turned back to the window.

"I have many business interests. A man I work with told me a story. A story about a collector who lives in a castle. Someone broke into his castle and stole a book. He wants it back, and he wants to find the man who took it."

"He knows it was me."

"Yes. Leon Havertz hired a man to find you."

"Any idea who Havertz sent after me?"

Evgeny made a bear-like noise. Harry's arm hairs rose. "What's that mean, Evgeny?"

"A bad man." Evgeny cursed in Russian. "A man with no conscience."

Harry stepped back from the window. Straight into a chair behind him. "You know his name?"

"No. But I know who he works for."

"Who's that?"

"Hamas."

Harry touched the back of the chair. "Leon Havertz sent a terrorist after me?"

"A mercenary. Havertz has used the group before to obtain artifacts. Hamas needs money, so they steal artifacts and sell them, and one of them has traveled to New York to find you. Stop worrying about relics and worry about yourself."

"Anything else you can you tell me about the guy Havertz sent?"

"I can tell you how to know it is him."

"How?"

"The man who is coming for you only has one ear. The other was shot off."

Harry made a mental note. "Any idea about his age, height, anything like that?"

"He is not young," Evgeny said. "That is all I know. This man has been sent to get the book you stole and bring it back. I do not think he will be sorry if you die."

Great. Just great. "Thanks, Evgeny. I owe you."

"You owe me the truth about my burnt scrolls. What else do you know about them now?"

"I've been kind of busy with my personal project."

"The French guy. Yes, I know. You have no time now for Evgeny, the man who is calling to save your life."

"You want me alive so I can solve the question of Pliny's scrolls."

"True," Evgeny said. "But also, I like you. I respect a man who is the best at what he does."

Harry sighed. "I appreciate that."

"I still need you to find the truth. Do not waste much time with this French guy."

"His name was Charlemagne."

"Yes, him. Hurry and close that one out. I will not be patient forever."

Harry almost cracked a smile. "I wouldn't expect you to. Give me a couple of days to work on the Charlemagne hunt. I'm headed to Switzerland tomorrow. I'll work on your project as soon as I'm finished there."

Evgeny grumbled something along the lines of acceptance. "Do not forget," Evgeny said. "My patience can run out. There are always other relic hunters."

"I thought I was the best."

"You are the best until someone else is better."

Harry chuckled. "Any advice about how to handle this Hamas guy?" Harry asked. "Maybe you could spare a squad of bodyguards for me."

"No. I need them all. You want my advice on how to deal with this man?"

"I do."

"Shoot him. Do not hesitate; do not ask him a question. When you see him, shoot."

"What if it's the wrong one-eared guy?"

"Buy extra bullets."

The line went dead. Harry checked again that every door was locked; same with the windows. He then sent a text to Joey Morello saying someone might be looking for Harry in the neighborhood, and if anyone started asking questions, tell him. This was Morello turf. Unless this guy got someone to talk, finding Harry wouldn't be as easy as the guy might assume. People around here watched out for each other. Harry could count on every single neighbor to have his back. Was it enough?

Having his own backside in danger was one matter. The fact it could put Sara in danger was another. Any fatigue he'd felt was gone when he called her. *Pick up. Pick up.* His hand grew tight on the phone as it rang.

"Is anything wrong?" Sara asked without preamble.

Harry let out a breath. "Why do you ask?"

"It's late. I wasn't expecting you to call."

"Where are you?"

"I'm at work."

"Are you alone?"

"Alone? Not exactly. There's an entire security team here, along with any number of my colleagues who are working late. I'm in my office. Am I alone in the building? Not at all." Her words sharpened. "Why?"

"I just spoke with Evgeny Smolov. About the guy I borrowed the illuminated manuscript from."

"You mean stole."

"Pay attention. That guy knows who I am. He sent someone to get his book back." Sara didn't respond. "Did you hear me?" he asked. "There's someone coming after me. Which means they could come after you." Still nothing. "Sara, this is serious."

She finally spoke. "A man is coming to collect the book you stole. Why don't you give it to him and avoid trouble?"

"Give it to him? I can't do that."

"Why not?"

"This isn't the sort of guy who'll say 'thanks' and leave."

"Are you certain?"

"I'd rather not find out." He didn't tell her who was supposedly coming for it. Even his promise to always tell her the truth had limits.

"Then leave it somewhere for him to find."

"What if we need it again? There could be information inside we don't know about yet. Information from Agilulph we'll need later to follow this path." No response. "Are you listening to me?"

"Mm-hmm."

"Sara, what the heck's wrong with you?"

"Nothing. There's nothing wrong with me at all. In fact, the opposite is true."

Harry went to the staircase and headed up to his bedroom. "You've lost me." He opened his closet and went to the far corner, standing on his toes to reach up and grab a case on the highest shelf. A bad taste appeared in his mouth. He didn't like guns. Never had. His father had taught him long ago that smart men didn't resort to violence. If that happened, it meant they hadn't planned well enough.

"Nothing is wrong. I'm doing wonderfully. As you will be in a moment."

The pistol had a dull shine when he lifted it from the case. He stopped, then set the gun back down. "Why will I be wonderful?"

"Because I can read Pliny's message."

Harry almost dropped the phone. "You can?"

"I decoded it only a minute ago."

His mind, normally useful, was empty. "You did?"

"Yes. I assume you'd like to know how?" Harry said he would. "Do you remember when I mentioned the museum has a replica of the Antikythera mechanism?"

"Yeah."

"I never saw it used, but I do recall being told it works. When I couldn't decode the message in Pliny's *Natural History* using the replica Evgeny sent, I was frustrated. But what if Evgeny's device simply doesn't work? We assumed it was accurate. Assumptions can be dangerous."

"You used the museum's replica instead of Evgeny's."

"Correct. Evgeny's replica showed us the hidden message in the scroll from Pompeii—the line of code at the bottom. It told us to look at page nineteen, beginning with the word *observe* and ending with *nature*."

"Which you did. It was gibberish."

"A random sentence about spices from the Far East, which didn't even begin with the correct word. No matter how I turned it around in my head, it made no sense."

"What did you find, Sara?"

"I asked a colleague if I could use the museum's replica for an experiment. He gave me the key to the exhibit, and as we speak, I am standing in front of the open case with the translated text from Pliny's scroll. When I used the same combination of letter, numeral and Greek mythological symbol, I had a different result."

"The letter *C*, the number *one*, and the symbol for *Chloris*, goddess of flowers."

"Yes. The museum replica didn't point me to page nineteen. It points to page twenty-three."

"Are the new first and last words on page twenty-three?"

"They are," Sara said. "The first word is *find*. The last word is *counselor*.

"And there's a sentence on the right page that begins and ends with those words?"

"I'll read it to you." She paused for a beat. "It says *find the Great One's tutor in the temple of Octavian and his counselor*."

Harry sat down on his bed, the pistol forgotten. His mind went into overdrive. "*Great One*. If you were Pliny the Elder, who would you call the *Great One*?"

"Alexander," Sara said.

"Alexander the Great. Who was famously tutored by a Greek philosopher."

"A tutor Pliny idolized," Sara said. "Aristotle."

Harry pumped the brakes. "Incredible, but what does it mean?"

"The answer lies across an ocean."

"Huh?"

"Across an ocean, in a temple dedicated to the Roman emperor Octavian and his counselor."

"I have no idea what that means."

"The man who would become emperor wasn't called Octavian as a boy. His name was Augustus, and when he ruled the Roman Empire, he required counsel. His closest counselor? His wife, Livia. Which matters to us because there is an ancient Roman temple bearing both of their names. The Temple of Augustus and Livia in Vienne, France."

"Is there anything there tied to Aristotle?"

"I don't know," Sara said. "Should we go and see for ourselves?"

Harry jumped off his bed. "Yes. I'll get tickets and we—" His brain caught up with his mouth. "Hang on." Harry sat back down. "You clearly weren't listening to me earlier. There's a man looking for me. A bad man who intends to get the illuminated manuscript back."

"I was listening. I said to give it to him."

"That's not how it works. You can't go to France with me. Being around me will only put you in danger."

"Harry, if I'm in danger, I *should* be with you."

"That's what puts you in more danger."

"Harry, I trust you. I know what you do can sometimes be risky. If I can't accept that, then I need to move on. My taking this position at a museum in New York is hardly moving on."

"Right now, I'm basically putting everyone I care about in danger because of what I do."

"I know you wouldn't be who you are if you couldn't do what you loved. Now, should I buy my own ticket to France?"

"Your own ticket?"

"I thought you were leaving for Zurich," Sara said. "Grossmünster Church. Or did you forget that?"

"That's become"—he searched for the right word—"complicated."

"I'm listening. The truth, Harry."

He'd backed himself into a corner here. Harry told her everything, about how Olivier Lloris was impatiently waiting for progress on his as-yet-unnamed Charlemagne artifacts, and how Harry's way of placating Lloris while keeping him on the hook included a meeting in Switzerland.

"Will you show him the illuminated manuscript?" Sara asked.

"I should give *him* the darn thing. Then this guy chasing me can go after Olivier."

"Why don't you?"

"I told you. It's not that easy. Guys like this, they make it personal. My guy says this guy will come after me now no matter what."

"He's a hired gun. He only wants the manuscript."

"I doubt that's all. But I'm talking about the collector here. He'll want to make me pay."

"Then how will it ever end?"

"I have an idea. But if it's going to work, I need to keep Evgeny happy."

"In that case, we buy tickets to France. With a layover in Switzerland."

He was really in it now. "Fine," he said. "Evgeny Smolov is paying. At least we'll fly first class."

Harry promised to call her with an update as soon as he had the flight information. He clicked off, looked down at the open firearm box on his bed, and then nearly jumped through the ceiling when his doorbell rang. Harry grabbed the gun and his phone at the same time. Only then did he notice a message on his phone. Joey Morello had texted. He was waiting outside.

Chapter 10

Brooklyn

Harry ran downstairs, leaving the gun in his room only after checking on his security camera that it was in fact Joey Morello on his doorstep. Mack stood on the sidewalk behind him. Even so, Harry reached into his coat closet and grabbed his shotgun before he opened the front door.

"Evening," Joey said. "Have a second?"

"Sure." Harry stepped back to let Joey in. "You waiting out here?" he called to Mack.

"Somebody's gotta watch youse guys' backs."

"I won't be long," Joey said as he walked in and closed the door behind him. He inclined his head toward Harry's left hand. "Expecting trouble?"

Harry looked down at the shotgun. "It's been a busy night," he said. "You here to make it even busier?"

Joey waved a hand. "No. I was down the street and thought I'd drop by. I need advice. But before that, tell me what's going on. Anything I can help with?"

"No, but thanks." Harry recapped the entire saga of the defective Antikythera mechanism, his plan to rope Olivier Lloris in even further, and how Sara had adroitly inserted herself into the middle of it all. The last bit got a chuckle out of Joey.

"She's a keeper, that's for sure. You're outmatched with her."

"True," Harry said. "Enough about me. What's on your mind?"

"Carmelo Piazza again."

"Is he asking more questions about your business?"

"Not mine." Joey dipped his head toward Harry. "Yours."

"My store?"

"No. Your personal project."

Harry had been candid about his plan to give Olivier Lloris the retribution he deserved. Of anyone in the world, Joey Morello understood the need to protect family. "How is Carmelo involved?"

"Carmelo's interference caught me off guard. I took measures to ensure that won't happen again."

Harry had been around long enough to know what that meant. "You have an informant."

"Carmelo has no shortage of enemies in Sicily. None of these conflicts has risen to the level of a true feud, but if he suffered some misfortune, these people would be pleased."

"And you found one close to Carmelo to tell you what they know."

"A woman who works in his household. Carmelo owns horses. This woman cares for them and has other duties on the property. She is everywhere, yet unnoticed. Her father had a brother who lost an eye years ago in a bar fight." Joey lifted an eyebrow. "A fight with one of Carmelo Piazza's men."

"Sicilians never forget."

"The woman sent word today that she overhead Carmelo discussing you with Olivier Lloris."

"She is certain it was Olivier?"

"Positive."

"What were they talking about?"

"Your activities. Mine as well. It seems Olivier is still unclear about your motivations, and he is getting impatient."

"I'm meeting him in Switzerland in a day or two to show him the illuminated manuscript and what we learned."

"Trying to build trust?"

"That's the plan." Joey indicated his agreement. "What will help you?" Harry asked. "Should I forget about the meeting?"

"I would never tell you how to handle your business," Joey said. "But if you want my opinion, I say keep moving ahead. Let me handle this interference behind the scenes. I'll use my source to stay on top of what Carmelo is planning. Right now, those two scumbags are only talking. If it looks like action is coming, we'll handle it." Joey went to the window and slid the curtain aside to reveal Mack at his post, his oversized head slowly turning back and forth, looking up and down the street.

"Agreed," Harry said. "There's one complication with the issue."

"What's that?" Joey asked. Harry told him about Leon Havertz sending a terrorist to retrieve the book. "I might just give Olivier the manuscript," Harry said. "I don't need it any longer, and if I give it to Olivier, I can whisper in a few ears that he has a new illuminated manuscript."

"Not a bad idea, but it may not solve the problem of the guy coming after you. He's under contract to find you. Havertz will only think you sold it. And he still wants you punished."

"True. I don't have any other good options, though. Not with this guy after me."

"You want my help handling this guy?"

"No, I can take care of it. He's missing an ear. Can't be too hard to spot."

"Let me know if that changes," Joey said. He reached up and rubbed the back of his neck. "I spoke with Gio Sabella about Carmelo."

The elder statesman among the five families. A man who had known Joey's father, Vincent Morello, his entire life, had come over from Italy at the same time as Vincent. The head of the Sabella family could have taken over as head of the five families in New York when Vincent was murdered. Instead, he had offered his support to Joey, the Morello heir.

"What does Gio think?" Harry asked.

"He reminded me the ocean is not as big as it used to be. Information travels quickly. If other families believe Carmelo is making me look foolish and I do nothing about it, my reputation suffers. That would be detrimental to me and everyone I care for."

"I assume Gio had a solution."

"His advice is to seek reconciliation, not war. A formal apology from Carmelo would go a long way toward smoothing this over. Carmelo acknowledges what he did. His reputation takes a hit. I not only show I can handle this sort of adversity, but handle it in a way that's better for everyone. I don't want an all-out war with a Sicilian clan."

"Are you going to take his advice?"

"Yes. In fact, it's a chance for me to return a favor. Franco Licata was the man who told me about Carmelo's dishonorable behavior."

"You're going to use Franco as the intermediary to send a message to Carmelo Piazza."

"You got it. Franco delivers my message to Carmelo. He does it quietly, which gives Carmelo a chance to handle this in private, which is more than he deserves."

"It also elevates Franco in the view of Carmelo Piazza," Harry said. "Makes it clear Franco is close with Joey Morello. Even better, it insulates him from suspicion. Carmelo won't think Franco is the one who told you about what Carmelo was doing."

"Right on all counts," Joey said. "Now all I have to do is hope Carmelo doesn't do anything stupid. Like start a war anyway."

"You sure you want Carmelo to know we're aware he's been checking on me?"

"Franco will only tell Carmelo I'm aware of him asking about Rose Leroux." That was what had started all this. Carmelo had quietly asked about Rose Leroux because Olivier Lloris was getting impatient waiting for his Charlemagne artifacts. "Your name won't come up," Joey said. "If Carmelo thinks all I know is that he was asking about my business with Rose Leroux, he'll have no need to involve Olivier Lloris in this, which keeps you out of danger. But you still have that one-eared mercenary coming for you."

"I almost forgot."

"I don't want to push Carmelo harder than necessary. For all of our sakes, but especially for yours. Having you running around Europe puts you too close to Sicily for my taste."

"I appreciate it, Joey. I'll be fine."

"That's what people say right up until they're not fine." Joey stepped toward the door. "That's enough worrying you for now. Well, almost." He stuck his hand out, and Harry shook it. "Remember, this could go badly with Carmelo," Joey said as he opened the door. "I can't be sure how he'll take it."

"If he has any brains he'll give you an apology." Harry shrugged. "Except people with brains don't do what Carmelo did."

"That's what worries me." Joey stepped out onto the front porch. "Watch your back in Europe, Harry. It could get ugly."

Harry didn't blink. "I'll keep my eyes open. It's Olivier Lloris who needs to be worried now."

Joey stepped back toward Harry and embraced him before turning and heading down to his car, where Mack stood waiting. Harry didn't wait for the car to vanish, didn't watch Joey leave. He turned, locked the door, and headed straight upstairs. Tomorrow would be here soon and he needed all the sleep he could get. He fell into bed and his eyes slammed shut.

A blaring noise ripped them open. He tried to move and failed. One arm was nothing but pins and needles. One eye opened as he finally gained control of an arm and reached for his buzzing phone. The time displayed on it indicated several hours had passed since Joey had left and Harry had crash-landed in bed. Joey had just been here. Why was he texting Harry already?

Harry opened the message. He groaned, closed his eyes, and rolled back over, wide awake now. He couldn't get the single sentence from Joey out of his mind.

Franco spoke with Carmelo. Didn't go well. More to come.

Chapter 11

Zurich

Mountains rose above green valleys, their snow-capped peaks casting shadows across the landscape as Harry looked out of his window. The pilot's update that they were about to land in Zurich had woken Harry from a deep sleep. And if that hadn't worked, Sara had smacked his shoulder from her seat beside him. He grumbled, but not so loudly she could hear him. What was the point of flying first class if you couldn't sleep most of the way?

Passages from Pliny's *Natural History* came drifting back to him as he shook the cobwebs from his mind, along with bits of trivia he'd discovered while reading those passages. That ancient Romans believed there were seven planets. That the highly prized purple dye used for fabrics came from a species of snail. That pepper had been considered as valuable by weight as gold. Pliny also described his disdain for perfume. On that point, Harry could agree.

Harry recounted what he'd learned as their plane taxied to the gate.

"It's interesting," Sara said. "Did you find anything about Caligula?" Harry shook his head. "I found one story," she said. "Pliny told an anecdote about how, when Caligula was about to be deposed, he smashed a pair of incredibly rare crystal cups so his successor couldn't have such luxurious items."

"Sounds like a great guy."

Limousines lined the street where he and Sara exited the airport. They found a taxi, Harry rattled off the name of their hotel, and they were off.

The hotel was less than a mile from their true destination, and its daily rate would have put Harry in the poorhouse. Good thing Evgeny Smolov was paying for it. Their taxi wound past the sparkling waters of Lake Zurich, while the rugged peaks still loomed in the distance.

Thirty minutes after Harry and Sara walked through the hotel's front door, they were back on the street and headed toward their first stop. Not Grossmünster Church. Before that, Harry had a date with an impatient collector at a nearby park. A park with plenty of exits, and more importantly, plenty of public visitors.

Sara wanted to stand watch while Harry met Olivier Lloris, but Harry put his foot down. She could go to Grossmünster and get a head start, or she could wait at the hotel. Sara chose the church. Keeping her as far as possible from Olivier was his goal.

In the park, well-heeled businessmen carrying briefcases walked among nannies pushing strollers as Harry, a manila folder tucked under one arm, took a circular route to the fountain where Olivier was to meet him. Olivier wasn't at the fountain yet. No surprise there. The man had thrown a tantrum when Harry told him to be in Zurich on such short notice. Showing up on someone else's timeline was not an Olivier Lloris thing to do.

Harry had specifically asked to meet Olivier in person, not because he wanted to attack the man but so that he could forge a connection. That's how trust was built. Face to face.

Harry circled the fountain, passing a group of senior citizens as they practiced yoga in a grassy space. This time he noticed one man. Not Olivier. His lackey, name of Benoit Lafont, who had met Harry in Paris. Benoit stood near the fountain, hands in his pockets, dapper as ever in a three-piece suit and stylish hat.

Harry walked straight to the waiting man. Benoit didn't move an inch until Harry was next to him. Harry glanced around at the other people near them. "Where's Olivier?" Harry asked without facing Benoit. "My instructions were for him to come."

"Good day, Pepe."

Harry almost groaned. Benoit had used the first French name that had popped into Harry's head when he'd met Benoit outside the Louvre. Poor choice.

"Mr. Lloris sends his apologies," Benoit said. "He is unable to be here. I represent his interests."

"Then tell him I'm unable to sell him any further artifacts." Harry took the folder from beneath his arm, waved it once at the man, then put it back and walked away.

"He will be displeased."

Harry didn't bother to turn. He kept walking.

"Pepe." Benoit waited until Harry turned around. "A moment, please."

Harry walked back as Benoit lifted a phone to his ear, muttering something in French Harry couldn't catch before the phone disappeared. "Mr. Lloris has cleared his schedule," Benoit said. "He will see you today."

"Very funny. Where is he?"

"I'm right here."

Harry spun around. Olivier Lloris had materialized behind him. "Back off," Harry said. "You're making me nervous."

"Shall we walk?" Olivier lifted an arm toward the middle of the park. "I prefer walking while I talk. More privacy."

"You follow me." Harry started walking in the opposite direction. Olivier caught up with quick steps. "Tell Benoit to get lost," Harry said. Only after Olivier told Benoit to fall back did Harry look closely at him. "Why bring the backup?"

"I have enemies," Olivier said.

"And I'm one of them?"

"I don't know."

"I'm not. I'm a businessman, same as you." Harry handed the folder to Olivier. "Have a look."

Olivier stopped walking, took the envelope and removed several images of the illuminated manuscript. "Pictures of elephants," he said after flipping through. "And a map of"—here he put the paper close to his face—"Burgundia." Olivier looked up. "Why are you wasting my time with this nonsense?"

"That nonsense is how I found the next location on Charlemagne's trail. Check the last image. The one showing a line from Agilulph's bible."

Olivier flipped to it. "I do not read Latin."

"It's about a monk named Columbanus and a path marked by mythical beasts of thunder and fury." Harry waited long enough for Olivier's face to tighten. "Columbanus was an Irish monk who built monasteries around Ireland and Italy. Charlemagne provided him with financial support. You figure out what thunderous beasts he considered mythical."

"Elephants."

"Elephants are not native to Europe. Virtually no European alive at the time would have ever seen one. They only had drawings, often fantastical ones at that."

"Elephants were a myth to them."

"Correct," Harry said. "Which is how Agilulph hid his message. He used elephants." Harry inclined his head toward the top page in Olivier's other hand. "That one, to be specific."

"Where is the illuminated manuscript?" Olivier asked.

"In a safe place." A note sounded in Harry's mind. Not of alarm. Of opportunity. "You collect illuminated manuscripts?"

"I collect many items."

"I'll sell you the manuscript after I finish my search."

Olivier continued to look at the paper in his hand. A woman on rollerblades buzzed past them and the paper fluttered. "Agreed," Olivier said. "When will I have it?"

"The sooner you let me get on with this search and leave me alone, the faster you get it." Harry looked back toward Benoit. "You have any other goons following me around I don't know about?"

"No one is following you."

Good to know. "Give me space and we both get what we want faster."

"A fair request." Olivier put the papers back in Harry's manila folder. He did not return it. "Benoit will give you a number. Call me when you have made progress."

Harry didn't react, at least not on the outside. Had Olivier Lloris just given up a measure of control? It seemed so. "Agreed," Harry said.

Olivier motioned Benoit over and had him give Harry a business card that showed only a phone number and Olivier's initials. Harry stuck it in a pocket, turned and walked away from the men without another word. He took a random path out of the park, stopping twice to check for any sign of a tail. Olivier might be starting to trust Harry a little. If so, perfect. Harry, however, wouldn't make that mistake. No one stood out as he looked around him again, so he exited the park and walked in the opposite direction of his hotel, found a cab and took it in a circle back to the park, then headed on a meandering route to a different hotel one block down. Harry pushed his way through the spinning front door, headed for the restaurant, and walked into the kitchen as though he belonged. No one questioned him as he moved quickly past harried waiters and cooks, the rich aromas chasing him out the back door to a remarkably clean alleyway. Only then did Harry go to his hotel.

He called Sara from the lobby and told her to meet him there. Harry stood against the wall and kept alert until Sara arrived. He put one hand in a pocket, the reassuring smoothness of his ceramic knuckledusters easing the last vestiges of concern regarding Olivier.

Sara stopped beside him.

"Ready?" he asked.

"Follow me."

He hurried to keep up as she marched through the lobby and headed outside. Vendors offering sandwiches and ice cream shouted for customers as they walked alongside the waterfront overlooking the Limmat River. Harry told her what had transpired with Olivier Lloris in the park.

"You are certain he did not try to follow you?" Sara asked.

"If he did, I lost him."

"Interesting that you offered to sell him the illuminated manuscript."

"I came here to earn some trust. He was clearly interested in it. It's one more way to get to him when the time comes."

Sara did not inquire further. "I see him."

Harry spun around. "Where?"

"Not Olivier." She pointed skyward. "Him. Up there."

Harry looked up and found a giant staring down at them. A stone king, sitting on a throne cut from the side of one massive tower rising from the church only a few short blocks away. Grossmünster Church, with Charlemagne looking down on all below. Safety netting covered the king, while evidence of scaffolding along the exterior walls suggested his royal backside was in the midst of repair work. Thankfully, that was the only evidence of construction in sight.

"There he is," Harry said.

A pair of white stone towers rose above the rectangular church, twice as high as any other building around. Harry and Sara stopped at one end of the plaza fronting the church, both craning their necks to look up at the towers as Charlemagne looked down. "We know this is where King Clovis conquered the Alemanni tribe," Sara said. "And then where Charlemagne's horse stumbled, inspiring him to expand the church. The question is, what do we do now?"

Harry pointed at the pair of ceremonial bronze doors marking the entrance to the church. "Charlemagne's on both of those. He's on the side of one tower. Chances are there are more images of him inside. I say we look at each, see if we can identify any ties to Agilulph or the path."

"Elephants, perhaps?"

"Exactly what I was thinking," Harry said. "Come on. A service is just letting out. Should be plenty of cover inside."

He led the way, dodging through the stream of people slowly trickling through normal-sized doors alongside the huge bronze ones bearing Charlemagne's face. The street sounds of Zurich disappeared the moment they stepped inside, with only muted conversations and quiet footsteps echoing gently inside the building. Harry pulled Sara to one side and leaned close to her ear. "You take that side." He pointed to their right. "I'll take the other. Text if you spot anything interesting."

Harry stood in front of the entrance a moment longer, looking over the rows of pews stretching ahead. There were two sections of wide benches, separated by a central walkway leading to the altar at the far end. He glanced up at the semicircular arches supporting the towering ceiling. Hallways lined the second level, and sunlight of all colors fell through the stained-glass windows high in the walls. Another ornate stained-glass window glowed behind the altar.

Harry spared them only a glance. No imagery of Charlemagne was to be found in any of the glass. Harry headed for the long walkway on his assigned side of the rectangular church, passing between thick support pillars until he reached the far wall. This time when he looked up, the ceiling was closer, though still well out of reach. He examined the underside of the second level. How thick was its floor? Not thick enough for a man to walk upright in, should he somehow manage to get inside. He'd seen churches before where not everything was as it seemed. Hollow stones, hidden levels, secret chambers. Right now, Harry needed to think like an architect. Did anything seem off?

Nothing did. He looked down the long hallway. Recessed bulbs gave muted lighting, throwing a burnt orange glow over the stone walls. Harry waited for his eyes to adjust after the bright light of the central area. He blinked. A half-dozen statues were set into alcoves. He looked across the nave and saw six statues lining that exterior hallway as well.

He moved to the closest one on his side. A man, no shocker there, though not one he recognized. An engraving on the base told him this was Saint Felix, one of Zurich's patron saints and one of the three guys whose tomb Charlemagne's horse had supposedly tripped over. A fortuitous fall for the church, because soon afterwards, money had spilled from the king's pockets to this place. Felix had his hands out in supplication or blessing. He wore a hooded frock, and fortunately, still had his head. According to legend, Felix and his sister were beheaded for converting to Christianity.

Harry looked left and right. The only other people in the long hallway were two women, both leaning on canes, both facing away from him. Harry slipped into the narrow space between the back of the statue and the alcove wall. He checked low and high, finding nothing out of the ordinary on the statue's rear. A few curse words and one scrape on his arm later, Harry turned to check the alcove wall, with the same result.

The two old ladies didn't turn when Harry stumbled back out from behind the statue. He straightened his shirt and moved on. The smooth stone walls offered no help. Same with the ceiling. The next statue down the line was Regula, sister of Felix and fellow saint. Regula's statue also had her head, and it also offered nothing to suggest Agilulph's path ran through her. Harry had made it halfway to the third statue when he passed the mouth of another hallway branching off at a ninety-degree angle. The stone walls that formed it were the same off-white as the rest of the church, the ceiling curved in Romanesque fashion. Here, too, recessed modern lighting offered muted illumination. A small placard at eye level told Harry what lay ahead. "A crypt," he said to himself. "That's promising." He checked the wall on the other side of the new hallway. *What's that?*

"Harry." Sara grabbed his arm as she spoke, spinning him around. "Did you find anything?" she asked. "I did not. You should check my side to be sure I didn't miss anything."

"I did."

Sara frowned. "You already checked my area?"

"No." Harry pointed over her shoulder. "I found something." Sara turned to where he pointed. "An elephant," Harry said.

Sara angled her head. "It's small."

"It's an elephant carved by a person who's never seen one before."

With its narrow legs and rather slender torso, the animal in question could have been from any of several different species if weren't for the elongated trunk. And one other aspect Sara couldn't see in the shadowy light.

"There's the trunk," Harry said in hushed tones. He stepped closer, pulling her with him. "And there's this."

Sara drew in a sharp breath. "*C.M.*," she said, reading the two Latin letters aloud. One had been carved into each of the elephant's hind legs. "Carolus Magnus."

"Charles the Great. Think this is what we're after?"

"Agilulph used elephants in the illuminated manuscript to indicate Grossmünster Church," Sara said. "Using elephants again is consistent. It's still impossible to know what it means without having read the actual manuscript."

"Look where the trunk's pointing."

"Down the hallway."

"Toward the crypt." He gestured ahead. "Ladies first."

Sara moved down one side of the hallway while Harry took the other, and they checked each stone as they went. Harry peered into an open doorway and found filing cabinets lining one wall, with an empty desk against the other. A cold fireplace was beside the desk. The next room down had no filing cabinets and, like its neighbor, a single desk. Unlike its neighbor, this one had a monk seated at it, his back to them. Harry withdrew his head from the doorway and crept quietly onward.

"Nothing on my side," he whispered to Sara. She shook her head. *Nothing here either.*

They reached a staircase with steps leading downward, though at least these were well-lit. A glance passed between Harry and Sara. Her eyes narrowed. He shrugged and set off, stopping at the bottom of the stairs. In a moment, Sara joined him. They were at a T-junction with a perpendicular hallway. They could go left or right, but not ahead.

"Which way?" Sara asked. She pointed to a sign in German. "There are crypts in both directions."

"Right sounds good to me."

"Why?"

He tilted his head back. "Look behind you."

She turned around. "Oh. Right it is."

Sara leaned closer to get a better look at a second elephant engraving on the wall. The animal was identical to the first, except this time its trunk pointed to the right. They moved in that direction, passing open doors leading to burial chambers on either side. "Don't you want to look in those?" Sara asked after Harry walked past the first one.

"These are newer vaults," Harry said. "You can tell by the stonework. No more than two or three centuries old. We want the older openings." He pointed ahead. "That way."

They kept walking. The tunnel bent ahead, moving toward the river. "Look up," he said. "Notice anything?"

"The stonework is much rougher here," Sara said.

Harry reached an arm overhead. Not a tall man, he could nearly brush his fingers on the stonework. "Lower, too. This is an older section. Where we want to be."

The doorways carved into the walls on either side became more irregularly shaped, the cuts rougher, everything smaller. There were still electric lights on the walls, and a carpet runner covered the center of the walkway, but Harry noted the smoothness of the floor stones on either side of the runner, worn slick by centuries of foot traffic. Harry scanned left and right as they walked.

"We must be getting near the exterior walls now," Sara said.

"Maybe. Maybe not. This tunnel likely predates most of the building above it, and the tunnel almost certainly dates to Charlemagne's era. Zurich looked a heck of a lot different back then. Same with the church he built."

Harry passed another door. He stopped so fast Sara ran into his back. "This is it," he said.

An engraving covered the wall inside: Charlemagne in his royal glory, standing with his feet on the ground and the tip of his crown touching the ceiling. He held a massive sword in one hand, while the other grasped a book. A cape flowed from his shoulders to make the king even more imposing. A beard reached from his chin down to the oversized brooch holding his cape together.

"Look at the book," Harry said.

Sara took in a quick breath. "The same elephant is on it."

"Now his trunk points straight up." Harry touched the end of the trunk. "No, it's actually angled toward Charlemagne."

"What does it mean?" she asked.

Harry didn't respond. An image had come to mind, indistinct and hazy, hovering at the edge of thought. Something he'd seen recently. He closed his eyes.

Her voice broke the stillness. "Are you okay?"

He raised a hand to silence her. The trunk pointing upward. Charlemagne's image, carved into a stone wall. He'd seen this image before. There were so many engravings of Charlemagne, their details blending into a jumbled mess… *Think.* Harry pressed his lips together and smacked his hand against the wall. Not too hard. It was stone, and he didn't want to break—*break*.

"Broken." His eyes opened. "It was broken."

Sara looked up and down the hallway, then at him. "What was broken?"

"The stone around Charlemagne's head," Harry said. "Around his crown. It was *broken*."

"I have no idea what you mean."

Harry stepped back from the wall and looked up at Charlemagne. The cape. The brooch. The beard. "The sword." He pointed at the image. "This exact image is in the illuminated manuscript. On the page with the map telling us to come to Zurich."

Sara looked at the image. "Are you certain?"

"I'm sure. Except the one in the manuscript had debris flying around Charlemagne's head, and some type of design beside it. That's why it stuck with me. I didn't understand what was flying around his head." He turned to face her. "They were pieces of broken stone." He smacked the stone wall again.

She gave him a dubious look. "That seems like a stretch."

"I think it's Agilulph telling us how to find it."

"It?"

"Whatever the manuscript is meant to show us." Harry pointed at Charlemagne again. "This image is the same as the one from the manuscript. It's not a coincidence. It's a marker."

"A marker to what?"

"To something hidden behind that wall."

Sara leaned back a fraction. "You're not serious."

"Think about it." Harry struck a pose in an approximation of the carved Charlemagne image. "Charlemagne's holding a sword near his head." Harry pretended to hold a sword so the tip was near his ear. "In the manuscript, Charlemagne has broken stone flying around his head, and he's wearing a golden crown." Harry aimed his imaginary sword at the wall. "A crown exactly like that one." Harry lifted his other hand. "All while he's holding a book, which looks an awful lot like the illuminated manuscript."

"Which tells you to break a hole in a stone wall."

"Exactly."

"A *gray* stone wall with a crown carved on it. A crown that is decidedly not golden."

Harry shrugged. "You have a better idea?"

"I do not."

"Then help me find something to smash through that wall."

Harry backtracked down the hall, with Sara at his heels, stopping at each open crypt chamber as he passed to poke his head inside. Nothing useful in the first one. Same with the second. He ducked into the third and found the same. Harry lifted a hand to stop Sara from going any further. He motioned for her to get close to him. "There was a monk in the office ahead," Harry whispered in her ear, pointing at the doorway in question. "And another office beyond that one. An empty office." Inspiration struck. "With a fireplace in it."

"A fireplace that may have a poker."

"I'm hoping. Stay here. I'll be right back."

Harry moved down the hallway, hugging the shadows on the opposite wall as he moved toward the occupied office. He paused outside the entrance and peered in. The monk had vanished. A good sign? He'd take it. Harry tiptoed silently on and then leaned his head around the entrance to the next office with the fireplace. He found it empty and slipped in. No poker. No fireplace tools at all. Nothing to help him break through stone.

Harry frowned. His gaze traveled up the wall to a point above the fireplace. His frown disappeared. "That should do it."

It took him longer than he liked, but a minute later Harry was back in the hallway and moving quietly toward Sara, again checking the monk's office and finding it empty. Sara emerged from a shadow in the hallway as he approached. She lifted one eyebrow, looking at what he held. "No fireplace tools?" she asked. He shrugged. "Perhaps this is divine intervention."

"Funny." He hefted the object in his hands. A cross, over a foot tall and nearly as wide, made of solid iron. "Keep your voice down." He glanced toward the heavens. "You never know who's listening."

The crown atop Charlemagne's head nearly touched the ceiling. Harry, even standing on his toes, did not. "Boost me up," he told Sara.

She didn't argue, but went down on one knee, clasped her hands together, and held steady as Harry stepped up, keeping one hand on the wall for balance. Burying any tinge of doubt that maybe Charlemagne wouldn't want to have one of his churches desecrated, Harry leaned back and took aim.

The iron cross hurtled at the stone wall above him. Harry closed his eyes an instant before impact, turning his head aside as flying chips of stone filled the air. Harry opened his eyes again to find the intricately carved crown had been obliterated. The stone on which it was carved remained intact. "Watch out," he told Sara. "I'm hitting it again."

His arm went back, the cross hit the statue again, and more stone chunks flew. Again, then once more, and another time until, at last, Harry tried to pull the cross back and it wouldn't budge. The end he'd been smashing against the stone had stuck in the wall. His chest tightened. *There's an opening there.* The wall wasn't solid stone. He twisted and pulled until the cross came free.

"Are you finished?" Sara asked through gritted teeth. "I can't hold you forever."

"Look at this."

"I can't," she said, her voice tight. "Describe it."

"There's a hole in the wall."

"Do better."

"I broke through the stone."

"What can you see?"

"Nothing yet. Hold on." He cracked the cross against the wall twice more, breaking down more of the stone in front of him. Thick dust filled the air and he looked down. "Watch out." Without waiting for a response, he dropped the cross onto the carpet runner as gently as he could. It *clunked* softly. Harry looked at the stone floor beneath the runner a moment longer. Why was the stone beneath them a different color from the stone on the wall? It was much lighter, and he hadn't noticed until he had this bird's-eye view.

"Let me down," Harry said. He dropped to the ground. "You're lighter than me," he said, going to one knee. "I'll boost you up."

Harry fished out the penlight he kept in one pocket, handed it to Sara, then boosted her up. "Break away more of the stone with your hands," Harry said. "I cracked it, so most should come loose." He didn't say that he'd left it for her so she could be an active partner in the search. She'd asked for that back in Brooklyn. He was finally listening.

"Harry."

"Won't it come loose?" He looked toward the iron cross. "I can use the cross again, but I have to put you down fi—"

"There's something in here."

Her voice made him go very still. "What?"

"Gold."

He nearly dropped her. "Sorry," he said when she yelped. "Can you reach in?"

Sara didn't respond for some time. He kept still, not wanting to knock her off balance. He waited for as long as his patience allowed, which was not long at all. "Sara, talk to me."

"Look."

He craned his neck. "Holy smokes."

Sara held a crown. A circlet of gold, dotted with precious stones in the shape of a cross. There was a purple amethyst, a blue sapphire and a green emerald. Lines in the gold showed it had been made of four golden plates, fused together in a simple design. Sara turned it slowly to inspect the entire circumference. "You were right," she said softly.

Harry searched for an appropriately self-satisfied response. He wasn't fast enough.

"This may be one of his missing—*oh*," she said, cutting herself off. "You were more correct than we realized."

"What are you talking about?"

"There's more here inside the opening. Take this."

She handed the crown down to him. He took it while keeping her balanced. It was heavier than it looked. The fiery sparks from the green, blue and purple gems dazzled him momentarily.

"It's red," Sara said from above. "I believe it's a ruby."

Harry tore his gaze from the crown and looked back up at her. "A single gemstone?" he asked.

"Yes. It's standing upright inside here." She grunted. "I can't move it."

Alarm bells rang in his head. A ruby, standing upright? The illuminated manuscript had shown a golden crown on Charlemagne's head, with chunks of rock falling after the king hit himself with his sword. Harry closed his eyes. *Think*. There hadn't been any red jewels on the crown, at least that he could recall. The only red had been that little dot with an *X* through—

"Don't touch it." His shout rang through the hall. "Stop."

Her weight shifted and he nearly dropped her. "There," she said. "I got it. I pulled—"

The floor shook. Harry's vision blurred and the stones beneath his feet quaked as he shouted, "Put it back. It's a trap."

Sara stumbled from her perch on his leg. He'd remembered too late. The red dot with an *X* through it on Agilulph's map. A warning. Don't touch the red gemstone.

Harry kept the crown in one hand and his other on Sara's leg as the quaking intensified. He lost his grip on her and twisted to the side as the stone floor cracked and dust billowed up, stinging his eyes. Sara was shouting as her foot slipped off his leg, and Harry reached back to catch himself.

The stone floor collapsed. Harry plummeted into a void of darkness, the world turning black as a rumble of stone filled his ears. Harry fell, how far he couldn't say, one hand latched onto Charlemagne's crown and the other grasping out for Sara as she twisted in the air.

He crashed down onto a hard surface. The walls stopped rushing up. The shaking stopped. Harry bounced, twisting as he began to slide down an incline. Unable to stop his descent, he flailed, grabbing at thin air and trying to dig his feet in. He caught only a glimpse of Sara before he turned weightless once more. He floated for a beat, nothing but black and dust and sharp rocks all around him, before the ground rushed up at him. The first part of him to hit it was his face.

Harry coughed. He cracked one eye open. A faint light shone above him. The fingers on one hand wiggled, a good sign. He clenched his other hand and let out a sigh. The crown was still there.

"Harry?"

Sara. Harry pushed himself up and got to his feet. "I'm here."

"Where are we?"

He shielded his face as a beam of light blinded him. "Not in my face," he said.

Sara lowered the penlight and he coughed, blinking rapidly as he looked around them. They were in a passage of some sort. A wet tunnel. He looked down and found a trickle of water running to one side of him. "You okay?" he asked.

"I think so," Sara said. "Are you?"

"Yeah. Part of the floor collapsed." He looked at the rectangular hole perhaps fifteen feet above them. A narrow chute had been beneath the false floor, and it had funneled them to this spot below. "I should have warned you," he said. "The floor in front of Charlemagne. The stones were different. I noticed it when you boosted me up."

"Next time, say something."

Harry ignored her. "What is this place?" He stood still. "I don't like it."

Sara aimed her light all around. They were in a circular tunnel, one with deep grooves cut into the wall on either side. No light came from anywhere other than the hallway above them. "Moving the ruby triggered the floor collapse." She stood amid the broken stones. "This could have been much worse."

"That's why I'm worried. Agilulph warned us not to touch the red stone. The penalty for ignoring his warning won't be a bruised tailbone." Red sparks flashed by his foot as Sara moved her light. He reached down and found the large ruby, which went into his pocket. *Score one for the good guys.* He frowned, his nerves tingling. Harry lifted a hand. "You hear that?"

Sara turned an ear to the wall. "It sounds as though stones are moving."

"Stay still." A faint trembling came from the ground beneath his toes. His stomach went cold. "We need to get out of here. Now."

A loud *snap* split the air and a sudden movement grabbed his eye. "The channels in the wall," Harry said. "They're shifting."

Sara's flashlight beam shot over to the wall and revealed a rope inside one of the wall channels. A rope whizzing past in a blur. She turned to the channel on the other wall. Same deal. A grinding noise came from the darkness of the tunnel.

"The ropes are pulling something." Harry whispered it to himself. "Toward us."

"What did you say?"

Harry didn't speak. He grabbed her arm and took off, pulling her with him, leaping and twisting over the fallen floor stones. The ropes were flying past now, the floor was vibrating, and in the darkness behind them the low rumble of moments ago had turned into a thunderous roar. Sara's light raced across the walls as they ran, their legs burning, lungs aching in the dusty air, feet slipping on the water.

They were too slow. Harry turned to glance over one shoulder and saw it coming. He saw it, but he didn't believe.

The ropes racing along on either side of them were pulling death toward Harry and Sara. Two huge stone elephants careened toward them on a wheeled platform, the ropes attached to either side, hurtling the elephants forward. Their trunks were like spears flying toward them, coming impossibly fast, gaining on them no matter how hard they ran.

"We have to jump," Harry yelled. "They're catching up." His words came in bursts as he jammed the crown down the front of his shirt. "Jump and grab the trunk of the one closest to you. Then pull yourself up and over."

"It will kill us."

"Just do it."

Seconds later the elephants were on them. Harry hesitated, then shouted, "Now!"

They both jumped, each grabbing hold of one of the stone creatures' trunks. "Climb up," Harry screamed above the din.

The tunnel couldn't go on forever. Harry had no intention of being in front of this thing when it ran out of room. He clambered up and over the elephants as they bore down on them. Sara did the same, and they scrambled up and over the giant carved heads, clutching the wild stone eyes and slab-like ears as handholds, then sliding down over the elephants' neck and onto their backs.

"Look out!" Sara cried, and Harry spun to face forward again. A wall waited ahead. They rose as one and leapt back into the darkness behind the elephants an instant before they crashed into the wall.

Harry lost sight of Sara as he rolled over and over, finally coming to a stop on the stone floor. He lifted a hand to his face and found it was soaking wet. He rolled so the jagged curves of the crown stuffed down his shirt didn't jab his chest as he called out. "Sara? Can you hear me?"

Nothing. He called out again, straining his voice this time. "Answer me," he shouted. "Where are you?"

"Right beside you." Her hand latched onto his shoulder as a beam of light blinded him. *Would she never learn not to shine that thing right in his face?* He blinked water from his eyes. "Turn that flashlight off," Harry said, squinting. "It's too bright."

"Harry."

"What?" He dug the crown from his shirt. The darn thing was digging a hole in his chest.

"Look."

She grabbed him by the shoulders. Harry nearly dropped the crown as she twisted him around. He realized the light he'd been avoiding didn't come from a flashlight. Harry's legs moved of their own accord, helping him stand up from the rubble of what he now saw had once been a wall. The crown remained clutched in one hand.

Water dripped from his fingertip when he pointed ahead and down. "That's the river."

Three long steps from where he stood would have seen Harry tumble out of the open tunnel and plunge into the Limmat River ten feet below. Harry moved carefully between the broken stones and peered over the edge.

The two stone elephants lay at the bottom of the crystal-clear river. The carved beasts had burst through the side of a retaining wall by the church. Harry looked across the river to a boat dock, currently empty, then pulled his head back into the tunnel.

"Let's go," he said. He tucked the crown in his waistband. "There are going to be a lot of people coming down here to investigate what just happened. We need to be gone."

Sara looked up and down the tunnel, still seemingly trying to absorb what had happened. "Where? We don't know what comes next."

"First, somewhere quiet. I need your help."

"With what?"

He grabbed her hand and pulled her in the direction of the crypt. "Deciphering a message." She angled her head in confusion as they began to backtrack through the tunnel. "A message carved into the crown," Harry said. "On the interior. A message from Agilulph."

Chapter 12

Manhattan

Nora marched out of the subway as the first streetlamps flickered to life overhead. She passed two uniformed officers on the sidewalk and glared at them, though the men didn't notice her. Good thing, too, because it wasn't those two she wanted to throttle. No, that was a different pair of NYPD patrol officers who should have known better than to try and inventory the contents of a man's trunk. A man Nora was minutes away from arresting for trafficking in ancient Chinese vases, some of them nearly a thousand years old.

The two uniformed cops had pulled the guy over for cruising through a red light on his way to sell the trunk-load of artifacts. A sale Nora and her team had worked for months to set up. A sale the trafficker never made it to, because he was too busy trying to convince the two cops to let him off with a warning.

Nora gritted her teeth at the memory as she waited to cross the street. She had seen what was unfolding and tried to warn them on the radio before it was too late, but the two uniforms hadn't answered in time. All they had to do was let the guy go. Give him a warning. Do anything but dig through his car's trunk and pull out the box of artifacts.

A box that was heavier than it looked. The officer had dropped it, leaving every artifact as ruined as Nora's bust. She would have caught the suspect in the middle of a sale, could have brought much more serious charges against him, then used those charges as leverage to offer him a deal. Nora didn't care about the trafficker. She cared about his *supplier.* The next guy up the criminal food chain was the real prize.

The light changed. She blew air from her nose. *Forget about it.* She couldn't change what had happened. Those patrolmen had no idea the bust was about to happen. Could they have answered their radio sooner? Yes, but that was over and done with. Now the seller had lawyered up, claimed he had no idea the artifacts were real, and Nora knew he would get off with nothing worse than a fine. Forget any leverage for a deal. And now the supplier Nora really wanted would keep moving artifacts through other sellers.

She passed an ATM tucked beneath the overhang of a bank entrance, bathed in bright security lights. This was her neighborhood branch, one where Nora knew the tellers by name. She kept one eye on a man in a baseball hat taking money out of the machine as she passed, then looked away. Her block was quiet. Safe, too. Neighbors watched out for each other.

A pair of teens flew past her on the sidewalk, the wheels on their skateboards rumbling as they zipped by close enough that she threw them a wicked look over her shoulder. They didn't bother to look, but when she turned forward again and resumed walking toward home, a tiny bell dinged in her head. The man who had been at the ATM was walking behind her, well back but headed in her direction. Why had he caught her eye? It wasn't like the sidewalks around here were ever empty. Yet this guy was on her radar now.

She closed her eyes. What was it? She couldn't see his face, not with that hat pulled low over his eyes, so there was no way to recognize him. The guy didn't look intimidating, which she knew meant next to nothing. The guy was a guy getting money out of the bank, she told herself.

Keep this up and you'll turn into a punchline. Nora pushed the thought from her mind. What she needed was some takeout and a movie. Might be time for an old Mel Brooks flick.

She ordered food from a delivery app on her phone as she approached her apartment building. Ever cautious, Nora walked past its front entrance without stopping, went to the next corner, and crossed the street so she could backtrack and stand directly across from her building. She paused behind a parked car and looked around. The guy in the ballcap had passed her building entrance and disappeared around the corner. She took a breath, let it out long and slow. *See? Nothing.*

She jaywalked over to her front door and used her keycard to unlock it. One of the four elevators was open and waiting. Nora rode up to her floor, set off down the hallway, keys in hand, and paused outside her front door. She lifted her chin, closed her eyes, and took three deep breaths. The same routine she used every time she arrived home. One of her colleagues had told her she needed to relax more, and instead of telling the woman to mind her own business, Nora had tried a new tactic. Each night, she stood outside her door and took three deep breaths before entering her apartment. Her idea was to consciously leave her troubles outside.

She unlocked the door, pushed it open and walked in. She couldn't shake a nagging feeling there was something about that guy at the ATM. Why? Hard to say, so she pushed it aside. She locked the door behind her, and her keys went on a wall hook beside the door as she slipped out of her shoes, setting them in their assigned spots on the floor inside her closet. Her handbag went on its hook as well.

"Let it go." Saying it out loud worked for the moment, clearing her mind as she pulled a half-empty bottle of wine from the refrigerator. "Let it go," she repeated as she grabbed a wine glass from the row of glasses in a cupboard, taking a moment to adjust the one behind it so they were in a straight line. Must have bumped it earlier and not noticed. She usually noticed things like that.

Her glass of wine went on a coaster. The throw pillows on her couch were stacked in a corner, out of sight. She grabbed the remote, flicked her television on, and took a sip from her glass. *This is more like it.*

She sat up so fast wine nearly splashed onto the carpet. "His ear. It was his ear."

That's why the man at the ATM had caught her attention. The detail that drew her in. Earlier that morning a man had walked into the same local coffee shop that she frequented, had stood in line behind her. A man missing one ear.

Maybe the guy had just moved here. Who knew what brought people to the neighborhood? She took another drink. Maybe she did need to relax.

Her phone buzzed. "You outside?" Nora asked. The food deliveryman said he was. "Come in." Nora buzzed him in and clicked off, setting her glass down on the coaster and heading to the door. Nora opened the closet and took her handbag out. She liked to tip in cash, in case the deliveryman decided not to tell the restaurant about the tip. If that happened, well, so be it. Nobody could say Nora Doyle wasn't willing to bend the rules.

"Hello," she said as she opened the door. Nora looped the strap of her handbag over her arm, ready to take the bag of food, and held out the cash as she looked up at the man's face. "Thank y—"

The deliveryman only had one ear. Her food smashed to the floor as the deliveryman grabbed Nora by the throat and shoved her back. She grabbed his hand and dug her nails into it, twisting as she stumbled back to keep her balance. She jabbed at her assailant's face with her other hand, digging for a soft spot, an eye, anything.

The man growled as he dodged, smacking her hand away and tightening his grip to cut off her air. He was much stronger than she was, and she couldn't keep this up for long.

She took another step back, then regained her footing and held fast. The man pushed, trying to topple her, and Nora resisted. He pushed harder, which was exactly what she wanted. Nora resisted, then she didn't.

The strap of her purse was still looped over her arm, and the bag spun wildly when she grabbed his shirt and changed direction; she was now simultaneously pulling him closer to her and moving swiftly backwards, dragging him with her—right back into the wall she knew lay right behind her. At the last moment, she twisted, still gripping his shirt, and spun them both around, slamming his back into the wall before driving her shoulder into his chest and smashing her forehead against his nose.

His hand slipped free and he gave a howl of pain. Nora sucked air as she let go of his shirt and scrambled back. Blood dripped from his nose as he moved toward her. He lunged for her handbag and used it to pull her back toward him. She tried to slip free but only managed to wrap the strap further around her arm. He bent down, drove a shoulder into her belly and flipped her up into a fireman's carry before tossing her almost effortlessly toward the couch. Nora crashed onto her coffee table and felt it crack beneath the sudden impact.

In a flash, the man was standing over her. He grabbed a fistful of her hair, pulling her up toward him so they were almost nose to nose. "Where is Harry Fox?" he growled.

Nora froze. "What?"

Spittle flew from the man's lips. "Where is he?"

She drew one hand into a fist and punched him in his wounded nose.

He shrieked but held on. He straightened, lifting Nora off the ground and throwing her toward the sliding glass doors that led to the balcony. Glass exploded as she crashed through the door, hit the railing outside, and dropped heavily to the floor. Her vision blurred as she looked up to find the man standing over her again. "Tell me where he is."

"He's away," Nora said. She let her voice shake. "Not here."

"Where is he?"

Nora lifted a hand. "Stop, please. I'll tell you." Her other hand was beneath her. The hand with the purse wrapped around it. "He's only been gone for two days."

The man grabbed her shoulder with one hand; the other was balled into a fist and ready to strike. "Call his mobile," he said. "Right now."

Nora pulled her purse out from under her and slipped her fingers into it. They found what she needed. "Let me up and I'll call him."

The man tightened his grip and began to haul her up. Nora feebly tried to help, reaching one hand up to grab the railing. Her other hand came out from beneath her and went toward his arm. "Help me," she said, her words strained. "My ankle. I think it's broken."

The man kept a grip on Nora's shoulder as he reached for her other arm. The one reaching for him. Nora gritted her teeth. Wait for it. Wait for it. *Now.*

Snick. The man's mouth opened in surprise.

Nora shot up from the ground and smashed a knee into his groin. When the man crumpled, she pulled his arm closer to the railing and locked the handcuffs to it. One end was already secure on his wrist. The other latched shut on the railing.

"No!" He screamed in vain, trying to get loose as Nora backed out of reach. His eyes bulged and blood streamed from his nose. "I'll ki—"

Nora spun, and her foot smashed off the side of his head. The blow dazed him, and he smashed against the railing. Nora shot forward, grabbed his feet, and flipped him over the railing like a bag of laundry. He screamed again, a shrill cry that was abruptly cut off when the full weight of his body came to bear on one wrist. The wrist handcuffed to Nora's railing.

The cuffs held. The bones in his wrist did not.

"Hang tight," Nora said as she turned and went back inside.

The man's cries trailed her as she grabbed her phone and called for backup. "I need a couple of squad cars," Nora said to the dispatcher after identifying herself. She watched her assailant swing, nothing but fifty feet of air between him and the sidewalk. "No hurry," she said. "I need to finish my dinner."

Nora stood in front of the two-way mirror looking into the interrogation room. She watched the one-eared man as he sat at a scuffed table, his left arm cuffed to a metal loop on its surface. His other arm was in a splint. The guys in the ambulance said he had a broken wrist. They also said they'd never had to pull someone back onto a balcony before. Usually they met them at ground level.

Gary Doyle stood beside Nora, watching her watch the man. "You said you noticed him hanging around your neighborhood yesterday morning?"

"At a coffee shop," Nora said. "And no, I'd never seen him before that."

Gary's face remained impassive. His words, though, were hard. "He knows Harry. He knows you are familiar with Harry. Familiar enough that he expected you to know where to find Harry. All of which is a concern."

"For me or Harry?"

"Both. The target was Harry. The question is, why? Is it because of what happened with the Cana family? Is it because of another operation with your team? Or something else?"

"Harry might be able to tell us." Nora checked her phone. "If he ever calls me back."

"He hasn't returned my call either." Gary lifted his chin toward the seated man behind the glass. "He hasn't said a word. No identification, and so far, his fingerprints have not registered a hit in any system that we can access."

"If you haven't found him by now, you won't." Nora rubbed her throat and winced. There'd be a heck of a bruise there tomorrow. "English isn't this man's first language."

"That describes roughly a quarter of the people in this city."

"That's not what I mean. I can tell from the way he talked."

"I thought he didn't say much."

"He told me to call Harry's *mobile*. Not his cell. That's a European term."

Gary agreed. "So he's from overseas. That accent could be from any number of countries."

"Nothing came back from Interpol on his prints?"

"Not yet." Gary tapped a finger on his chin. "Between us, I'm not holding my breath. This guy doesn't strike me as an amateur. More like a pro whose luck ran out when he tangled with you."

"It was nearly my luck that ran out."

"Indeed," Gary said tersely. He checked his phone again. "What the devil is Harry doing that he can't return our calls?"

Nora bit her lip. Should she tell him? She looked up at her dad, past the prosecutor's mask, through the fiery Irish beard. Underneath it all he was still her dad, and he was clearly upset about what had nearly happened. *Might as well tell him.* "Harry and Sara are in Zurich."

Gary's head snapped around. "Switzerland? Why?"

Nora gave her father a broad overview of Harry's search, though Gary knew not to ask too many questions. "To check out a church. Supposedly there's a connection between the church and the illuminated manuscript he..." Her voice trailed off before she rallied. "Procured from Germany."

"What connection?"

Nora shook her head. "No idea. Sara only told me where they were going. She didn't say what they were after."

"Call him again. I cannot let you go home without knowing why this man tried to kill you."

Nora's pocket vibrated. She pulled her phone out. "Speak of the devil." She showed Gary the screen. "It's Harry." She connected the call. "Where are you?" Nora asked.

"You wouldn't believe me if I told you."

"Try me. And if the answer's Zurich, I'm way ahead of you."

"How did—never mind."

"You were saying I wouldn't believe you?"

"We're in Zurich, yes. The part you won't believe is we just took an unguided tour of the city sewer system."

"Gary's with me," Nora said, putting the phone on speaker. "You have our attention. Why are you in the sewer?"

The man sitting on the other side of the glass soon fell from her thoughts as Harry described their near-disaster. "We went back into the church and acted confused like everyone else," Harry said as he concluded the tale. "Walked out past the authorities and church staff and here we are."

"Aren't you filthy?"

"Yes, but we're safe. And the best part? The crown we found has a message on it."

Gary couldn't stay quiet any longer. "What does it say?"

"I'll let you know as soon as we get somewhere private."

Nora raised a hand to silence her father. "Quite the story. Now it's my turn."

"Your turn?" Harry asked.

"A man just tried to kill me."

Chapter 13

Zurich

Harry stopped in the middle of the sidewalk. "Are you okay?" he asked, putting his own phone on speaker.

"I'm fine," Nora said.

Harry grabbed Sara's arm and pulled her under the canopy of a shop storefront. "Say that again," Harry told Nora. "Sara's with me."

Nora repeated that she was fine.

"What happened?" Sara asked.

"A man snuck into my apartment building and attacked me," Nora said. She recounted him posing as a food deliveryman and bursting through her door when she answered. "He was hanging around my building looking for me and overhead the real deliveryman speak with me before I let him in. I know because the deliveryman reported my assailant threatened him outside my building, stole my food and told him to get lost. I saw the guy who attacked me twice earlier that day. At the coffee shop, then again walking on my way home."

"You recognized him from that?" Sara asked. "That's incredible."

"It helped that he only had one ear."

Harry's blood ran cold. "What did you say?"

"I said he had one ear missing," Nora replied.

"No."

"Yes," Nora said. "You think I'd make that up? He's sitting in an interview room on the other side of the glass from me right now. I'll send you his picture."

"I can't believe he found you," Harry said quietly.

Gary jumped in. "It seems you know something, Harry. Out with it."

"He was looking for me."

"He was," Gary said. "How did you know?"

"Someone warned me to watch for a one-eared man."

Gary was not letting up. "Explain."

"Sara told you about the illuminated manuscript. I stole it from a collector in Germany. The collector sent that man to get it back."

"How did he find me?" Nora asked.

"No idea."

Gary scoffed. "No idea? You nearly caused Nora's death."

"Hold on a second," Nora said. "Whoever told that guy how to find me likely knew we were related, and that I would know where to find you."

"Who knows about our connection?" Harry asked. "Do people at your work?"

"No," Nora said. "I keep my private life out of the office."

"He may have spoken with one of the Cana family members in prison," Harry said. "No one else in my orbit would talk."

"Someone did," Gary fired back. "Nora nearly died because of it. Now she has police protection at her home for the foreseeable future. I'm not certain we can trust your associates."

Harry clenched the phone. His gaze narrowed, and he ignored the hand Sara laid on his shoulder. "Gary, you want to blame me for this? Go ahead. I didn't sell Nora out. Those *associates* you're so quick to accuse are loyal people. They'd never turn on me." Gary tried to speak, but Harry rolled on. "Why don't we talk about you. What was it you said before I left? That you can't help me anymore? So, if you want to talk about letting people down, look in the mirror. You were pretty quick to toss me aside."

Sara grabbed the phone. "Are you two finished?" she shouted. Heads turned on the street. Sara grabbed Harry's arm and pulled him into the alley beside them. "Arguing doesn't help anyone," Sara said in a lower tone. "Harry and I are here in Zurich, far away from this man. Nora is the one in danger. As are you, Gary. If you two want to argue, do it another time. We all have work to do."

"I'm with her," Nora said.

Harry clenched and unclenched his fists, but he kept his mouth shut and waited.

"Sara is right," Gary eventually said. "I let my emotions get the better of me."

Harry shook his head. "Yeah, me too."

"I never meant that you would be abandoned," Gary said. "I apologize if that is what you heard."

"Forget about it. It's all good."

"You guys can hug later," Nora said. "And quit worrying about me. This guy is going to be in jail for a long time. Whoever he is. Worry about your own necks. You said the collector in Germany sent this man to find you?"

"The German is Leon Havertz," Harry said. "He's rich, and he wants the book back. I knew to look out for a one-eared man because a friend of mine knows someone who works for Havertz."

"Tell your friend to have his informant keep his eyes open," Nora said. Harry said he would. "I'll call my contact at Interpol," Nora continued. "See if she knows anything about a one-eared hit man."

"Are you calling Guro?"

"I trust her," Nora said. "She knows how to ask questions discreetly."

Guro Mjelde, the Interpol field agent based in Oslo who had called in a favor to get Harry out of jail in Greece. A jail that employed several corrupt cops who hadn't wanted Harry to leave. "Smart move," Harry said.

"The smart move would be for *you* to call Guro," Nora said. "You're good at what you do, but even the best can use help once in a while."

"I thought you were calling her."

"I am. To tell her to expect your call."

A year ago, Harry might have said he didn't need or want help. A year ago, he was a different man. He knew enough to take good advice when he heard it. Usually.

"You're right," Harry said. "As long as Guro isn't prohibited from helping me."

"I have no authority over an Interpol agent," Gary said.

"Text me after you speak with her," Harry said. He paused. His gaze flicked over to Sara, who gave him a questioning look. "One of us will be in touch," he said quickly. "As soon as we know what we found."

He clicked off. "You hang on to this." Harry pulled the crown from inside his shirt and handed it to Sara. "We need a quiet place to talk." He grabbed her hand after she hid the crown under her coat. "The hotel sounds good to me."

Sara didn't argue, but the quizzical look on her face never fully disappeared as they walked at pace back to their hotel. Once they were inside their room and the deadbolt was secure, Sara removed the crown from her shirt. She sat at the desk and turned the light on, angling it to fall on the letters carved on the interior of the circle. "Latin," Sara said. "Difficult to read. Find me some paper and a pen."

Harry stood up in slow motion, though Sara didn't appear to notice. "What did you mean earlier when you said *missing*? Right when we found the crown." He took unhurried steps toward a notepad across the room. "You said it could be *one of his missing*, then you stopped."

"Missing crowns," Sara said. "Have you never heard the story?"

Harry shook his head. "Whose crowns?"

She set the crown on the desk and faced him. "Reliable historical accounts indicate Charlemagne used three crowns throughout his life. The most famous one still exists today. It's called the Crown of Charlemagne, and it was used to crown every French king from Charlemagne through Napoleon the third, the last monarch of France."

Harry paused by the notepad, intrigued. "Where is it now?"

"In the Louvre."

"What about the other two?"

"One was melted down during the French civil war between the Catholics and Protestants."

"That's two," Harry said. "So we're missing one."

"It was supposedly lost to history," Sara said. "No one knows what became of it after the reign of Phillip the second, several centuries after Charlemagne. No images of it exist, though there are contemporary descriptions given, stating that the king wore it almost daily. Allegedly it was a massive affair."

"Sounds like the Crown of Charlemagne was impractical for daily wear."

"Exactly. It was too big to wear outside of formal ceremonies, so Charlemagne had a smaller crown made, without as many jewels or decorative elements."

Harry stopped halfway back to her, the notepad and a pen in his hands. "You don't happen to know what the smaller crown may have looked like?"

Sara picked up the crown and held it in front of her. "It has been described as a circlet of gold, dotted with precious stones in the shape of a cross. It had a single amethyst, a single sapphire." She touched each stone in turn as she spoke. "And a single emerald."

Harry couldn't keep the grin off his face. "I don't suppose you want to swing by the Élysée Palace and tell the president we have their missing crown?"

Sara considered. "A year ago, I would have said yes. However, you appear to be influencing my decision-making process. I believe I should study this crown more carefully before making any conclusions as to what it is."

"Agreed."

Sara stuck her hand out for the notepad and pen. Harry did not hand them over. "We need to talk about something," he said.

"After I translate this inscription." Sara waggled her fingers.

He continued to hold on to the pen and paper. "I need your help," Harry said. "With the Charlemagne pursuit."

"I'm trying to do that. Currently you're stopping me. The paper and pen, please?"

Harry pursed his lips for a moment. *May as well just say it.* "I need your help with Charlemagne, and I need that help to happen in New York."

Sara tilted her head, one hand still out. "In New York?"

"I need you to figure out what comes next with Charlemagne while I finish deciphering the Antikythera code."

Sara's hand dropped. "You don't want me here any longer."

"I don't want to delay progress on either front. The Charlemagne search is moving and we'd be foolish to ignore it. At the same time, we can't ignore what we've learned from the Antikythera. Whatever comes next is likely at the Temple of Augustus and Livia in Vienne, France. Not in Zurich."

"It's also not in New York." Her words came with an edge. "Not to mention you've never laid eyes on the temple. I've been there. I would be an asset."

Fighting this battle would never work out in his favor. "You're more than an asset. You're also the right person to follow Charlemagne's trail. You're the best person… the *only* person I trust with it."

"No, Harry. I'm an Egyptologist. Nothing more."

"You're incredible at this. I know skill when I see it."

"Stop pretending this is about anything other than that you want me to go."

"I'm not pretending. I want to solve both mysteries without getting us killed. You're the best person for the Charlemagne question while I'm focused on the Antikythera and all the questions it brings." He lifted one hand, palm up. "But I'm doing a disservice to everything we're after if I think half of my attention is enough. I need your help. You're the only person who can do it."

She stared at him, her expression impenetrable. Harry managed to keep his gaze on her face as his mind whirred. Would she understand he meant every word?

"I assume you want me to stay with Nora," Sara said. "For protection."

"It would be the smart move," Harry said. "Or Gary could assign a protection detail to you. Based on certain threats you may have received."

"Threats that do not exist," she said. Harry shrugged. She continued to look at him, her mouth closed, eyes unblinking.

"I'll go," Sara said. "What you say is logical. My time is better spent on the Charlemagne pursuit. If you believe I can do it more safely from New York, so be it."

Harry didn't hide his relief. "Thank you." He thought about grabbing his phone out of a pocket, then pushed that thought aside. No need to make any mention of Guro Mjelde right now. He didn't want Sara to think he needed to get rid of her to make room for Guro. That wasn't true, but Sara would be hurt by her dismissal, and when people felt pushed aside, they saw ulterior motives where none existed.

Sara put her hand back out. "The paper?"

Harry handed it over, along with the pen. "Want me to get your ticket home?"

"That would be helpful." Sara put the notepad on the desk and clicked the pen open. The crown's amethyst flashed a brilliant purple when she angled the crown toward the light. "I assume you are leaving for Vienne shortly?"

"As soon as I get your travel booked."

"I suggest you notify Evgeny Smolov of your plans." She glanced in his direction. "Telling him we made progress in spite of the defective replica he gave us should help curb his impatience."

Harry looked at the ceiling and groaned. "Maybe I shouldn't."

"Why not?"

"How do you think a man like Evgeny Smolov will react when he learns his replica didn't work? Whoever made it for him will be lucky if all they lose is their job."

"Phrase it diplomatically."

It would have to be a heck of an email to placate Evgeny. "I'll do my best. But you're right: it may buy me some patience. If he has any at all."

In short order Harry had booked a ticket home for Sara and a flight for himself to France. He looked up from his phone. Sara hadn't spoken the entire time, the only sound coming from her desk the scratching of the pen on paper. She turned the crown this way and that to catch the light, then made notes on her pad. Harry silently watched her work, though he couldn't do anything to quiet the voices in his head. Was this the right move? More importantly, would she be safe in New York?

He looked back down at his phone and began tapping out a message. Guro Mjelde's day was about to get a bit more interesting.

Chapter 14

Vienne, France

A Roman temple stood incongruously in the middle of a modern French city. Harry looked up at its towering columns supporting an intricately designed portico. This temple had stood nearly untouched for two thousand years while the ancient city of Vienne modernized around it. Harry looked right and left as he jogged across the street, passing tourists seated beneath wide umbrellas on the plaza fronting the temple as the sun continued to climb overhead. The temple roof ran straight into a hillside behind it that had been cut out to accommodate the structure. The top of the hill itself overlooked the temple and offered an excellent vantage point from which to view the area.

Or at least it would have, if anyone was allowed to climb the hill. Sturdy fencing kept potential explorers from getting more than twenty feet up the grassy slope. Harry stood with his hands on his hips, gazing appreciatively up at the riot of color rising above him, the striking blue of wild sage alongside intensely yellow daises providing a bright contrast to the marble and concrete buildings below. Wide steps fronted the rectangular structure on every side except the rear, where the hillside touched the building.

Pockmarked columns stretched skyward on either side of him as Harry walked back under the portico and crossed the flat stone area leading to a pair of metal doors. One door was open, and a man sat behind a small counter outside it. He didn't even try to hide his wide yawn as Harry paid the token entrance fee and walked into the chilly interior. Harry stepped to one side, into the darkness behind the closed front door, and paused.

Columns lined either side of the rectangular interior, stretching ahead of him. Frescoes decorated the walls on one side. Some sections of the painted scenes were still vibrant, while some were more faded. On the other side of the interior, images had been created from stone mosaic laid into the walls. The stone inlay side had statues in recessed portions of the walls, the inlay and statues together forming a complete work of art. On the fresco side, freestanding statues were set between the columns.

A simple altar table stood at the front of the temple, set on a raised platform. Doorways opened to rooms on either side of the platform. A statue of Jupiter seated on his throne was positioned behind the altar.

The statues on the fresco side were not original to the building; most were Roman loot from past conquests. Those statues had been placed here only within the past hundred years or so, for one simple purpose. They were here to attract tourists and their entrance fees.

Harry looked left. He looked right. The only other person in sight was one guard making a slow round of the temple. His eyes were down, looking at his cell phone. He didn't pay Harry the slightest bit of mind. Harry took one step toward a fresco on the left when his phone buzzed. He pulled it out. A message from Guro. *I spoke with Nora. Call when you are free.*

Guro Mjelde had been on vacation when Harry tried to contact her before leaving Zurich. He hadn't expected to hear from her this quickly. Why Guro would interrupt her vacation to see Harry was beyond him, but Nora told him Guro took her job with Interpol seriously, and if Nora vouched for Harry, Guro would be there to help him.

Harry had not promised Nora he would tell Guro what he was doing. Or that he didn't intend to turn over anything he recovered. Guro was a safety net, to be used only when and if he needed her help, and needed it badly.

Harry put his phone away. He sighed, then pulled it back out and sent a brief message to Sara. *Any luck?*

The reply was immediate. *Focus on the task at hand. We'll talk later.*

He pocketed the phone. Sara was right. Harry had one mission. To *find the Great One's tutor in the temple of Octavian and his counselor.* Octavian had been known as Augustus in his youth. His wife Livia was his closest counselor, and this was their temple. Now, his task was to find anything relating to Aristotle, tutor of Alexander. Alexander, also known as the *Great One* in Roman times.

Aristotle had died three hundred years before this temple was built. He'd lived hundreds of miles from Rome, and over a thousand miles from Vienne. What about Aristotle would stand out to Pliny the Elder? Aristotle was not only a renowned philosopher; he was much more. He wrote on topics from linguistics to economics, psychology to the arts. Harry had to search for some link to Aristotle in this temple. He had no shortage of options.

The building was only so big. He'd find it, whatever *it* was. He stepped closer to the nearest fresco and looked up. It was an image of the Greek centaur Chiron standing with Achilles. The creature with the upper body of a man on the lower body and legs of a horse stood beside the Greek hero, one arm around Achilles' shoulder as the centaur pointed at something out of the picture. Nothing about the image seemed connected to Aristotle, so he moved to the next one. A single image of Ares, the Greek god of war. Both frescoes so far were from Greek myth, not Roman. Was it because Rome had repurposed so many Greek myths to use as their own? Or did this subtly point to another purpose?

Hard to say. He filed that away and moved on to the third fresco, this one along one of the longer sides of the building. An image of the Greek hero Perseus, who, according to myth, had beheaded Medusa. Nothing to do with Aristotle. Beyond that lay more images from Greek myths, none of which Harry could connect to Aristotle. He reached the end of the long wall and found himself in front of the entranceway to parts unknown.

A stanchion stood on each side, supporting a black rope blocking his path to the entrance. A sign in the middle of the rope told Harry this section was closed. He glanced over his shoulder to see the lone guard standing by the front entrance talking with his colleague at the ticket booth. Harry leaned over the rope, pulled a penlight from his pocket and flicked it on. The light revealed a single chamber ahead. Scaffolding fronted the bare walls of a room under repair.

Harry leaned back and slipped the penlight in his pocket. The guard at the front door was still chatting with his friend. Another rope barrier steered Harry in front of the altar as he crossed to the opposite wall. The statue of the Roman god Jupiter behind the altar caught his eye, mainly because it resembled several statues of Zeus, the Greek god on which the Roman deity was based. The simple design decorating the wall behind Jupiter was one he'd seen before, a large four-sided, diamond-shaped figure containing a second, smaller square image.

His pocket buzzed. Sara. Harry pressed the phone to his ear and whispered. "What's up?"

"Have you spoken with Guro?"

"Not yet." *And it could be a while,* Harry thought as he explained where he was. "I'll call her once I'm done here."

"I had a thought."

"This can't be good."

"Listen to me. While I appreciate Nora's intention, I can't help but think Guro's involvement comes with certain concerns."

Harry stopped beside one of the massive columns. "Concerns?"

"Guro is an Interpol agent." A pause. "You are a private citizen who isn't bound by the same legal constraints."

"That's diplomatic of you. In other words, I don't worry about legalities because that's her job."

"That is one way of saying it."

He liked this new version of Sara. "Sounds like you think working with Guro may not be in our best interests."

"It crossed my mind."

"You think I should politely decline her assistance?"

"I think that's a decision only you can make. However, if you decide Guro isn't the right person to assist, I have a second option." Harry didn't respond. "A person you've worked with before," Sara said.

Harry wracked his brain. Nothing. "Who?"

"Dessi."

The train of his thoughts derailed. Not a minor derailment. A massive, tanker-cars-piling-up-and-deadly-chemicals-sloshing-together-before-exploding derailment. "The anarchist?" Harry nearly yelled it. He looked around. The guards hadn't noticed. "She's insane."

"Dessi Zheleva is a respected professor of history at a Bulgarian university."

"She gave me her car and a gun thirty minutes after I met her so I could evade two murderers. Then she agreed to take my car and distract them." Harry ran a hand through his hair. "Dessi is a lunatic."

"I would say you just described a valuable field operative."

"Who wants to overthrow the Bulgarian government and bring about a return of ancient Thrace. Sara, she's bonkers." Harry waited. Sara didn't respond. His mind kept working. "She is reliable in a tight spot," he finally admitted. "But we don't really know her. She's a friend of a friend."

"I have confidence in my friends. And theirs."

How did he manage to find such lunatics? "I'll think about it," Harry said. "You raise a good point. If you trust Dessi, I should too. Even if she's nuts."

"Yes, and thank you."

"In some ways, Guro being an Interpol agent could be a headache down the road," Harry said. "I'll hold off on calling her for the moment." He kept going before she could respond. "Any updates on that guy who attacked Nora?"

"He hasn't said a word. He has an attorney now. I suspect his silence will stretch on."

"At least he's locked up," Harry said. "One less guy to watch over my shoulder for."

Speaking of watching. Harry looked back and found the security guards still in conversation near the entrance. Harry pulled an earbud out of his pocket and stuck it in one ear. "Can you hear me?" he asked.

"Yes." Sara's voice banged his eardrum. "Where are you?"

"Inside the temple," he said with a wince as he lowered the volume. "There are frescoes on one side, and ornate statues on the other."

"See any ties to Aristotle?"

"No." Harry looked back at the guards. They still weren't paying him any mind. "It's empty here today," he said. "I have the place to myself. The frescoes are all about Greek gods, which is interesting given this is a Roman temple."

"It's possible the Greek theme is meant to convey a message."

"That this Roman temple has ties to a certain Greek philosopher?" Harry said. "I thought of that."

"What about the statues on the other side of the building?" Sara asked. "Are they Greek images as well?"

Harry didn't respond. He was too busy staring at the picture in front of him.

"Hello?"

Harry may have been moving his mouth, but he couldn't be sure. He couldn't focus on anything but the wall, on an image made of what he now realized were not different cuts of inlaid stone, but tiny ceramic tiles glued to the wall. They formed an image of two men. "I found him," Harry managed to say.

"Who?" Sara's voice was hard. "What are you talking about?"

"See for yourself." Harry snapped a picture of the wall and sent it to her. He waited. It didn't take long.

"It's him," she said. "It's both of them."

Two men faced each other on the wall. One had a beard. His hands were up near the other man's face and he was leaning forward, as though by the force of his presence he could convey a message. The other man was clean-shaven and held an open book in his hands, and appeared to be listening closely to the first man. Both wore flowing robes, and the bearded man was standing with one shoulder exposed, in the Greek fashion.

"That's Aristotle," Harry said. "I recognize him."

"It is," Sara said. "He's speaking with Plato. Is there any writing in the book?"

Harry leaned closer to the wall. "Nothing."

"What about on their robes, or any notes or marks on their bodies?"

"No and no again." The image was of two men engaged in a debate or discussion. Harry gave each of them a second look to confirm it. "There's nothing on either of them." His gaze went up. "Nothing above them." His gaze went down. "Hold on."

Three images were below the two men, down at the bottom of the wall, partially hidden in shadow. Harry knelt to get a better look. "There's more—whoa."

"There's more what?" Sara asked. "I lost you."

It took Harry a second to find his voice. "There's more to the picture."

"What do you see?"

The next step. Or at least part of it. "It's coming your way." He snapped a photo of the bottom and sent it to Sara.

"What in the world are those?" she asked.

The images were made of even smaller ceramic tiles than the rest of the picture. Three images, one at the bottom on the far left of the picture, one in the center and one on the far right. He wasn't sure what they meant, but that wasn't as important as what lay below them. "Forget these images for a second," Harry said. "Look below them."

A sharp intake of breath told him she'd spotted it. "It's nonsense."

"This nonsense looks an awful lot like the string of nonsense we found in Pliny's scroll." Harry ran his finger over the second line that began with two numbers, a five and a seven followed by seemingly random letters. "It's similar to the pattern we saw in Pliny's scroll," he said. "Which was a code."

"Describe the symbols to me," Sara said. "I'll enter them on the

Antikythera. If it's the same code, the device should adjust itself to give us the starting letter in the substitution cipher. If we're lucky. The symbols, please?"

"Right." Harry used his phone's light to illuminate the wall. "The first one is a circle," he said. "The one in the middle looks like a half-moon, maybe, or a block turned on its side. This last one I'm not sure about." He angled his head. "It's a squiggly line. Might be a… I don't know. A lightning bolt?"

"No."

Harry frowned at her response. "It's just a guess. I don't know what it is. It does sort of look like a lightning bolt."

"It is."

"You're losing me here. Do you agree it's a lightning bolt, or—"

"Listen to me," she said. Harry knew that tone of voice. "No, it's not a squiggly line. And yes, it is a lightning bolt. They're symbols, Harry. What do they represent?"

A circle. A half-moon. A lightning bolt. Three symbols that represented a larger message. He blinked and it hit him. "The lightning bolt stands for a Greek god."

"Zeus," Sara said. "And the first symbol isn't a circle. It's the letter *O*. The next one is the Roman numeral *C*, which stands for the number one hundred. These are instructions for the Antikythera."

"Any chance you can get to the museum right now?" Harry asked.

"I'm already here. Stay on the line."

Harry continued his circuit of the room, pretending to examine the remaining images in turn for the guard's benefit. Not that the man charged with keeping order inside paid him any attention. He glanced over at Harry once for a grand total of three seconds, then kept on talking with his colleague.

"Are you still there?"

He jumped when Sara's voice sounded in his ear. "I'm here," he said. "Did you get the Antikythera?"

"I'm standing in front of the case now," she said. "My colleague left a key to the exhibit in his desk. He said it was in case I needed it for further study."

The Antikythera had three marked circular rows on it, Harry remembered. One row of letters, one of numbers and one of symbols.

"Put in those three." Harry began slowly making his way back toward Aristotle.

"I'm working on it."

Silence filled his ear as Harry walked, pausing at each image on the wall to look up, though he didn't truly see anything. All he could focus on was the occasional *click* coming through his earpiece. What was taking so long?

"The letter *O*, the Roman numeral for one hundred, and Zeus's lightning bolt," Sara finally said. "All of them are on the dial. Hold on. It's realigning itself."

"What letter is above the number one now?"

"*K*. Any *K* on the wall represents an *A*. Any *L* is a *B*, and so on."

"The numbers are five and seven," Harry said. "Page fifty-seven in *Natural History*."

They each worked to translate the cipher. Harry pulled up an image of the Latin alphabet on his phone. On his phone *K* showed as the eleventh letter of the alphabet, but for Pliny's purposes here, it was the first.

It took him a minute to translate the letters on the wall. "It says—"

"—*Empedocles truth*." Sara beat him to it. "Is that what you have?" she asked.

"Yes," he said begrudgingly. "I had it."

"It's not a race." Sara paused. "Though I would have won." She kept going, over his grumbling. "Do you know the name?"

Harry stopped grumbling. *Do I ever.* "Empedocles was a renowned philosopher who lived before the time of Socrates. He proposed the theory of there being four classical elements. Earth, water, fire and air."

"A belief system that held for two thousand years," Sara said. "I wonder what Pliny has to say on the matter."

Harry looked toward the entrance. The guard who had been leaning against the wall talking to his buddy outside was gone. "Uh-oh."

"What's wrong?"

Harry stepped back from the wall and nearly jumped out of his skin. The security guard was right behind him.

"*Bonjour.*" Harry blurted it out, horrible accent and all.

The guard blinked. He lifted his chin. *"C'est beau."*

What the heck did that mean? Saying hello about exhausted Harry's knowledge of the language. He went with the fallback plan, his best answer in a pinch. Poorly accented English, the sort a native Arabic speaker might have. "My French is bad."

The guard didn't hesitate, replying immediately in English now. "I said, it is beautiful."

"Yes, it is. Very beautiful."

The guard nodded, touched his hat, and moved on, shoes clicking on the stone floor as he walked back toward the entrance. "Sorry about that," he said quietly. "Had to chat with a guard for a moment."

"I found Pliny's message."

"*Empedocles revealed the elemental nature, but it is only in his fire, and the danger of knowledge, where we reveal the lightning strike of truth.*"

Harry ran it through his head once more. "Elemental nature? That could be a reference to the four elements he believed comprised the universe."

"Including fire," Sara said. "Based on the context in this section I can see Pliny is implying that *change* or *evolution* is the driving force behind the universe, that if we want to understand what drives the universe, we must understand it is always changing. It's really an early version of the idea of evolution and that the species or group that best adapts to a changing environment will survive. Fire brings change as it turns wood to ash, clay to pottery. You get the picture."

"What I don't get is what it has to do with this temple." Harry examined the image of the two men in front of him again. "And I don't like that part about danger. Or that lightning strike stuff."

"I'm surprised Pliny excluded the other three elements. The four create a cycle. Each element is only one quarter of the total circle. They can't stand alone."

A side of. "Say that again," Harry said.

"That each one is only a quarter of the total circle."

He turned to his left. "A total circle. Or a total square if you use a straight line instead of a curved one, wouldn't you say?"

"I suppose so, yes."

Harry stepped back from the wall, turning to fully face the temple's rear wall. "That's the answer."

"What are you talking about?"

"Look at this." He snapped a photo of the rear wall and sent it to her.

"I see an altar and a statue of Jupiter, and I'm talking to a man who will be very sorry if he doesn't explain himself this instant."

"Look behind Jupiter. What do you see?"

"A design. A large square with a diamond inside it."

"Exactly. A four-sided symbol."

"It's a symbol of an *idea.* Of four ideas. Earth, water, fire and air." The intake of breath again. "The Empedoclean elements. It's the symbol for those elements and their qualities."

A square contained within a diamond. Each point on the diamond represented an element, while each point on the square inside the diamond stood for a quality. "The outer, diamond-shaped design is the elements. One corresponds to each point on the diamond. The square inside of it details the qualities assigned to the elements on either side."

"I don't see any labels on the diagram," Sara said. "And I don't believe it matters."

"Because Pliny already said where to look."

"Fire," Sara said.

"Which is at the very top."

Harry frowned. "I think I need to use Jupiter's statue so I can reach the upper point on the diamond shape. That's where *fire* is in the Empedoclean elemental chart. And that's where I need to go."

"What makes you think there's anything up there?"

"Pliny's message. That, and the fact this temple backs up to a hillside. There's only dirt and rock behind that wall. At least that's what everyone thinks."

Less suspicion graced her words now. "What will you do once you climb Jupiter?"

"Take a closer look at that topmost point on the design, for starters. It's so far up on the wall I bet no one's physically touched it for centuries." He knelt as though to tie his shoe, giving him a direct view of the front door while keeping him low. "I'm going for it," Harry said. "Mainly because my gut says this is right."

"An infallible source."

"Ninety percent of the time it's right every time." Harry stood. "I'll be in touch." He went to end the call, but didn't. "Hey," he said. "Does Nora have those towels and the bathrobe you like?"

"A robe and towels?"

"Like the ones I bought you for my place."

"No, Harry. She does not."

"Just checking. I'll call you."

He clicked off. Partly so she didn't have a chance to argue, and partly so she would remember how awesome he was for getting her those overpriced cotton luxuries. But mostly because the wandering guard had once again found his way to the front door and was chatting with his buddy in the booth outside. Harry looked at the rear wall. He looked back at the security guard. *It's probably far enough.* Far enough that any noise Harry made climbing Mount Jupiter could go unnoticed.

One way to find out. Harry quietly crossed the floor, veering around the altar until Jupiter stood just above him, ten feet of sculpted marble. Harry viewed Jupiter not as a statue, but as a ladder. If he climbed up on Jupiter's lap, grabbed his shoulders and hauled himself up to stand on those shoulders, the top of the diamond-shaped design would be within reach. Nothing to it.

Three long steps took him to the statue's base. Harry glanced back.

The guard wasn't looking in his direction, so he vaulted himself onto Jupiter's lap before grabbing hold of the big man's head and pulling himself up so his feet were bunched together on a shoulder. Harry got his balance and then stood to his full height with care. He turned around.

The guard still had his back to him.

Harry turned back and reached out to touch the top of the diamond design. Fire was at the top of the Empedoclean elemental chart, though this design had no labels. Harry leaned closer to the wall. No writing, but it wasn't entirely bare. *I was right.*

An upward-pointing triangle had been carved above the tip of the diamond. Faint, hand-etched, but definitely there. The alchemical symbol for fire. He pushed on the triangle. Nothing happened. He frowned, and pushed harder. Still nothing. This had to be a button or lever—some way to access the next step. He pushed again, grunting this time, his teeth clenched with effort. He leaned his weight into it and pushed with his legs.

One foot slipped. Harry reached out and grabbed the first thing he could reach. He twisted, caught hold of Jupiter's staff and held on tight to keep himself upright. His foot swung loose and his fingers tightened on the staff in a death grip—so hard his thumb broke through the stone staff.

His heavy breaths filled the air as he went still. A look back found the guard still with his back to Harry, oblivious to what was happening. Only then did Harry's brain catch up. He looked at his hand, at the thumb that had broken through the staff held by the statue. That wasn't possible. His eyes widened. *Found you.*

He had pressed an invisible button at the top of Jupiter's staff. The ground vibrated. Softly, as though a huge truck was rumbling at some distance away. He looked ahead, left and right. Motion at the edge of vision caught his eye. Harry turned.

A panel had opened in the altar.

One section of the altar's rear side had receded on itself to reveal an opening—in an altar that had appeared to be made of solid stone. Harry stared at the gap. He looked toward the front door. The guard whose back had been turned now faced him. *Oh no.* But both hands were stretched overhead: he was yawning, his face toward the ceiling as he leaned backward. Harry dropped and landed behind the altar as the guard's hands came down and he straightened. The last glimpse Harry had of the guard was him looking straight ahead as Harry fell.

He hit the ground and went down on all fours. He tensed, not moving. The soft, slow *click* of footsteps told him the guard was moving again. Harry scrambled to the far side of the altar and peered around. The guard had his arms behind his back and was walking the same route he'd traveled before, moving at a leisurely pace. Harry ducked back behind the altar and wracked his brain. Had the guard's route included walking behind the altar or in front of it? In front of it. As long as he kept to that pattern, he wouldn't see the open slot in the altar and wouldn't know what Harry was doing.

The penlight came out of Harry's pocket. He aimed it at the darkness of the newly opened entrance and flicked the beam to life.

A set of steep stairs descended into the ground.

He leaned into the opening. The stairs sloped down to the right. Five steps led down to a landing, then turned ninety degrees on a path leading into the hillside. *I was right.* He reached down and touched the first step. His fingerprints remained in the thick dust. The step didn't move at Harry's touch, didn't do anything at all. That would have to be good enough for now.

He touched the first step with his boot. Nothing happened, so he went down a few more steps and looked back. There was no way to close the panel behind him now. He'd have to take his chances. He descended the five steps to the landing, turning so he could look down the steps heading deeper into the hillside. He aimed his penlight to the bottom. A floor came into view, at least twenty feet down. This staircase was even steeper than he had realized. There was a good chance he'd break his neck if he tripped.

Stone walls and a low stone ceiling were all close enough for him to reach out and touch. Musty air dried his throat as he descended. A cool wave of air snaked down his shirt in the darkness as he walked, chasing his flashlight beam down the stairs. Harry paused halfway down to the floor, looking back toward the light from the open panel and listening for signs the guard had discovered this entrance. He heard nothing.

Harry continued downward until he stood on the final step, where he played his light over the walls. He had entered a wide chamber, although the ceiling remained low. Support pillars lined the walls. He hesitated, then stepped from the last stair down to the chamber floor.

Snap.

He looked down. A broken length of string lay at his feet. It had been stretched across the stairway in front of the final step, and he'd missed it because the string was practically invisible, a translucent fabric resembling a spider's web. His fists clenched. Nothing happened.

He let out a slow breath. Whatever was meant to happen had not. He almost laughed. *Better to be lucky than good.*

He turned to face the wall to his left. No writing or markings. Then the wall to his right. Nothing. Only then did he aim his light ahead into the chamber's darkness.

Stone slabs covered the rear wall. White stone, similar to the stone used for the temple above. This hidden space could have been created by Pliny. No, not could have—had been. There were Latin letters inscribed in the stone at eye level, with another row of nonsensical letters carved below the Latin. Two letters preceded the lower row of gibberish. Harry checked his phone. No service. He snapped a photo of the letters on the wall, then translated the Latin words in his head.

Only one man saw two long-haired stars at once. Find him in history and follow his path to locate what is cold and wet.

"Long-haired stars." Harry's whisper sounded like a shout in the quiet. He stood as though electrified. "Comets. He's talking about a comet."

Ancient Greeks and Romans believed comets signaled changing

fortune. Good or bad, they couldn't say, but when a comet raced across the sky it meant change was coming. The word itself came from a Greek phrase. "Long-haired stars," Harry said to himself. "*Aster kometes.*" This descriptive Greek phrase had given birth to the English word.

Only a few men in history were famously associated with comets. Mark Twain was born in a year when Halley's Comet appeared in the skies, and he had died in a year when it returned. Another person, however, was much closer to Harry's purpose. "Aristotle wrote of once seeing two comets at the same time," he said to himself. He was the only man Harry knew to have seen two long-haired stars at once.

He needed to call Sara. The answer to this riddle lay in the story of Aristotle seeing two comets at once. A story told in *Natural History*. Time to go. Harry put his boot on the first step and started up.

The step dropped. Harry stumbled, pitching forward before he threw a hand out and caught himself on a higher stair. What the heck? He was nearly lying flat on the steep stairs when he looked back to see what happened.

The first step had fallen into the floor. Not cracked in half. Not had a piece break off. The entire step had dropped into the floor.

He felt it before he saw it. The rumbling started in his gut, home of the internal compass that almost never failed. His legs and arms shook as the vibrations intensified, his teeth chattering and vision blurring. Dust spewed from below him to coat his nose and throat, his eyes burning as a cloud of grit and debris filled the air. He squinted through the haze.

The second step had turned so the flat top was now angled down toward Harry. He blinked and the third step did the same. *It's turning into a slide.* A slide to trap an intruder at the bottom and prevent them from climbing out.

He had to get to the landing or he'd be stuck down there. Harry backed up as the fourth step up began to turn, then the next one after that. He charged forward as the steps continued turning, the sixth and seventh twisting as he leapt for the next one, his boot skidding on an angled step as he kicked to propel himself upward.

His lead foot caught on a step as it began to turn. Harry kicked off with it again, jumping to stay ahead of the onrushing change. This time his lead foot got to a still-level step, but when he pushed down to jump again that step gave way and he stumbled, arms flailing for balance, as the shaking intensified. The light that came from the temple above had been reduced to a soft blur, barely visible through the haze.

He flung an arm down as he fell. His hand found an upturned step and he pushed, kicking at the angled ground of already-turned steps to push up, toward the light. His boot had just enough purchase to keep him moving. He reached, caught another step and pulled, legs churning as the hazy speck of light grew closer and the rumble became a roar and the steps continued to fall.

I got this. He kicked toward the landing, now so close he could reach out and touch it, the safety of its level floor nearly within reach. He gave one last desperate kick upward, toward the edge, both hands outstretched as the last steps turned.

He grabbed onto the lip of the landing. One hand held. One didn't. Harry fell back, his weight swinging him around as he kept a grip on the smooth stone rim. He swung to one side, bounced off the tunnel wall, then swung back. He stuck a foot out to stop his swinging before it ripped his hand free and sent him back into the chamber below.

Harry's shoulder burned. His lungs ached. His eyes watered. But he held on.

He gritted his teeth, pulled himself up as far as he could and threw his other hand toward the ledge. It caught, and he began to haul himself up. The toes of his boots slid across the now-angled staircase as he moved up an inch at a time, keeping his grip on the ledge until he managed to throw one elbow up, then the other. His boots moved all the while, almost of their own accord, before the tip of one caught in a tiny groove and then he was up and over the ledge, rolling and ending up on his back.

The dusty air tasted like ambrosia as he gasped, lungs heaving, not moving. The short stairs leading up to the temple waited behind him.

A pebble smacked off his forehead. Harry frowned.

The ceiling rattled. More debris fell. A *crack* split the air, and before his brain could give orders Harry jumped up and dove for the shorter staircase as the ceiling collapsed. He landed on the stone steps with a bone-jarring smash.

A giant stone block had crashed onto the flat landing. One final assault from Pliny for anyone who managed to make it up the staircase. Harry could only shake his head. *I bet Pliny warned me.* He thought back ruefully to the encoded missive scratched across the chamber wall.

"Mon Dieu."

Harry looked up the stairs. The guard looked back down. *"Es-tu blessé?"*

Harry replied without thinking. *"Je vais bien."*

The guard's eyes narrowed. "Your French is much improved."

Chapter 15

Manhattan

"I appreciate you looking into it for me," Nora said. "I'll keep trying."

"Remember, our job is a journey," Guro Mjelde said. "One step leads to another, then one more. Eventually you find answers."

"I know. It's frustrating sometimes, but that comes with the territory." Nora rubbed her forehead. "I'll figure out who he is."

"I know you will. And I will help. I promise I will not stop looking."

"I appreciate it. Let me know if you hear anything from Harry."

"I will," Guro said. "He said he would be in touch."

"Don't worry," Nora said. "I'll set him straight if he doesn't play ball."

Guro didn't know everything about Harry, though she knew enough. "He is a field man," Guro said. "A man of action. Men like that decide to work with others in their own time. I can wait."

Nora thanked her Norwegian friend and clicked off. At times like these she wished she wasn't on speaker. Then she could slam the receiver in its cradle. Maybe even break the phone. Then she'd feel better.

Stop it. Any therapist would tell her violence was not a useful form of expression. Nora would tell the therapist exactly what they could do with that opinion. And then she'd be in more trouble.

"Guro's right," Nora said to herself. "I'll figure out who he is. Eventually."

She looked out the window of her office. Manhattan stretched out in front of her, or at least the sliver of it she could see between skyscrapers, all the way to the East River. Someone out there knew about the man who had broken into her house, who had tried to kill her. She'd find them eventually. Then she would make someone pay.

A knock sounded on her open office door. "Special Agent Doyle?"

Nora turned to find a strange face leaning around the door frame. "Yes," she said.

The body beneath the face came into view. "My name is Craig Boulder. I'm with the mayor's office."

Nora's back stiffened. "Hello."

"May I come in?"

Nora gestured to a chair across from her desk. She did not stand when Craig stepped in and closed the door behind him. "Do you have five minutes?" Craig asked as he sat down. "I won't take long, I promise."

Craig's suit was well cut. Same with his hair. Nora's suspicion level ratcheted up a notch. "I can spare five minutes." She leaned over the desk. "Do you have any identification?"

"Of course." Craig smiled with practiced ease, showing perfect teeth.

She took the card Craig had removed from a pocket. A city-issued identification card for one Agent Craig Boulder, Department of Investigation. Her eyes narrowed. The word *Temporary* ran across the top of his card in bold print. Nora kept hold of the card when she looked up. "You're temporary?"

"I'm a consultant."

"For?"

His smile never wavered. "The mayor's office. Department of Investigation."

"What are you investigating?"

"Background information."

Answers like that shouted *lawyer*. "Who's your supervisor?"

Craig gave her a name. This time she had to scratch a non-existent itch by her ear to cover the reaction. Craig's boss was the head of the mayor's re-election committee. A committee, she had heard through the grapevine, that was now focused on lobbying the governor of New York in regard to the expected resignation of the lieutenant governor. "I see."

She handed his identification back. "What's on your mind?"

"A recent operation against one of the organized crime families in the city," Craig said. "Involving the Cana family."

"A successful operation," Nora said. "What about it?"

"It was successful." Craig sat back in the chair and crossed one leg over the other. "Impressive work. I'd like to ask you about how it happened."

"Why does the mayor's re-election campaign want to know details about the Cana family?"

Craig didn't flinch at the broadside. "I wouldn't know," he said. "My assignment has nothing to do with his re-election."

Sure. Nora waved a hand. "Fire away."

Craig made a show of opening the leather notebook on his lap. A metallic pen flashed when he took it out of his suit jacket pocket. "Apparently, the information that led to Altin Cana's arrest was provided by a confidential informant." A pause, which Nora did not fill. "A confidential informant you cultivated."

"Is there a question coming?"

"Who was the informant?"

"That's confidential."

"What information did he give you?"

"Who says it's a man?"

Fewer teeth this time. "What did he or she tell you?"

"The informant told me about a murder Altin Cana committed. That eventually led to a warrant for his arrest. I'm sure you know the rest."

"An arrest during which several dozen felons were found in possession of various firearms and narcotics. Most will be in jail until they are eligible for retirement. Some, much longer. The result of your work is that the Cana family has ceased to exist."

"You got it."

"Back to the informant," Craig said. "A member of the district attorney's team convinced a judge the informant's name should be redacted in all court documents. For his protection."

"His or her."

"This member of the district attorney's tea—"

"—is my father." Nora cut him off. "We can get that out of the way."

"Yes."

Nora glanced at her watch. "Is there a real question here?"

Craig uncrossed his legs, his elbows finding his knees as he leaned toward her. "Did you or your father fabricate evidence in order to convince a judge to issue a warrant for Altin Cana's arrest?"

A thunderclap filled Nora's head. Silent to everyone else, it rattled her thoughts until they were a jumbled mess. *He knows.* Somehow Craig knew Harry had altered a recording so it implicated Altin Cana in the murder. It didn't matter that the crime boss had ordered dozens of them himself in the past. He hadn't ordered this one. He'd been framed, and Craig knew that Nora knew.

She reached for the coffee mug on her desk. It was empty. She took a sip anyway. Nora set it down, narrowed her eyes, and kept her voice flat. "No."

"Did you or your father facilitate the release of a man named Harry Fox from Greek police custody recently?"

The wave of that question crashed over her. She stood firm. "I have no idea what you're talking about."

"Harry Fox was detained in Thessaloniki by the local authorities. He was transported to the police station for possible charges related to antiquities crimes. A member of Interpol arrived…" Here Craig finally checked his notebook. "A woman named Chara Markou. She took control of the investigation and released Mr. Fox." Craig looked up. "Is any of this familiar?"

"Can't say it is."

"Did you or your father assist Chara Markou with facilitating Harry Fox's release from custody?"

"Am I in trouble? Because from where I sit this sounds like an accusation. Without evidence."

"Please answer the question."

"No, Craig Boulder. Neither I nor my father had anything to do with the man's detention in Greece recently."

"You're certain?" Nora didn't bother answering. "This is important, Ms. Doyle."

"I'd be very interested to know why. All I hear is a political consultant trying to undermine my credibility."

"It's not your credibility in question." Craig closed his expensive notebook. When he spoke again, his voice was softer. "I am not your enemy."

"Could have fooled me."

"I am, in fact, working to protect someone close to you."

Nora's head of steam evaporated. "You're what?"

"Attempting to determine if there is any reason for concern regarding the recent actions of you or your father. Any actions that would prove"—he looked to the ceiling as though for inspiration—"concerning, should they come to light."

"Why would you be concerned about what I did? Everything was legitimate. I followed the rules and we busted Altin Cana. It was a solid bust. The city is a safer place today because he's not on the streets."

"I agree," Craig said. The smile returned. "My concern is not focused on you."

"This is about my father." She looked at Craig. At the pocket holding his badge, the one given to him by the mayor's re-election committee chairman. A man worried not only about getting his boss installed as lieutenant governor, but also about keeping his boss's influence strong at City Hall. How? By placing people he trusted as backfills. Top of that list? The district attorney's office.

"I am concerned with maintaining the mayor's unblemished public image." Craig inclined his head toward her. "Yours as well, Ms. Doyle."

Nora wanted to agree with him. She wanted to tell Craig she knew he was right and they needed to be prepared for what came next. She wanted to, but she'd been around too long and seen too much. Craig Boulder wanted her trust and he was darned good at his job. A little too good, in her opinion. "I'm happy to answer your questions," Nora said.

Craig switched back into interrogator mode. He repeated the question about fabricating evidence. And the one about helping Harry get out of that police station in Greece. Nora answered consistently and confidently, lying through her teeth. An emphatic *No* to each one.

Any trace of congeniality was gone from Craig's face. "Ms. Doyle, I wouldn't want to find out you've been less than forthcoming."

She tried to bore a hole through his skull with her gaze. "I'm certain."

Craig let her last denial linger in the quiet office. "Thank you," he finally said. The notebook closed. "I appreciate your time, Ms. Doyle."

"My pleasure," Nora said. "One question for you. If that's permitted."

Craig was already on his feet. "Of course."

"When is my father being appointed district attorney?"

Craig's eye gave a barely noticeable twitch. "I'm afraid I don't have any insight into that matter," he said. He put out a hand, which she shook. "Thank you, Ms. Doyle."

Craig wasn't out her door two seconds before Nora called her dad's cell. "Pick up or I'm breaking down your door," she muttered as it rang.

"Hello," Gary Doyle said, his voice bright. "What's going on?"

"Where are you?"

"In my office."

"I'm coming up now. We need to talk."

She made the trek up to Gary's office in record time. His secretary barely had a chance to get her head up before Nora flew past, slamming Gary's door shut behind her. Gary was seated behind his battleship of a desk.

"Hello, Nora. What's on your mind?"

She aimed a finger at his face as though it were loaded. "Why didn't you tell me?"

"Tell you what?"

"That you're being appointed as the next district attorney."

Gary set his pen down. He nodded slowly. "I wondered when that rumor would start."

"It's not a rumor, Dad. I just had a consultant hired by the mayor's re-election chair in my office." Her words came faster. "Guess what he asked me about?"

"Perhaps you should have a seat," Gary said.

"I will not have a seat. I will stand here as long as it takes to get a straight answer out of you."

Gary sat back in his chair. "To answer your first question, I have no idea if it's happening."

"They don't send consultants snooping around without a reason."

"No, they do not. However, nothing is official."

Nora's face grew hot. "Stop being a lawyer. Tell me everything you know."

Gary fought to keep the bemused look off his face and failed. "Don't take this the wrong way, but you would have been an excellent interrogator."

"Do you really want to mess with me?"

His hands came up. "I do not. Fine, I'll talk. Like you and everyone else in the city, I have heard the lieutenant governor is resigning due to health concerns. As I told Harry, that means—"

"Hold on." Nora leaned across Gary's desk. If her face had been warm before, it was steaming now. "You told *Harry* about this?"

Gary Doyle, seasoned prosecutor, fumbled for words. "It, well, it came up as part of a different conversation."

"What conversation?"

"A different one," Gary said. "Now, if you will stop interrupting me, I'm trying to answer your question." He gave her enough of a look to keep her quiet for the moment. "The current governor will appoint a replacement if his lieutenant resigns."

"Which is widely expected to be the mayor. I know."

"Leaving a vacancy in City Hall that your boss will be eager to fill. Assuming the current D.A. wins the special election, that means there needs to be a new district attorney." Nora aimed her loaded finger at Gary again. "You."

"Speculation, but yes. It could be me." Gary adjusted the knot on his already-adjusted tie. "I have heard whispers that the D.A. has me at the top of his list as a replacement."

"Putting you in the pole position for the next election cycle." Nora crossed her arms. She still did not sit. "Do you want the job?"

Gary shrugged. "It's not the sort of offer you refuse."

"You're spending too much time around mobsters."

"And you're not?"

The finger came back. "This is about you, and how you're keeping things from me." Nora stepped back. "Does Mom know?"

"I operate under the assumption that your mother knows everything."

"She didn't tell me." Nora threw her hands up and screamed. "What's wrong with you two? How can you keep this secret? My dad's about to be appointed the interim D.A. and you don't even tell me?"

"If anyone in a two-block radius was not aware, they are now."

"It's not funny." She lowered her voice with effort. "I told the investigator I didn't know anything about the confidential informant in the Cana case, and I didn't know anything about how or why Interpol got Harry out of a Greek prison."

A dark shadow crossed Gary's face. "I see." He rubbed his lustrous red beard. For some time, he looked at his desk. When Gary finally looked up again, he wasn't the father she'd known and loved her entire life, a man who would move mountains for her. He was Gary Doyle, Assistant District Attorney. A man who put criminals away for life. "Were your answers truthful?"

If there was ever a time when Nora could read between the lines, it was now. This was her choice. Her decision. He would back her either way. But she had to decide.

It was no choice at all. "They were," Nora said.

"I see." Another rub at the beard. "Then we have nothing to worry about. Should this man approach me, I'll tell him the truth." Gary's face tightened. "The same truth you told him."

"Good."

"Good." Gary nodded. His next words were soft, so low Nora had to move closer to hear them. "Nora, your mother told me something once, and it stayed with me. She told me there is very little black and white in this world. It's filled with gray areas, where right and wrong aren't absolute. To me, that means doing my best to make not only the right decision, but the best decision. I believe you do that as well. Including today."

Gary knew she'd told a lie. He didn't care. He had her back. "Is this because you want to be district attorney?"

"I never asked to be the D.A.," Gary said. "Though I wouldn't turn it down. Either way, my mind is at ease. I believe our decisions served the greater good. I'm not looking back."

"Neither am I." Nora paused. "Thanks for being a great dad."

"Oh, I'm not great every day, but I try." Gary sat back in his chair. "Was the man who interviewed you courteous? If not, I'll find the guy and let him know how I feel about anyone intimidating my daughter."

Nora smirked. "I didn't let him off easy."

"That's my girl." Gary picked up his coffee mug, looked into it, and frowned. "Speaking of Harry," he said as he put the mug back down. "What is he getting himself into now? The last I heard he was making his way from Zurich to somewhere in France."

"After kicking Sara off the case."

"I understand the sentiment. Regardless, Sara is not an adversary I'd care to face often."

"Lucky for him she's focused on their original task."

"The Charlemagne pursuit."

Nora nodded. "Which requires more research, from what she told me. Harry is looking into the burnt scroll information."

"A burnt scroll from an exiled oligarch."

The words came out of Nora's mouth before she could stop herself. "Harry can handle himself."

Gary raised an eyebrow. "If you believe it, then so do I."

Nora sat down in the chair now, looking at her father, but barely hearing what he said. Who was she, jumping to Harry's defense so quickly? Harry did what he pleased even when he was supposedly working for her. He didn't listen. Ran off without thinking. The sort of things she couldn't stand. And she was defending him?

"Have you heard from Harry?" Gary asked.

Nora shook her head to clear those thoughts away. She'd deal with Harry later. Namely by remembering to put him in his place. "No," Nora said. "Let's fix that."

She dialed Harry's number, put the phone on speaker and set it on Gary's desk. Several rings passed before Harry answered. "Hey."

Nora looked up at Gary. "Are you running?" she asked Harry.

"Not now," Harry said.

"You sound out of breath."

"I am."

"Can you talk? I'm here with my dad."

What could only be called extreme hesitation filled Harry's voice. "Hey, Gary."

"Hello, Harry. Before you ask, Nora knows everything."

"About what?"

"Everything."

"Oh. Okay. Thanks for the heads up."

Nora waved a hand to silence her father. "Why are you out of breath?"

"I had to run from a museum security guard. I'm still walking fast. Don't want him to catch up."

"Hold on." Gary stood from his chair. "*Why* are you running from a security guard?"

"Did Nora tell you I was going to the Temple of Augustus and Livia here in Vienne?" Gary said she had. "I found a passage under the altar. There was a staircase leading down to a chamber. The chamber had a message from Pliny. Part of it was in code. I didn't call Sara to use the Antikythera to decipher it. Big mistake. Nearly got myself killed when the stairs turned into a slide and the ceiling collapsed. I got out, but the guard wasn't thrilled. So I ran."

Gary looked at Nora, his mouth slightly open and eyes wide.

"I'll explain later," Nora said to her father. "Harry, where are you now?"

"Headed back to my hotel, then I have to talk to Sara about Aristotle and comets."

"I have no idea what that means."

"Me either." He took a few sharp breaths. "Hey, I have to tell you something. I don't think Guro is the right person to help me."

"Because she's in law enforcement?"

"Right. The sort of help I could use now is, well, it's the more versatile kind."

"The kind unbound by the constraints of the law."

"You said it, not me."

Nora rubbed her forehead and asked the question for appearance's sake. "Anyone come to mind?" She already knew the answer.

"That lunatic professor. Dessi Zheleva."

"Sara's associate."

Gary jumped in. "Who is Dessi Zheleva?"

"You want to take that one?" Nora asked Harry.

"Dessi is a Bulgarian professor who's basically an anarchist. She's scary, smart, and she saved my life a few months ago. I trust her."

Gary took it in stride. "I see. And how can this anarchist scholar aid you?"

"By watching my back."

"That's what Sara was doing," Nora said.

"She was, and she did a fine job."

"What can we do to help from here?" Nora asked.

"Tell me about the guy who attacked you."

"Nothing to tell," Nora said. "He isn't talking."

"In that case, I have to call Sara. She has access to the Antikythera. I need it to decode a message I found on the chamber wall. I think that will tell me where to go next. Call her later. She'll get you up to speed."

The line went dead. Gary's hand went back to his beard before he spoke. "What's the Antikythera?"

Nora sighed. "It's a long story."

"Where's Harry going next?"

This time Nora smiled. "He's following Pliny the Elder's footsteps."

Chapter 16

Paris

"On three, everyone. Mr. Lloris, please look this way."

Olivier Lloris dutifully turned to face the central photographer. He smiled, ignoring the pinch of the unfamiliar construction worker's hard hat against his skull. He pushed the brand-new shovel in his hands down into the dirt. People on either side of Olivier squeezed closer to get in the shot as one of the photographers counted down, shutters clicked, and the image was captured.

"Thank you, everyone. That's what we needed."

Olivier handed the shovel and hard hat to one of the organizers, then started shaking hands. One after another until each person had posed for a photo with the generous benefactor whose donations had paid for all this. Olivier smiled over and over until finally the person who would truly make this happen stood in front of him.

"Thank you, Mr. Olivier." The woman beamed as she shook Olivier's hand. "Your generous gift will help children for decades to come."

"It's my pleasure," Olivier said. He meant it. "My school never had enough books when I grew up. If I can give even one child in this neighborhood a better opportunity to learn, it's all worth it."

"This new school will do that," the woman said. "I'll make certain of it."

"You're the right administrator to lead this facility." He patted her on the shoulder. "I'm counting on you."

The woman beamed. Olivier turned for one last photograph before waving the cameras away. "Watch out," he said. "The backhoes are ready to go. School opens in twelve months and counting."

Everyone laughed. On cue, the closest backhoe roared to life, and then people really did scatter, just in case the driver meant business. The school would sit on a formerly vacant lot in one of Paris's poorest neighborhoods. The press coverage was great, but he wasn't doing it for the accolades. Olivier really did know what it was to grow up with nothing.

"Mr. Lloris, do you have time for a few questions?"

He kept a blank face as the reporter approached. "Who are you with?" Olivier asked. His face relaxed when the reporter named a local paper. As long as it wasn't a national paper, he was fine. They tended to ask questions he didn't appreciate. "I have a few minutes," Olivier said.

The basic stuff came first. Why donate money for this new school? Do you see more schools in your future? Softballs, all of them, and Olivier offered the smooth answers this reporter expected, falling into a familiar routine. Until it wasn't.

"You said you understand what it is like to have tough times," the reporter said. "Does that drive you to give back?"

"It does. I'm happy to do this."

"Tough times," the reporter continued. "Such as when your tire business had that unfortunate fire. Does that experience play a role in your philanthropy, the knowledge it can all change so quickly?"

Olivier's jaw tightened. He looked more closely at the reporter. A young guy. Barely out of school. "You must be mistaken," Olivier said quietly. "I never experienced such a tragedy."

The kid's face went red. "Oh, my. I'm sorry, sir. I must have mixed up my research."

Olivier's face softened. "It was a competitor's facility that was destroyed. And yes, it was a tragedy. From which I learned a valuable lesson."

The kid brightened. "Which is?"

"Everything can be taken from you in an instant." He clapped the reporter's narrow shoulder and pulled him in close. "I don't like to talk about that fire," Olivier said. "It has nothing to do with why we're here today. Don't print anything about it."

"Of course, Mr. Olivier. I won't."

"Excellent." He pushed the kid away. "Now, please excuse me. I have an appointment."

The young reporter was all thanks as Olivier turned and stepped into the back of his waiting car. His bodyguard sat behind the wheel. "To lunch, sir?"

"Yes. Don't worry if we're late. The man I'm meeting wants to sell me something. Let him sit."

The man Olivier was meeting had a Roman statue for sale. Nearly two thousand years old and recovered in the United Kingdom by construction workers building a new parking lot. Did Olivier want it? Yes, he did. That didn't mean he would let the seller know.

Olivier settled into the seat of his luxurious sedan as it slid away from the curb and merged into traffic. The reporter's question remained in his ears. The kid couldn't know the truth, couldn't have asked it that way intentionally. So why had Olivier bristled at the question? The problem was Olivier had set the fire himself. No easier way to get ahead of the competition than to turn their business into a smoldering heap. That's the part he didn't want to talk about.

That fire had changed Olivier's life. At one time, he had been merely a skillful painter forging paintings that mimicked other artists, often long dead and famous. That talent had led to the next phase, his purchase of a tire manufacturing business, and when his chief competitor's operation had gone up in flames, suddenly Olivier was the only game in town. That's when he'd started making real money.

That fire was Olivier's first step in building a business empire.

A buzzing phone pulled him back to the present. An Italian number was on screen. *Carmelo Piazza.* "What is it?" Olivier asked in English when he connected the call.

"Joey Morello knows."

"Knows what?"

"That I've been asking about his business." Carmelo spoke quickly. "You know what that means?"

"That people in your organization talk too much."

"It means Joey Morello knows I disrespected him."

"I am sure you are not the first."

"You do not understand. You're not Italian."

Dieu merci. "Deny it. Sow doubt and say it strongly."

"To lie is even worse."

"How?"

"If I say it is a lie, then I am calling the person who told him about it a liar. It is a second insult to Joey. He will not let it go."

These Italians and their unwritten codes. "Then what do you propose?"

"I propose you find the solution. You are the cause of this problem."

Olivier almost laughed. *He does have a backbone.* "You agreed to my offer. It was a business transaction, nothing more. Don't view this as a problem. View it as an opportunity."

"To get myself killed."

"To expand your territory."

Silence. The kind Olivier had learned to let stretch on. "How would I do that?" Carmelo finally said.

"Find out who talked. It isn't one of your men?"

"Impossible."

"Then it is someone from another clan. Someone Joey Morello knows. A person he respects. Find that man, and you will find your new territory. Only another clan leader would call Joey Morello. Not a foot soldier. The clan leader who whispered in Joey Morello's ear is the man you will take down." The car's supple leather seat pressed against Olivier as they made a turn. "You are a clan leader. How would you view a fellow leader who intrudes on your business?"

"Unfavorably."

"Joey Morello should be able to handle his own business. Relying on others is a sign of weakness. And no one needs a weak leader."

"Learning who talked will be difficult."

"Find him, then start whispering in the right ears. It is easier to attack his reputation than confront him directly."

"Reputation is everything."

"Then ruin his. The man is meddling in other people's business. Ruin his reputation first. After that, taking his territory should be easy. It doesn't matter what you did. Accuse him of worse. That's how you do it." Did this man know nothing about how to fight dirty?

"It could work."

And just like that, Carmelo was on board. "Good," Olivier said. "One other item. Do not interfere with Harry Fox. I need him to be left alone. For now." He didn't tell Carmelo that he wanted Harry Fox to complete his hunt for the Charlemagne relics.

"I understand," Carmelo said.

The line went dead. Olivier leaned back in his seat, tapping the phone against his chin. He should have been thinking about his impending statue purchase and how to drive down the price, but another thought intruded. That reporter's question kept playing in his head. If the reporter had decided to dig into Olivier's background, he could have learned enough to discover that Olivier had built up the capital to buy his tire company by creating and selling counterfeit art. Art that hung on the walls of unsuspecting private collectors today.

Hard to say, but all of this led him to think about another possible problem: Harry Fox. The Morello man was working for Olivier now. Working to locate relics on his behalf. Could Olivier trust Harry Fox? Or was he blinded by a desire to possess relics tied to Charlemagne?

Harry Fox hadn't given any indication there was more to the relic hunt than making a profit on what he found. Yet Olivier had a feeling this was more than it seemed. A mirage. He had no proof of other motives. That's why he dialed Carmelo's number.

"I had another thought," Olivier said when Carmelo answered.

"About the plan?"

"Not the one to expand your territory. About my relic acquisition. I am not certain I can trust Harry Fox."

"You should only trust family."

"I don't have any family, so I need you to send a man after Harry Fox."

"The Morello man?" Carmelo barked a laugh devoid of humor. "If you think Joey Morello is angry now, see what happens when I try to kill his man."

"I don't want you to kill anyone. I want you to follow him. Nothing more."

"Why would I follow the man you hired to recover a trinket?"

"It is not a trinket, and you will do it because I will pay you."

"I am listening."

"Send a man to tail Harry Fox from a distance. See where he goes, what he does. Do not interfere with his work. Do not bother him in any way. I only want a pair of eyes on the man. Do you have anyone who can handle the job?"

"I know someone." Carmelo named a price.

Olivier swallowed his true feelings on the number. "Agreed," he said. "I will call you back with where to find him."

"What if my man discovers where to find this artifact you seek? Would that be worth anything to you?"

Olivier opened his mouth. He closed it. *Would it?* Yes. It would. "No," he lied. "I need you to leave him alone. Do not get in the way of my plans."

"Plans change," Carmelo said. "My man can be persuasive."

Olivier hesitated. "I am not interested."

"I believe you are. My man will learn where to find your artifact."

The thought of saving money by stealing instead of buying took center stage in Olivier's head. "How will he do this?"

"By following, and by listening. Then, by being persuasive."

The restaurant where Olivier would meet the statue seller came into view ahead. "Start by following him," Olivier told Carmelo. "Once your man knows more, we will talk. I will send Harry's location shortly."

He clicked off and told his driver to circle the block. Olivier called Harry's phone. His relic hunter did not sound pleased when he answered.

"What is it?" Harry asked without preamble.

"Have you made any progress?"

Harry barked something sharp, a reply Olivier didn't quite catch. Not because he couldn't hear Harry. Because he was listening to the background noise. Harry was in a crowd. A crowd of people speaking *French.*

"Did you hear me?" Harry's sharp words pulled Olivier back to the call. "You want this done, leave me alone."

"Then I will trust you are a man of your word," Olivier said. He let that linger, listening closely. Yes, the conversations in the background were those of native French speakers. They spoke the softer French of people in the southern regions. "An update is not unreasonable."

Harry grumbled. Olivier listened. *He's in southern France.*

"I'm making progress," Harry said. "That's all you need to know."

Olivier pressed the phone to his ear and caught the sound of a train coming to a stop. He couldn't make out the automated voice announcing the name of the stop over the loud music, jazz of some sort. His eyes went wide. *Jazz.* "I can't hear you," Olivier said. "The music is too loud."

Harry raised his voice. "I said that's all you need to know. I'll call when I have more."

The line went dead. Olivier smacked his leg. "Live jazz music. That's the key."

Harry was in a French city, likely a southern one. One with public transit, but more importantly, a city where Harry could be in the middle of it and have his conversation overpowered by jazz music. A quick check on his phone gave Olivier the answer. He congratulated himself before sending a message to Carmelo.

Harry Fox is in Vienne, France. Find him.

Chapter 17

Germany

Moonlight glinted on the polished blade in Leon's hand. The ceremonial dagger had an ivory hilt, inlaid with gold and a single ruby at the bottom. It had belonged to his father and grandfather. Before that it had belonged to a line of German barons whose family had fallen on hard times. The dagger was a symbol of status and power—everything Leon Havertz's family had earned.

That acquired status and power had been passed to Leon, and he would care for that legacy, ensure it remained untarnished. From now on, at least. His hand tightened on the dagger. If the walls of his office weren't made of stone, he would have hurled it at the wall across from him.

"Sir?" The voice of his security chief sounded from the doorway.

"Come in." Leon waited for his employee to cross the wide room, passing between a mounted broadsword on one side and a crossbow on the other, until he stood to the side of and slightly behind Leon's overstuffed chair. The ever-present fire crackled in front of them as Leon studied the dagger. His employee waited for orders. "You may speak," Leon eventually said.

"I have an update on the man we sent to New York."

"Yes?"

"He is in police custody."

Leon nearly jumped from his chair. "How?"

"He was arrested in the home of a city employee. He assaulted a member of law enforcement."

"He failed." Leon turned and threw the dagger at the wall behind him, shouting as he did. The dagger hit the wall with a muted thud and fell to the ground. Leon stood, his face burning, his breathing heavy. He looked at the security chief. The man looked away. Leon took a long breath, collected himself, then turned to face his employee.

Harry Fox had escaped. That was all that mattered. "I need another man." A moment passed, then one possible solution flashed across his mind. "Bring me my phone."

The security chief reached into his pocket and handed Leon a cell phone. "You are dismissed." Only after the chief had left did Leon dial a number. The same number he'd dialed to reach Marwan the first time, before Marwan failed him. Marwan had told Leon long ago he would always be able to reach him – or someone in Marwan's organization – on this number. Hopefully that held true.

The ringing stopped. Leon spoke quickly. "Marwan is in jail."

A noise sounded. Possibly a throaty grumble, so low he wasn't sure. When the person on the other end finally spoke, it was in soft tones. "How?"

"He was arrested. That's all I know." It wasn't Leon's concern what happened. "His job is not finished."

"No matter."

"Wrong," Leon said. "I paid half a million dollars for Marwan to recover my property and arrange a conversation between myself and the man who stole from me. He took my money, but I do not have my property."

"That is your problem."

"Are you not a man of your honor?" He took a shot in the dark. "Is your family not honorable? Marwan failed to complete our agreement. Can your family not be trusted?"

"Do not insult my family. He is my brother. I should kill you."

"You should fulfill the agreement."

"I do not worry for you. I worry for my brother."

"Your brother is safe enough. If you want to see him again, you will need money. For lawyers. Money for your cause. Money that I have."

Silence met his words. *Excellent.*

"I will pay you the remaining half million dollars," Leon continued. "In exchange, you will locate Harry Fox, retrieve my property, and dispose of him."

"That was not the agreement."

"Your brother failed. The terms have changed." Something in Arabic or some other heathen tongue came through the phone. "That is my offer. Do you accept, or will your brother live out his life in an American prison?"

It didn't take long. "I accept."

"My banker will bring the diamonds to your jeweler."

"Where do I find this man Fox?"

"He travels under a false passport with the name Daniel Connery. I will send you his current location."

Leon clicked off. He called for his security chief, gave the orders, and within an hour had the last location Daniel Connery's passport had been used and a description of Harry Fox sent off to the second Hamas man. Harry's last passport activity was purchasing a rail ticket from France to the German city of Trier. He would arrive there early the next morning.

Leon sat in his chair for a moment, still holding the phone. He typed a message and sent it. *Send proof of his disposal.*

Only seconds passed before the response arrived. *It will be done.*

Chapter 18

Trier, Germany

"Sorry I'm late."

The woman he'd last seen in Bulgaria as she drew two killers away from him glared at Harry. Glared down at him, for she was nearly a head taller. "Do not let it happen again." Then Dessi Zheleva grabbed him in a bear hug, one she stepped back from nearly as soon as it began. "It is good to see you."

Harry looked across the familiar cityscape of Trier as the early morning sun painted everything with soft light. Pointed towers on the tallest buildings rose above the city; rolling green hills rose and fell in the distance. The university campus on the horizon stirred something inside him. Sara's old office was there. The office she'd had before moving to America. He had a pretty good idea of where to find the street on which they'd first met. Right after a couple of skinheads had decided to pick on a guy with darker skin. A guy named Harry Fox. A guy, it turned out, who had just made more than a friend to watch his back. That chance meeting with Sara changed Harry's life.

"Good to see you too," Harry said. "Thanks for coming. Road work held up my train."

What should have been an eight-hour trip had turned into twelve due to his train being delayed. Thankfully, he'd booked a sleeper car and rested most of the journey.

"It is no problem." Dessi shifted her weight from one foot to the other as she spoke. She touched the mass of dark, curly hair on her head, then pulled her hand away in a flash. "Sara told me only to meet you here. Why?"

The intensity of her gaze. That's what Harry remembered most about Dessi. She was a force unto herself. "That's all she told you?" he asked. Dessi said yes. "And you still came?"

"Why wouldn't I come?" She was so serious he almost laughed. "Sara is a friend," Dessi said. "She would not ask for a favor unless it was necessary."

"Fair enough."

Dessi went on as though he hadn't spoken. "A favor to meet a—what did you call yourself? An expert in rare antiquities?"

"I am. I have a store now."

"The artifacts have proper documentation?"

"Everything on my shelves is completely aboveboard." He didn't mention the items not on shelves. "Perfectly legit."

"I am certain this is true." Her face said otherwise. "Now tell me why I am here. And then you will tell me what happened in the Valley of the Kings."

The valley where Harry had uncovered the truth behind Spartacus. The Spartacus who nearly toppled Rome. "Deal," Harry said. "It's the least I can do after what you did for me."

Dessi waved a hand. "I distracted two goons."

"Two goons with guns who wanted to kill me."

"If you are alive, they are goons, and useless ones. No more." She stuck a hand out, palm up, and motioned with her fingers. *Out with it.*

"You're here because I found a message from Pliny the Elder hidden beneath a Roman temple in Vienne, France."

Dessi nodded as though that were the most unremarkable statement she would hear all day. "You are not working with the government?"

Not this again. "No, Dessi. I'm not. In fact, my government connection told me I'm on my own for a while. Seems the last time I helped them it brought too much unwanted attention."

"That is what you get for helping the government." She spat out that last word as though it were poison. In her mind, it was. "What did you find in the temple?" He told her about the message involving comets and Aristotle. "That does not relate to Trier," Dessi said.

"Not on the surface. Pliny is telling us to find a passage in a book he wrote called *Natural History*. A passage about Aristotle seeing two comets at once." He hesitated. "Are you familiar with the Antikythera?"

"Do you believe there is any chance I am not?"

"Figured you were. The device can be used to decode messages in Pliny's book. Messages that reveal a path he left behind."

Another nod, perhaps of mild interest this time. "What is at the end of this path?"

"That's what I'm trying to figure out. The path protects something he didn't want Emperor Caligula to have."

"What is it?"

"He called it the *Great possessions*. No idea what he's talking about, but apparently if Caligula got his hands on them, these possessions would reinforce the idea that Caligula was a god and the reincarnation of Jupiter. Pliny knew that would be very bad for most Romans."

"The history books are not kind to Caligula," Dessi said. "Pliny was probably correct. Caligula was crazy." She smiled. "I want to find them. Where does Pliny's path lead in Trier?"

"To the Imperial Baths."

Lines creased her forehead. "A Roman bath complex. That is a logical choice."

Harry had expected every response up to and including utter craziness with Dessi. But he didn't expect that. "What do you mean, logical?"

"The bathhouses were a central part of Roman life. They were built to last. A good place to leave a message."

Dessi Zheleva was a lot of things. A possible anarchist, borderline nuts, and completely fearless. She was also as sharp as they came. "Exactly my thoughts," Harry said.

Dessi's head twisted as she looked around the train station. Nothing but morning pedestrians to be seen, and plenty of them. "Why are we standing here?"

Harry angled his head. "Because I just got off the train?"

"Time to go." She turned and walked off without another word.

Harry scrambled to catch up with her long strides. The imposing spires of Trier Cathedral caught his eye. It was the oldest church in Germany. Sara had told him that.

"Watch out," Dessi said abruptly.

Harry bounced off Dessi's back and stumbled. "Why'd you stop?" he asked.

"To get in my car." Dessi opened the door of a car as European as any Harry had seen. "Get in," she said as she folded herself behind the wheel.

"Didn't they have any smaller ones?"

"You are not funny."

Harry tossed his bag in the rear seat and hopped in beside her. A tight fit. "I'm disappointed," he said.

Dessi turned the key and stepped on the gas in one motion. "You cannot mean with me."

"Your car."

A scowl crossed her face. "Speak plainly."

"The blue Toyota Corolla you let me borrow in Bulgaria. That's what I was hoping to see again."

"You made fun of my car."

"And for that, I am sorry. That car saved the day."

"I flew here." Dessi took both hands off the wheel, pulled an elastic band out of her pocket, and tied her hair back off her face, using one knee to navigate as she hammered the gas, pumped the brakes, then accelerated. "Or else I would have it."

He reached for the wheel as a sharp turn appeared ahead. Dessi slapped his hand away. She did not reach for the wheel. "Hands off."

Harry grabbed the *oh crap* bar above the window. "How's Rhesus?" he said, to distract himself from impending death. Rhesus was Dessi's Newfoundland, a massive dog Harry suspected was the only living creature Dessi truly loved. A dog he'd nearly gotten killed when she helped him escape the two gunmen in Bulgaria.

"He is fine. No thanks to you."

"I'm still really sorry about that."

"Sorry would not bring my dog back to life if he had been shot." Harry absorbed her words in silence. "It is good he was not," she continued. "Rhesus is a warrior. A true Thracian. Like me."

Harry managed to keep a neutral expression as they screeched to a halt for a red light. History wasn't Dessi's profession. It was her life, shaping her view of the world. Dessi's worldview came through the lens of a Thracian citizen. An ancient Thracian. One whose honor, courage and steadfast resolve were unflinching. Her life's goal was to educate the modern world on what it had lost. That goal was why this woman with the promising scholarly career had ended up in the backwaters of rural Bulgaria.

"Glad to hear he's healthy," Harry said.

Dessi finished with her hair and both hands went back to the wheel. Harry relaxed. Slightly.

"What do you know about the baths?"

"Not much."

"Pay attention."

Harry sat back as Dessi talked. The Roman baths were built adjacent to natural hot water pools, complete with an underground sewer system and labyrinthine tunnels used by staff and patrons. The large bath complex served not only as a bathing house, but as a place to socialize. Dessi made it clear that not everyone had equal access during Roman times, with women having limited rights. Apparently, the baths were separate from an area holding toilets and servants' quarters, with an adjacent open area serving as the exercise grounds.

"Sounds like a relaxing place."

"Such amenities were not seen again for over a thousand years," Dessi said. "Where does this message from Pliny the Elder tell you to go?"

Shadows filled the car as a row of clouds covered the sun. "I'm not certain. The passage in *Natural History* said Pliny visited the baths at Trier, and it mentions how refreshing the water is. Specifically, it says the water is 'cold and wet'."

"The pools are hot. Never cold. That is wrong."

"I think it's telling us what to look for," Harry said. "How familiar are you with the classical elements?"

"Earth, water, air and fire. Empedocles first posed the idea. Aristotle and Hippocrates expanded upon it."

"Remember the chart? A diamond shape with a square inside it?"

"Each point on the diamond represents an element. Each point on the interior square describes the phases between elements." Dessi turned to look directly at Harry. "The description between water and earth is *cold*. Is that the connection from Pliny's text?"

"Not bad, Dessi. That's it." He pointed at the windshield. "Stop sign ahead."

She may have glanced through the windshield. Then again, she may not have. He pitched forward as she smashed the brakes. "I am driving. And that is simple."

He couldn't come up with a single point to refute hers. "Lucky for us, I guess."

Dessi accelerated around a turn. Harry fell into the door a moment before she swerved into a parking spot alongside the road. Harry held on until the engine was silent. By then Dessi was out of the car and motioning for him to follow.

"We're still in the city," Harry said as he unfolded himself from the seat and stepped out.

"They are the Trier baths. Where else would they be?"

The only thing he could see were local businesses. A bistro. A hair salon. "Where?"

"One block this way."

A block later the baths revealed themselves. The sky had clouded over completely as they walked past a small bank and the view opened ahead. Stone ruins sitting on two square blocks of green park. Harry chased Dessi across several lanes of traffic and found himself on an elevated sidewalk looking over the baths. Ancient Roman walls still stood all around.

"The baths are at a lower elevation than the city. Do you know why?" Harry did, but she didn't give him a chance to respond. "Because many tiny layers of soil or debris built on each other gradually."

"Trier is literally built on top of Trier," Harry said.

"You are not entirely stupid."

"You and Nora would get along just fine," Harry said under his breath.

"What did you say?"

"I said let's get moving." Harry took the lead this time, forcing Dessi to follow him into the site. Partial ruins stood to their right, two-story remnants of the bathhouse, which had once been circular with large openings for windows. It looked a bit like a much smaller version of the Colosseum, if half of it had collapsed. Underground tunnels cut through the grassy central area; metal guardrails prevented tourists from falling in. Other openings with staircases leading underground indicated that more tunnels were present and entirely covered.

Harry made it to a wide, modern staircase leading down to ground level before she caught up. "Ever been here?" Harry asked as they descended together. "I haven't."

"Yes."

"Any suggestion on where to start?"

"Yes." Dessi looked around. A few tourists dotted the grounds, and several groups milled about at the base of the stairs, most using guidebooks and oversized tourist maps. Dessi held her tongue until they reached a set of metal scaffolding, out of hearing range of anyone else.

"Pliny told you the water was cold and wet," she said. "You believe this ties to the classic elements." Dessi grabbed his arm to keep him from going further. "Have you seen any other symbols related to the elements?" Harry told her about the image behind Jupiter in Vienne. "Given that," Dessi said, "we should look for the elemental symbol for water."

"An inverted triangle," Harry said. "Pointing down."

"Your usefulness improves." Dessi pointed toward the grassy area ahead. "That is where we begin."

"The tunnels," Harry said. "Good place to hide something."

"I expect Pliny did not imagine it would take anyone so long to find it."

Harry could only shake his head as he followed her toward the closest underground access point. The woman had a way with words. "What about comets?" Harry asked, more to prod her than because he believed it. "The *Natural History* text started with the fact Aristotle was the only man Pliny knew who claimed to have seen two comets."

"Comets were not understood at the time. Pliny was a philosopher as well as a scientist. A man of reason. Reasonable men understand simple communication is the best. I believe he would use water to communicate, not comets." Dessi raised her hands to indicate the baths around them. "We look for the water symbol."

"Dessi, you are also not entirely useless."

Dessi's back stiffened. She didn't break stride, didn't turn to look at him, so Harry's smirk went unseen. Moments later they stood in front of an open staircase leading to the tunnels below. Dim lights lined the rough stone walls on either side. Harry's phone vibrated. He pulled it out to find a text from Nora. What it contained made him rip his gaze from the screen and look around, peering at every face.

Dessi noticed. "What is wrong?"

"The airport police got back to Nora."

"What about?"

"The man who attacked her. Nobody knew who he was, so Nora took a shot in the dark and called in a favor from an officer at JFK."

"Nora believes the man flew to America."

"It was a guess. Her contact scanned the footage of all international arrivals for two days before she was attacked. A facial recognition program found the guy. He flew in from Beirut on a Lebanese passport."

"They have his name."

"Not because of the passport, because it was stolen. Or at least that's what the owner said when police in Lebanon knocked on his door."

"He may have willingly given it to the man who attacked Nora."

"You'll be shocked to hear they're related. Cousins."

"Only a fool would require more proof to know the truth," Dessi said. Harry's scowl shouted agreement. "Now they know his name," she continued. "Nora is safe."

"The cousin in Lebanon said he had no idea when his relative stole the passport. The police say otherwise. The man who attacked Nora is Marwan Qassad. He's a known Hamas operative."

"Hamas would have only one motive to attack your sister. Money."

"Marwan is known to work as an operative for hire." Harry ran a hand over the stubble on his chin. "Kidnapping, extortion. Murder. He's also suspected of trafficking cultural relics."

Harry didn't have to say the worst part out loud. Dessi didn't miss much.

"The Hamas man asked about you," she said. "He sells relics. You are the reason he went to New York."

"Thanks for reminding me."

"What is done is done. Your sister is alive. That man is in jail." For the first time since he'd met her several months ago, a change came over Dessi's face. It softened. "The past is where we will find the truth. It is also where some people choose to hide from difficult times. Do not live in the past. I do not."

"Are you kidding? It's your entire existence."

"Wrong. It is where I learn. The past teaches me how to live now." Dessi clapped a hand so hard on Harry's shoulder he winced. "Live as your sister did when she was attacked. With strength. The strength to follow this trail."

Harry did his best not to shrink from the caring, intense woman peering into his soul. "Thanks, Dessi. I think you're on to something."

"Good." She gave him a thump on the shoulder. "Now, the tunnels."

"Not yet." Harry looked around again. "You had the same idea I did. That Hamas guy isn't the only terrorist in that group, and they still want the money."

"Yes. There could be a second man coming. Nora must be ready."

"One of my friends is keeping an eye on her." He did not mention said friend was the *capo dei capi* of the organized crime families in New York City.

"What about your store?"

"What about it?"

"Does it exist?"

Harry rolled his eyes. "Yes."

"Who is watching the store while you are gone?"

"I hired an employee."

"Is he an expert in rare antiquities?"

"Not even close. He's more of a technical wizard." Harry waved away her questioning look. "He's a good guy to have around." He indicated the staircase. "Ready?"

"Stay here." Dessi moved down the stairs without further explanation. Harry protested to no avail, then was left to stand by himself while she disappeared into the dim tunnel below. Thirty seconds later he had gathered up a head of steam and moved to follow her. Who did she think she was, leaving him behind?"

His foot had barely hit the first step before she came back out of the darkness at pace. "This is not the tunnel," she said.

"How could you know that?"

"Bathing areas had a common arrangement. There is the *tepidarium*, the warm room. There is the *caldarium*, the hot room. And the *laconicum*. The dry, hot room." Dessi pointed to different areas of the larger complex in turn as she spoke. "Do you see where each is?"

"One is on each side."

"Yes. North, east, and south."

Which, if you didn't have a compass, was behind them, to the left, and also ahead. "That leaves west." Harry pointed to their right, across the wide expanse of kempt grass and walkways. "What's that way?"

"The vestibule. Where the servants and slaves waited for their masters."

Roman citizens often had slaves, and the richer ones had servants as well. "You think that's where we need to look." She opened her mouth, but he connected the dots too quickly. "You think we should look there because it's the invisible part of the baths. The part only servants and slaves used."

"An excellent place to hide what you do not want to be found."

"How do we get there?"

"Servants and slaves moved in the shadows," Dessi said. "Out of sight."

"They used the tunnels."

"Yes. That is where we must go."

Dessi turned away from the stairs, heading across the surface toward the far side. They passed people standing or walking in twos and threes. Both scrutinized each face they passed. Harry leaned closer to Dessi and spoke in low tones. "I have no idea who we should be looking for."

"A Hamas terrorist."

"And you would know a terrorist if you saw one?"

"I trust my instincts."

A cloud covered the sun as they followed a paved walkway across the grounds. Paths jutted off at various angles, leading toward partially standing walls, underground tunnel access points, and in one case, an opening to a sewer tunnel big enough to drive a truck through. Dessi studied the people they passed, as did Harry, each searching for someone who stood out in any way.

"Do you have a picture of the man who attacked Nora?"

"I will in a second." Harry texted Nora, asking for one, and explained why. Her response was almost immediate. *Sara told me Dessi would save your sorry butt.* Harry chuckled and turned his phone so Dessi could see. "Your fanbase is growing."

"You should listen to them." His phone buzzed again and she grabbed it from him. "The picture is here."

A man to whom the years had not been kind stared back at them from Harry's screen. Cavernous lines ran upward from the corners of a hard mouth. His nose had been broken more than once. All this, in addition to a missing ear, gave him a dangerous edge Harry could almost physically feel.

"Now I know what to look for," Dessi said as she handed Harry's phone back.

Harry tried to hide his thoughts. "What native language would he speak?"

Dessi didn't hesitate. "Arabic. The language of Lebanon."

"Ever been there?" Dessi said she had not. "I was. Once. The road signs are in Arabic and French. Which means there's a very good chance our man also speaks French."

"It is no matter. I know what to look for. A man without a soul." She indicated the photo. "A man like him."

Harry pondered that as they approached another staircase leading below the ground. "Stop." Dessi threw her arm out and held him fast. "This is it."

An opening resembling a large sewer tunnel with an arched overhang lay ahead of them. "How can you tell?" Harry asked.

"The image." She pointed to the outline of a single person carved above the arched entrance. "It is a man wearing livery. Not a toga. Only Roman citizens wore togas. Their servants and slaves did not. They wore uniforms or clothing with symbols representing their master. This is a servants' tunnel."

Harry peered into the distance at the far-off faces of other visitors. "I don't see anyone without a soul." He was only half-joking.

"I cannot see anyone." Yet she waited, still looking around.

"What is it?" Harry asked.

"I cannot see him. But I feel there is danger." Another moment passed. "We must move quickly."

This morning Harry would have scoffed at such talk. Feelings didn't stop an enemy. Intelligence and preparation did. That was before he saw the face of the man who'd tried to hurt Nora. Before Dessi Zheleva's certain conviction in herself had changed his mind. Harry wasn't dismissing Dessi's thoughts now. One hand went into his pocket, touching the ceramic knuckledusters that had saved his backside more than once.

Satisfied for the time being that they were not being followed, they went down the short staircase.

At the bottom, brick and stone had been stacked and mortared to create the tunnel's entrance. They stepped inside, and here they faced their first choice. "Left or right?" Harry asked.

The larger tunnel almost immediately branched off into two narrower ones. White lights ran along the upper walls of the wider section, but inside the two narrower tunnels the only lighting came from dim yellow bulbs hanging from the curved ceilings; their light did not extend very far.

"There is scaffolding in the left tunnel," Dessi said.

"Let's take the right one."

"Why?"

"Scaffolding means repair work," Harry said. "Repair work means people digging into the walls, or maybe a wall partially collapsed. People poking around inside means it's more likely they would already have found anything there is to find. Like a message or hidden area Pliny may have left behind."

Dessi agreed, and they veered right. Damp glistened on the walls. Harry's boots left footprints on the stone floor after he trod in a small puddle. The stone and brick around them were smooth. They passed the first pool of light, the gloom surrounding them once more as a second pool of light in front of them beckoned.

"What are these niches for?" he asked.

They had passed several of the carve-outs, sections in the wall about the size of a window. "Storage," Dessi said. "They would have had doors on them in Roman times."

"Ancient supply closets," Harry said. A thought from years ago came back, of a broom closet in a Roman church near the Colosseum, a place where he'd found a relic tied to a long-dead Roman military commander. A man named Lucius Artorius Castus. A man who may have inspired the legend of King Arthur. "Might be something in these." He poked his head in the nearest one. "Or not."

"What we want will not be here. We are too close to the public bathing area. The servants' passages go deeper. We must look back there."

It made sense. Still, Harry gave each alcove they passed a quick inspection, finding nothing. An opening in the ceiling here allowed weak natural light to filter through. Harry glanced up and saw dark clouds looming above.

"We're running out of tunnel," he said after passing one more empty alcove. Their path ahead split again, two tunnels branching to the left and right. "Let's try the scaffolding trick again."

"It did not work this time. We have found nothing."

"Ye of little faith." The left and right options had equally dismal lighting. Again, one had scaffolding. "Work is happening to our left. Let's go—"

A noise cut through his words. Dessi grabbed his shoulder and pressed a finger to her lips. Her breath was warm when she leaned close and whispered, "Did you hear it?"

"Sounded almost like a cough," he said in equally soft tones. "From above."

They turned as one and looked to the sickly gray light filtering down behind them from the opening carved in the ceiling. They waited. Nothing.

"Could have been someone walking past," Harry said. "Or the wind, maybe."

"Or it is someone after us."

They stood still, listening, for another minute. Then Harry's feet grew antsy. "Probably nothing," he said. Dessi appeared unconvinced. "Let's get moving," Harry said. "The longer we stay here, the more time someone has to catch up." He tilted his head toward the right tunnel. "That way. Come on."

Dessi followed when he started walking. The lights were dim here, somehow dimmer than those they'd passed so far. Deep shadows dominated the tunnel, which seemed to narrow as they walked.

"How did they move around down here?" he asked aloud. "It's awful."

"They had no choice."

Harry paused beside another alcove. "I can't see anything in this dim light."

"The clouds." Dessi pointed to an opening above that would have let in sunlight if there were any. "They block the light."

A penlight came out of Harry's pocket. "I could see in the last tunnel. The lights in this one are horrid. And yet the alcoves are bigger now, nearly floor to ceiling." His light flashed on and he looked up. He went still. "Dessi."

"Be quiet," she said from a few steps ahead.

His voice stayed the same. "Dessi."

"Did you not hear me? Be quiet."

"Come back here."

She must have caught the tone in his voice, because she came back to his side. "What?"

"Look at this wall."

His penlight beam lit up the alcove. An image was engraved on the brickwork. "It's a triangle," Harry said. "Inverted."

Dessi brushed past him and reached out to touch the triangle, carved into the wall at eye level. "It looks as old as the bricks."

"Bricks." Harry ran back to the T-intersection, retracing his steps until he stood in front of the last alcove. "Stone." He ran back to Dessi. "This alcove is brick," Harry said. "The others are made of stone. If I dug a hole in a wall and wanted to cover it up, I'd use brick, not stone. Easier to build with." He touched the wall. "Or if I wanted to build something like a door or false wall, I'd cover it with brick." He turned, scouring the ground for a moment until he found what he needed. "Get another rock." He showed her the one in his hand. "And start tapping."

Tap-tap. Tap-tap. One after another, Harry tapped the rock against each brick, starting at the top and going down the row. "Listen to the sounds," he said. "One might be hollow, or there could be an opening behind it. Find that odd sound and we find our way in."

Dessi went to work, grabbing a stone from the floor and joining his search. Their tapping echoed in the narrow chamber.

"I found it."

Harry stopped tapping. Dessi hesitated, then knocked her stone again on one specific brick. It was the only brick completely contained inside the inverted triangle. "Do you hear it?" she asked.

"It sounds hollow." Harry almost knocked her over when he jumped forward, his face inches from the brick as he knocked and listened. "Not this one. It's solid. But there could be a space behind it."

"Why?"

His answer was to use the edge of the stone he'd tapped with to gouge at the mortar and send chunks of it flying. "Look," he said. "This brick is only for show. I can stick my finger in here and pull it out."

Once he'd chipped a hole in the mortar it was easy to pull more out, for only a thin layer of mortar kept this brick in place. Harry dug out one side, while Dessi worked on the other.

"Ouch." Pain arced through his finger when he tried to dislodge the brick. "Part of it is stuck." He aimed his light at it, and a flash sent white spots across his vision. "There's *metal* in here. Like a channel or a track."

Dessi shouldered him aside, digging her own smaller fingers into the crevice. Before he could warn her that perhaps Pliny had added another layer of security, Dessi had begun shoving the brick, growling as she pushed. It held for an instant before clouds of dust blew out of the wall and the brick rattled back on metal tracks, falling abruptly into the wall and forcing Dessi to jolt a half-step forward until the brick held fast.

Ancient gears rumbled. Tiny stones fell free as the wall vibrated for a beat. Harry pulled Dessi with him as he stepped back and to the side, clear of what might come next. Mortar cracked. Harry jumped, and Pliny's next mystery revealed itself. Hinges hidden beneath the mortar creaked as a window-sized piece of wall swung open toward them—a piece inscribed with the inverted triangle. Harry pulled Dessi farther out of the way as the triangle slowly moved toward them. Dessi moved to slip around the hanging section and look inside.

"Wait." Harry grabbed her arm. "We don't know what else Pliny left."

Dessi didn't argue, though Harry still kept a tight grip on her shoulder as she leaned to see what waited. He counted to ten, then counted once more. "We should be good," he said at last. In truth, he had no idea, but they weren't going to solve the mystery from this side of the open wall.

He released his hold on Dessi's shoulder, and she scurried around the piece of wall, Harry right behind her. They both stood still as Harry's penlight lit up a message hidden for two thousand years.

"Can you read it?"

Harry started at Dessi's question, loud in the tunnel's quiet. "It's Latin," Harry said. "And yes, I can read it." He recited aloud: "'*Seek the lofty sanctuary of he whose divine hands gave birth to the icon of human agony*.'"

Dessi repeated parts of it to herself. "Divine hands. Human agony. It could be the Christian savior. The man who died in agony for all humans." She pointed to what looked like a dull rectangle, slightly larger than a deck of cards. It sat in a recessed portion of the wall, a portion that appeared to have been cut specifically to hold the rectangle. The rectangle had writing on it. "What is that?"

Harry reached out and touched it. "A wax tablet," he said. "This writing is in code." Numbers preceded a seemingly random sequence of letters. "The same code I found at the other sites. We need the Antikythera to translate it."

"A message about the Christian god, perhaps."

"I'm not so sure. You know any Christian sanctuaries not tied to Jesus? I sure don't. That's a lot of options."

"True. What do you—"

"Quiet." Harry put a finger to his lips. "You hear that?" he asked in a whisper.

Dessi nodded. "Footsteps."

"Come on." Harry carefully pulled the wax tablet from its recessed perch and pushed on the section of wall. It rumbled shut, though anyone looking closely would see the disturbed mortar. He handed the wax tablet to Dessi. "Hold this." She took it without a word, her eyes wide. "Follow me," he whispered.

He made it one step before she grabbed him. "That is toward the noise," Dessi said quietly as she stuffed the tablet in her pocket. "Go the other way."

"I want to see who it is," Harry said. "Could be just another tourist."

"What if it is not a tourist?"

"Then we deal with it." Harry raised his voice to speak normally. "Come on," he said, and started walking. He flicked off his penlight as they made it to the next pool of weak light. The gray sunlight was not far ahead, backlighting the silhouette of someone walking down the stairs toward them. Harry put one hand in a pocket, his fingers slipping into the familiar comfort of his knuckledusters.

On they walked, Harry forcing them to move slowly. The shadowy outline solidified into a person. A man with a baseball hat pulled low over his eyes, with a shade of skin much like Harry's. Or maybe that was the guy's beard. His eyes flashed as he looked toward Harry and Dessi, then darkened as he looked down at the ground. The hidden panel in the wall was still close behind them, too close for them to stop and pretend to look at any other part of the tunnel.

Harry's heart picked up speed. This man coming at them wasn't looking around. He was walking straight toward them, and fast.

Harry played a hunch. "*Bonjour.*"

The man responded at once. "*Bonjour.*"

A low voice, not threatening. So low Harry barely caught the reply. Dessi's hand latched onto Harry's shoulder as the man approached, and it took everything he had to keep from shouting as her fingers dug into his flesh. He blinked, the man's shoulder brushed his, and the moment passed. Harry kept his gaze ahead and his feet moving. The man would see their discovery soon.

A burst of coughing sounded in the tunnel behind them. The man had probably breathed in some of the dust from their recent excavation. Harry looked back to find Dessi wide-eyed. He beckoned for her to keep walking and hurried to the staircase to ground level, where he raced up into the murky day. He paused halfway up. "Wait," he told Dessi, who was several steps below him. "Listen."

They could no longer hear the man's footsteps in the tunnel.

"He's stopped," Dessi said. "He spoke French. And it was him coughing above us before. The sound came through the hole in the ceiling."

"He could be just a guy with a cough," Harry said, not really believing his own words. He grabbed the rickety handrail on the stairs and leaned farther down. He closed his eyes.

"Subhan Allah!"

A cold wind blew through Harry's soul. "Come on." He grabbed Dessi's hand and dragged her away.

"What was that?" she asked as they flew along.

He was moving fast. Not so fast he didn't notice how easily her long strides kept up with his shorter ones, though, so he picked up the pace. "Did you hear him?"

"I couldn't understand what he said." They were running through the temple ruins now.

Harry replied as rapidly as he could manage, "He said *Glory is to Allah.* Something people say when they're surprised."

"He found the message."

"Head for your car," Harry said. "We're out of here."

The wind had faded to nothing now, and weak shafts of sunlight had managed to break through the cloud cover.

Maybe it was the adrenaline in his veins. Maybe it was instinct.

Whatever the reason, at that moment a long-haired man across the site caught Harry's eye. He was moving at top speed. His ponytail bounced and his goatee glistened in the sun as he ran on a course headed straight for Harry and Dessi.

They raced out of the site and into the city street. Dessi burst ahead of him, across the street and down the sidewalk toward her parked car. Harry looked behind him and caught a glimpse of the long-haired man as he exited the site and stopped, looking left and right. The scowl on his face turned to a wicked grin when he looked ahead and locked eyes with Harry.

"He's coming after us," Harry shouted. Dessi picked up the pace, digging in her pocket for the keys as she ran. They reached the car, and Dessi pressed the key fob to unlock it. She jumped behind the wheel and fired up the engine as Harry ripped the passenger door open and almost fell into his seat. Dessi gunned it, whipping the car into traffic and accelerating as he hauled the door shut.

But the long-haired man had caught up with them. He reached out and got one hand on the trunk, grabbing the lid where it met the rear windshield. Dessi whipped the steering wheel around, tires screeching as they veered into a side street. There was a shout of rage as the long-haired man lost his grip, rolled heavily against a parked car and scrambled back to his feet. Dessi jumped a curb, missed the corner of a building by inches, then accelerated back onto the street.

"Focus on the road," Harry shouted. She got them back on course as Harry turned to look through the rear window. The long-haired man stood in the middle of the street, watching them.

"Where do we go?" Dessi asked breathlessly.

"Anywhere away from here. I need to think."

He needed to think about the two men. And he needed to ask himself the right questions. Had the man in the hat been following them? The long-haired one certainly had. Were they together? Perhaps. Perhaps not. That would mean two people were after him. Two men with a reason to chase him down. Two men who likely wanted him dead.

Chapter 19

Manhattan

The phone on Gary Doyle's desk buzzed. A call from his secretary.

"Yes?"

"There's a man here to see you, Mr. Doyle."

Gary's eyebrows came together. "I don't have a meeting on my calendar."

"Correct, sir. He does not have an appointment."

"Who is it?"

A moment passed. "A consultant with the mayor's office. The Department of Investigation."

Gary's jaw tightened. "What's his name?"

"Craig Boulder, sir."

The temporary consultant. Showing up unannounced? Fine. Gary Doyle could play this game. "Send him in."

Craig Boulder radiated charm as he strode into the office. The quick smile he flashed could be described as disarming. Gary immediately went on high alert. "Hello, Mr. Boulder." Gary came around from behind his desk and shook Craig's outstretched hand. "How may I be of assistance?"

"Thanks for seeing me, Assistant D.A. Doyle," Craig said. "I only need a few minutes of your time."

Gary gestured to a smaller table with four chairs around it along one wall. "Have a seat." He took one as Craig did the same. "I must admit you have me at a disadvantage."

"How is that, A.D.A. Doyle?"

"Please, call me Gary. What I mean is that while I'm familiar with most of the mayor's departments, yours is not one of them."

Craig didn't waver. "Surely you've heard of the investigations department?"

"I know it exists."

"I'm here for a friendly chat. Just a few questions."

Gary pressed his lips together. Craig was up to something. "Fire away, Mr. Boulder."

The easy grin stayed, but any sense of congeniality vanished. "Why did you assist a member of the Antiquities Anti-Trafficking team in a suspected smuggler's escape from police custody in Greece?"

Gary wasn't born with a poker face. He'd earned it over the years. It went into full effect now. "I'm afraid you're confused, Mr. Boulder."

"Call me Craig."

"Right. Well." Gary let that word stretch out. "Craig. You are confused. That never happened."

There was a notebook on Craig's lap. Leather cover, monogrammed initials in the corner. Probably a fancy pen inside. Craig didn't open it as he spoke. "You never assisted Agent Nora Doyle with a case involving an accused artifacts trafficker in Thessaloniki?"

"No, Craig, I did not. Care to tell me how you came by this misinformation?"

"Various sources."

Craig was ready to launch another verbal broadside. Gary beat him to it. "Tell me again what you're investigating, Craig? I don't believe you mentioned it."

"The purpose of my investigation is a private matter for the mayor's office, Gary. That's all I can say."

"In that case, this meeting is over." Gary did not get up as he gestured toward the door. "You may see yourself out."

Did a spark of panic flash across Craig's face? Gary thought it did. Craig stayed seated and put his hands out, palms toward his adversary.

"This is an important matter we're reviewing." His voice dropped, and Craig leaned forward. "Important for the mayor, and for you."

If the fool believed Gary didn't know what this was all about, the mayor needed better lackeys. "Craig, you're here to see if there's anything in my recent past that may embarrass the mayor if I'm considered for interim district attorney."

To his credit, Craig didn't back down. "If that's true, and I'm not saying it is, you'll understand why it's vitally important for you to be honest with me."

Gary's mind went back to Nora. To what Craig had asked her, how he'd tried to trick, cajole and then outright threaten her. Craig Boulder had come after his daughter for doing the right thing. Now it was his turn. "I understand," Gary said. "And I repeat myself: I have no idea what you're talking about."

"Several officers at the Thessaloniki police station say otherwise. I also cannot, for reasons beyond my understanding, contact the Interpol agent involved." Craig flipped his notebook open, though his gaze barely settled on the page. "Agent Chara Markou, who is based in Athens. She is known to collaborate with a Norwegian agent, Guro Mjelde."

Gary gave his best impersonation of a man thinking hard. "Can't say I've heard of either of them. And may I offer a thought?"

"Yes."

"It will be challenging trying to force an agent of an international law enforcement team to speak with you. The mayor's authority extends only to our city limits."

Craig was not impressed. "We do what we can with what we have."

Enough of this nonsense. "What you have is hearsay, conjecture and speculation. What you lack are facts or evidence. You have nothing."

Craig folded his hands in his lap. "I hope we have cooperation here in our system." When Gary didn't dignify that with a response, Craig kept going. "You mentioned you are aware the mayor may be considering a succession plan. If the mayor were considering the future of this office after his time here is over, he would require reliable men. The best men—

or women—to carry on the tremendous work he has started." Craig steepled his fingers and peered over top of them. "People whose past actions would not cause embarrassment. The district attorney must be beyond reproach."

"A person who does the right thing."

"Always."

A face came to Gary's mind as he studied Craig studying him. His wife's face. Dani Doyle, the strongest woman he knew. In the running for the wisest, too. A piece of advice she'd given him over the years jumped out. *The world isn't black and white. It's gray. Do the right thing, even when it's not black and white.*

Gary made a mental note to thank Dani tonight. Gary stood from his chair. "Craig, I always do the right thing. Always have, always will. That's all I can tell you."

Craig remained in his seat a moment longer. Long enough to realize this wasn't a battle of wills he could win. "The mayor will be pleased." He got to his feet.

Gary showed Craig to the door. He waited until the man went through the office suite door and disappeared into the hallway before speaking to his assistant. "I'll be busy for the next twenty minutes," Gary said. "If anyone calls, take a message."

His office door closed on quiet hinges, plush carpet muffling his footsteps as Gary went to stand in front of the window by his desk. He looked down on pedestrians the size of ants as they hurried through what must be a cold wind. Gary had meant it when he told Craig he always did the right thing. He was an attorney, and he chose his words with care. He had not told Craig he always acted within the law. There was a reason it was called a legal system, not a justice system. The law sometimes failed to achieve justice. That's when Gary worked in the gray areas, looking for a way to do the right thing.

He put his hands behind his back. His weight shifted from one foot to the other. The right thing for his family, and the right thing for his office.

He pulled his cell phone from a pocket and called the only person he could.

"Good afternoon," Dani said when she answered his call.

"Hello, dear."

"What's on your mind?" she asked.

Gary hadn't been able to hide anything from Dani for a long time. "Why do you think there's anything on my mind?"

"You don't call me in the middle of a workday without good reason."

"Hearing your voice is reason enough to call."

"You never were very skilled at casual flattery. Now, what's the matter?"

Gary recounted his conversation with Craig Boulder. Dani listened until he reached the part where Craig discussed the necessity of his past actions being beyond reproach. "Do you know what I thought of when he said that?" Gary asked.

"I do not."

"You."

"Me?"

"You offered a slice of wisdom one time that I felt was applicable here."

"Only once?"

He grinned. "Many times."

"The suspense is unbearable."

"You reminded me the world isn't always black and white. Sometimes the things we do, the decisions we make, occur in a gray area between absolute black and white, right and wrong."

"Where we do the best we can."

"Where we do what we know is the right thing." Dani murmured her agreement. "Which is what I did today," Gary said. "Or at least I believe I did."

"Did your decision make the world a better place?"

Gary considered. "It prevented an injustice. And it gave another good man a chance to do the right thing."

"Then you did the right thing." Gary kept quiet. He could tell more was to come. "You've made the best decision with the information you had. We all learn from decisions, myself included. Everything I've done, I would do again." She was referring to the gut-wrenching decision she'd made a long time ago to protect Harry, a son she wouldn't see again for nearly two decades. "I'm sure you made the correct choice today. It's important you believe that. In your heart."

His office window rattled slightly as the wind picked up. "I do."

"Remember that if you ever find yourself in the district attorney's chair. You always do the right thing. That's who you are."

"And I believe the right thing to do tonight is take you out for a nice dinner," Gary said. "Where we talk about anything but this."

Gary named the place and time to meet before clicking off. He walked around his desk and took a seat. His gaze went to a picture hanging on the wall. Not exactly one of many, as Gary had no interest in filling his walls with trophy photos. Each one on his wall or desk held special meaning. Including the one he looked at now.

A photo of Gary on his first day with the district attorney's office, taken on the front steps of this building. Two other people were in the photo. He stood in the middle, with Dani to his right, a man on his left. The district attorney at the time. A man whose time had come and gone, but one who had made an indelible impression on Gary for many reasons.

Ron Mitchell. His elections were mere formalities, for nobody could challenge Ron. He still held the record for largest margin of victory in a citywide election, because the opposing party couldn't find anyone to run against Ron. Born and raised in the city, Ron liked to say he knew every hot dog stand and bodega in town, and if you needed to know who made the best pizza, just ask Ron Mitchell.

He was also the most strategic man Gary Doyle had ever met. Calculating, yet caring in equal measure. Ron lived and breathed New York City. He loved it as only a born New Yorker could.

Gary still had Ron's phone number, and when he called it, the man himself answered. Good Lord, was it really Gary Doyle? Saints be praised. Was Ron Mitchell free for a quick drink tonight before Gary met his wife for dinner? Darn right he was. Gary suggested the time and location. That would be fine, and no, that wasn't too early. Ron was retired, after all. He did as he pleased, same as ever. See you soon, Gary my boy.

A short while later Gary ducked out of the office and made his way to meet Ron. The legendary D.A. was shaking hands with the manager when Gary walked into the restaurant to find Ron deep in a story about political escapades of decades past.

"As I live and breathe." Ron disengaged with the smoothest of skill. "Gary Doyle."

"Hello, Ron." Gary didn't offer his hand. He braced himself.

"It's good to see your friendly face." Ron didn't give Gary a chance. A bear of a man with the size to match his personality, Ron threw his arms out and pulled Gary in close, smashing the red beard into his chest and putting two of Gary's ribs in danger. Gary squeezed back for all he was worth, which wasn't much compared to Ron. "Gangsters and con artists high and low must quake in their ill-gotten shoes when you're on the case." Ron finally released Gary, who gulped air. "Well done with the Cana case. We won't be hearing their name again."

"Thanks, Ron. It was a team effort."

Ron laughed. "Modest as ever. We'll make a politician out of you yet."

"You're more right than you know."

Ron's eyes flashed beneath the bushy hedgerows he called eyebrows. "Is that so?" He wrapped an arm around Gary's shoulders. "Then we must talk, my friend."

The manager showed them to a high-backed booth tucked into the far corner. Ron wasted no time once they had two glasses in front of them. "You said you have a dinner date with your lovely wife," Ron said. "Which means your time is valuable. Why are you wasting it with an old lug like me?"

Gary sipped his drink. "Because I need your advice."

"Then I'd say you are in dire straits, my friend. However, one item that is never in short supply from me is advice."

"You've heard about the lieutenant governor?"

"Every alderman from here to the state line knows the lieutenant's health is failing. If I were a betting man"—and here Ron winked—"which I am certainly not, I would wager the poor man is out before the holidays."

"A few months at most."

"Meaning the governor has to move some of his chess pieces." Here Ron leaned closer, though it did little to corral his booming voice. "Say the mayor becomes lieutenant governor. Then the city needs a mayor. The district attorney is ambitious, and people seem to like him. Do you?"

Gary would have been caught off guard as a young man. Now, he knew Ron too well. The guy kept people on his toes. "I would likely vote for him."

Ron winked again. "So you and everyone else votes the D.A. into City Hall. Which requires a new D.A., one who is initially appointed."

Ron sat back. He took a drink. Ice rattled when he set it down. "How did I do?"

Gary put his hands up. "I surrender. You must have a crystal ball."

Ron chuckled. "More like crumbling vertebrae and too much experience. I've seen this story more than once." He stuck his hand out. "Should I be the first to offer my congratulations to the newest district attorney?"

"All I have now is speculation and rumor," Gary said.

"Rumors in this town are more reliable than the truth. Except when they're not." A *thunk* sounded when one of Ron's thick fingers tapped the table. "Figuring out which is which keeps you ahead in this game."

Gary needed Ron to be straight with him. "Alright, I believe it's more than likely that I'll be considered should events play out as you describe."

"Someone official tell you that?"

"A contractor with the Department of Investigation spoke with my daughter recently."

"Nora? She's a peach. Great work on that Cana job. I heard her fingerprints were all over it."

"It was her operation. Her team makes my job easy." A waitress came past and they ordered another round. "Nora is part of the reason I asked you to meet me."

Worry lines materialized on Ron's face. "Something wrong?"

"The consultant who interviewed Nora came to my office today. Asked me some pointed questions. The same as he did with Nora."

Ron grunted. "Digging for dirt."

"Exactly. The mayor's image must remain untarnished."

"He going to find anything?"

"No."

"Then forget about him. Let him spin his wheels."

Their drinks arrived. Gary took a sip. "It's a little more complicated."

"Isn't it always." Ron crooked a finger and waved it toward himself. *Out with it.*

"The investigator kept asking Nora about a confidential informant in the Cana case." Gary looked around. Nobody paid them the least bit of mind. "That C.I. is the entire case. The investigator wanted to know why the C.I.'s name was redacted from every document connected to the case."

"You took down a bunch of murdering gangsters. Of course the C.I.'s name would be protected." Ron waved a dismissive hand.

Gary hesitated for half a breath. "I agree."

Ron missed nothing. "What else is there?"

"He asked why one undercover operative tied to Nora's team was quickly released from a Greek jail when Interpol intervened."

"Now that, Gary, is a story I'd like to hear."

"The short version is this man likely broke several minor Greek laws. Trespassing, possibly the destruction of protected antiquities. He was detained by local police who Nora had reason to believe were on the payroll of a local criminal organization. Could she prove it? No. Do I think she was right? Yes."

"That's how Interpol got involved."

Gary responded in a low voice. "Nora called in a favor. She has contacts. The end result was a Greek Interpol agent stepped in and took custody of the man in question. She then released him."

"Which is of no concern to this city. At worst a reporter could write an article and make allegations." Ron tapped the table again. "But that could be a problem. The mayor's image and all that. What did you tell the investigator?"

"That I had no idea what he was talking about."

"Good."

"I'm interested to hear what you think."

"About what you told the investigator? I think you should tell that guy to jump in the Hudson."

"On that angle, we're in agreement. Speaking directly, I believe I've done the right thing. The right decision isn't always the legal decision. I'm having trouble with that."

Ron nodded slowly. He took a drink, looked at his watch. A big watch. "We have a few more minutes," Ron said. "Let me tell you a story." A deep breath. "Back when my knees didn't ache and I had a full head of hair, a man called my office. Wouldn't give his name, wouldn't tell my secretary much of anything, but he insisted he needed to speak with me. She put him through, and this guy told me he had something big I needed to see. Now, you know how many cranks are in this city. I started to tell the guy to pound salt, but, and I can't say why, my gut told me to listen." Ron took a drink. "He mentioned the name of a man in the Department of Finance. A big shot. The caller says he has proof a city financial leader is funneling money from tax revenue into his own pocket. I ask him how he knows this is happening. You know what he tells me? That he has the man's personal ledger. I ask him where he got it. He tells me he broke in and stole it."

"Meaning the big shot is going to know the ledger is missing."

"You have to remember, this was long before computers, so it's plausible. I tell my caller if he has proof, he needs to bring it in and show me. The guy says he can drop it off somewhere. I tell him no way. I need to speak with him in person. You know what the caller says?" Gary shook his head. "He tells me he can't—if I see his face, he's dead. And I believed him. I told the caller he could cover his face if he wanted, and we could meet in a public place."

"He agreed."

"Told me to come right then, alone, to a nearby park. I walked out of my office and headed straight to the park. There's a man sitting on a bench, a scarf covering half his face and a hat pulled low. There's a big green ledger in his lap. I sit down. He opens the ledger and turns it, page by page. Account numbers, check amounts—a prosecutor's dream. I'm ready to get this case rolling when he drops a bomb on me. The informant, because that's what he is now, flips to the end of the book, points to the most recent withdrawals. Large withdrawals, along with purchases in the same amounts. Purchases at a diamond wholesaler who also sells gold. One I happen to know plays fast and loose with accounting records."

Gary took a breath as Ron barreled onward. "Financial guy was turning the money into diamonds and gold. He was getting ready to run. To run fast and run far. Out of my jurisdiction." Gary finished his drink. He did not speak.

Ron continued. "There was one more issue. The finance guy who was doing the stealing had some family connections to Boston, and the Boston mafia. The city was a different place back then. Connections made the man, and connections put some bad men in places of power." Another deep breath, and a sigh to sail a boat. "I didn't have much time. Either start an official inquiry, and undoubtedly tip the guy off, or move faster. To me, it was a matter of right and wrong, not legal or illegal."

"What did you do?"

"I took the ledger and went straight to a precinct near the financial guy's house. Where I knew a detective I could trust. I gave him the ledger, told him to say he'd found it while searching a house. A house he'd visit soon. Then I walked across the street and called that station from a pay phone. Gave an anonymous tip there was a robbery in progress. That I saw the intruder was armed. Said to send help, and send it fast."

Gary found his hands were clenched tight. "You gave them the financial guy's address."

"Bingo."

"Good Lord, Ron. That was risky."

"Cops show up at the guy's house. They have to clear it, of course, make sure there's no armed intruder inside. Guess what they find in the basement? Gold bricks. Piles of them. They found the diamonds too."

"And the ledger?"

One corner of Ron's mouth lifted. "My detective friend *found* the ledger in the basement. The ledger that showed everything."

"Did the informant survive?"

"As far as I know he's still in the city. Nobody could prove the ledger came from anywhere else. The thief knew someone set him up; he just didn't know who."

Gary chuckled, then asked a question even though he already knew the answer. "Who prosecuted the case?"

"A young district attorney who believed in doing the right thing." Ron looked at his watch. "You'll be late for dinner." The two men stood from their seats. "And Gary?"

"Yes?"

Ron shrugged into his coat. "It's never wrong to do the right thing."

Chapter 20

Trier, Germany

"Pull over here."

Harry pointed toward a street running up the hill on one side of the road. "I think we lost them."

Dessi parked her car by the sidewalk and they both got out. "Where are we?" she asked, looking around.

Harry pointed to a sign across the street. "Outside a Roman amphitheater."

Only then did Dessi see it. "I cannot read German."

A grassy hillside hanging on to the last vestiges of summer rose behind them. Harry pointed down the sidewalk. "The entrance is ahead. Let's go inside and talk. There's plenty of open space, and we can talk in private."

"We should stay in the city. More people. More places to hide."

"Do you really think that guy is going to look for us at an open Roman amphitheater? It's the last place he'd stop."

Dessi did not argue as Harry led her toward the entrance ahead. He looked back and forth. A path had been cut through the hillside. Stone walls stood on either side as they walked through a passageway to a giant circular area. A tiered hillside encircled the stone wall perimeter of the flat amphitheater floor.

"This used to be the main stage," Harry said after paying the modest entry fee. "The hillside is tiered because there used to be rows of seating." Modern staircases had been added to allow tourists to move around on the grass. Perhaps a half-dozen small groups moved around the open area in twos and threes.

"I could not read the sign, but do you truly believe I have never seen an amphitheater?" Dessi asked. "There will be cellars under our feet. A place for animals, for prisoners, for storage. We should not go down there. Those places are haunted."

Harry paused in the act of grabbing his phone. "Haunted?"

"By the spirits of the dead."

Harry had been around Dessi enough to know arguing was a poor decision. "Above ground it is," he said. He managed to get his phone out, then loosed a choice word. "It's dead. Does your phone have any juice?"

"Yes."

"Call this number." He rattled off Sara's cell and said whose it was. "We need her to translate the wax tablet."

Dessi punched in the number, then pulled the tablet from her pocket as the phone rang.

"Hello?" Sara answered, her voice cautious.

"It's me."

"Harry? Whose phone is this?"

"Dessi's. Mine's dead."

"Where are you?"

"At the Trier Amphitheater." He told Sara about the false wall under the baths, the man with a hat who had spooked them, and the second, long-haired man who had chased them to their car. "He nearly caught us," Harry said. "Even got a hand on the car. Until Dessi hit the gas."

The gray skies had started to clear and rays of sunlight filtered through. Harry touched Dessi's arm and pointed toward a staircase leading to the tiered hillside. "Let's go up there," he said to Dessi. "Toward the tree line at the top. More privacy."

Dessi followed as he put the phone back to his ear. "Are you at the office with the Antikythera?" he asked.

Silence met his question as Harry reached the top of the stairs, walked parallel along an old row of seating, then continued climbing toward the upper levels. "Sara, you there?"

"I am."

Another flat area, another short set of stairs. "Do you have it?" he asked.

"I'm at Nora's, and yes."

"What's that mean?"

"The Antikythera by my office is the only one that works correctly. I replaced the one on display at the museum with Evgeny's bogus replica, and the museum device is here with me at Nora's."

Harry whistled. "Great work."

"I'm holding it now. What is the message?"

Dessi was listening. "Tell me again what the numbers and letters mean."

"The numbers indicate a page in Pliny's book *Natural History*. The gibberish letters are a substitution code. Sara uses the Antikythera to translate the gibberish letters into words, two in total. The first and last words of the message on the specific page in Pliny's book. He embedded the messages in his book so everyone could see it, but no one recognized it."

"What about the three images above the numbers and letters?"

"They tell Sara how to align the dial." He explained how the dial had three rings, each of which had to be aligned with the corresponding symbols before the dial would reveal which letter of the alphabet was the starting letter. "It's a substitution cipher," Harry finished. "If the dial indicates the letter *B*, then we know every *B* is really an *A*, the *C* stands for the letter *B*, and so on. Once we know that, we know where to look on the page."

"I'm ready," Sara said.

Dessi handed the wax tablet to Harry, who recited the combination of a number, a letter and a Greek mythological symbol for Sara. "I have them entered," Sara said. "The dial is adjusting." Harry looked around. Nobody at the site seemed aware of them. "Got it," Sara said. "The first letter is *M*."

"That means any *M* on this tablet is really an *A*."

Harry read off the page number. "I have it," Sara said. "What are the letters?" Harry read those off, one at a time, until Sara had translated the first and last words she needed to locate Pliny's message. "*Inspect* and *air*."

Harry inclined his head toward the trees as they waited. "Let's get in the shade," he said. "Harder to see us in there."

They had just stepped beneath the nearest tree when Sara found it. "It's here," she said. "The words are both on this page. It's a passage about Pliny's travels to study sculpture around Greece. It says *inspect the masterful work of Agesander. His skill is a cyclone of emotion, the air*."

Dessi frowned. "That is not a sentence."

"There's more," Sara said. "But that's what Pliny wants us to read."

"Air is one of the classical elements," Harry said. "Could be we're looking for the elemental symbol for air wherever we go."

"Any idea where that is?" Sara asked.

"Pliny's talking about an artist of some kind. The words *masterful work* and *skill* tell me that."

"With certainty?" Sara asked.

"They suggest it," Harry said. "But this doesn't fit with the message from the baths."

"Are there always two messages?" Dessi asked.

"No," Harry said. "This is the first time. And I have no idea who Agesander is."

"I do," Sara said. "Thanks to the internet. I'd never heard of the man. Agesander was a Greek sculptor in Pliny's time."

A thought struck Harry. A page from *Natural History* that he'd read on his flight from New York. "I think I read that name in Pliny's work," Harry said. "Now it's ringing a bell."

"Agesander's most famous work is a statue called *Laocoon and His Sons*. It's a depiction of a mythological Trojan priest named Laocoon as he and his sons are being attacked by sea serpents."

"Sounds lovely," Harry said.

Dessi wasn't so sure about it. "The message from the baths was not about a sculpture. It is about human agony. Perhaps about the Christian god whose agony they believe grants eternal life."

"Does the sculpture still exist, and if it does, where is it?"

"It's in the same place it has been since Agesander created it," Sara said. "In a castle on the island of Cyprus. The castle has a sanctuary containing over a dozen of Agesander's sculptures. Including *Laocoon and His Sons*."

"We must inspect this statue," Dessi said. "He mentions air. We should look for that symbol."

"Not bad, Dessi." Harry put his hand out and offered her the wax tablet. "Mind holding on to this?"

Dessi took the tablet from him. Or tried to. Harry didn't let go. "Hang on." He pulled the tablet back. "Did you see these?"

"What?" Dessi asked.

"There's writing on the back side." He angled the tablet so the rear side faced skyward to catch the light. "Letters. They're so faint I didn't see them until just now."

"What does it say?" Sara asked.

"Gibberish again," Harry said. "More code. Sara, see if the substitution code we used to read the front of this tablet works for the back side. *M* is the first letter, standing in for *A*."

"Read the letters again," Sara said. Harry did. "Got it," Sara said after several beats passed. "It says *Beware the gift of Prometheus*."

"Fire," Harry said. "He's talking about fire. Prometheus stole fire from the gods and gave it to humanity."

"Could it mean to avoid fire symbols?" Dessi asked.

"Not a bad guess," Harry said. "We can read up on Prometheus on our way and figure out what else he might have done that we should avoid. We're heading to the airport. Sara, I'll call you from there."

Sara wished them luck and clicked off. Harry handed the phone back to Dessi. As he did, movement over her shoulder caught his attention. A man walking on the street beyond the amphitheater entrance. A man with long hair who, as Harry watched, stopped by Dessi's car and leaned over the trunk. Harry squinted. "Dessi, turn around and look at your car."

She did. "What is that man doing?" A sharp intake of breath. "He looks like the man from the baths. Is it him?"

"Looks an awful lot like him." As they watched, the man leaned over further and reached for the rear window, where it met the trunk. He reached down into the gap between the trunk and window, then stood and turned to reveal his profile. The man held a small circular object in his hand, held it to the light. It flashed, and Harry knew. "It's him," Harry said. "I'm sure of it."

"What is he putting on my car?"

"He's not putting anything on your car. He's taking it off." Harry's eyebrows furrowed. "That's why he smacked your car as we drove off. He wasn't trying to hang on. He put that thing in the slot between your trunk and the window where we wouldn't see it. I bet it's a tracking device with a magnet on it. That's how he found us."

Clouds moved and the sun peeked out more. "It is him," she said. "I am certain. We must go."

The man put a phone to his ear. Harry's nerves tingled. "I don't like this," Harry said quietly. "Who's he calling?"

Harry twisted around. He went still as a man walked out of the tree line thirty feet away with a phone pressed to his ear. The man didn't look at Harry, but his words carried over the open grass to reach Harry's ear. Italian words. *No, not Italian.* "That's Sicilian," Harry said. "He's speaking Sicilian."

The man looked up. His gaze met Harry's, and Harry hesitated a beat too long. The man kept the phone pressed to his ear while he reached into a pocket with his other hand. Harry blinked, and the hand came back out gripping a pistol.

He grabbed Dessi's arm. "Run," Harry shouted, taking off toward the entranceway.

Gunshots boomed. The first geyser of dirt erupted near Harry's foot. The second was even closer. Harry surged ahead of Dessi as they ran toward the exit. "Not to the arena," Harry yelled as other tourists looked around. People now began shouting and running; one bearded man stood still, watching in wonder. "Too open." He steered her toward the tree line and waited for the next shot. It never came. The long-haired man came at them, waving his arms and shouting in Sicilian. *He's telling the other man not to shoot.*

"Into the arena," Harry yelled as he ran downhill. There were a few other tourists running there, not enough to get lost in but enough to provide some cover.

They raced down the stone stairs and took a running leap into the oval arena. Long-hair mirrored their path to cut them off, while the shooter stayed straight on their tail. Harry's feet pounded the ground as he ran, waiting for the *crack* of a shot, for the searing pain of a bullet. Dessi kept pace at his side. No gunfire chased them.

"Up the other side," he told her. Cutting across the arena forced the long-haired man to either make a perilous leap from the highest point on the hillside, or loop around the front entrance to cut them off on the far side. He saw Harry's intent and looped around to avoid the ankle-breaking jump.

Got you. Harry skidded as he hit the brakes and reversed course. Dessi shouted a question he didn't catch. The shooter went to jump to the arena floor as Harry raced back at him. The shooter's face screwed up, but it was too late. He had committed and was already jumping. His arms wheeled, his feet kicked, and he hit the ground. Harry was ready, timing it so he arrived an instant after the shooter's feet touched down. The shooter landed, Harry jumped, and when he kicked both feet out in a flying leap, they connected hard with the shooter's chest and sent him airborne. The shooter twisted as he flew. Harry fell heavily back to the ground; the air was forced from his chest on impact. He blinked and sat up. The shooter screamed and spun like a thrown doll, one leg at an impossible angle as he flipped before stopping in a heap.

Harry didn't need a doctor to tell him that guy wouldn't walk anytime soon. The shooter's gun lay a short distance away. Harry ran and kicked it as far as he could, then spun around to find Dessi staring at him, open-mouthed. "Back this way," Harry told her, waving his arm in a *this way* motion. She darted back. Harry scanned the far hillside for any sign of long-hair, finding no one in sight except for the swarthy, bearded tourist, still looking on, his face a mask of bewilderment. The guy wasn't even moving.

"What now?" Dessi asked breathlessly as she made it to his side.

"We get out of here fast."

The gunman didn't do anything but howl and grasp his shattered leg as they bolted back the way they'd come, up the stairs and toward the tree line. Long-hair appeared on the far side a moment before Harry and Dessi stepped into the shade beneath trees on their side. He looked over at his comrade in the arena. He hesitated, leaning toward the way he'd come, then turned and ran into the arena. Carefully, it seemed. He didn't want a broken leg as well.

"I can hear them talking," Dessi said. "What are they saying?"

The men's voices carried up the hillside with surprising clarity. "Not sure," Harry said. "It's Sicilian." He did not explain that their words were thunderclouds portending trouble for Joey Morello. "Back to the road," Harry said. "We can't take your car."

"He removed the tracking device." Dessi stayed in front of him as they raced through the trees. Light flashed between barren branches as the clouds came back and briefly turned the sun into a strobe light. "My car is fine."

"They removed one tracking device," Harry said. "There could be others."

"We cannot drive to Cyprus. We must fly."

They came out from beneath the trees. The street fronting the arena was barren of pedestrians. Police sirens sounded in the distance. Dessi looked up to the sky. Her eyes narrowed. Harry looked up to find her staring at a large bird circling overhead. An eagle.

"You will fly there alone." Dessi's words were level, unhurried. "It is your destiny."

"Me? We're in this together."

"It is not my destiny. I was meant to help you on the path. Only you are meant to find the end." She pointed skyward. "The eagle is an omen. I know what I must do." Dessi touched her chest. "I will distract those men. I will take my car. If they follow me, you will have more time." Dessi grabbed him by the shoulders and pulled Harry close. Her eyes seemed to come alive as she looked down at him. "Follow the path. Find the truth. I am only meant to help you."

"Dessi, that guy had a gun."

"And now he is injured. This is a rental car, not mine. I will lead them on a chase. By the time they realize, you will be on a plane."

"Look, I appreciate it, but that's crazy. You won't be safe."

Dessi grinned. "No one gets out of this life alive, Harry. But do not worry about me. It is not my destiny to die today. The gods are not finished with me yet."

Dessi was bonkers. And on his side. "How are you so sure?"

"The eagle is a sign of victory. We are not meant to lose this race. Also, I see that." She pointed to his chest. Harry looked down to find his amulet, a golden square with Egyptian glyphs on it, hanging outside his shirt.

"What about it?" he asked as he quickly tucked it back under his shirt.

"I have seen you touch it when danger is close," she said. "It brings you luck. So go, and, when we meet again, tell me what you found."

Without another word, she turned, ran for the car and hopped behind the wheel. The engine whined, rubber chirped on asphalt, and in moments she was out of sight. Dessi could handle herself, Harry knew, and now he needed to do the same. He popped his head over the wooded hillside to peer down to the arena floor. Long-hair had his injured friend draped over a shoulder and they were making their way to the exit as fast as they could.

Harry turned to run, then hesitated. He looked back. The bearded tourist was still standing across the arena by the trees, watching without expression as long-hair helped his friend out of the arena. The bearded guy hadn't moved an inch the entire time. Harry shook his head and ran toward the city center to find a taxi to the airport and a castle filled with statues.

Chapter 21

Larnaca International Airport
Larnaca, Cyprus

Cargo planes roared down the runway, one after another, big business for an island as small as Cyprus. Harry pulled his rental car out of the airport parking lot, squinted against the falling sun and pointed the hood north before flooring the gas pedal. The car's navigation system said an hour's drive would bring him to his target on the Kyrenia mountain range in Northern Cyprus. Saint Hilarion Castle, an ancient Greek and Byzantine stronghold overseeing a vital mountain passage, a fortress from which the castle lord had controlled trade and demanded taxes for passage. A castle where fortunes had once been made. Perhaps, a place where one more fortune waited.

The Mediterranean's sparkling waters faded in his rearview mirror as he raced into the heart of Cyprus. The road rose and fell as he moved past groves of olive trees and forests of pine running up the sides of hills and small mountains. The Troodos mountain range rose to the west, its massive peaks soaring above dark valleys where the sun rarely fell, though the mountainside sparkled as the sun brought its light to the evergreen trees.

Barely six hours before, he'd watched Dessi race away from the amphitheater in one direction, while he'd sprinted off in the other. Harry had caught a cab to the airport and booked a flight leaving for Cyprus within the hour. He'd bought a burner phone in the airport and texted the number to Joey and Dessi. She had messaged him before he left, then again moments ago, her news the same each time. No sign of the long-haired man who spoke Sicilian, nor of his injured friend. If they were tracking her car, they were doing a good job of staying hidden. Dessi was at the airport now, about to fly back to Bulgaria. Excellent news that she was safe, Harry thought, but there were still too many unanswered questions.

Who were these two men? It seemed safe to assume their interest in Harry was connected to the Pliny hunt. How did they know it existed? And how had they found Harry? Who did they work for, and where were they now? Harry had a guess who'd sent the men. He'd shared his thoughts with Joey Morello, and Joey thought the same.

Harry's phone buzzed. "Speak of the devil," Harry said as he answered. "What's the word?"

"Nothing good." Joey Morello sounded like a man who could use a stiff drink. "Franco Licata just got back to me." Franco was one of Joey's closest allies in Sicily, the clan leader who'd alerted Joey that someone named Carmelo Piazza was meddling in his affairs. "Word on the street is one of Carmelo's guys is in a German hospital with a broken leg. No one is sure how it happened."

"Except you."

"Except me."

"What about the long-haired guy?"

"He fits the description of a well-known Piazza clan soldier."

Harry groaned. "Great. Now we have Sicilians and Hamas terrorists on our tail."

"You think the guy with the cough from the baths is with Hamas?"

Harry passed a small winery on one side of the road, long irrigation lines strung up and down the rows. "I don't know. He responded in French when I spoke to him, then he talked to himself in Arabic."

"When he saw the hidden compartment you left hanging open."

"Yeah, then."

"Hardly proof he's a terrorist."

"You know how often there's hard proof in what I do."

"Not often."

"That's about right."

"Then keep your eyes open for any bearded guys wearing a hat. Did this guy have a beard?"

"I couldn't tell. And you're not funny."

"I'm kidding. In all seriousness, you must have bought yourself a little time by putting one of Piazza's goons in the hospital. Is there any way the other one could have followed you?"

Joey knew about Dessi using her car as a distraction. Harry shared Dessi's update that she hadn't seen any sign of the men since she left the amphitheater. "It's a good sign," Harry said. "But hardly conclusive. They managed to track us to Germany. I have to expect someone will show up in Cyprus."

"What do you really think? Your honest opinion."

"Honestly? I doubt they followed me here. The wax tablet is the only way to know about Saint Hilarion Castle. They'd have to overhear me talking about it, or have a bug on my phone, which they didn't and they don't. I used the Daniel Connery passport."

"How do you know they can't track your phone?"

"Because I'm using a burner," Harry reminded him. "And I mailed my other phone back to Brooklyn. With the battery taken out."

"Right. That should take care of Piazza's remaining guy. What about the other one?"

"You mean the one who may or may not have a beard and a cough?" Harry shook his head. "Odds are it's all in my head. And I know you asked me about this so I could talk myself off the crazy ledge."

"Just trying to be a friend."

"Carmelo Piazza is still sticking his nose in your business."

"Shooting at one of my best friends is more than sticking his nose in it," Joey said. "He's looking for a fight. A fight I don't want. A fight I likely can't avoid. Not after what he did."

"Who else would know those were Piazza's men in Germany? If

nobody knows, who cares?"

"The problem is I know. If someone finds out I knew what Carmelo was up to and I didn't do anything about it, that's all it takes. Reputation is everything in my world, Harry. Lose it and it never comes back."

Joey was right and Harry knew it. "You want me to call Olivier Lloris, tell him our deal's off and he isn't getting any artifacts from me?"

"And deny you vengeance? No, don't do that. Olivier Lloris has it coming. Pay him back for what he did, and leave Piazza to me."

Harry's voice was low when he responded. "That could mean a war."

"Yes," Joey said. "It could." Several moments passed in silence before Joey continued. "Stay alert, stay alive, and we'll deal with this when you get back to Brooklyn. Anything I can do right now to help?"

"You're keeping an eye on Sara. That's all the help I need."

"She's fine," Joey said. "My guys put the word out that if anything happens to Sara or Nora, I'm coming after the guy who did it."

"You're better than the U.S. Marines," Harry said. The peaks of a new mountain range came into view ahead. The Kyrenia range. The one he wanted. "I'll be in touch," Harry said before he clicked off. Joey would take care of keeping Sara safe. But right now, Harry had another problem in front of him—how to follow Pliny's trail into Saint Hilarion Castle.

Shimmering waters appeared to the east as he drove out of a low-lying area. The sparkling faded as cloud cover rolled in and the road rose ahead of him. An oceanfront fishing town hugged the coastline, while trees and scrub grass grew undisturbed further up the mountainside. He passed several cars parked alongside the road as he drove, most likely belonging to hikers now somewhere on the slopes. None of the cars drew his attention. No one would park this far down if their destination was the castle. Scant few roads wound up the sloping hill, the only thread tying this ancient fortress to the modern world below. An ancient fortress Harry knew was undergoing a repair.

The site had been closed for weeks. His research on the flight over had revealed myriad repairs underway, necessitated by the local population's opposition to moving Agesander's sculptures to a modern museum. Despite the castle and its defensive walls having stood for two thousand years, the same couldn't be said for the roof. Progress on repairs had been slow and the museum remained closed.

A visitor center and empty parking lot came into view. Harry motored past them without slowing. He drove up the steep road, passing a defensive wall twice as tall as a man stretching from the visitor center to a lookout tower at the upper peak. The road forked in front of him. Right took him along the castle's defensive wall. Left would eventually send him further up an adjacent peak's side and to points unknown. A thick patch of trees ahead on the left caught his eye. *Left it is.*

The setting sun's bottom edge nearly touched the tallest mountain peak when he pulled off the road a distance beyond and above the visitor center, bumping over uneven terrain until his car was inside the thick line of evergreens. The chilled air brought goosebumps to his arms when he stepped out of the car. Long shadows stretched ahead, the engine clicking as it cooled while Harry checked his pockets one last time. Burner phone, knuckledusters, wax tablet. All check. The car keys went under a nearby rock and he was off.

He skidded and slipped down the steep mountainside, pausing behind a thick tree trunk to scan the road in both directions before stepping out into view. No cars in sight, though he did see a lone hiker in the distance. A hiker wearing a hat. His stomach tensed. *Easy, Harry. Not everyone in a hat is after you.* Still, he watched the man walking for a minute longer. The guy never looked Harry's way, never did anything to draw attention, only moving up the hillside in a direction that would take him to a lookout point offering a clear view of the town below and the ocean beyond. If the man was trying to get to the castle, he was taking a hard path.

I'll be in and out before anyone knows I'm here. That thought set his mind at ease. He moved across the road and found shelter between two trees, that same thought running through his head again and again. He was here and had a job to do. Didn't matter if he wanted to do it or not. Evgeny Smolov was the sort of friend he needed. Or acquaintance, or ruthless exiled oligarch, or whatever you wanted to call him. A man you didn't want as an enemy, but if a particularly desirable piece of whatever Pliny left behind didn't make it back to Evgeny, so be it. Harry would use it to lure Olivier Lloris ever closer. Harry's boots dug rhythmically into the dirt as the ground rose beneath him. *It's going to work out fine.*

The castle's exterior defensive wall towered above him, a wall of rough and sharply uneven stone mortared together. He wouldn't want to try to scale the wall under enemy fire, but doing so on a quiet evening with no one else around didn't take long. Once on top of the wall Harry found thick thornbushes growing beneath him on the other side. He couldn't risk someone spotting him, so it was crouch, leap, and fly. Arms wheeling, he reached for the open ground beyond the row of bushes.

He almost made it. One foot hit the very top of a thorny bush and sent him spinning. He crashed to the ground and rolled on impact, ending up on his backside with no apparent broken bones. "Smooth move," he told himself. Harry got to his feet and brushed the dirt from his pants before limping to the nearest tree to take stock.

Mossy stone paths wound through the grounds. The defensive wall continued straight for a short distance before turning ninety degrees and running straight up the mountain to meet one side of the peak, directly below the watchtower. Harry looked up at the tower, then his gaze traveled down the mountain to a plateau not far below it. A plateau with a two-story structure on it. The castle hall, where guests were greeted and business was conducted. It also contained rooms for the commander and the object of Harry's search. The sanctuary.

That's where Harry would find the statue. And if his interpretation of Pliny's message was accurate, the elemental symbol for air.

Wind scythed across the rockface and made him shake as he moved up the hillside, pausing at each tree to cast an eye around for other intruders. He forced himself to move cautiously, to linger in the growing dark and to ignore the rapidly cooling air. The odds were that even if the Sicilians still wanted to find Harry, they wouldn't be here this quickly. As for the Hamas connection, that was a worry for another day. He'd probably have to lean on Joey's connections to get those guys off his tail.

Today was for Pliny's search.

The hillside rose above him, now too steep to climb without a path. He veered off to take one of the stone walkways, nearly running as it took him first away from the castle hall above, then switch-backed on a direct path for his target. An empty guard's checkpoint funneled him into a narrow stairway, the ancient stone walls seeming to press in on either side before he emerged at the top to find a short trail leading to yet another staircase, this one cut out of the side of the hill and with an unlit floodlight at the top. Harry raced up the stairs to a landing that finally opened into the first level of the hall.

One hand stayed on the cold metal rail when he reached the last step. A sweeping view of the city by the dark water of the sea stretched out before him. The first streetlights came to life in the fishing town, with headlights moving up and down the narrow streets. The lights on shipping boats further out to sea flashed on as the sun continued to fall, the deep blue ocean water dimming to black, mirroring the darkening sky above. Harry stood motionless, letting the scene take hold of him. Pliny's riddles, the Antikythera, Hamas terrorists coming after Nora, all of it fell from his mind for a moment.

Light exploded behind him. Harry jumped as the floodlight burst to life and nearly sent him tumbling over the narrow metal handrail. The light had an engine like a tank, rumbling and buzzing as it sent its powerful beam over the mountain below. He steadied himself, both hands tight on the handrail, and looked down on a long shadow stretching across the mountainside. His own personal Bat-Signal.

He jumped away, his shadow leaping with him for an instant before vanishing. Anyone looking at the castle from below knew he was here now. Any intruder, the cops, the mayor, even the dogs at the local shelter. Nothing he could do about it except get in and get out.

He jogged across the open plaza toward the castle hall entrance, veering close to the far handrail to get a look. He leaned over and looked down. A sheer drop, two hundred feet at minimum. He stepped back. Stay away from that side.

He found a dark shadow by the entrance and stood in it. A glass enclosure projected out from the original castle's main entrance; the new door, at the back of the enclosure, was all glass and steel. Scattered around were rows of scaffolding and sawhorses, ladders and piles of material. A major roof renovation was underway, with a sign on the door informing visitors the target re-opening was some months off. Harry hugged the stone mountainside and craned his neck until he could peer through the side of the glass enclosure, leaning close and shielding his eyes against the glare of more floodlights than he'd realized were there, all of them now lighting up the night at various points around the site.

He peered through the glass exterior wall. Tarps covered the floor inside, with more building materials, toolboxes and stacks of shingles stacked throughout the space. Ongoing construction meant plenty of ways in and out. Safe ways? Probably not. Harry stepped back from the glass wall and looked up. Exposed ductwork ran across the ceiling. *That could work.*

He stopped at one toolbox tucked against the front wall, a big one. It was unlocked. He grabbed a screwdriver, went to the nearest scaffolding and climbed, the metal poles and wooden boards creaking under his weight. The top level was even with the enclosure roof. Harry leaned over and slid between the metal pipes, the scaffolding wobbling only a bit as he stepped onto the roof and knelt. The wind was fierce up here, hard enough to knock him off balance if he weren't careful. He found a ventilation shaft cover, bent over it, and used the screwdriver to unfasten the cover, which he set down beside him.

A gust of wind promptly whipped it off the roof, down onto the plaza, and sent it flying away with a loud screech. He slid into the large air duct and got on his hands and knees to crawl forward. The shaft was wider than the one in Harry's house. Even so, his shoulders bumped off the sides with each move. Dust filled his nose and burned his eyes. A square of faint light lay several yards ahead, filtering through a metal grill below him in the duct. Harry stopped when the light was in front of him. His screwdriver made short work of detaching the cover.

Anyone inside the hall would have seen a head poke out from the air shaft, look in every direction, then disappear back inside. A moment later, they would have seen a man dropping from inside the duct and landing softly on the floor. But no one was there to see. Harry kept low to the ground and surveyed his surroundings.

He was in the middle of a long entranceway. Giant photos of the ancient castle grounds covered the walls, with informational stands beneath each picture ready to enlighten visitors. More construction material was stacked around the walls with little evidence of progress. The ceiling had been cut open in different areas. A single large bucket sat below the largest hole. It did not have any water in it.

Darkness waited beyond the entranceway. Darkness broken only by dots of light along the edges of the floor and glowing red exit signs above various doors. Vague forms distorted by the dim light waited at the edge of sight. The sanctuary. Harry kept to the perimeter, penlight in hand but not turned on until he reached the threshold and stopped, one shoulder pressed against the wall. He flicked the penlight on and aimed it ahead toward the hall's rear wall, stone and original to the castle. Harry's light brought a fearsome creature to life.

A bearded man, ten feet high and carved from white stone, stared down at Harry. Standing on a pedestal, the giant had biceps thicker than Harry's waist and he clutched a hammer fit to crush mountains in one hand. The open eye in the middle of his forehead told the story. A cyclops, the one-eyed mythological creature in Homer's *Odyssey*, here depicted as the son of the sea god Poseidon. Harry turned his light to the next statue and found the sea god himself waiting, equally imposing and holding a three-pointed trident in one hand while the other pointed ahead.

Agesander had created these statues. A jolt raced from his feet to his forehead. *This is the path. I was right.*

The rectangular hall stretched ahead, so far it must have been partially carved into the mountainside, far enough that his light didn't reach the end. Harry moved to a side wall, skirting around statues of the Greek king Odysseus, the Greek goddess Athena, and a muscular young man clad only in metal greaves and carrying a wineskin. He spared each only a glance, staying alert for the room's main attraction. Halfway down the castle hall the walls changed from drywall to ancient stone, the original castle walls. He reached out and his fingers scraped over the rough surface. His light stayed ahead, pushing back the darkness until it revealed the statue he'd come so far to find. Laocoon and His Sons.

Laocoon had been a priest involved in the mythical Trojan Wars, which had pitted the Greeks against the Trojans. According to Virgil's *Aeneid*, Laocoon and his two sons had attempted to reveal the true purpose of the Trojan horse by running it through with a spear, but the Greeks hidden inside had made short work of the three Trojans. In other versions, Laocoon suffered similarly undesirable fates through various misfortunes, nearly always with his sons.

Harry walked to the statue's base. His light started on the pedestal, moving upward to reveal the bare feet of three men. Laocoon in the middle, one son on either side. Two large snakes were wrapped around Laocoon's legs, as well as around the legs and arms of his sons, ensnaring all three in their grasp. None of the men was clothed. One snake had buried its fangs into Laocoon's hip, while the second had already delivered its poison to one of the sons; the youth was frozen in the process of falling lifeless to the ground.

The hair on Harry's arms rose. Laocoon's agony had been exquisitely carved, his mouth open and eyes to the heavens as though beseeching the gods for salvation. His sole surviving son looked to his father, silently asking for protection that would not come. Harry could almost hear their cries and smell their fear. A shudder passed through his chest.

Harry stood motionless for some time. When he shook his head to clear it, it seemed as though the edges of the world came back into focus. No wonder Pliny offered the highest of praise for Agesander's work, and no wonder, either, that this masterpiece was often called "the prototypical icon of human agony."

Harry frowned. Pliny's chosen passage in *Natural History* said *inspect the masterful work of Agesander.* But for what? *His skill is a cyclone of emotion, the air.* The references to the classical elements had guided him so far.

He looked past the statue's torturous beauty. At the stone, at the men, the snakes. The answer must be there. His light fell on Laocoon first. Prominent muscles bulged as the priest fought for his life and those of his sons. Laocoon's flowing hair and his beard framed a mouth open in a silent scream. A close look at the sons on either side yielded the same result. Nothing tied to air.

Harry stood back. "Air," he said aloud. "An upward-pointing triangle, bisected by a horizontal line." Did anything in the statue resemble that, a pair of arms coming together to form a point with a snake across them, perhaps? He checked. No.

"Where are you?" Laocoon did not answer. "Air," Harry said, not as quietly as intended.

A *bang* sounded. Harry spun, sending his beam of light racing across the walls. Nothing moved behind him. No shadows flickered; no footsteps followed. He flicked his light off and kept still, eyes moving back and forth across the open hall. A full minute passed. He shook his head. The wind was blowing hard out there. Might have been the grate cover he'd lost control of, still flying around. The statue drew his attention once more. Maybe he wasn't looking at this the right way. As in, check around back, you dummy.

The base was easily fifteen feet wide and half again as long. He bent low to check every inch from the ground up, circling the entire base one step at a time. Nothing. He did the same with the lower portions of each human figure, from one son to Laocoon then to the other son, then checking the snakes as well. Again, nothing. He stretched his back and sighed. Time to climb.

He grabbed part of the closest snake. He stopped. "Air," he said. "That's what I have to find. The air."

He paused again. What if it wasn't merely the symbol he sought, but also a direction, a way to find the symbol? If so, one place on the statue stood out. Three places, in fact. "Their mouths," he said. "Emotion is expressed with your voice, your mouth. The way you produce air."

Laocoon's knee looked sturdy enough to support his weight. Harry stepped up on the big man's leg, grabbed a shoulder of one son and leaned over to check his open mouth. A tongue, beautifully carved, but nothing else. He hopped down and went to the other son, this time using one snake's thick body as a step. Up he went, the ancient stone cold under his touch. Again, a tongue waited inside the son's mouth, nothing more. He stepped down and immediately went back to Laocoon's knee, stepping on it and using a stone arm to balance himself as he rose to his full height. Not quite enough. He stood on his toes, rising the last few inches needed to see inside the priest's mouth. Detailed teeth, a textured tongue, and nothing else. Harry's chest deflated. He blinked. The stone inside Laocoon's mouth sparked. *What's that?* He pulled himself closer to look at the roof of Laocoon's mouth and saw it.

"The air symbol," Harry said, blood coursing through his veins loud enough to drown out the words. "I knew it."

An upward-pointing triangle bisected by a horizontal line was carved into the roof of Laocoon's mouth. Harry knew what to do next. He reached into the mouth and pressed the symbol.

"*Scendere*!"

The shouted Italian command filled the room. *Get down!* Harry spun, lost his grip and fell to the ground. He twisted to get up, scrambling to his feet as running footsteps pounded closer. He made it to one knee before a light flashed on, blindingly intense and right in his face. Harry raised an arm to protect his eyes.

A pistol appeared in the light. Aimed at Harry. "*Non muoverti.*" The voice was disembodied, coming from behind the light. In case Harry didn't understand, the gun jerked sharply, and the phrase was repeated.

"I'm not moving," Harry said in fluent Italian. "Get that light out of my face."

The light retreated several steps. Harry squinted under his arm, peering beyond the brightness. He drew in a sharp breath as a face came into view.

The long-haired man from Germany parted his lips. "What did you find, Harry Fox? What did you find?"

Chapter 22

Saint Hilarion Castle, Cyprus

Harry glared at the light as he stayed still, kneeling on the stone floor. "I didn't find anything."

The long-haired man shook his head. "Do not lie. You talk too much for a man who lies. I could hear you. You found something." His eyes flashed. "*The air symbol.*"

Darn. The guy must have been watching as Harry scaled the statue. Harry was losing his edge. "Who are you?" Harry asked.

"Tell me about the symbol."

Harry knew darn well who this guy was. "Does Carmelo think it's a good idea to interfere in Joey Morello's business?" Harry asked.

"Never heard of him."

"Carmelo or Joey?"

"Either." The gun waggled. "The air symbol. Now."

"What air symbol?"

"You said you found it when you looked in the statue's mouth." Long-hair inclined his head toward Laocoon.

"Never heard of an air symbol."

BANG. The bullet knocked a chunk of stone from the statue's base. A divot appeared directly beside Harry's foot. "Talk," long-hair said.

Harry's father had taught him a lot about relic hunting. He'd also taught him about much more. Near the top of that list was if someone had a gun, run. Since Harry couldn't run, he had to buy time until he could. "It's a carving on the roof of Laocoon's mouth," Harry said.

Long-hair frowned. "What's Laocoon?"

Harry pointed to the priest. "That's his name. Laocoon. The symbol is inside his mouth."

"What does it have to do with Charlemagne?"

Thought so. "Nothing."

"You're after an artifact connected to Charlemagne."

Either Olivier Lloris or Carmelo Piazza hadn't given this guy the whole story. Harry kept silent, thinking, and then the dots connected. Olivier was looking into Harry now. Why? He either didn't trust Harry or he was impatient. Possibly both, so he'd hired Carmelo Piazza to do some digging, and Carmelo had sent this genius. A genius who'd gotten the drop on Harry, to be fair, but the guy barely knew anything.

"I'm not sure who's telling you that, but they're wrong." Harry pointed at Laocoon again. "I'm here for a different relic. Your boss messed up."

"I work for no one." Long-hair chewed on Harry's words for several beats. "One relic or another; doesn't matter. What's next?"

"That's what I was trying to figure out. Point that gun somewhere else while I think. Shoot me by accident and you get nothing." Keeping his hands where long-hair could see them, he slowly rose to his feet.

Long-hair didn't respond. He did lower the gun a fraction so Harry's knee was in danger instead of his chest. Harry turned back to the statue, put his hands on his hips, and stalled. He made all the right motions, leaning to one side, then the other, and grunted as though what he saw made sense. His mind raced all the while to slot pieces of this puzzle together. Joey's informant had told them Olivier had hired Carmelo because he was losing patience with Harry. Had Carmelo suggested Olivier speed the process along by gathering more than intelligence?

Possibly. Harry stepped closer to the statue and continued his charade. Olivier and Carmelo knew Harry was chasing a relic tied to Charlemagne. They had no idea he was also following Pliny the Elder's trail for Evgeny Smolov. That would explain why this goon was here. He'd followed Harry to Germany, tried to corral him there and failed, then somehow tracked him to this Cyprus mountaintop.

Harry turned. "How did you find me?"

"Stop talking and keep looking."

"I need to know because I might have missed something in Germany. You were there. You chased us out of the baths. You made me miss something. I need to know how you found me."

A line of nonsense, but long-hair didn't know that. Harry pressed on before the guy could think. "If I know how you found me, it could help me figure out what I missed." He waved an arm toward Laocoon behind him. "You want me to find the relic for you? Tell me how you found me."

Evidently long-hair's fear of Carmelo outweighed his intelligence. "I heard you talking in that stadium."

The Roman amphitheater. That's where Harry had realized the men following them were Sicilian—when he'd overheard the gunman talking on his phone. That guy had been at least thirty feet away from Harry, standing up near the tree line. If Harry could hear them, they could hear *him*. He closed his eyes. *Darn*. "You heard me say Saint Hilarion."

"Easy to follow you when I knew where you were going."

Harry scowled and turned around to face the sculpture once more. His dad wouldn't be happy with him right now. "I have to climb up here," Harry said.

His mind whirred as he stood in front of Laocoon and rested a hand on the massive stone knee. Carmelo had likely convinced Olivier he could deliver the Charlemagne relic faster by putting pressure on Harry. Pressure in the form of gunmen. A terrible plan, but one that would make sense to a gangster like Carmelo. He used money to make problems go away, and Olivier had plenty of money to pay for it.

None of which meant Harry would be shot at the end of this. He could keep following Pliny's path even with this moron holding a gun to his back. The longer he took, the more likely he'd have a chance to turn the tables on the gunman, and even if that never happened Harry could show long-hair that whatever they found had nothing to do with

Charlemagne. The guy clearly lived in fear of his boss. Harry could probably even bargain his way out of this with Pliny's relic. Assuming he found it.

Great plan. It was a terrible plan, but it was all he had. "The symbol is on the roof of his mouth," Harry said again as he pulled himself onto Laocoon's knee. "I have a flashlight in my pocket. I'm going to pull it out so I can see what I'm doing. Don't shoot me."

"Nice and slow."

Harry paused as though to get a better grip on the statue. *Just keep long-hair at bay.* Escape, or bargain his way to freedom. He stepped up so his face was level with Laocoon's open mouth. Out came his penlight, slowly, and Harry clicked the light on before holding it between his teeth. The symbol wasn't much bigger than a silver dollar. Harry reached between the stone teeth and extended his forefinger. His nail grated over the grainy stone, catching on the carved lines as it moved, then sliding freely. Until it caught again. Harry blinked. His shoulder quivered as he held tight and dragged his nail over the interior again. Same result.

A thin carved line encircled the symbol. Harry bunched his fingers and pressed the triangle. Pressed it hard. His teeth clenched on the metal penlight as he pushed, leaning into the statue for leverage.

The symbol vanished. It retracted into the roof of Laocoon's mouth as Harry pushed harder, pushing until his fingers disappeared entirely. The stone stopped moving, held for a moment, and then he heard it.

Click. A noise inside Laocoon's head, as though Harry had tripped a latch. He went still.

Long-hair opened his big mouth. "What is it?"

"Quiet." Harry leaned his ear toward the statue's mouth and shoved the penlight back in his pocket. Laocoon's mouth was emitting a noise, right at the edge of hearing, a noise that wasn't quite a noise. His vision twitched. His toes tingled. "It's starting to *vibrate*," Harry said to himself. He touched the statue. The statue held still.

There was a loud *snap* of cracking rock. Harry leapt, landing on the ground, ready to run as the sound of stone grating on stone filled the room. He jumped to one side, looking back at the source of the noise, the room's rear wall, part of the original castle wall. A cloud of dust shot out from the center of that rear wall as a dark line appeared.

"It's opening," Harry shouted above the noise. "Move back."

He used Laocoon's statue for cover as the dark crack widened and revealed a door. A section of the wall fell inward on itself to reveal a hidden opening. Harry peered over at the darkness. He could not tell if anything peered back. Out came his penlight and he aimed the beam at this new door. Were those steps?

"Don't move," long-hair called out from behind Harry. The guy had stood farther back, as Harry had warned him to do a moment ago. Now he came forward, gun out. He stopped ten feet from Harry. "What is in there?"

"No idea." Harry stepped closer to the opening and moved his light around, trying to get a better look. "That's what I'm going to find out."

"Stop."

Harry looked back over his shoulder at long-hair. He lowered the penlight. "You want to go first?" A shadow shifted beyond long-hair's shoulder, close to the castle hall entrance. Harry glanced at it for a beat. *What is that?*

"Why would you not go in first?"

"You ever walk down an ancient hidden staircase before?" Harry asked. Long-hair stayed quiet. "Didn't think so. Could be a false floor, or maybe a few spikes waiting. Or maybe you'll get lucky and there's gold in there."

Long-hair didn't move. He kept the gun up as emotions ran across his face, the main one being indecisiveness. Harry shook his head. There wasn't time for this. "You want to shoot me, go ahead." He turned to the dark entrance. "I'm going inside."

"Stop," long-hair shouted, then walked over to Harry, his gun leading the way. "You know what's in there. Tell me."

"I have no idea."

A bead of sweat dotted long-hair's forehead and he slipped into

Corsican as he shouted at Harry, ranting about the truth, as best Harry could tell.

"I'm not lying," Harry said.

More shouted Corsican cut him off. The gun waggled in Harry's face. Harry leaned back, lifting his hands in the air, ready to bolt as long-hair leaned closer and the gun came so close Harry could see his reflection in the barrel and—

Light flashed and thunder filled the room. Long-hair jerked. He looked down at his chest. Another flash lit the gloom behind him and the Corsican shuddered once more. A dark patch spread on his chest. His gun never fired. Long-hair looked at Harry, surprise on his face. He blinked once and then collapsed.

Chapter 23

Saint Hilarion Castle, Cyprus

"Do not move." The words were spoken in English, out of the murky dark ahead. The shape of a man appeared, only an outline until the speaker walked forward into the dim red light. A bearded man holding a gun. "Move back," the man said, his words roughened by a lifetime of cigarettes. "Quickly."

Harry looked down. Long-hair lay on his stomach with two bullet holes in his back. Harry looked up. "You shot him."

The bearded man did not respond. He was now no more than twenty feet away.

Harry's vision sharpened. "What do you want?" He studied the man's face.

"The book," the man said. "The book you stole."

Harry played a hunch. "Sorry about your buddy in New York. Havertz must really value that book."

The man's face twitched. "I didn't take the book," Harry said. "But I know who did."

"You stole it from a man in Germany. Your face was on camera. The same face is on your passport. A passport with a different name."

The pieces came together for Harry now. Leon Havertz had hired Marwan Qassam to find the book. Somehow Marwan had found Nora and gone after her while trying to get to Harry. Marwan failed, so Leon had hired this guy. Who had followed Harry by tracking the Daniel

Connery passport. His jaw tightened. They knew about Nora, which meant they could know about his whole family—and about Sara. Olivier Lloris wasn't the only person threatening Harry's loved ones. Harry would have to take care of that.

Harry considered carrying on the bluff, but this guy knew too much. "You must really want that book." He gestured to the dead man again.

"I want to be paid. If he shot you, I could not find the book. So I shot him."

"The book isn't here. I'm here for something better." The gunman's face made it clear he was listening. "The man who hired you is a collector. Go back to Havertz with a new relic and you'll make even more money. Maybe enough to get Marwan a good lawyer, good enough to get him out of jail."

"Do not speak of my brother."

The way he said the word told Harry *blood relative*. "Okay," Harry said. "What's your name?"

"Azrael."

Great. The Islamic and Christian angel of death. "Azrael, I'm here to find out what's waiting behind that wall. So I'm going in. Don't shoot me."

"Wait."

Harry stood still. Azrael stepped toward him. "Turn around," Azrael said. Harry did as ordered. "Arms out." Again, Harry complied. A few beats passed, and Harry heard the sound of Azrael checking his gun. The noise of metal sliding on metal made his chest grow tight. More steps as Azrael came closer.

"Argh!"

Harry turned to see Azrael stumble, arms spinning as he fell. The pistol flew from his grip, clattering across the floor as it slid toward Harry and stopped by his feet. Harry grabbed it, twisting as he brought the gun to bear on Azrael, who was on the floor. "Don't move," Harry said.

"Wait." Azrael lifted a hand toward Harry, palm up.

"Bad move, Azrael." Harry looked around. He needed rope, or a zip tie, something to keep Azrael in place for a while. Movement caught his eye. "Stay put," Harry said.

Azrael did not. He started to rise, getting to one knee.

"I'm serious." Harry gripped the pistol in both hands, one finger on the trigger. "Stop it."

Azreal stood. His face was flat, even calm. "Go ahead," he said. "Shoot me."

That's the last thing Harry wanted. "One more step and I will," he said. "I don't want to."

"No, you do not." Azrael took a step toward Harry.

Harry put pressure on the trigger. Any more and it would go off. He closed one eye and sighted down the barrel at Azrael's chest. "I'm serious, man. Stop moving."

Azreal's hand slid around to the middle of his back. He kept reaching, and Harry yelled at him to stop. Harry took a breath. "Last chance." Azrael made a grab for whatever was back there.

Harry pulled the trigger.

Click.

Blood roared in his ears. He pulled the trigger again. *Click.* Azrael laughed. "I was wrong," he said. "You will do it." A pistol appeared from around his back. A semiautomatic, small and deadly. "Only this one is loaded."

Harry's chest sank. What he'd heard with his back turned was Azrael pushing the plunger to eject the shells before he'd tossed the gun toward Harry.

"Throw it," Azrael said.

The gun clattered on the floor as Harry tossed it away. "Now what?"

"Now your fingerprints are on the murder weapon," Azrael said. He waved the pistol. "Go."

Harry turned and walked around Laocoon toward the dark opening. Wind whistled from deep inside the darkness. His penlight revealed steps leading down beyond the reach of his light. The ceiling of this path led upward, giving the sense of a large, open space ahead. The steps were carved by hand. The rest of the cavern was not. Harry turned and looked back at Azrael. "You coming?"

"I will follow you."

Harry shrugged. He leaned down and played his light across the first step. A thin layer of dust covered the rough stone. No lines suggested pressure plates to step on. He checked the walls and found them equally unremarkable. It didn't feel like a trap.

Tiny dust clouds bloomed with each step as he descended into the gloom. A light appeared behind him and Harry turned to find Azrael had a flashlight out as well, stepping directly on Harry's footprints down the stairs. The pistol remained in his other hand. Not ten steps down, their combined lights pushed away the dark to reveal a cavern. Fifty feet wide and twice as deep, it was a natural cave that once had been open to the world, before Pliny had it covered with a stone on hinges. Quick, bright flashes shot back at Harry from higher on the walls as he aimed his flashlight around the room. A bowl set atop a pedestal off to the left caught his eye. Harry walked over to it, reached up and peered inside. He touched the interior. His finger came back greasy. "Oil," Harry said. "There used to be oil in here."

He looked to the nearby wall. A torch sat in a sconce. Behind it a sheet of polished metal reflected Harry's penlight. *That makes sense.* "I'm lighting that torch," Harry said. "It's going to get bright in here."

Flame sprouted from his lighter, catching on the dry torch, which crackled and popped as sparks flew before it blazed strong enough that Harry leaned back. The polished metal behind it caught the new light and sent it at an angle across the wall to another metal mirror, then on to the next and on again until the single torch filled the cavern with an amber light. Harry saw a second torch on the opposite wall and walked over to light it as well, doubling the light.

"What are those?" Azrael asked, pointing, as the flames burned bright.

Two statues stood in front of them, twenty feet from the bottom of the steps, stone gods looking down on two intruders. Poseidon on the left, bearded and muscled with his fearsome trident. Athena on the right, goddess of wisdom, daughter of Zeus, was looking toward Harry with an enquiring expression.

"Look at their torsos," Harry said.

Each statue had a recessed area roughly the size of a shoebox carved into its navel. "There's writing on them," Harry said. "It's Latin."

Azrael stayed well clear of Harry as he studied first the room, then the statues. "What do they say?" he asked.

"Do you read Latin?"

"No, but I can shoot you if you lie to me."

Fair enough. Harry leaned over to read the engraved words on Poseidon. "Listen," Harry said before he read the message aloud.

"*The skin of Helios who defends Rhodes.*"

Harry moved to read the second message, written on Athena. "It's the same message," he said. "Word for word. The only differences are the images beneath the inscription."

Harry pointed to the image on Poseidon, a circle with two bisecting lines in the middle of it, as though someone had circled a plus symbol. "That stands for *earth*," Harry said. He pointed to the Athena image, a triangle twisted ninety degrees so it looked like an arrowhead, with a dot on the pointed end. "This is the ancient symbol for metal, usually iron or bronze. I'm not sure what they mean here."

Azrael indicated the written words. "Tell me what those inscriptions mean."

"Helios is the Greek sun god. Rhodes was a prosperous trading center in Greek times, and it grew to become one of the Roman world's most prominent locations for art and science education." Harry hesitated. There was something else, something he was missing. Something big. *Big.* He laughed out loud. "Of course."

"What?" Azrael asked.

"Helios didn't defend Rhodes. He celebrated the *defense* of Rhodes." Azrael's face suggested he wasn't following. "Ancient Greeks had to defend their cities against any number of enemies," Harry said. "The Macedonians laid siege to Rhodes for over a year. The siege failed, and when the Macedonians left, Rhodes built a statue celebrating the victory." He waited. Azrael didn't speak. "The Colossus of Rhodes," Harry said. "It's one of the seven wonders of the ancient world. The largest statue in existence at the time. A hundred-foot-tall statue of Helios."

"The sun god Helios."

"That's what the inscription references. I'm not sure about this *skin* part."

Harry's mind churned, one image coming back over and over. The Colossus. No, not only the Colossus of Rhodes, but colossi. More than one of them. A section of Pliny's text discussed colossi. Information about their design, the proportions, and the materials used to build them. Miracles of engineering that seemed impossible until you understood how it was done. The miracle lay in the construction. In using certain materials to give the impression of solidity where none existed.

The passages came back to him, part of a chapter on metallurgy. Pliny wrote of using iron rods to frame the thin, metallic exterior of a statue. An exterior, in Rhodes, made by melting their defeated enemies' weapons and repurposing the copper and bronze to form a thin but strong shell. To form a *skin.*

"I understand it."

Azrael stepped closer. "Understand what?"

Harry lifted a finger to stay any further talk. The statue of Poseidon called to him, and he leaned closer to inspect it. A moment passed. He found what he was looking for.

"I understand the question." Harry turned to look at the pistol trained on him. He didn't have a choice. But he could give Azrael a chance. "And I need your help."

Azrael's face made it clear what he thought of that. "Why do you need my help?"

"Pliny left this trail to hide something. He wanted people who thought like him, who believed what he believed, to follow it. He never expected someone would search alone. That's why I need your help." Harry indicated Poseidon and Athena in turn. "The message is the same on each statue because they're meant to work together. Look at the symbol for earth on Poseidon. See what's around it?"

Azrael kept his distance as he went to the statue and gave it a closer look. "There is a line around it."

"It's the same type of device as Laocoon's statue. It's a button. The symbol on Athena is the same. They're both buttons, and we have to press them at the same time. The message on each statue is a riddle. A riddle about the Colossus of Rhodes. That's what the symbols are for." Athena's stone arm was slightly rough as he ran his fingers over it. "The *skin* of Helios is pointing to the Colossus of Rhodes. To the exterior, which was made of bronze." Harry pointed to the symbol on Athena. "And stone, for support." He indicated the symbol on Poseidon. "They're far enough apart that one person can't do it alone."

Azrael had as close to a trusting look on his face as Harry had seen. "What will happen if only one is pushed?"

"Nothing good." Harry lifted a shoulder. "Besides, if I'm wrong, we haven't lost anything."

Azrael's gaze shifted from one statue to the other. He did not speak.

"You want another relic to sell?" Harry said impatiently. "Help me push those buttons."

Azrael's response caught him off guard. "Are you not worried I take the relic and then kill you?"

"You still need that book. I was serious when I said I don't have it here, but I can get it." Harry kept going. "Put that gun away and help me get through whatever else stands in the way of us finding Pliny's relic. You can have the book for free within a month." A beat passed. "And half of whatever Pliny's relic sells for. I have bosses too. A guy I'd rather not be working for, but I can't change that, so half of what we find is the best I can do."

"You treat me as a fool," Azrael said.

Harry sighed. "Don't say I didn't offer." A heaviness settled on his chest when he moved to stand in front of Athena. Azrael was still standing in front of Poseidon. The statue's trident was pointed at Azrael's waist. Azrael's pistol stayed aimed at Harry. "On three," Harry said. "One. Two." Harry turned his head away. "Three."

The two buttons moved easily enough. In fact, they hardly made a noise. Not that Harry would have heard it over the sound of Azrael's scream.

Apparently, Pliny had never intended for both buttons to be pressed. He did leave a riddle with one correct answer, however. The skin of Helios was made from copper and bronze. From metal. Not from earth.

When Azrael pushed the earth symbol the trident thrust forward, impaling him, lifting him into the air and holding him in place. Harry looked over at the grisly sound of stone being thrust through flesh. Azrael went up. The pistol flew through the air. Harry reached out and snatched it in one smooth motion.

Azrael hung limply as the ground rumbled and a section of the rear wall opened. Light flashed inside the dark opening. Sparks, and moments later the *whoosh* of fuel catching. Torches caught, light bloomed, and Pliny's final test came to life.

It was a new cavern. One with torches burning high on the walls to reveal a myth come alive.

"The Labyrinth."

Chapter 24

Saint Hilarion Castle, Cyprus

Harry grabbed the other pistol with his prints on it before walking past the statues to find himself in another cavern. Equally wide and long, it sat just five short steps below the first one. Facing him was a stone maze that in Greek myth was guarded by a creature with the head and tail of a bull and the body of a man. The Minotaur.

Harry didn't need his penlight to see the entire chamber, but he aimed it around the perimeter. No Minotaur in sight, though that did little to ease his mind. He slipped the pistol into his waistband. What was this place?

Stone walls twice his height formed the circular maze whose outer edges touched the cavern walls on either side. He couldn't simply walk around it. Ropes crisscrossed the room immediately above the maze walls, strung in a way that made it impossible to scale the maze walls without running into at least one rope. The ropes were strung taut from wall to wall, connected to a series of pillars rising from floor to ceiling. The pillars were decorated with imagery from Greek myth, none of them pleasant. The three-headed dog Cerberus, hound of Hades. A Gorgon, one of the female monsters with snakes on their head instead of hair, with Medusa being the most recognizable one. A Griffin, with a lion's body and the head and wings of an eagle. And, of course, several Minotaurs. All had ropes strung between them. Ropes Harry would break if he tried to walk across the maze walls instead of through the maze itself. His gut told him breaking any rope by going across the top was a bad idea.

Each creature's image had an open mouth, a mouth pointing down to the maze. He had no intention of finding out what might come spewing or shooting from those mouths if he knocked down a rope.

He checked the floor as he walked straight toward the maze entrance, an opening between the two rounded stone walls of the outer perimeter large enough for two men to walk through together. Harry's gaze went to Latin writing inscribed on the wall, adjacent to the entrance. His voice echoed slightly as he read it aloud.

Those who seek to protect the Great possessions must follow my encyclopedia. Use these lessons inside to find safe passage through the Labyrinth. My possessions await.

"His book again." The message referenced Pliny's *Great possessions* and *Natural History*. How did Harry follow a book through a maze? He looked left, right, up and down. Danger above, nothing anywhere else. "Ahead it is."

Shadows danced at his feet as he stepped through the entrance and stopped just inside it. He checked his phone. No service. *Great.* A stone wall to the right forced him to go left. He looked up, stretching an arm overhead toward the strung ropes. He could touch them if he jumped. He did not jump.

He began to walk, his fingertips brushed the curving walls on either side when he stretched his arms out, following the path as it bent to the right. With each measured step he studied the floor before moving ahead, searching for, but not finding any indication of, a trap. Pliny had instructed his compatriots to follow *Natural History* to make it through here. Harry had read that book end to end. Well, skimmed it. It would have to do.

The pathway continued bending until he was nearly to the cavern's rear. There, he found another T-junction, and once again, a stone wall blocked his path, forcing him to choose a direction. Left or right. This time, the choice was not so simple. Dozens of strands of rope had been strung tightly between the walls, blocking his path forward in both directions. He'd have to push through the rope to continue, no matter which way he chose. But, again, which way? A message carved into the wall ahead of him appeared to hold the key.

Astronomy—the Planets

A single number lay on either side of the phrase. An *8* on the left, and a *7* on the right.

"It's a test," Harry said to himself. "A test about *Natural History*. Astronomy is one of the books."

Pliny was wagering that those who served Caligula wouldn't know Pliny's teachings, and wouldn't be able to correctly follow his reference. The first encyclopedia, *Natural History*, consisted of ten books on separate topics. One of the topics? Astronomy.

"How many planets did Pliny say existed?" Harry's thoughts went back to reading Pliny's text on the plane from New York. He'd read some portions more closely than others. Including the one on astronomy.

Pliny would have listed the planets known to exist at the time, a list including celestial bodies not recognized as planets today. "The sun and moon are included," he said. Astronomers at the time had known of Mercury and Venus. Add in Earth and that made five. What else?

"Planets named after Roman gods. Mars and Jupiter." He closed his eyes. "And Saturn. Not Uranus or Neptune—they were too far away to be seen then. And forget about Pluto."

He counted again. The sun and moon. Mercury, Venus, Earth, Mars, Jupiter and Saturn. Eight planets. He started to turn left.

Wait. Eight was wrong. His hand was on the ropes to the right, those blocking the path marked by the *8*, ready to push through. He stepped back. "Romans believed the earth was the center of the universe. It wouldn't count as a planet in Pliny's book."

Long ago he'd learned to trust his gut. Deliberate, consider, then act. Hesitation killed. Except when it saved you. He turned and began shoving his way through the ropes blocking the path marked with a *7*.

Ropes snapped as he surged through. Snapped rather easily, he noticed, his weight carrying him forward until he broke through the last bit of webbing and stumbled to a halt. Arms out, head twisting, he looked for a threat. None appeared. *Phew.* "I knew I was right," he told himself.

The path led deeper into the circular maze, this time bending left. The passageway was narrower than it appeared from the outside, the walls thick, and he moved ahead as before, with one eye on the floor. He noticed where each stone panel had been mortared into place, and though the mortar had been smoothed, he could see without much effort where one panel ended and the next began. Somehow that seemed important. Pliny was meticulous in all he did. He didn't do things haphazardly. The mortar seemed, well, sloppy.

He looked up the cavern wall. A monster looked down. One of the Gorgons, the writhing snakes on her head seemingly alive, fangs bared and backs arched as though ready to strike. The Gorgon's mouth was open, and he noted circular openings cut into her body directly above the ropes crisscrossing the entire maze structure, each rope strung from the exterior walls led down to a wall in the maze. Including the wall he walked beside, in fact. The holes in the monsters were aimed everywhere across the maze. He couldn't go anywhere without at least one of the monsters looking down on him. He stopped walking. Each of the mythological creatures carved on the pillars had the same openings, with ropes directly below each opening fastened to various portions of the maze wall as well. What was this about?

The next choice appeared before him. The path led to an opening and another stone wall beyond it. He could go no further unless he chose a direction. Right or left, with each path again blocked by ropes strung from wall to wall. Another Latin inscription had been engraved in the wall ahead of him.

Metallurgy—death to counterfeiters.

Metallurgy had saved his life earlier tonight. He recalled how the skins of colossi were made—copper and bronze from melted enemy weapons—but as for remembering the entire chapter devoted to this topic? He did recall a passage about how metallurgic technology could be used to prevent counterfeiting.

To the right of the inscription he saw the words *Cast copper and silver.* To the left, *Struck gold and silver.*

Two different combinations of metal. Two choices on where to turn. Only one was correct. Harry closed his eyes and pictured the text describing counterfeiting. "Copper and silver were combined with other metals to make fake coins. Nobody does that with gold."

Gold was too valuable to mix. If a counterfeiter wanted to mix anything with gold to increase the weight, it would not be silver. No, copper and silver was the combination used by counterfeiters. He was sure of it.

Harry went right. The ropes barring his path offered token resistance as he pushed his way through and marched ahead.

A light pulsing sounded at the edge of his hearing. Harry paused, his internal alarm starting to ring. The ropes above him began vibrating like strings on a guitar, and as he took one hesitant step back, the mythological Minotaur statue on a pillar above him spat a cloud of dust from its mouth.

A spear slammed into the ground by his feet, sticking point-first in the stone. Harry turned and ran back to the last intersection.

Ropes above him cracked and snapped as the pulsing turned to rumbling. The rope netting above the maze shredded as first one and then another spear zinged through, each one narrowly missing him. His legs churned as he reversed course and took the path he'd avoided, the one marked as *Struck gold and silver.* He passed the wording, smashed through that rope barrier, and it hit him. *Struck.* Roman gold coins weren't cast—only counterfeit coins were cast. The metals didn't matter. The *process* did.

A crack split the wall ahead as he raced in a loop for safety. One of the mortared seams broke with a sound like a shotgun as Harry ran past. He felt the air move behind him, and an instant after he was clear, the entire section of wall collapsed into the tunnel. A spear zipped past his shoulder, banged off the wall ahead and nearly hit him as it bounced back. He accelerated. Thunder boomed all around, the mortared joints cracking as entire sections of the wall broke loose. The maze was collapsing around him, spears were flying, and the only way out was straight ahead.

Another intersection appeared. Harry paused to duck low in front of the carved words. Dust filled the air as a joint beside him cracked and started to give way. The Latin script jumped back and forth as the crumbling maze blurred his vision. He put one hand on the wall for support and leaned close to the message.

Caligula's hubris.

Two drinking cups were engraved on the wall to his right. He saw a nearly identical pair on the left, though that pair was cracked in half. "Broken crystal," Harry shouted, and bolted toward the damaged cups.

He crashed through the ropes, and sparks flew as the point of another spear hit the wall beside Harry. The stout wooden shaft grazed his face, and when he reached up, his fingers found a gash and wet blood. Pliny had passed a final judgment on Caligula with that metallurgic reference to his conceit. Harry leaned forward as the path continued winding around and the walls kept collapsing. An explosion of debris ahead forced him to run blindly through a dust cloud, squinting as the pulverized stone stung his eyes. He wiped tears away and then jerked backwards as a section of wall collapsed in front of him. His foot caught on the rough stone and he went airborne, arms flailing. He landed hard on the stone floor, rolled, bounced off a wall and sat up groggily, his brain rattling.

He jumped to his feet and dodged to one side as a stone slab crashed down where he'd been lying a breath earlier. He skirted the fallen section of wall, made a final turn, and then the path straightened. An open doorway stood ahead, a square of darkness in the chaos and destruction.

But the floor leading to the door had vanished, leaving an empty hole too big for him to jump.

The entire maze was collapsing. Whatever mortar or support was holding the last pieces upright gave way now with a series of loud cracks, and stones began to fall inward. Harry gritted his teeth and buried the alarm bells clanging in his head. *I can make it.*

He took several steps back, then surged ahead as fast as he could. His foot hit the last inch of floor and he leapt. He leaned ahead, reaching for the doorway, fingers out and legs pumping in mid-air as he flew forward.

Gravity took hold. He sank, falling more than flying now, the ground leading to safety slipping past as he stretched both arms out, his fingers splayed and mouth open as he cursed them all—Pliny and Caligula and Leon Havertz and Evgeny Smolov—for putting him here. His fingers touched the lip of the floor ahead.

He missed.

He slammed into the wall, his fingers still scrabbling for purchase, and the stone grated his nose as he fell. A brown blur sped past him. He grabbed for it.

He stopped sliding. His shoulder screamed and his fingers burned as he latched onto a spear embedded in the wall. He hung there, bouncing and swinging slightly with his own momentum, the endless darkness beneath calling for him as he dangled and held tight. Harry flung his other hand up onto the spear, then, coughing and grunting, tried to pull himself up. He swore to any gods listening he'd never doubt them again if he could just get out of here. Another pull and he hauled himself high enough to swing one foot onto the spear. It held.

Feet kicking, knees banging, Harry wrangled himself up to stand on the spear, holding onto the wall for balance, then clutched at the lip of the doorway above him and pulled himself over the edge. Panting, he fell heavily onto his back to stare at the ceiling above as he gasped for air. His head fell to one side and he looked toward the maze. Or what remained of it. The walls had collapsed. The strung ropes had fallen. He peered through the dusty haze at nothing but rubble. Azreal's body was under there somewhere. Harry closed his eyes. *I tried to warn you.*

After a moment, he clambered to his feet and looked ahead. A shadow lurked in the darkness. A large shadow. There was something here, and it was close. Very close.

He flicked his light on. The floor ahead was smooth, solid stone, with no lines in it or ropes across it. His pool of light moved ahead until it revealed a wheel. A massive wheel, twice Harry's height. "It's *iron*," he said. The spokes, the exterior, all of it was iron. An intricate carving of a lion's head decorated the wheel's center. Harry stepped toward it and colors began to flash in the beam from his penlight. Green, red, blue. All brilliant, creating a dazzling rainbow. Harry's mouth opened as he kept moving his light up. The flashing continued, with one additional color. The dull glimmer of gold. He moved the light higher and nearly fell over. "It's a golden temple."

Ionic columns rose ten feet from their gilded bases. Every inch of every column was covered in gold. Precious stones were embedded in their surfaces—emeralds, rubies, sapphires and diamonds. The gemstones continued onto the curved ceiling, and there were yet more on the winged goddess statues standing watch atop each of the four corners.

Latticework adorned a rectangular container in the middle of the columns. Harry angled his head. "That's a tomb." One fit for a king or emperor. But who?

The thick layer of dust on the ground muted his footsteps as he made a circuit of the tomb. Bas-relief sculptures decorated the tomb's upper portion, showing regal elephants and fearsome lions. The tomb itself sat on a carriage, with harnesses for horses to pull it. Harry walked full circle and stood before the tomb's entrance for the first time. On either side of it, two golden lions sat on their haunches. Above it was an inscription.

"Impossible." Harry's balance wavered. His head grew light as air. *A name.* A name written in a language he could not read, though it didn't matter. A name revealing the truth behind everything. *Ἀλέξανδρος*. "*Great possessions.*"

Epilogue

Brooklyn

Harry stood outside his shop and took a second to admire the craftsmanship of his new sign. *Fox & Son.* As always, his spirits lifted when memories of his dad flooded in. If he was watching, Fred Fox was in for a treat today.

A soft chime sounded when Harry pushed through the door. "Morning, Scott."

The second-ever employee of Fox & Son looked up from his seat behind the counter. "Morning, Harry." He rescued the glasses hanging precariously on the edge of his nose. "Rested and relaxed from your trip?"

Harry had returned to Brooklyn a few days earlier and had been to the store only once. He had not shared the details behind his European trip with Scott. Perhaps, in time, he would. "I am," Harry said. "Is Sara here?"

"In your office."

"Any news?"

"Your software system was archaic. I fixed it."

"It's not even a year old."

"May as well have been from the Dark Ages," Scott said. "Don't worry, we're good now. Even the Pentagon couldn't hack into our database now."

"How much did it cost?"

"Nothing."

"Nothing?"

Scott smirked. "I called in a favor from an old friend."

"Be careful or you'll get yourself promoted." Harry walked past the counter. "Thanks."

"The website is on my to-do list for today," Scott said. "We'll be the first hit on every search engine soon."

Good thing Scott already had more money than he'd ever need. Otherwise, Harry wouldn't be able to afford him. He followed the scent of rich coffee through the showroom to his office. The door was open. Sara waited inside, seated behind his desk. An open shoebox sat on his desk.

"Morning," Harry said.

"Have you heard from your friend? I use the term loosely."

That would be Evgeny Smolov. "Earlier this morning. His new Cypriot contracting firm continues to oversee repairs at Saint Hilarion Castle."

Sara lifted an eyebrow. "No one is questioning the sudden change in ownership?"

"Evgeny described himself as a silent partner in the business. One partner who controls everything and who has managed to keep our discovery secret."

"While he takes items from the castle to one of his personal museums." Sara frowned. "That man terrifies me. Stay on his good side."

"I think delivering the greatest treasure collection since Tutankhamun's tomb will do that."

"A collection the outside world will never see." Sara shook her head, but only for a moment. "He is shrewd."

Sara Hamed was not easy to impress. However, discovering the tomb of one of history's most legendary leaders inside a series of hidden caverns behind Saint Hilarion Castle had done it. An empty tomb.

Harry grabbed one of the coffee cups from his desk and sat in a visitor's chair. "I wonder where his body is?"

"Some would say exactly where it should be."

"Meaning still hidden well enough that no one can exploit its discovery for personal gain?"

"If you were one of my students, you would get an A."

Harry grinned and sipped his coffee.

The name on the tomb had been written in ancient Macedonian. Harry couldn't read it, but he recognized the name of one of history's greatest military leaders. *Alexander*. King of Macedon and Persia, Pharaoh of Egypt, and a man whose tomb had never been identified. However, the location of his funerary carriage was not lost. At least not to Harry Fox and his friends.

The historical record stated that when Alexander died, his body was preserved, placed in a golden coffin and then in a carriage built to resemble an ancient Greek temple. A carriage decorated with precious stones and covered in gold. Alexander's remains were to be transported back to his native Macedonia for interment, in a ceremony fit for the most powerful man on earth. The procession required sixty-four horses to pull the massive tomb.

However, dead kings left empty thrones, and men fought for those thrones. Alexander's generals engaged in a series of conflicts over who would control the vast empire. One of those generals wanted possession of Alexander's body to lend weight to his claim. The funerary procession was ambushed, the rolling temple stolen, and thus began the saga of Alexander's final resting place. The tomb was taken to Egypt and interred in Memphis. Decades later it was moved to the Egyptian city of Alexandria for reburial, and then later it was removed and placed in a communal mausoleum, where it stayed for more than a century.

Then Caligula came into power. The likely insane emperor intended to use Alexander's remains to demonstrate to all that he was not merely an emperor, but a god. Pliny the Elder learned of his plan and conspired with like-minded Romans to secrete Alexander's movable tomb inside a mostly unknown castle in Roman Cyprus.

How did Harry know all of this? A scroll inside the empty golden coffin of Alexander told him the story. It detailed everything except the final location of Alexander's body. That would remain a mystery. What would not be a mystery was Pliny's reason for leaving a trail to the tomb.

Sara seemed able to read his mind. "Pliny went to a lot of trouble to hide the tomb," she said.

Harry snapped out of his reverie. "And to make sure someone could find it if they needed to move it again. The Antikythera was brilliant."

"A dual-purpose machine that predicts astronomical positions and can also decode hidden messages," Sara said. "Even James Bond would approve."

"It's incredible, it's amazing, and it's never going to see the light of day."

"That bothers you?" she asked.

He shrugged. "Nothing I can do about it. You want to take on Evgeny Smolov?" She shook her head. "Besides, if that's what I think it is"—he tilted his coffee cup toward the shoebox on his desk—"I'm more interested in what's in that box than in Alexander's priceless tomb."

It must have taken a supreme act of will for Sara to accept that Alexander's empty tomb would remain lost, hidden in one of Evgeny's mansions, yet she did. "It is what you think it is," she said as she reached for the box. "And I have something to show you."

She lifted the lid. A black velvet bag lay inside, its surface interrupted by several raised points jutting upward into the fabric in a circle. She removed the bag and slid out the crown inside, laid the bag down, and set the crown on top of it. Harry set his coffee down and leaned close, so close his nose nearly touched the gold. "You believe this is the lost Crown of Charlemagne?" he asked.

"It is. I'm certain."

"How?"

"The metalwork and craftsmanship align with the period, and it matches everything historical records say about the crown's design. However, the reason I'm positive this is Charlemagne's lost crown is here. This—" And here she lifted one side of the crown and carefully removed a thin square of gold from the black bag. "And this." Sara lifted a square object from the shoebox. It was two pieces of plastic, screwed together, with a sheet of what he suspected was linen between them. Tiny, elegant handwriting covered the surface.

"Where did you find that?"

"Inside the crown." She tapped the gold square. "This is a cover for a hidden compartment. The folded linen was inside." She tapped the sheet. "It's a message from Agilulph."

He pumped a fist. "We were right."

"It's Latin," she said. "Here's the translation."

"Thanks." He took the proffered sheet of notepaper, his gaze flying over Sara's meticulously neat script.

You have succeeded in the quest for peace, devoted follower of my Father. The prize gifted with the mythical thunder beast is secure, ready to maintain peace across his kingdom. Locate my Father where Anthony of the caves led his disciples. My Father looks upon the true path.

Harry read the note again before setting it down. "*Father* is Charlemagne. Agilulph is talking about what Harun al-Rashid gave Charlemagne along with the elephant."

"A water clock. With the keys to Jerusalem inside."

"So"—Harry drained his coffee—"when do we start?"

She took the translation back, then tucked the crown and enclosed message into the black bag and placed it carefully in the shoebox. "Once we discuss another matter."

"What's that?"

"The quality of your towels and bathrobes."

"My what?" he asked. Sara merely set her hands on his desk, fingers interlaced. It took him a second. "Oh, right. I take it you like them?"

"I have been at Nora's for nearly a week. I haven't had the chance to thoroughly test them."

"They're the same kind you have."

"It's not that I don't like them." A moment passed, and the way she looked at him made Harry take note. "Do you?"

Harry shrugged. "They're fine. What are you getting at?"

"That the towels are only a portion of the changes to come."

"What else do I need to change?"

"If you want me to stay at your home more often, you'll need to work with me on this. Or perhaps I'm mistaken, and you're not interested in having me at your house more often."

"What? No, you're not mistaken." The whir of air moving through ductwork sounded much louder, and his vision seemed to sharpen. Eventually his brain caught up. "Are you saying you want to move in?"

One corner of her lip turned up. "Eventually, perhaps. Right now, I'm open to visiting more often. Provided some conditions are met."

"Conditions?"

The familiar, faint scent of lavender came across the desk as she leaned closer. "I assume the new towels and robe you purchased were to entice me to visit more often. I appreciate the gesture. It's touching, and my answer is yes, I would like to spend more time at your home. Given this, I suggest you purchase new cookware."

"There's nothing wrong with my pans."

"For use as blunt objects to incapacitate intruders, no. For cooking, they are atrocious." A line creased her forehead. "Are new pans a problem?" He grumbled. "I'm sorry?" Sara asked. "I didn't catch that."

"No, it's not a problem."

"Excellent." Her phone was sitting on his desk, and she glanced at it, then rose from his chair. "I'll send you recommendations. You can handle it from there."

"Hold on." Harry jumped up as she started to walk out. His coffee cup nearly went flying and he fumbled for a second to get it under control. "Are you coming over tonight?" he asked as he put the cup down. "I won't have the pans by then."

"I can't come tonight." She didn't break stride. "Unless my plans change."

"Where are you going now?"

The soft chime indicating a customer had walked in sounded from the store floor. "To say hello to Nora."

"Nora? What's she doing here? And we have to talk about this."

Sara turned, the curl at one side of her lip spreading. "Get the pans. Then we'll talk."

That's all she gave him before Nora's voice sounded from the store, and a moment later she had her arms around Sara.

"Glad one of you had the courtesy to invite me over," Nora said. She released Sara, walked straight to Harry's desk and sat in his personal chair. "What's in the box?"

Harry muttered a greeting. "Make yourself at home."

Nora glared at him, then turned to Sara. "What's in the box?"

"Charlemagne's lost crown."

"Interesting." She spared a quick look at the black bag. "Did you tell him?" she asked Sara.

"I thought you would want to do it."

"Tell me what?" This was getting out of hand. Sara dropping the maybe-moving-in bomb, then Nora showing up and stealing his chair, and now secrets. "You guys are up to something and I don't like it."

Sara sat beside him. "Nora has news to share."

Harry waved a hand. *Out with it.*

"It's about Gary," Nora said. "Nobody knows this except Mom, me and Sara. If I find out you spilled the beans, you'll be sorry."

"I have no doubt." He lifted a finger. "Let me guess. Gary finally found another department willing to take on the loose cannon known as Nora Doyle."

Nora didn't even blink. "Anybody ever tell you how funny you are? No? Didn't think so."

A quiet chuckle sounded from Sara's chair. "Don't encourage her," Harry said.

"The mayor invited Gary to his office yesterday," Nora said. "Along with the district attorney. They discussed a hypothetical situation."

That could only be about one topic. "Hypothetical as in what Gary may do if certain staff changes occur?"

"Right. Beginning in the lieutenant governor's office and ending in the district attorney's," Nora said. "They were feeling him out."

"To see if he wants to be the D.A.'s backfill," Harry said. "Sitting in for an elected official is a lot different than being part of that official's team. He'd be the face of the office now."

"And receive all the criticism and accolades that come with it," Nora finished.

"Including building his name recognition and getting a head start when elections roll around." Harry rubbed the stubble on his chin. "I'm guessing Gary said he's in."

"Yes," Nora said. "This hypothetical situation will come to pass as soon as the lieutenant governor resigns, and eventually my dad will be the new district attorney."

"Good for him." What Harry also meant was *good for me.* Having his stepdad as the D.A. could come in handy if trouble came calling.

Which it did at that very moment. A text from Joey Morello flashed onto his phone. *Stop by when you can. Need to talk about E.S.* Harry responded that he'd be over shortly.

"That looks like a business face," Sara said.

"It's Joey. He wants to chat."

Nora crossed her arms. "Whatever it is, stay out of trouble. We're all under the microscope for what happened in Greece. Understood?"

"I'll keep my head down. Promise." He could promise nothing of the sort.

He stood, and the two women stood with him. Nora turned and headed to the door. She paused at the threshold. "Don't forget about the pans."

"I wo—how did you know?" Harry's gaze narrowed at Nora's back. He whipped his head around to look at Sara. Sara didn't move. "You talked to Nora about this?"

"Sara needed to be certain she wasn't making a mistake." Nora turned her head so one eye looked at Harry over her shoulder. "She didn't take my advice."

He was left to gawk at her back as she walked out. What sounded suspiciously like muffled laughter from Sara made him look back. "You asked her opinion?"

"I have no comment." Sara hooked her arm through his as she walked past. "Walk me out."

Sara wrapped him in a quick hug, then said she'd call after work. Was she coming over tonight? Maybe, maybe not.

Harry watched her handbag swing gently as she headed off down the sidewalk toward a subway entrance. How he would ever survive living with Sara Hamed remained a mystery. He turned and headed in the direction of Joey Morello's house. The walk to Joey's stronghold deep in the heart of Brooklyn passed quickly, and Harry managed to not think about any changes in his life for most of the journey.

Joey's base of operations in the neighborhood was a fortress, though from the outside it appeared to be no more than a larger house on a normal residential street. Only people within the Morello family knew the windows were bulletproof, security cameras monitored every inch of the block from positions on Joey's house and those around it, and that every person living on this block either worked for the Morello family or had a relative on its payroll. In short, this wasn't simply another Brooklyn neighborhood. It was a Morello stronghold, and woe unto the person who brought trouble to Joey Morello's doorstep.

Harry walked up the front steps. The door opened and he came face-to-barrel-chest with the executor of that woe. Mack, possibly Harry's oldest friend in the Morello family.

"Aladdin!" Two big arms spread wide and grabbed Harry with friendly force. "You handsome little guy. How you doing?"

Harry held his breath until Mack lowered him back to the ground. "Not bad, Mack. Not bad at all. How are you?"

"Bored stiff." Mack closed the front door behind Harry and settled his bulk into a chair beside it. One of his hands rested lightly on a shotgun leaning against the jamb. A gun Harry knew was loaded. "The boss said you was coming. He's in his office."

Harry thanked the man who had given him one of history's least original and possibly most insensitive nicknames, then headed down the hall. The door to Joey's office was open, and his friend's voice rang out as he approached. "Come in, Harry."

The *capo dei capi* of New York's organized crime families stood from behind his desk. "Thanks for coming so quickly. Too early for a drink? From what Evgeny tells me, we have a reason to celebrate."

Harry winced. *I never told Evgeny about the defective Antikythera replica.* He'd been meaning to do that, except he didn't want Evgeny to shoot him. Maybe that was a secret best kept. "A drink sounds great. Irish coffee?"

"You read my mind." Joey set the coffee maker burbling and hissing and then moved to lean against a windowsill. "Was the find as impressive as Evgeny made it sound?"

Harry took a seat in front of Joey's desk, turning the chair to face his host. "Alexander's tomb?" he asked. Joey nodded. "Every bit," Harry said. "Had to be a thousand diamonds. Rubies, emeralds and sapphires, too. And every inch of it covered in gold. The only thing more impressive would have been finding Alexander's body inside of it."

"Evgeny still thinks you might be able to find it. How, I have no idea, but once he gets an idea in his head it sticks."

"Getting your way every time for decades makes people"—and here Harry searched for the right phrase—"believe in themselves."

Joey smiled. "He certainly believes in you. And now, it seems, in me."

The coffee machine made an odd noise. Apparently, it was done. "How's that?" Harry asked, as Joey prepared their drinks.

Whiskey went into each coffee mug, followed by a splash of Bailey's. "Evgeny asked if I could recommend a bank to handle an investment he's making in renewable energy. He's expanding his holdings to include American wind farms. He didn't sound surprised when I told him that's exactly the sort of niche investment the bank I now own specializes in handling."

"He already knew."

"He knew everything, and this morning he wired me ten million dollars to invest. There's another ten million coming next month." Joey handed Harry his mug, then lifted his own. "To you, Harry. Cheers."

Mugs clinked. They drank. "Twenty million earns you a nice fee," Harry said.

"Twenty million isn't the best part. If this goes well, Evgeny said he knows a few people looking for places to deposit their cash. Friends of his."

Evgeny Smolov's friends were like Evgeny. Filthy rich. Usually with an emphasis on the "filthy."

Harry shrugged. "It's a good day to be in the renewable energy banking business."

"All because of you. I'll be sure you get your proper cut."

Harry shook his head. "You've done enough for me."

"What's right is right," Joey said, then his face darkened. "Any word from Olivier Lloris?"

"I spoke with him last night. Told him two guys showed up and tried to kill me. You should have heard him. He was shocked, I tell you. Shocked. It took him about three seconds to ask if I had any idea who the men worked for." Harry sipped his drink. "I lied and said they looked like freelancers."

"Did he buy it?"

"Olivier wants Charlemagne's artifacts, especially the crown, and he wants to avoid trouble with you. He bought it, and I also suspect he trusts me a little more now because he thinks he outsmarted me."

"Enough to get you close enough to pay him back?"

The steam from Harry's mug drifted in front of his eyes. "I'll find out soon enough. I haven't told Sara about Olivier wanting the crown. That's a battle for another day. Right now, I only have to worry about Leon Havertz."

Joey grinned. Harry waited. Joey kept quiet. "What aren't you telling me?"

"Evgeny had a word with Havertz."

"Oh?"

"I told you Evgeny was a good friend to have. He told Leon Havertz to forget about the stolen illuminated manuscript. I suspect certain promises were made. Promises of bodily harm, likely. Along with financial ruin and a painful death. Havertz got the message. You can forget about him."

The day was getting better and better. "That's half our problem gone," Harry said. "Any word on Carmelo?"

Carmelo still had to answer for intruding on Joey's business. Trying to kill Harry was bad. But even Harry knew the true issue lay in the challenge and disrespect, for there was nothing worse in Joey's world than that. It could not go unpunished.

Joey's mouth tightened. "I've been told he denies everything. I know he did it. Which means other people know, and that could force my hand. I don't want a feud with Carmelo. His clan may be small, but he has strong allies."

"This could get complicated."

"Unless I handle it alone." Joey set his mug down. "Carmelo could apologize and seek forgiveness. Between us, I'd accept, but him coming to me is unlikely. He may keep trying to sabotage me from Sicily by working with other families to undermine my authority here and abroad."

"You could take the fight to him," Harry said. "Not wait to see what he does next."

"That's what my father would have done." Joey shook his head. "But our world has changed. I want peace. The only thing I know for sure is I can't sit back and do nothing."

"You'll figure it out," Harry said. "And I'll help you. It won't be the first time we get into trouble together."

The darkness lifted from Joey's face, if only briefly. "And we usually get out of it together too. Thanks."

Harry's phone buzzed with an incoming call. "It's Sara," he said. Joey waved at him to take it. "What's up?" Harry asked as he connected the call.

"The message." Sara was breathless, as though she'd been running. "It's more than a message."

"What is?"

"The letter from Agilulph in Charlemagne's crown. Agilulph gave directions. The message is a set of directions."

Harry bolted out of his chair. "To the Caliphate gifts?"

"Yes."

Author's Note

The Antikythera mechanism is at once both a testament to the brilliance of ancient Greek scientists and mathematicians, and an example of humanity's innate shortcomings, all on display in a lump of rock surrounding corroded bronze gears, plates and fragments. At the time of its discovery many scholars felt it simply couldn't exist, for it was too advanced, too complex, to truly be a model of the solar system as it was known in ancient Greece. They were wrong.

But I'm getting ahead of myself. That's the real story, and we'll begin with the facts. The Antikythera mechanism was discovered in 1901 in a Roman-era shipwreck off the coast of Antikythera, a Greek island on the Aegean Sea. A crew of sponge divers found the wreck nearly one hundred fifty feet down, and, saying nothing of their incredible lung capacity, they uncovered quite a few objects, including statues, jewels, coins, and an odd lump of bronze and wood. The corroded lump was unremarkable compared to the other treasures, so it went largely unnoticed for two years, sitting in a museum storage room. A gear wheel embedded in rock was soon found in the lump, and for a brief period scholars investigated the odd contraption, some even identifying it as an astronomical clock, which wasn't far off.

However, interest waned, and it was nearly fifty years before the find was investigated further. Research continued, and in 1971 X-rays of the fragments were taken that revealed how the inner workings likely operated. Only then, nearly a century after its dramatic recovery from the depths, was the mysterious machine more fully understood. The hunk of corroded metal was, in fact, a machine to predict locations of the known planets, eclipses and stars decades in advance, using techniques of a complexity that wouldn't be seen again for over a thousand years.

Since its rediscovery, this mechanism has intrigued humanity, and the popular culture references aren't limited to this novel. Astute readers will recognize the Antikythera from another fictional story: *Indiana Jones and the Dial of Destiny.* The Antikythera is the MacGuffin in Indy's latest adventure, the driving force setting into motion one of the more incredible stories I've ever seen. If you've seen the movie, you'll know George Lucas's version of the mechanism is quite different from the actual Antikythera, and also bears zero resemblance to my version of it. I loved what they did with the mechanism in *Dial of Destiny*. So much, in fact, that it inspired me to create my own take on what it could be used for. Pliny the Elder, *Natural History* and all the fascinating locations in this story have nothing to do with the mechanism. Or at least, nothing I'm aware of.

Also, as interesting as the Antikythera may be, it's far from the only factual historical reference in this tale. Below you will find an overview of where the truth ends and fiction begins, related to many components of Harry's latest adventure.

Harry's near-disaster of an invasion into Leon Havertz's German castle (*Chapter 1*) includes quite a few suits of armor, including a gold-plated suit he correctly identifies as one to be worn while watching a battle, not fighting it. The suit described is based on the field armor of King Henry VIII, which can be seen today in the Metropolitan Museum of Art in New York's Central Park.

What Harry recovers from the castle is the missing link pointing forward on Agilulph's hidden path. The illuminated manuscript (*Chapter 2*) is a figment of my imagination, but the Irish Saint Columbanus truly existed and is known today for founding monasteries across Ireland and Italy, including Bobbio Abbey, which is discussed in this book. The abbey was dissolved in 1803, but many of its buildings still exist, and in the Middle Ages the abbey housed one of the most important libraries in Europe. However, Columbanus died in 615, more than a century before

Charlemagne was born, so any connection between the saint and Charles the Great is fictional. The story of Charlemagne's elephant, though, is not.

Charlemagne did not only wage war. While his reputation today is that of a masterful ruler who unified most of Western Europe through conquest, an equally important tool in his expansion arsenal were alliances. After all, an enemy you don't have to fight is the best enemy of all. Charlemagne brokered a key alliance with the Abbasid Caliphate, or empire, led by Caliph Harun al-Rashid. A mutual interest in increased trade and the Spanish region led to this arrangement, as both leaders understood that peace begat prosperity on all sides. Also, they had enough enemies to fight, namely the Umayadd dynasty in the Iberian Peninsula. Envoys traveled between Charlemagne's court in what is now northern France and the Abbasid court in Baghdad, and one of the many gifts exchanged was an Asian elephant named Abul-Abbas, which was almost certainly the first elephant to be seen in Europe since Emperor Claudius invaded northern Europe seven centuries earlier. Such an animal would have been as foreign to Charlemagne's people as a penguin from Antarctica. Though Abul-Abbas was certainly the most attention-grabbing present, there were other impressive gifts, including a water clock with animated mechanical knights, along with a much smaller gift: a set of keys, given by the Abbasid Caliphate to Charlemagne, keys to the Church of the Holy Sepulchre in Jerusalem, the holiest site for Christians in the world. The keys symbolized the Caliphate giving nominal control over the church to Charlemagne, though some would say the Caliph, in his quest for peace and prosperity, had in effect promised control of the entire city to Charles the Great. This will become important to Harry's story very soon.

Among Evgeny Smolov's many possessions are charred scrolls found in Pompeii. Unreadable, of course—until the advent of computed topography (*Chapter 2)*. The method described in this story is real and has been used to reveal the contents of charred scrolls, though to my knowledge none has yet been from Pompeii or suggested the existence of any hidden historical trails. The technology has only been developed and deployed within the past year, so it is possible there is incredible knowledge waiting to be revealed, knowledge lost for centuries that may in turn lead to even greater discoveries. I would like to think so, and we will see what the future holds.

Among the many lost works from ancient times, Pliny's *The Student (Chapter 2)* is notable in that we have first-hand references to the contents, so even though the work in its entirety is no longer extant, the work is not entirely lost. One notable quote from the story is "the orator is trained from his very cradle and perfected," a quote referenced by Pliny's nephew and adopted son, Pliny the Younger. It is a real quote, though if those words hold the key to a greater mystery, I am unaware of the connection. One of Pliny's works that does exist and has been widely studied is what many call the world's first encyclopedia, *Natural History.* This book *(Chapter 2)* is the largest single piece of scholarly work to have survived from the Roman Empire. The actual work is divided into more sections than I indicate in this story, as I've adjusted the format to allow for a smoother narrative flow and for simplicity's sake. *Natural History,* in fact, consists of thirty-seven books and is divided into ten volumes. Topics referenced in this story that are truly covered include astronomy, meteorology, mining and statuary, but there are many more as well, ranging from anthropology and human physiology to medicine and, interestingly, magic. This voluminous collection wasn't finished when Pliny the Elder died trying to rescue friends and family during the eruption of Mount Vesuvius, which buried Pompeii, so his adopted son, Pliny the Younger, picked up where the Elder left off *(Chapter 2)*, publishing the remaining twenty-seven volumes not yet publicly available when his father perished.

As mentioned earlier, Bobbio Abbey is real and was founded by the itinerant Saint Columbanus *(Chapter 3),* who traveled with the aim of spreading Christianity throughout the world—a goal supported by one of Charlemagne's predecessors, King Clovis *(Chapter 5)*, the first Christian Frankish king. He conquered the Germanic Alemanni tribe, who lived alongside the Romans during the precipitous decline of the Western Roman Empire following the first sack of Rome in 410 A.D. by the Visigoths, a topic focused on in one of Harry's prior adventures. The Alemanni battled both the Romans and Franks, ultimately suffering defeat at the hands of Clovis and spending the next three centuries under the Frankish thumb before ultimately becoming part of the Holy Roman Empire. Such is the way of the world, with nations coming and going, the more enduring legacies being found in their cultural contributions, which often exist for centuries or more after their flags no longer fly.

Harry and Sara discover Zurich is a stop on Agilulph's path by deciphering a message cloaking the city name in a question about Charlemagne. It's a question about a legend involving three tombs, the tombs of saints who patronized Zurich and upon whose graves Charlemagne supposedly built a great church called Grossmünster, a church anyone in Zurich can visit today along the banks of the Limmat River. The legend is quite real, at least as far as legends go. As to whether Charlemagne's poor horsemanship led to the founding of a church that still stands to this day, I cannot say with certainty whether it truly occurred, or if it was the invention of an enterprising clergyman who realized a legend about Charlemagne would attract more pilgrims and the coin they brought. Odds are we'll never know, but I have an opinion.

The exterior of the church is as I've described it, complete with two towering spires and a recessed statue of Charlemagne on one exterior wall. The stained-glass windows and open central area are real, but anyone visiting the church won't find any of the statues I reference inside, as I created those to help the story flow. The same is true for the underground chambers in which Harry and Sara locate Charlemagne's crown. As far as I know, there are no below-ground tunnels or chambers containing statues of any sort. However, I imagine an enterprising explorer—equipped with proper tools and permits—could, in theory, find their way from one of these imaginary tunnels to the Limmat River. Would you be carried there on the back of a stampeding herd of stone elephants? Probably not, but it can't be ruled out entirely.

And if that explorer did find an artifact, say a crown, perhaps, it would not be *the* Crown of Charlemagne *(Chapter 13)*—a crown that was quite real and that likely never sat atop Charlemagne's head. The crown of this name was most likely created for Charlemagne's grandson, Charles the Bald (I would have chosen a hat over a crown, but what do I know?), and likely appeared much as described in this story. The crown began as a simpler object, or at least as simple as a circle of gold decorated with jewels can be, then gradually become more of a showpiece over time as subsequent kings used Charlemagne's name for the reflected glory. The crown became more ostentatious with each passing coronation, until it was ultimately destroyed in the French Revolution. At that point it was one of eleven royal French crowns, though of those eleven, only one still exists, the Crown of Louis XV, now on permanent display in the Louvre.

It is a fact that Aristotle tutored Alexander the Great *(Chapter 9)*. The Temple of Augustus and Livia *(Chapter 14)* in Vienne, France, is real and can be seen today. However, it is not set hard against a hill, but instead sits in the middle of the city, and if you visit, you can enjoy a drink and a meal in one of the numerous sidewalk tables surrounding the popular tourist attraction. After quenching your thirst, though, you will be hard-pressed to find any image or message tied to Aristotle inside the temple, as none exists. The image of Aristotle speaking with Plato is in fact based on a real-life work called *Relief of Aristotle and Plato* by Luca della Robbia, a piece that can be seen in the Florence Cathedral in Florence, Italy. The image is as described, and I used it as-is to hide another message on Agilulph's path.

The true layout of the temple's interior is wholly unlike what I detail in this story, mainly due to size, as the real temple isn't much bigger than a large house. The Temple of Augustus and Livia has stood in Vienne for two thousand years, but it has not remained untouched. At times it has variously been a parish church, a commercial court, a museum and a library before being restored to its original state in the latter half of the nineteenth century.

Harry and Sara discover a variant of the classical elements diagram on the rear wall of the temple in Vienne, a factual representation of the idea proposed by Aristotle and Empedocles to explain the natural environment in more easily understandable terms and components. Similar explanations existed across ancient cultures ranging from Greece to India, with the basic elements consisting of fire, air, earth and water. The chart also detailed qualities tying the elements to each other. For example, the quality tying fire to air is *hot*, as fire is hot and dry, while air is both hot and wet. Moving counterclockwise around the circular diagram, the next element is water, which shares with air the quality of being *wet*. Through this association, ancient scholars attempted to make sense of the world through classification, and despite some inaccuracies, such attempts in no small way gave birth to modern scientific thought.

While investigating the Temple of Augustus and Livia, Harry is forced to think on his feet and deceive a security guard as to why he's so interested in vague symbols carved into the temple wall. Harry uses thickly accented French and English to disarm the guard, tricking him into believing Harry is a tourist whose first language is Arabic, and the guard soon leaves Harry alone. Harry's command of several languages has been discussed in earlier stories, but I want to take a moment here to address the specifics of why Harry speaks so many languages, and to point out an editorial decision I made in the interests of telling a more fluid story, a decision many readers may not know of. Harry's parents are Fred, whose ancestry is European, and Dani, whose ancestors came from Pakistan. I made the decision to have had Dani expose her son to Arabic as a child, which is the reason Harry speaks it fluently. However, the *lingua franca*, or common language, of Pakistan is Urdu. This is the primary language of around seven percent of Pakistani citizens, but it is widely written, spoken and understood throughout the nation. Arabic is the religious language of Pakistan, with a majority of the nation's Muslim population having exposure to and an understanding of the language, but I want to remind everyone that Pakistanis are not Arabs and do not speak Arabic. I took the liberty of having Harry speak Arabic fluently in large part because so many of the artifacts he comes across have ties to lands where Arabic is spoken.

Harry's final challenge in the temple is a statue of Jupiter *(Chapter 14)*, which he must summit to get a better look at the fire section of the classical elements diagram. In his conversation with Sara before climbing, he tries both to convince her he's on the right path and to ease her concern by saying "ninety percent of the time it's right every time." This, of course, is nonsense, but it's a very specific piece of nonsense. The inspiration for this bit of inanity comes from two world-class comedic sources: Yogi Berra, the Hall of Fame catcher for the New York Yankees, and the movie *Anchorman.* Yogi had countless quips and witticisms, and those made him larger than life, a baseball player who transcended the sport—impressive for a guy who won thirteen World Series rings, more than anyone else in baseball history. The saying I borrowed from is "Baseball is 90 percent mental. The other half is physical." As for *Anchorman*, Paul Rudd's character is discussing a brand of cologne and its effect on women when he states, "They've done studies, you know. Sixty percent of the time it works every time."

Harry locates a triangle on Jupiter's staff *(Chapter 14)* shortly after his quip, a triangle that opens a hidden chamber beneath the altar. While the triangle is, in fact, the alchemical symbol for fire, Aristotle never would have used this to indicate a hidden access button, because Aristotle didn't practice alchemy. The medieval precursor to modern chemistry, alchemy didn't exist in the Western world until after Aristotle died. However, I thought it made for a better story, so I fudged the timeline.

The conflicted character that is Olivier Lloris goes from the opening of a new school he's funding to a meeting with an artifacts dealer in an attempt to purchase a millennia-old statue found in a parking lot *(Chapter 16)*. This may sound crazy, but it really happened in 2023 when a British construction worker unearthed the marble head of an eighteen-hundred-year-old Roman statue while digging out ground for a parking lot on the Earl of Exeter's property in Stamford. The head is believed to be part of a statue that came from Italy in the mid-eighteenth century after a past earl purchased it. How it came to be in the ground for centuries, though, is a mystery.

Of all the reasons for Harry Fox to run into trouble, music is a new one in this book. His location is betrayed during a call with Olivier Lloris because of music Olivier hears in the background. Jazz music, to be specific, which allows Olivier to piece together enough information to know Harry is in Vienne, France. The Jazz à Vienne festival that (indirectly, of course) nearly gets Harry killed is real, and occurs in the southern French city every year in June and July. The timing of the actual festival does not align with the setting of this story, which is toward the end of the year, but I thought it was a neat way for Harry to get into trouble, so I moved the festival back a few months.

A major turning point in the story takes place at the Trier Imperial Baths in Germany, which is also where Harry's involvement with Sara began several years earlier. The baths are a wonderful setting for the confluence of events bringing both sides of Harry's pursuit together, but in truth it would have been impossible for Pliny to secrete any messages or clues in the baths, because they weren't built until the fourth century, over two hundred years after his death. The three principal areas or rooms—the tepidarium, the caldarium and the laconicum—are real and comprised the standard layout for public baths. The vestibule in truth would have been much smaller, but I made it a larger, almost equal, section of the grounds for story purposes.

Pliny points Harry to a final location in Cyprus by referencing a Greek sculptor named Agesander *(Chapter 20)*. Pliny praises Agesander's work in the highest terms, specifically calling out a statue called *Laocoon and His Sons*. The statue and Pliny's praise of it are real. Pliny mentions the statue in his writings, praising it as one of the finest pieces of art in the world. It has truly been called "the prototypical icon of human agony" in Western art, and it can be seen today, not at Saint Hilarion Castle on the island of Cyprus, but at the Vatican Museums in Italy. Agesander was a real sculptor, or at least a team of sculptors who worked together to produce a number of works. None of these are at Saint Hilarion Castle, and there are no ties between the castle and either Pliny or Agesander. I created those ties for the purposes of this story. Beyond that, it would have been impossible for Agesander's work to be purpose-crafted for the castle, as it wasn't built until at least 1000 A.D., a millennium after Pliny's time. Additionally, any visitors to the castle will not find statues crafted by Agesander, an indoor museum or an enclosed church of any sort. The castle is a ruin, having been dismantled by the Venetians in the fifteenth century to salvage the stone for other defensive purposes. The outer grounds and parking area are approximately as described, though there are no spotlights to surprise any nocturnal visitors, nor, to my knowledge, are there any hidden caverns inside the mountain.

The alchemical symbol for earth resembled a plus sign like the one Harry discovers on a statue of Poseidon *(Chapter 23)*. It is the correct symbol for that element, though the symbol for metal is one I created out of thin air for this story. Pliny truly does discuss metallurgy in *Natural History*, though he does not specifically discuss colossi and their construction. However, the Colossus of Rhodes was allegedly built in part by using the melted weapons of defeated foes, and I chose to treat that as fact for this story because I think that's pretty neat. As for another important clue Harry must decipher—and almost fails to do so—astronomy is indeed a topic covered in *Natural History*. Classical astronomers did truly count seven planets, which included the sun and moon. Given they subscribed to the geocentric model in which the earth was the center of the universe, our planet wasn't among the seven. Another topic in Pliny's encyclopedia nearly proves to be Harry's undoing—that of coinage, specifically the methods of counterfeiting coin *(Chapter 24)*. Struck coins are made by hitting a piece of hot metal—whatever one the coin is made of—with a hammer-like object containing a design. The design is imprinted on the hot metal, and you have a new coin. Cast coins are made by pouring liquid metal into a die and letting it cool. Roman coins were produced using both methods, but the casting process offered a more efficient way to mass-produce counterfeit coins, a fact Pliny bemoans in *Natural History*.

The basis for this story is that Pliny the Elder created a mysterious path to thwart the ambitions of his nemesis, Emperor Caligula. The final test Harry must pass as he races through the labyrinth relates to a story about Caligula himself. In Roman times crystal was highly prized, a status symbol only the very richest could afford—men like Caligula. The story I borrowed from states that a certain Roman emperor destroyed two crystal cups when he learned he was about to be deposed, but the truth of the matter is that the emperor was not Caligula, but Nero. In other words, the story about the destruction of crystal cups is true, but I changed the destroyer from Nero to Caligula so it fit with my own story.

All of Harry's efforts lead to one final prize, the destination in this story, the object he's after the whole time even if he doesn't know it: Alexander the Great's funerary cart. This is a real artifact, documented in the historical record, but the mystery concerns what happened to it, where the cart ultimately ended up, and whether it still exists at all. It is a fact that Alexander requested to be buried at a specific temple shortly before his death, and it is also a fact that this wish was completely ignored by several generals wishing to use Alexander's body as a tool for personal gain—sound familiar?

Alexander's body was placed in a funerary cart identical to the one Harry found in Cyprus. It was a massive affair requiring sixty-four mules to pull it. The team charged with moving it was overseen by a Macedonian general named Perdiccas, and it included a group of road builders, just in case they ran out of suitable road en route to Macedonia. The trouble started when another Macedonian general named Ptolemy I (who would go on to found the Ptolemaic dynasty, of which Cleopatra was the last ruler—yes, that Cleopatra) hijacked the ponderous procession to bolster his claim to Alexander's empire through possession of the body. Ptolemy conspired with the man leading the procession, a General Arrhidaeus, to hijack the procession and take Alexander's corpse to Egypt. However, such a massive carriage didn't move quickly, and it wasn't long after the heist that Perdiccas learned of Ptolemy's treachery. He sent a "task force" of armed men to recover the carriage from Ptolemy's men, but unfortunately, he didn't send enough.

Ptolemy expected this to happen and sent his own force, a much larger one, ostensibly tasked with giving Alexander's corpse a military welcome befitting the conquering hero. In fact, it was an insurance policy against exactly what Perdiccas did, and it worked to perfection. Alexander's body was interred at Memphis in Egypt around 321 B.C., and that is where the historical record becomes fuzzy.

Within a century his body was relocated to Alexandria by one of Ptolemy's descendants, then moved again by another descendant to a different location in Alexandria. Roughly two centuries later, Julius Caesar visited Alexander's tomb, and around this time Cleopatra—a descendant of Ptolemy—looted Alexander's tomb to help pay for her and Mark Antony's unsuccessful war against Octavian. Some time after that, Emperor Caligula supposedly stole Alexander's breastplate (at least it wasn't made of crystal), after which the records are even less precise. Various lootings and possible relocations are mentioned, though by 400 A.D. it is remarked that the tomb has basically been forgotten, with the most distant claim of seeing the tomb coming around 1500 A.D. when an Andalusian diplomat writes that he visited it.

How much, if any, of this is true? It's impossible to say. All that can be said with certainty is that Alexander's tomb is lost and remains one of humanity's more enduring mysteries. Various scholars have suggested dozens of locations, and numerous excavations have been undertaken, none successful. Perhaps it was destroyed, or perhaps it was looted until nothing remained, sending Alexander's bones and treasures to every corner of the globe. Despite the utter lack of credible evidence, however, interest in the tale remains strong and searches will likely continue for centuries to come.

Which brings us to the end of this chapter in Harry's adventures. A new threat is looming on the horizon, a threat that Harry must now face head-on if he wants to keep his family safe. A threat from the man who upended his life. A man who seems to have no idea what's coming for him. A man Harry should not underestimate, for Olivier Lloris has already decimated Harry's childhood, and would not hesitate to bring the full force of his anger to bear should he discover Harry's true intentions. Plus, Harry bought those new towels and bathrobes. He can't let Olivier get the best of him now. The next adventure will center on the impending clash between Harry and Olivier, forcing a conclusion to this quiet war in a decidedly loud fashion.

I hope you enjoyed reading this story as much as I enjoyed writing it. Thank you for joining me on this journey. I'll see you again soon.

Andrew Clawson
May 2024

Excerpt from

THE CHARLEMAGNE ACCORD

You can get your copy of THE CHARLEMAGNE ACCORD at Amazon

Chapter 1

Kharkiv, Ukraine

A barrage of missiles blasted through the night sky. Harry hit the dirt.

A gravelly voice chuckled without humor. "They are not shooting at us."

Harry got off the ground, staying low as he brushed dirt from his sleeves. He turned to look at the man behind him, sitting in the stern of a small boat. "Can't be too careful."

"A careful man would not be here."

Hard to argue with that. Harry crouched as he looked around. The river flowed unquietly behind him. Armored vehicles were parked in a line against a low-slung rock wall. Helicopters rumbled in the distance, their navigation lights moving steadily in the darkness. Sporadic gunfire punctuated the interminable noise coming from the nearby front lines.

"I won't be here long." Harry's breath fogged the chill air. "Now what?"

The bearded man behind Harry had smeared dark camouflage face paint on his nose and forehead. Only the whites of his eyes glowed under the moonlight. "Now I leave. I will see you soon. If you survive."

The burly man spun his tiny boat around, vanishing into the darkness across a river flecked with white. Harry swallowed, his throat dry. *Thanks for the reminder.*

A small, open-top jeep drove past not far away, the engine whining softly, two soldiers inside. Russian soldiers, both wearing white-and-black snow camouflage fatigues.

White-and-black. He lifted one arm. An arm clad in white, black and blue camouflage. "Wait." He turned to find nothing but darkness. The man who led him here was long gone. A man who gave him the wrong color camo. Another jeep rumbled by as Harry turned to watch it move. The two soldiers inside had white-and-black camo fatigues on. No blue.

He needed to get his hands on a pair of those fatigues. His Pakistani-American heritage made him stand out even with his mouth shut. Without those fatigues, his life expectancy would be measured in minutes. This place was crawling with Russians. Not surprising, given the front lines of Russia's ongoing invasion of Ukraine were only a few short miles away.

A tank roared to life in the distance. Harry pressed his back against the stack of wooden crates providing cover. What had he been thinking? This morning he woke up on a soft bed on a yacht in the Black Sea. A yacht owned by an exiled Russian oligarch named Evgeny Smolov. If pressed, Harry would say Evgeny was somewhat of a friend, though the sort of friend who might toss Harry to the sharks if Harry was no longer useful. One of Evgeny's personal helicopters had ferried Harry – along with a shipment of black-market arms – to a quiet field outside of Kyiv. The Ukrainian soldiers waiting for them unloaded boxes of anti-aircraft missiles, replaced them with several briefcases filled with cash, and then loaded the missiles and Harry into a waiting vehicle. One quick stop at a Ukrainian military outpost later, Harry found himself clad in the wrong color of fatigues as he sat on the back of a motorcycle, clinging to a burly, bearded man whose idea of subtle infiltration behind Russian lines consisted of racing their bike at full speed across unmarked fields and hoping they didn't run into any Russians.

They hadn't, which is why Harry was still alive. For the moment. And this was only the first step of his mission. A personal mission that began when he found a hidden message inside the lost crown of Charlemagne the Great. A message indicating there was another message waiting, hidden in a centuries-old church in Ukraine's second largest city. A city now controlled by the Russian military.

Gunfire chattered nearby. Harry went still until loud Russian and harsh laughter filled the air. He didn't speak much of the language, but clearly someone had a strange idea about how to have fun. It soon died, and he turned to peer around the crates. A towering monastery peered back.

In daylight the golden domes and pointed spires might fill believer's hearts with joy. The towering walls and colonnaded bell towers made the faithful pause in their tracks and look to the heavens. Tonight, it did nothing of the sort. Bullet holes and darkness turned this religious destination into a grim reminder of all that was wrong with the world. One belltower had been reduced to little more than rubble, while many of the stained-glass windows had been blown out. He looked through a jagged hole large enough to drive a tank through into what had once been a hushed sanctuary. Now the harsh mobile spotlights of the Russian army displayed charred pews and scorched marble floors. The sight of it brought a much different feeling to Harry's chest.

The Russians had turned this holy place into an operations base, a staging point for attacks on the Ukrainians nearby. Harry shook his head. *That's not my problem.*

He was here for one reason, and one reason only: locate an image of Charlemagne in this church, one of Ukraine's holiest. This specific church dated back to Charlemagne's time and was a cave monastery, meaning it had originally been built inside existing caves. Over time it had grown, the imposing outbuildings taking hold while the caves became nothing but a memory. Or, Harry hoped, a hiding place where the next step on a royal path waited for him to find it.

All he had to do was get past a small army of Russians and then hope he was in the correct place. The message in Charlemagne's crown pointed him here. He was almost certain.

"Stop wasting time," Harry told himself. Another jeep went past, dirt flying as the tires churned. Harry's gaze went to a tent across from him, a tent big enough for a half-dozen men, but this tent had its front flap pulled open so he could see inside. Light spilled from the open flap, reflecting off the dented bumper of a rusty pickup truck beside the tent. A single man stood in the light, sitting on the edge of a cot, brushing his teeth. Nobody else was inside with him. Harry's eyes narrowed. *Those could work.*

He stood and marched across the muddy road, acting as though he belonged. The darkness would shroud him enough to keep anyone from noticing he had the wrong color uniform. Should, at least. He stumbled over a frozen clod of earth as he walked, shoulders hunched and head down, one more miserable soldier stuck here in the cold. A slight pause at the entrance, a look either way. No one around. Harry ducked into the tent.

"Privyet." Harry muttered the word and walked past the soldier, not giving the guy a clear view of his face.

The soldier offered an unintelligible response, still brushing his teeth. Harry twisted to keep his back to the man, went back to the flap and let it fall loose. The soldier behind him did not look up. Several other cots lined the tents interior. All were empty. No spare fatigues in site. Too bad.

A flashlight on the ground beside one cot grabbed his eye. A big one, the sort you could see a long way with. All metal, and when he picked it up, darned heavy. *This will do.* He turned to find the man still hunched over, brushing his teeth. The soldier reached for a bottle of water as Harry walked beside him and lifted the flashlight.

Bang. The guy never knew what hit him. One second he was brushing his teeth, the next he was out cold on the canvas floor. Harry moved quickly, first stripping the man's clothes off, then removing his own and donning the stolen gear. A tad loose, but it would do. Now he looked like a real Russian soldier. Which left one problem. The actual Russian soldier lying at his feet who would soon wake up.

Harry ran to the flap, lifted it and peered out at the truck parked outside. A truck with a metal cover over the bed. The sort which locked from the outside.

He dropped the flap, pulled the shoestrings from a pair of combat boots by one cot, and in short order the soldier's hands and feet were bound. A length of fabric made a decent gag, so when Harry pulled the man to his feet and manhandled him out of the tent, the guy couldn't move. Thankfully, he was still unconscious, and remained so as Harry pulled him into the shadows outside the tent, dragged him to the dented pickup truck, and hefted him into the bed. Harry nearly locked the bed cover before running back into the tent and grabbing a couple of blankets, which he threw over the soldier before snapping the lock shut. It would keep the guy from freezing, but more to the point, it should keep the noise down. He glanced at his watch. He had fifteen minutes, tops.

A camo hat went on his head as he stepped out of the darkness and walked toward one side of the commandeered monastery. The message from Charlemagne's crown ran through his head.

Locate my father where Anthony of the caves led his disciples. My father looks upon the true path.

Anthony of the Caves had been a monk who lived in what would one day become Ukraine. He died a thousand years ago, having founded two major cave monasteries, both of which still stood today. One in Kiev. The other here in Kharkiv. Given the message written on Charlemagne's crown had been written by the great king's personal abbot, *my father* could only mean Charlemagne. Now all Harry had to do was find a king who had been dead for a thousand years inside a sprawling monastery filled with Russian soldiers.

One corner of his mouth lifted. *Nothing to it.* Frozen dirt cracked under his boots as he marched toward the monastery entrance, passing tents and hastily-erected metal sheds as he followed the ragged path. An entrance with a guard posted outside. His gaze shifted to the massive hole in the wall, a hole far away from the hustle and bustle of the front door. A hole big enough to drive a tank through. A hole without a guard posted outside.

A soldier stepped out of the metal shed beside Harry. The man never looked at Harry, never stopped walking as he crossed Harry's path and kept going, his eyes on the pistol in his hands. A pistol, Harry noted, in the process of being loaded. The shed door whined as it closed. A shed door with an unfamiliar Cyrillic word on it. Harry reached out and grabbed the door an instant before it clicked shut. He couldn't say why, only that his gut told him to. He peeked inside. "Would you look at this?" he whispered to himself. A look over his shoulder found no one watching before he slipped inside and shut the door behind him.

Shelves of weaponry stretched out before him. Row after row of automatic weapons. Boxes stacked alongside with writing on them, numerals indicating what sort of ammunition they held. And other boxes as well. Boxes which caught his eye. "Leave it to the Russians to leave their armory unattended." He shook his head and went directly to a box not with numerals on it, but words. A word he thought he knew. He lifted the lid and confirmed it, reaching in and pulling out a pair of grenades, which he stuffed in his pockets. An adjacent box contained rocket launchers; the ammunition helpfully stored nearby. He had no need for a rocket launcher right now. If things went sideways, well, at least he knew where to find them.

The wind kicked up as he walked out of the armory and headed straight for the monastery's gaping wound. The guard at the front door never noticed the man keeping to the shadows as he marched to the hole some fifty yards away. No one challenged Harry as he darted inside, wind whistling around him to send tiny snowflakes through the air until he made it past alternate rows of charred pews and overturned chairs to an interior doorway which remained intact. Broken glass jingled across the floor as he walked, hesitating as he touched the door handle, the carved wood cold on his ear when he leaned against it. He listened for any sign of life on the other side. He heard nothing.

A skin-tingling screech sounded when he pushed the door open. He kept pushing until the door opened enough for him to sneak through into a stone corridor. The noise returned when he closed the door, though this time it was muffled by the roar of airplanes flying overhead. Flying low, from the sound of it. He turned away from the building's front and walked deeper into the monastery. Weak yellow lights along the ceiling guided him. A painting sat propped against the wall to one side, the nail from where it had fallen still sticking out of the wall at eye level. He paused long enough to verify it wasn't Charlemagne before moving on. The lights overhead flickered, his shadow dancing across the walls. The next painting had managed to stay on its hook, this one of a saint he didn't recognize from a religion he barely understood. Eastern Orthodox Christianity was not in his wheelhouse, not by a long shot.

Which made it easier in some ways. His target was simple. Charlemagne. The Father of Europe wasn't the sort of man painters or sculptors tried to disguise. Harry had seen enough images of the man to make recognizing him easy. The hard part was finding him in this place. His research hadn't uncovered any paintings or sculptures or other images of Charlemagne inside, which didn't mean there weren't any to find. The path laid out by Agilulph was meant to be followed. Too bad Agilulph never counted on Russian forces occupying this holy place.

Light beckoned as the hallway dead-ended ahead. Bright light, the sort a military-grade spotlight would give off. Harry moved to a shadowy alcove as the corridor ended. He leaned out to find another corridor running in either direction. A closed door waited to one side. A chapel with high, curving ceilings and several statues lining the walls was on the other. He stepped out, heading for the statues.

The doorway behind him banged open. Harry straightened his back and marched instead of walked, never turning as harsh Russian words filled the air from the voices of several men. The voices of men used to giving orders. Harry turned, stepped back into a convenient shadow and saluted, his chest going still.

Three men. All had stripes on their shoulders. One looked at Harry as they passed, his eyes narrowing. He hesitated. Harry tensed.

The man looked away and walked onward. Harry waited until they disappeared into a different hallway before he took a breath. *That was luck.* And hoping to keep getting lucky was worse than no plan at all. His watch revealed nearly five minutes had passed since he locked that soldier in the truck. Ten more and he'd be pushing what little luck he might have left.

Four statues were in this chapel, and it was the work of a few moments to verify none were of Charlemagne. Cross this one off the list, and he truly did have a list in mind. A mental list of all the larger rooms in the monastery. Rooms where worshippers would gather. Rooms built to impress those inside them. And from the viewpoint of a worshipper from the Middle Ages, what was impressive? Statues, paintings and other iconography. Including, he hoped, a representation of Charlemagne. The sort of object or item this church would keep around for a thousand years, not bury in a storage closet somewhere.

The muted noises filtering in from outside seemed to intensify as Harry completed his circuit of the room and returned to where he'd saluted a minute ago. Moonlight turned red as it fell through an unbroken stained-glass window to paint the marble floor beside him. He walked to a large passageway to his right, behind the pulpit on which countless preachers had given sermons, and darted into the dim passage before breaking into a run. It was not a short journey, as it connected the main church to a second one, and from there additional tunnels would connect the second church to others. Such was the nature of this and many other cave monasteries. They began in caves, and later outbuildings were added so it became a large complex instead of a single structure.

A slightly smaller, square church waited for him. Nobody was inside this one, only rows of empty pews and another vacant pulpit at the front. Oil paintings covered one wall, while a golden chandelier hung above the central nave and stained-glass windows let weak light inside. The oil paintings were of religious men looking rather miserable. Charlemagne was nowhere to be seen. He pulled up a mental map of the path he'd plotted through the monastery. His next move was through a doorway underneath one window of a giant cross that took him to the adjacent structure. The door opened silently. Harry watched his footing as his boots smacked off the stone floor. His watch glowed softly in the darkness. A watch with a tracking device in it. The Ukrainian soldier who dropped Harry outside this Russian camp had a device to track the watch's location so he knew when Harry was approaching their rendezvous point. The soldier would be ready to spirit Harry to safety, regardless of if the Russians were hot on Harry's tail.

At least the guy said he would. Except given the flat terrain around here, he'd see Harry coming from a long way off, and if Russians were chasing Harry would the guy truly wait? Without the threat of Evgeny Smolov's wrath hanging over all this, probably not. Harry's best chance lay with the soldiers greed and fear. Greed for more of Evgeny's weapons, and fear of his retribution. Otherwise, Harry was as good as dead. He shook his head and pushed that worry aside. Find Charlemagne first. Worry about the rest of it later. A doorway stood in front of him. Harry reached for it. One step at a time. That's how you stayed alive in this game. He pushed the door open.

A platoon of soldiers stood on the other side. Over a dozen men turned in unison as Harry stepped into the church. One man stood at the head of the troops, still barking orders.

Uh-oh. He didn't think. He saluted.

The man at the front shouted. Not at Harry. At all of them. Discipline, or something akin to it, ran strong in these men and the puzzled faces turned away from Harry and back toward their leader, each man shouting something Harry didn't understand. His heart was pounding too loudly for him to hear much of anything, so he made a rumbling noise that was lost in their voices and fell into line. Nobody looked back as the commanding officer turned on a heel and began marching toward a set of tall doors set into the church wall. Two soldiers ran ahead to open them before their leader had to stop. A gust of air flew into the chapel and Harry's breath turned to steam as he kept pace with the moving troops until they were outside and the doors clanged shut. Or one door, at least. Harry turned to find one of the doormen had set his gun down and was cursing at a stuck door. A solid kick from the soldier got it closed.

Exhaust billowed from the row of tanks and armored vehicles waiting outside, every one of them with headlights glowing and engines running. The two door-holders ran back to their places, passing Harry as the troop headed for the vehicles. The bright vehicle lights made him squint against the darkness.

He stopped marching. The troops continued. Harry turned ninety degrees and ran for the closest cover he could find. He dove behind a metal container, the frozen ground rattling his teeth as he crashed down and skidded into the darkness. He hit the container wall and went still, listening. The troops marched on. Harry got to his feet and poked his head around to look. Not a single soldier turned back. No flashlights landed on his face. He watched until the troops rounded a curve in the road and vanished. Only then did his breathing slow, any noise he made masked by the sound of rumbling tank engines.

Safe, for now, but that wouldn't last long standing behind a metal container. What was this thing, anyhow? The corrugated metal was streaked with dirt. He kept a shoulder on the wall as he leaned around the front again to find a door had been set into that side. A sign on the door caught his eye. A Cyrillic word he wouldn't have been able to read a few minutes ago. Now, though, it made perfect sense. *Armory.* Harry could only shake his head. *A mountain of weapons, and these guys leave it unlocked.*

The fact anyone with a pulse around here could walk in and take whatever they pleased sharpened his senses. Get caught and it's all over. Nobody was in sight when he looked up and down the road, and the burbling engines covered his footsteps as he ran back toward the chapel and slipped through the doors, once again unlocked. Doors which opened silently, thank goodness. A moment's hesitation inside found no one in sight, though he'd be hard pressed to see anyone in the gloomy light filtering through a handful of stained-glass windows. He stepped one side, his back to the wall. Metal clattered in the still dark.

He looked down. *A rifle.* Why was there a single rifle leaning against the wall in here? It took him a second. That soldier who had opened the door must have left it here. Well, he could find a replacement easily enough with unlocked armories every five steps. Harry set the gun back where he'd found it and pulled a penlight from his pocket, clicking it on so a narrow beam of brilliant light cut through the chapel. He looked down. A marble floor, undecorated. He looked up. He hesitated. A walkway ran the circumference of the ceiling overhead, hugging the wall like some sort of viewing platform. Standing room only, perhaps? Hard to say. His light went to the walls, flitting over statues not of Charlemagne and images of saints, none of them – *whoa.*

A man had been painted on the wall. A beardless man wearing plain robes, standing with his eyes forward. A thin circle of gold sat on his head. A golden crown. A crown lost to history. A crown Harry recognized, because he had found it hidden under the streets of Zurich barely a month ago. The lost crown of Charlemagne.

"It's him," Harry said to himself. "Without a beard."

The crown gave it away. Without it, Harry wouldn't have looked at this man twice. Even with the crown it was hard to tell who this man was. Charlemagne imagery always showed him with a beard. Every single image Harry had ever seen. Until now. "Found you." Harry tilted his head. "What are you looking at?"

This painting of the incognito king was above the chapel's main entrance. Charlemagne looked directly across the room to the rear wall, his gaze traveling through a decorative wooden piece behind the altar. The priest would stand in front of this big hunk of wood, and a nice piece of wood it was, for it had been carved into a giant cross. Harry's gaze narrowed. Was that writing on the cross. He stepped closer and was able to look past the cross, back to the rear wall, and he stopped. The rear wall also had writing on it. Latin letters, cut into the stone. His gut told him to check there first.

Why carve a message into the actual wall? To make sure it stayed there, that's why. The man who left this trail had been deliberate. Abbot Agilulph meant for his messages to last, messages hiding a prize with the power to preserve an empire.

His footsteps echoed softly off the high ceiling as he moved toward the rear wall, aiming his flashlight at the Latin lettering and sending a silent thank you to his father for giving him a first-rate classical education. At least the language part of it. No self-respecting treasure hunter should go into the field without first knowing how to read this foundational language of the Western world. The letters on the rear wall came into view when he stood beside the cross. His mouth opened. He stopped walking.

I follow the heavenly path to look down on Agilulph's cross.

His actual name. Not a reference, or a vague allusion. This specifically called out the abbot, a brazen clue left in plain sight. Like all good clues, you could look right at it and never know what you were seeing. It only made sense if you knew of the path's existence. But why change tact now? Agilulph was a man who operated mostly in the shadows. Yes, he left clues where anyone could find them, but the trick was knowing those benign images or messages *were* clues on a path to one of history's lost treasures. Only then could the end be found.

"He's being direct now." Maybe it was because Agilulph's message was on the far edge of Charlemagne's world. Maybe something else. Hard to say after a thousand years. Harry had learned long ago it probably didn't matter. Follow the clues. Find the treasure. Stay alive.

"What is his *cross*?" Harry barely got the words out before his head turned. Toward the giant wooden cross beside him. A cross with writing on the front. He leaned back until he could see the letters, also Latin. *No way.*

For the glory of God. Standard stuff. What came next was not. Agilulph's name was inscribed on the cross, directly below the phrase honoring his god. It was the sort of inscription one made when donating a significant piece to an institution. "Agilulph brought that cross here," Harry said to himself. "That's what the message means. Charlemagne is looking at the rear wall *and* the cross."

The rear wall told him to *look down on Agilulph's cross* by taking *the heavenly path,* whatever that meant. His gaze went to the cross. A cross big enough to stand on, come to think of it. His gut told him to look higher. To look all the way up to the walkway running halfway up the wall around the upper reaches of this chapel. A walkway he thought could be for overflow seating. "Or for getting on top of this cross." The central portion of the cross was almost level with the walkway, and with how the walkway was set up, it was hardly more than a short step from it to the cross.

This cross had Agilulph's name on it. The darned thing was more than big enough to hold something inside, and as Harry considered this, his gut shouted for attention. That sixth sense which kept him alive when things got iffy, a sense honed in ancient temples and on Brooklyn streets. Sometimes the correct answer was the obvious one.

He spotted a staircase leading from the chapel floor up to the circular walkway. His footsteps were painfully loud as he banged his way up the wood-and-metal stairs to the upper level, then hurried around until he stood at a point where he could look down on the big cross. From up here the top of the middle post looked plenty large enough to stand on. All he had to do was hop the guardrail.

He did. Harry stepped over, sat his posterior on the rail for a moment to gather himself, then stepped across. No more than a normal stride length and he stood atop the cross, now on a square of wood several feet wide and equally as long. An inch-thick layer of dust mushroomed as he stepped. He didn't feel like he was going to topple over, and if he did, chances are he'd survive. In his line of work, it was all about taking chances.

A distant rumbling that had followed his every step since he came within sight of this base grew louder. The noise of tanks, personnel carriers and aircraft coming and going, ceaseless background music ebbing and flowing now getting stronger. He hesitated, half expecting the doors to clang open and that platoon to storm through, guns drawn. Nothing happened. He shuffled his feet and squatted. He nearly fell over when one toe on his boot caught in the wood.

What the heck? There was a gash in the wood. Moving with care, he twisted to get a clear view and aimed his light at the cross. It was his luck to get this far, then trip on an ancient defect and break a leg. Of all the – *that's no gash.*

An engraving came to life under his penlight. "That's his signature." Harry blinked. "Charlemagne's signature."

GET YOUR COPY OF THE HARRY FOX STORY
THE NAPOLEON CIPHER,
AVAILABLE EXCLUSIVELY FOR MY VIP READER LIST

Sharing the writing journey with my readers is a special privilege. I love connecting with anyone who reads my stories, and one way I accomplish that is through my mailing list. I only send notices of new releases or the occasional special offer related to my novels.

If you sign up for my VIP reader mailing list, I'll send you a copy of *The Napoleon Cipher*, the Harry Fox adventure that's not sold in any store. You can get your copy of this exclusive novel by signing up on my website.

Did you enjoy this story? Let people know

Reviews are the most effective way to get my books noticed. I'm one guy, a small fish in a massive pond. Over time, I hope to change that, and I would love your help. The best thing you could do to help spread the word is leave a review on your platform of choice.

Honest reviews are like gold. If you've enjoyed this book I would be so grateful if you could take a few minutes leaving a review, short or long.

Thank you very much.

Also by Andrew Clawson

The Parker Chase Series

A Patriot's Betrayal

The Crowns Vengeance

Dark Tides Rising

A Republic of Shadows

A Hollow Throne

A Tsar's Gold

The TURN Series

TURN: The Conflict Lands

TURN: A New Dawn

TURN: Endangered

Harry Fox Adventures

The Arthurian Relic

The Emerald Tablet

The Celtic Quest

The Achilles Legend

The Pagan Hammer

The Pharaoh's Amulet

The Thracian Idol

The Antikythera Code

The Charlemagne Accord

About the Author

Andrew Clawson is the author of multiple series, including the Parker Chase and TURN thrillers, as well as the Harry Fox adventures.

You can find him at his website, AndrewClawson.com

or you can connect with him on Instagram at andrew.clawson

on Twitter at @clawsonbooks

on Facebook at facebook.com/AndrewClawsonnovels

and you can always send him an email at:
andrew@andrewclawson.com.